FIRE

THE ELEMENTALS BOOK ONE

L.B. GILBERT

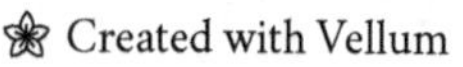 Created with Vellum

TITLES BY L.B. GILBERT

The Elementals Saga
Discordia, A Free Elementals Story
Fire
Air
Water
Earth

A Shifter's Claim
Kin Selection
Eat You Up*
Tooth and Nail
The When Witch and the Wolf

Charmed Legacy Cursed Angel Watchtowers
Forsaken

Writing As Lucy Leroux
The Singular Obsession Series

Making Her His
Confiscating Charlie, A Singular Obsession Novelette
Calen's Captive
Stolen Angel
The Roman's Woman
Save Me, A Singular Obsession Novella
Take Me, A Singular Obsession Prequel Novella
Trick's Trap
Peyton's Price

The Complete Spellbound Regency Series
The Hex, A Free Spellbound Regency Short
Cursed
Black Widow
Haunted

The Rogues and Rescuers Series
Codename Romeo
The Mercenary Next Door
Knight Takes Queen
The Millionaire's Mechanic
Burned Deep - Coming Soon

*As Lucy Leroux

DISCLAIMER

CREDITS

Cover Design: Rebecca Hamilton
http://qualitybookworks.wordpress.com

Logo Design: Juan Fernando Garcia
http://www.elblackbat.com/

Editors: Rainy Kaye
http://www.rainyofthedark.com/
Rebecca Hamilton
http://qualitybookworks.wordpress.com

Readers: Thank you to all of my readers, especially Priti Patel and Damien Leroux and anyone else I forgot!

1

He ducked into the dark alley, just steps behind her, biting back his excitement to finally have her alone. He couldn't give himself over to the pleasure until everything was ready. He'd made a few mistakes in the past when he'd gotten lost in the moment. The women had flaunted themselves and made him angry. It had been their fault. He had to remember to be firm with his girls, but not so angry that he became enraged. If he did, he lost control, and they slipped away so fast. That wouldn't happen this time. This one was special. Very special.

He'd been watching her for weeks. She was perfect. He had been wrong about the others. It never lasted with them because they weren't his one true love.

Diana. A clerk had called her that when she had stopped for takeout food.

The other women were nothing compared to her. Her perfectly formed features accentuated her soft skin and its fine pearl luster. Not a single blemish, not even a freckle. Just perfect, creamy, glowing skin. And her hair—deep red and shiny. He couldn't wait to run his fingers through it.

He crept farther into the alley, unable to believe his luck. The alley was deserted and dark was swiftly falling. No one would notice if she never came out again. He would subdue her and bring the van around to take her to his place.

Their place.

Images of the other women floated through his mind. He could judge them dispassionately now, and he knew why they were wrong. But *she* was perfect. She was his angel. And she'd been waiting for him. That was more-than-clear to him.

There was no man in her life. She was alone in the world, just like he was without her. He knew everything about her. She liked candles and Thai food, and she never watched television. He didn't watch television, either. He supposed there could be one in the bedroom of her sparsely furnished apartment. He had spent a lot of time peeking into her windows, but unfortunately none looked into her bedroom. He wanted to watch her sleep. Soon he would be in bed with her, next to her. . .inside of her.

They were going to be so happy together.

Taking another look at the garbage-filled alley, he wondered why she was in this neighborhood so late. Or why she had to have those bagels from the corner store. She went out of her way to get them. He'd tried them immediately after he'd seen her buy them. He didn't think they were any better than the ones just down the block from her place, but he didn't begrudge her choice. The fact that she detoured every day to this neighborhood where no one ever saw who came and went was a blessing to him. And now she'd entered this alley as the light was dying in the sky. It was like she was extending an invitation to him.

Except he had lost track of her. She should be just ahead. He peered around the dumpster—it was the only thing large enough for her to have hidden behind.

She isn't here!

He spun around, looking for any sign of where she had gone. With an inarticulate growl, he yanked up an empty crate sitting to the side and threw it at the wall so hard it smashed into pieces, knocking over a piece of plywood leaning against the wall. It slid to the ground, revealing a large hole in the wall of the adjoining building. He forced himself to calm his breathing and examined the hole. It was definitely large enough for his angel to have passed through.

"Fuck!" he muttered through gritted teeth.

If this was the way she had gone, then there was a chance she had heard all the noise he'd just made. He stepped back to size up the building. It was the back of decrepit warehouse. Why would his angel go inside there?

He looked around again. No, there was no other place she could have gone. He waited for a count of ten and then ducked into the hole. It was a large, dark space. He couldn't see much beyond the clutter surrounding the doorway. His angel wasn't anywhere to be found. Maybe she hadn't heard him. Relief flooded him. Maybe he still had a chance to surprise her.

He picked his way through the mess and stopped to listen. It was too quiet. He doubled his effort to stay silent in case she was nearby. For another few minutes, he picked his way, trying to move like the shadow he pretended to be. Reaching the midway point of the warehouse along the right wall, he paused. Light flickered from the back of the room.

A fire? He crept closer. Yes. It was definitely a fire. Maybe there were people here after all. Anger boiled inside him.

Is she meeting someone? A man?

His angel was really starting to piss him off. Maybe he wouldn't be so gentle with her.

He crept around a pile of broken crates. No one was there. He waited several minutes, hoping his angel would appear. . .alone. She had to have wandered farther into the warehouse. Impatient now, he walked out from behind the pile and up to the fire. A piece of paper lay on the floor on the other side of the fire. After looking around to make sure he was still alone, he knelt down to pick it up. It was an index card, a new one in pristine condition. He turned it around and read the words.

Got you, it said in a neat cursive script. He whirled around.

And there she was. His angel. But something was wrong.

Very wrong.

———

DIANA SMILED AT THE KILLER. "Hello, Donald. I've been waiting for you."

Donald Stevens, rapist and murderer of over a dozen women, stopped in his tracks. His narrow, greasy face froze in a mask of surprise. It was comical with its wide gaping mouth and protruding eyes that she had to stifle a laugh. But soon Donald's astonishment faded, his expression transforming into a dark and predatory hunger. He shifted his weight, broadcasting his intention to rush her.

With a disgusted shake of her head, Diana extended her hand to the fire. His eyes widened as the flames leapt to her hand. She smiled at him as she held it, cradling it in her palm like a treasure. He edged away.

"Well, Donald, you're disappointing me. I've been looking for you for a long time and, frankly, I expected more."

"How the fuck do you know my—"

Diana raised the fire to triple its size, directing the rush of air to throw the larger man into the wall. In a split second, she had her free hand around his neck. With one arm, she smoothly lifted him off the ground.

His eyes bulged, and his face turned a dark shade of red as he choked. Diana smiled coldly when panic seized him and he kicked helplessly in the air.

"You didn't honestly think you were the scariest thing walking this Earth, did you?" Diana whispered.

"Angel?" he wheezed as she released her grip on his throat a fraction.

"Not quite," she said with a twist of her lips before hardening her expression as the fire built up inside her.

Donald looked into her eyes, and as they changed, opened his mouth wide and screamed. Tired of having to touch him, Diana brought her other hand up and released the fire directly into his gaping mouth. His screaming was strangled as he clawed at his throat in a vain attempt to stop the flames. But it was running inside of him then, burning everything into ash from the inside out.

Diana finally let go and backed away as the flames consumed his torso. She stared down at the burning body, weariness rising as the adrenaline of the kill faded away. Sighing, she stirred the burning embers with the tip of her steel-toed boot.

She'd waited longer than usual to bring this one down. She could have just killed him as soon as she got to town, but she'd decided to wait, to snare him with his own trap. It seemed like poetic justice. She'd wanted revenge for all of those girls he'd hunted down and killed as if they were nothing.

Closing her eyes, she saw their faces in her mind. His victims faces were usually too battered to be recognizable to their loved ones, their bodies torn and broken. Like the two youngest who'd been living on the streets. He had kept those two the longest. . .and they suffered the most. That was why she'd put it off, letting him see her, desire her for almost a week and half.

It was too long for one predator, as Gia had gently reminded her last night.

I did take too long, Diana thought as the rush of vengeance faded and the dissatisfaction took over again. She watched the flames do their work, much faster than a normal fire would act on a body.

She used to live for this. The satisfaction used to last longer. If they were all this clean, this clear, it would be better. Punishing the guilty was what she was built for. Unfortunately, it seemed like more and more of these monsters kept turning up. Like the heads of a Hydra, she cut one down and two more sprung up in their place.

She waited for the fire to consume the last of the body, tossing the note she'd left for Donald on the dying flames. A few of his earliest victims had been taunted by notes just like it. They had found them in their homes and their workplaces, places they thought were safe until he proved otherwise. Satisfaction flared briefly again.

When there were only ashes left, Diana gathered her coat and made her way to the front door of the warehouse. There was no need to sneak out of the hole she'd made back in the alley. She walked into the darkness and closed the door behind her.

Walking past the shabby buildings and storefronts, she inhaled the cool night air. It was moist and heavy, but the overcast sky held no hint of a coming storm.

Too bad I can't make it rain at will. She always liked how it smelled after it rained.

Diana wrinkled her nose, silently acknowledging that she preferred firepower to water. Always had.

2

Diana unlocked the door to the apartment. She put her take-out on the table, one of the few pieces of furniture in the apartment.

Furnished apartments never had much of anything except for a used feeling in the air. She stripped off her uniform, the standard cargo pants and black tank she always wore with combat boots, and showered quickly. After pulling on clean clothes, she wrapped a fuzzy knit scarf from her pack around her shoulders.

The scarf was the one indulgence she carried with her from place to place. Gia had made it for her. Diana always waited till she was done with a case to take it out, unwilling to have it on as she did her work. It was like a reward after she finished a job.

Sighing, she looked around the bare room, glad she would be leaving it behind at first light. She was heading back to the east coast. Back to Boston.

And that was where this empty feeling started. After I took Katie home.

She pushed the thought away and pulled the candle on the bedside table closer. Sitting cross-legged on the bed, she called the fire with a flick of her finger. The wick on the candle flared to life, and she focused on the flame. Reaching out with her mind, she sent the image of the flame into the aether.

Though each of the Mother Nature's agents represented a distinct element, they were all bound together by the fifth, aether, which enabled them to communicate with each other. It didn't matter where in the world they were. All they had to do was commune with their element. In Diana's case, she simply lit a candle. No one ever questioned why a woman had so many candles.

Diana could feel the other three Elementals waiting through the aether. She winced slightly. It had been while since she'd talked to all of them as a group. She hadn't wanted them to gang up on her to move on from this case. But that also meant she hadn't heard how their missions were going, either.

"It's done," she said aloud.

"Good," Gia, the Earth Elemental, responded over the aether link. "Are you okay?"

"I'm fine," Diana lied.

"Are you sure?" Serin, the Water Elemental, chimed in.

Gia and Serin were the two most senior Elementals. Both had been in service of the mother for years. In Gia's case, centuries.

"Yeah, I'm sure," Diana said. "But it will be good to get out of here. I don't like the kind of cold they have here. Cold should not be humid."

"Wait till you get back to Boston," Logan said. "In summer, it's a pit."

Logan was the youngest Air Elemental in history. Gia considered her a prodigy, but Diana had decided not to hold that against her. And now she loved her. They all did.

"You lucked out before, not having to go there at this time of year. You'll miss Canada then," Logan continued.

"Should I skip the car and fly into your namesake this time?" Diana asked.

"How many times do I have to tell you I am not named after the airport!" she huffed, making Diana smile.

Logan had taken to her Elemental inheritance with alacrity, but she was still very young and easy to needle.

"We know, sweetie," Serin said. "Di's just winding you up. I have to get going. I have to head south for another disturbance."

"Any idea what's going down?" Logan asked eagerly.

In both age and experience, she was the youngest, and was still keen to learn everything she could about their missions.

"No real details yet," Serin supplied, "but there's a center. San Juan de Abajo, a small village on the coast near Vallarta."

Logan sighed. "You always get the best locations. Sometimes I wish I was Water."

"No, you don't," Serin said, a smile clear in her voice. "You would miss getting to whip up winds and storms and knocking guys three times your size on their butt."

"Hey, those guys were asking for it," Logan grumbled. "And they lived. Like they were supposed to."

With only four of them actively working at any one time, even some of the most knowledgeable magic practitioners didn't believe in Elementals. Sometimes a good scare was enough to straighten people out. And for those beginning to stray into the darker shades of magic, a good thrashing early on was easier and more effective.

Logan's last case was one of their preemptive attempts to stop such a situation from developing. She'd delivered a smack down worthy of a WWF wrestler, with a harsh reminder to stay within the parameters of the covenant.

The Mother had bound every Supernatural with a set of guidelines that over time had become known as the covenant. It was essentially a promise not to abuse the gift of magic she had given them. The covenant bound all Supernaturals to act only within certain boundaries. And of all the Otherkind races the Elementals policed, it was the witches that most often strayed outside those lines.

Logan had delivered her message to the witches in style, but there had been a running argument since that their youngest sister might be a teensy bit reckless. Her "warning" had landed several of the male witches in the hospital. The junior Elemental tried to manipulate her ability in ways that taxed her level of skill and control.

"Yeah, just be careful with the blow-back," Serin said.

Logan's blasts did sometimes get away from her.

"Okay, mom," Logan said, but she didn't sound annoyed.

They all knew Serin couldn't help but mother them.

"Well, I need to get going," Serin said. "I'll keep you posted on the situation once I know what is going on. Good luck in Boston, Di."

They could feel her withdrawal along the aether as she departed.

"I should go, too," Gia said. "I have some tracking to do tonight."

"Be careful," Diana couldn't help saying, even though she knew it was unnecessary.

Gia was the senior Elemental—the strongest and perhaps the wisest. But Diana always worried about her. It was Gia who had found Diana and told her she was an Elemental and at the back of her mind she feared Gia would disappear on her one day the way her own mother had.

"I always am," Gia assured her. "And...if you need to talk about anything at all, just call. Okay?"

"Okay."

Gia withdrew.

"Finally!" Logan breathed once she was gone. "I thought they were never going to go."

"So you heard something?" Diana asked, her heart sinking slightly.

"There are whispers in the wind about the little girl." Logan's voice was sympathetic.

It was one of the benefits to being the Air Elemental. The wind sometimes whispered useful things in your ear, but it wasn't exactly a reliable source of information. The echoes and fragments Logan heard were open to interpretation. But this time she sounded sure.

"What do you hear?" Diana felt both vindicated and chilled.

"Not too much, other than you were right. Katie's gone missing. . .again. No one has seen her in the last few weeks."

"What does the mother say?"

"She's missing now, too. But the little girl disappeared first. None of their acquaintances seem to know where they are, but they think the mother went in search of the little one."

"Any ideas of where to start looking?"

"There is a lead, but tread carefully on this one."

"Why?"

"Because, the winds speak of vampires."

Well crap, Diana thought.

DIANA LAY IN BED, staring at the ceiling. Logan's warning gave her a bad feeling about Boston. Not about the case of corporate malfeasance she'd been sent to investigate. But the other case, the one both Serin and Gia had said was over.

It had to be freaking vampires. *Ugh.* It was more than enough to keep her awake.

Little Katie should have been safe. Diana had made sure. Last year, she'd been sent on a monster hunt, much like the one she'd just finished. It was ironic that the ones she and her sisters called monsters were, more often than not, the completely human ones.

Diana sighed and shifted in bed. Sometimes the Supernaturals were far easier to stomach. At least one knew what to expect from them.

A child molester, a very prolific one, had taken Katie. He liked to keep his little girls for a long time, letting them get used to him. And once he'd earned their trust, he would strip it away, abusing them to the point of catatonia. Diana could still see Katie's haunted eyes, the light starting to bleed out of them. Diana remembered that look well. It happened to children who'd learned in the worst possible way that adults weren't always there to protect them.

Something inside Diana had broken after that case. The Mother had charged their kind with punishing those so evil they shifted the balance to the dark. But that was the crux of the matter. There had to be a dark side.

An Elemental wasn't a savior. They could track a killer to the ends of the Earth, but they didn't have the ability to identify a potential victim. The best they could do was track those peripherally involved in their cases. But that was only if they were among one of the Supernatural races. It didn't work with humans. Not unless they had done something bad enough to mark themselves.

Diana was sick of her inability to save the innocent. Intellectually, she knew she made a difference to the future victims a killer would've taken, but it had been cold comfort when she'd found that little girl.

There had been too many others that she hadn't been able to save.

Katie's mother, Brenda, had been so relieved to get her baby back. She had sworn she would never let the little girl out of her sight ever again. And Diana had believed her. The little girl's father hadn't been in the picture, only an aunt who had been very quiet in her presence. At the time, Diana had chalked it up to the FBI badge she flashed at them when she took Katie home. It was a useful tool in cases like those, when an Elemental had to mix with humans.

Diana shifted on the lumpy mattress and gave up rehashing the past, focusing on her plans instead. She would have to go inside the Boston vampire coven blind. She had no idea what connection they had to Katie's latest disappearance, but she knew enough about them to expect trouble.

The Broussards were the oldest and most powerful clan of vampires in the new world. They even outstripped most of the clans in the old world these days.

Normally she had no scruples over busting in and knocking heads, but the Mother hadn't exactly sanctioned this investigation. Her kind were supposed to be the clean-up crew.

Well, not this time, she decided.

And really, a little head busting is often the most effective approach.

3

Boston was hot and sticky.

Too sticky, Diana thought. She loved hot weather but hated the humidity. It felt as if she was swimming through the crowded Boston Gardens.

Am I near that Cheers bar? A drink would have been welcome.

Well, maybe next time. On impulse, she stopped for a piece of fried dough. She gobbled it down and ordered a second without a shred of remorse. Maintaining her firepower at optimum levels required consuming high quantities of calories. And she was going to need it tonight. In fact, she was going to have to add a few bread bowls of clam chowder at Faneuil Hall in the name of preparedness.

A couple of hours later, Diana was loitering in Louisburg Square's fenced-in park. She had spent the afternoon trying to track down Brenda, Katie's mom. But there had been no trace of her, and Diana wasn't willing to drop her current lead to hunt her down. Especially if Katie wasn't with her.

From her vantage point in the park, Diana could see the coven's townhouse. Most of the family homes in this area had been converted to apartments and condos, but the huge house was inhabited solely by the coven. Members often chose to take lodgings outside of the coven house, but many still chose to live inside with their brothers and sisters.

She would never understand why vampires and Weres chose to live piled on top of each other like that. Didn't they find themselves as insufferable as she did?

Apparently not, since they all vied to stay close to one another.

Even young vampires were irritating as shit. They made the mistake of believing their own hype, always dressing lavishly, throwing endless parties and employing humans to serve them in daylight. And the human servants delighted in their domestic drudgery! Though most of them did it for the status, a few really believed they would be made vampires if they succeeded in pleasing their masters.

On rare occasions, a human with some sensitivity to magic was turned, but it didn't happen often enough to justify the years of servitude.

It was enough of a challenge to turn a human from one of the vampire lineages. It took an amazingly skilled practitioner to wrap magic around a normal person and mold them into their own image. Of course, vampires didn't see it that way. To them, turning a human was a mystical act of creation unique to their kind. They couldn't see the parallels to the other groups of Supernaturals because it contradicted their mythos. And to vamps that was all that really mattered.

Vampires could breed a potential vampire the normal way, but only in the days before they turned. While still mostly human, a member of a vampiric line could mate to produce children. But they didn't do so as frequently as Weres and humans. And not all of their children were capable of being turned, a detail she was grateful for. More vampires meant more headaches for her.

Diana sighed and headed out of the square. Later that night would be a more appropriate time to visit the coven house. She needed to question its members about Katie's disappearance, and it would be better to do it before they dispersed to the city's Underlife, the network of shops and nightclubs that passed for civilization to Supernaturals.

She was almost out of the square when a prickling awareness at the back of her neck made her pause. Diana was being watched, and not by some stray human.

Despite the fact vampires didn't come out in daylight, she pulled her hood up and moved back to casually walk around the square. There was no one in sight that could have gotten her spidey senses tingling like that. And given the bright sunlight, it couldn't be a vampire.

Unless…

Most vampires conveniently burst into flames when they stepped into sunlight. To avoid smoldering, they kept to the night hours. Staying in the shadows wasn't enough since they were blinded by natural light, even reflected sunlight. It took a rare and unusually confident vampire to see past their kind's myths and long history to manipulate the magic around them enough to allow exposure to the sun. That didn't stop the vast majority of them from seeking out meaningless ritual after ritual that promised to turn them into Daywalkers.

Daywalkers were scarcer than Elementals, with a total of six confirmed in all of history. The last had been beheaded by an Elemental five centuries ago. So it wasn't likely there was one in this coven.

She was probably just too keyed up over Katie's disappearance and had imagined the sensation of being watched. Turning around, Diana shrugged off her suspicions and headed back to the waterfront.

ACROSS THE SQUARE, Alec released a shaky breath. He'd flattened himself against a far side of a brown truck. It was big and square, but still he felt exposed.

Damn, he thought, looking up to see the surprised and confused expression on the UPS driver's face. He slowly raised his head over the hood of the truck, but she was gone. Whoever she was. *Whatever* she was.

Smiling to the driver as if nothing strange had happened, Alec took out his phone for the special map application he'd had made to track the coven's servants. Noting a clear path through the front door, he slipped inside undetected.

Knowing where the servants were at all times helped. With vampiric speed, he moved upstairs and into his old room. He hadn't been back to Boston in years, but this room looked the same. Despite the fact he kept separate quarters near the waterfront, his mother insisted on keeping it exactly as it was. Except for the embroidered pillows he knocked off the bed when he sat down. Those seemed to have multiplied in his absence.

He'd never liked this room, with its blood red walls and black velvet accents. It looked like a damn bordello. But that didn't matter. He wouldn't be here much longer—not unless he found a lead in the disappearance of Pedro's son. He'd hit a dead end in his investigation, and he would have to move on soon, despite his concern for the boy.

Alec had been buried knee-deep in dusty books in a back room of an Oxford library when his informant in Boston had gotten in touch. The son of a long time retainer had disappeared under suspicious circumstances a little over a week ago.

Pedro had served the family faithfully for many years, but the coven heads, his parents Alden and Elva, had done nothing to find out what happened. He'd come home to investigate as soon as he could. But he hadn't found out anything—no trace of the boy or the people who had taken him. It didn't look like an inside job.

Small blessings. If he had found evidence that someone in his house was involved, it would have been a huge mess. But finding nothing also meant that he'd been unable to help. And now it looked as if there was nothing more he could do, not personally at least. If one of the other Supernatural groups were responsible, it would be up to them to investigate and mete out punishment. The covenants were very clear when it came to dealing with the Otherkind—Supernaturals not of your own race. And it was always possible that the taking of Pedro's son, Elias, was the act of a human predator.

If he didn't find anything in another few days, he would have his investigators keep looking after he left, for Pedro's sake.

Alden and Elva wouldn't be pleased if he left so soon, but Alec didn't like staying in one place too long. He chose to keep moving every few years, circumnavigating the globe on his various academic quests.

My long vaunted search for answers. The meaning of life, he mocked himself.

Of course, he hadn't called it that in the beginning. One search into the ancient world had led to another and so on. His plan had been to unlock the secrets of the ancients. The irony was that he'd been wildly successful..

If the secret of his discovery ever got out, it could shake the foundations of their society. The ability to walk in daylight was the vampire's holy grail. But his only major discovery hadn't given him the answers he'd sought.

Why did vampires exist? Had God the Father really turned their back on them? Or was it the Mother? Had they angered her? Was that why they were condemned to live in the dark? And why couldn't they convert any human they chose? That and other questions had plagued him for as long as he could remember.

All he'd found was more of the circuitous and empty gibberish that was ancient vampire lore.

Well, maybe his life was not supposed to have a deeper meaning. His studies kept him busy. He also had his duty, even if his own parents shirked theirs.

And with that thought, the near constant weight in his chest settled more firmly. He had visited Pedro earlier that day. The little Hispanic man was in terrible shape.

Alec had to look into the local Otherkind before he left. He usually got on well with members of the other Supernatural races, but in this case he didn't see an easy path ahead. His mind circled back to the girl in the square. He hadn't seen much, only a flash of white skin and dark red hair.

She's not a shifter and definitely not a Daywalker.

Once he'd finally been able to walk in daylight, he had wondered if another Daywalker might come out of the woodwork to approach him. But that hadn't happened.

Maybe the girl was a witch or a shamaness. His kind paid a lot of money to those tricky beings when they needed spells worked. But there hadn't been that specific vibration he always felt in the presence of one of their kind. All he had felt was a split second impression of immense power, and then a void as it was quickly masked. He debated telling Alden and Elva about it.

I was probably imagining the whole thing. Or it could have been a practitioner on vacation. A tourist even.

No, there was no need to panic everyone needlessly. Not that they would have the good sense to be scared if he sounded the alarm. The elders were in complete self-assurance on the superiority of their kind. But Alec had seen a lot in his travels, enough to wear away the unshakable certainty in vampire infallibility.

A noise behind him alerted him to another presence.

"Hello, Vincent," he said without turning around.

"What I wouldn't give to know how you do that," a droll, cultured voice returned.

Alec turned to see Vincent in the doorway. The other vampire was impeccably dressed in a black suit and a gold embroidered vest with a red silk shirt underneath. Not that Alec was a slouch in the wardrobe department. A good, if dramatic, sense of fashion was innate to most vampires he'd met.

Vincent was probably there to gloat. He had been rising earlier in the past few years, earlier than the hour Alec currently pretended to wake—a detail he was quite smug about.

"I didn't realize I had risen so late," he lied.

"Not so late," Vincent said, sounding pleased with himself. "But of course you're not used to the hours we keep here anymore." He paused. "I thought you'd like to know some fresh O positive was just delivered, since you didn't approve our current lineup of donors."

Alec nodded. "Thank you."

Blood was truly the only essential when it came to sustenance, but few of his kind admitted that they needed it sparingly, at most every few days for those but the youngest of their kind. Instead, most had blood every day, provided by their human servants or acquired by the local blood bank with a few healthy bribes. Daily intake was more for ritual and pleasure than survival. Killing the host was considered bad form, especially since almost all vampires could 'call' blood—control the flow of blood in themselves and their donor to ensure that they only took what was needed.

Alec made it a point to only consume what blood he truly needed, but it wasn't a popular position among his kind.

"What are you up to tonight?" Vincent asked, eager to report the answers to the elders should they ask.

"I might check out one of the clubs. What's hot right now?" Alec asked, deciding to take advantage of the other vampire's presence in his room, away from the many ears of the coven.

"Hmm. Taking an interest in the Underlife?" Vincent sounded intrigued.

His interest was probably justified, Alec reflected. When he lived here last, he wouldn't set foot in any of the supernatural nightspots for love or money.

"Why not? Things are a little *dead* after all that travel," he said as he got up and pretended to rethink his choice of tie.

Taking off the blue silk neckcloth that he'd put on that morning, he set it aside in favor of wearing an open collar.

"Well, right now, Whore is the place to be seen," Vincent said as he took a look around the room without appearing to do so.

"You're kidding right?" Alec's insides curdled a bit. "Did my parents have anything to do with that name?"

"No, it's owned by some practitioners. But the coven house has its own VIP section and private room for meetings. The usual setup. Your parents aren't into the club scene right now. More into exclusive soirées. Like tonight's." Vincent paused. "Your parents won't be pleased if you skip another one."

"I only got back last week and haven't been in the mood. But I'll be sure to drop by tonight before I go out," Alec said.

He'd avoided all of the parties his parents had thrown since his return, but after seeing Pedro it might be a good idea to play nice. The locals mixed with the Otherkind far more frequently than they would have you believe, and he might learn something useful.

Which means socializing, he thought with a shudder.

"Excellent! I'll tell your mother. She'll be so pleased," Vincent exclaimed with a huge smile.

He was practically out the door when Alec stopped him.

"Make sure she knows I'm only making an appearance. I don't want her turning this into a welcome home celebration."

He really didn't want to be the focus tonight. Or any other night.

"I'll be sure she knows your feelings on the subject. I should go help with the preparations. I have a few of my own invitations to extend. Ta-ta for now." Vincent whirled away with a flourish.

It's almost as if he's always wearing a cape, Alec marveled as the other man left.

Alec did not flounce or whirl, nor did he sweep out of rooms like he was in a ball gown. He wouldn't have known how even if he wanted to. But he still wondered how Vincent and all of his parent's other favorites always managed to pull it off.

4

Later that night, Alec was regretting his impulse to join his mother's party. He'd already been toasted twice and had roughly half the vampire population in the city paraded in front of him.

The damn female half. His parents had apparently decided to drop their more subtle efforts to persuade him to take a mate.

Alec smothered a yawn, annoyed they were resuming their campaign. The pressure to marry and produce a child before he turned had thankfully been abandoned when he had gone through his change early. Most turned after thirty human years or more. He had been an unprecedented twenty-four, a shocking event at the time. But after only a few hundred years reprieve, his parents had started hinting that the joys of taking a partner were a blessing despite the absence of children.

He had never felt the slightest temptation to find out if that was true. As for the steady stream of eligible female vampires being paraded in front of him, women were the last thing on his mind. Clearly his mother had chosen to ignore his polite requests that she stop matchmaking. He needed to speak to her about it, but he'd been avoiding a direct confrontation. His childless status was a sore point with them.

Eager to escape the inane conversation, he retreated to a chair near the fireplace and pretended to admire his mother's latest redecoration effort. It almost made him smile. The opulent ballroom, with its red silk damask covered walls, had some of the most elaborate chandeliers he'd ever seen outside a casino.

I feel like I'm in Vegas.

"Hello, Alec," a low female voice purred in his ear.

He turned away from the chandeliers to see Sylvan perched on the right arm of his armchair near the fireplace, a monstrously large piece that would have been at home in the grandest castles of Europe. Sylvan smiled invitingly and braced an arm above his shoulder. She couldn't get closer to him unless she sat on his lap.

She trailed her hand up his arm, looking as if she was going to climb on top of him any second. He shifted slightly, trying to dislodge her crawling fingers.

"Hi, Sylvan," Alec replied, his voice flat and discouraging.

Sylvan was the worst of his mother's potential daughter-in-laws. Her large breasts were almost completely exposed to the nipple, a dark green dress hugging every voluptuous curve. He'd never been into her, but Sylvan was tenacious. She wanted to be at his side at the top of the of the coven hierarchy, the mistress of the manor when his parents stepped down.

"It's good that you're finally home, Alec," she continued, her tongue curling around the syllables of his name.

Shifting in his seat, he stayed quiet.

Not pleased with his response or lack of one, Sylvan started again. "A little bird told me you were going to Whore tonight. You should come with me. They know me there."

Of course they do. "Oh, I think I might fly solo. Or I may not hit a club after all. I have some work to do," Alec said evasively.

Not for the first time, he wished vampires didn't have twenty-twenty vision. Cleaning a pair of spectacles could have provided a distraction. Anything to avoid direct eye contact. Sylvan was like the sun—a bright shining star that burned out your retinas if you looked at it too long.

"You've devoted centuries to your research," she replied, a hint of a sneer in her voice. "Your parents think it's time you settled down and took over your responsibilities here."

What responsibilities? Throwing the best party? Showing visiting dignitaries around town? Taking them clubbing?

"They've made that clear, but I'm simply not the marrying kind," Alec said with a deprecating smile.

"Don't compare a vampire bond to a *human* marriage," Sylvan spit out. "Our kind bonds for eternity. It is more than a stupid human marriage; it is a union of souls."

"Of course it is."

I will not roll my eyes.

"Don't roll your eyes at me!"

Damn.

"Anyway," Sylvan continued, regaining her purr with remarkable speed. "I know all the clubs from here to Miami, and most of the ones in LA. All the ones worth knowing, that is. You really should join me sometime."

"Maybe. . .sometime. But tonight is bad. I have some errands, and a few books to acquire."

That was a good one. Sylvan never read. *Not even sure she knows how.* A surprising number of vampires didn't bother to learn.

"Suit yourself. Just give me a buzz if you change your mind. I know everyone who's anyone. You've been out of the loop for too long," she said, rising from her perch in a smooth fluid motion that drew attention to her curves. "If you want to mix with the Otherkind, you need to know who the right people are. I can help you with that."

"Some social guidance would not be amiss," Alec said, reminding himself that his investigation was too important to brush her off outright. "Why don't you start now? Why don't you tell me about the local undesirables?"

"Really?" Sylvan asked, sitting back down on the arm of his chair in a flash. She leaned in conspiratorially. "Well, let's see. Where should we start?"

She turned to the room at large.

DIANA WAS outside the coven house, crouched in a treetop in the square. It was later than she had planned, but it seemed like the coven was staying in tonight. They were having a party, which meant the later she went in, the bigger the crowd. She'd rethought her plan and, if all went, she would circumvent the need for violence. Or at least major bodily harm.

Remember not to kill anyone. If they're not involved with Katie's disappearance, you'll never hear the end of it from Serin. The current generation of leaders for this coven hadn't met an Elemental before. She hopped down from the tree and headed to the house.

Time to make an impression.

5

Inside the coven house ballroom, Alec was doing his damnedest to get rid of Sylvan. He felt a little bad about it because she'd actually been helpful. He had a few leads now thanks to her, but gratitude only went so far. After downing the last of his wine, he excused himself to go get another drink. His mother could be counted on to serve only the finest vintages.

Alec studied the crowd from the relative safety of the bar. Everyone was dressed to kill, pun intended. But most humans would probably be disappointed in their parties. No vampires feeding off enthralled humans. No orgies or violence. Not even the hint of impropriety. The euphoria fresh human blood inspired was something best experienced in private. It would be hard to maintain the same level of vampire superiority if you've been seen *in flagrante delicto,* figuratively speaking.

He asked the bartender for a scotch and turned his attention back to the fireplace. He was doing a pretty good job of ignoring Sylvan, despite her pouty expression across the ballroom. He was subtly looking for the exit when he noticed the flames in the fireplace flicker. In unison—the whole blaze, which had a strange purple-blue color to it.

Stiffening, he walked closer while turning around to scan the room. Several others had noticed the fire's unnatural behavior. Everyone hushed and those closest to the fireplace moved away from it. Some were crowding near the doors when there was a sudden rushing sound like an animal howling in the sudden quiet.

All eyes turned to the fireplace. The once small flames leapt high, engulfing the entire space under the giant mantelpiece in an unnaturally bright flame. Alec was momentarily blinded. He covered his eyes with his hands. When they readjusted, he could see someone in the center of the ballroom. A young woman. One with dark red hair.

"Do excuse me," she said with a dazzling smile directed at his parents. "I didn't mean to interrupt. Well, okay. Actually, I did." She shifted her weight on one hip in a casual whole body shrug.

Elva's aristocratic face contorted into a mask of fury and outrage. Alden stalked toward the woman, his expression livid.

"How dare you?" Alec's father hissed. He didn't have to yell to get everyone's attention. All eyes were on him and their uninvited guest. "Who the hell are you? You can't be here!"

"Oh, I dare to go pretty much anywhere I want. But you're right. I should have at least knocked."

She raised her hand in a parody of knocking a door. . .but with each fake knock there was a real and extremely loud booming sound. It was so loud the chandeliers rattled.

What the hell? What witch could do something like that without an incantation? He hadn't seen her move her lips at all.

"I'm not impressed with your parlor tricks!" his father spit out.

The woman leaned in closer. "Who says it's a trick?" She spun slightly to take in the room around her. "Nice. A little too much velvet, though. Very nouveau bordello." Her full lips puckered a little.

She's beautiful, Alec thought for a long moment before he got a grip on himself. An unfamiliar vamp close to him turned and gave him a 'Are you completely crazy?' look.

Damn, must have said it out loud.

"Get the hell out of here, witch!" his father yelled, but it sounded more like a *b* than a *w*.

He grabbed the woman's arm but snapped back his hand like he had been burned. He gave a little grunt, blinking repeatedly. Then he seemed to shake it off and tried again.

Alec wanted to shout a warning, but he was frozen in place. His father's hand was smoking now, and there was a distinct smell of burned flesh in the air. Alden took two steps back, but his mother came forward shaking with rage.

"You can't be here," she shrilled as if her mate hadn't just been burned. "We have wards everywhere!"

"I'm aware of that," the stranger said.

The young woman was still calm and collected, her voice low and cool. It had a distinctly husky sound to it, one that was tweaking Alec's nerves. "But since I'm not a witch, they aren't really relevant right now."

"Of course you're a witch!" his mother yelled, spittle flying, completely losing her composure.

Okay, now that was really impressive. He couldn't remember the last time Elva had raised her voice.

The woman must have decided she was tired of getting spit on, and moved out of range. There was a sudden gasp, as if everyone in the room had exhaled collectively in surprise.

As the stranger walked across the polished marble floor, she made a circle around Alec's mother, leaving a set of small burning footprints in her wake.

The fire from each footprint flared with each step, leaving Elva completely encircled by flames. Panicking, she ran toward Alden. But before she could clear the edge, the circle of fire flared high and hot, trapping her inside.

A sudden crashing sound behind Alec made him turn around. Vamps and servants were scrambling out of the room, knocking over furniture and dropping trays of champagne as they went.

"What do you want?" His father's voice didn't sound right.

Alec turned back to the intruder, stunned to see her now ringed in a spiral of flame that moved with her, like it was a part of her. He inched toward her, trying to not make any noise. But she turned anyway, facing him directly across the length of the ballroom.

Alec stared into her eyes and the bottom dropped away from his world.

It really is one of them.

The woman turned back to his parents, but the image of those flame-filled eyes stayed with him. It wasn't a trick of the light or a reflection of the fire in the room. It was coming from inside of her. She was an Elemental.

"I want to know about the child," she said.

"Shit."

The Elemental cocked her head in his direction. *Crap. Bad time to think aloud.*

"What child?" His father sounded genuinely bewildered.

The Elemental produced a picture from god knows where. The fact that it wasn't burning up was proof that those flames weren't normal.

"This one. Her name is Katie. She should be safe at home sleeping right now, but she's not. And one of your kind knows something about her disappearance."

The Elemental's voice was cold and even.

"We don't know anything about that. We would never break the covenant and harm a child," Alden said, still confused.

That was true. . .mostly. They would never feed from or kill children. But allowing harm to come to them through some thoughtless action, well, that was a something Alec didn't want to think about.

"I didn't say you had done anything to her personally," the Elemental said as she reached out a small shapely hand and took hold of Alden's shirtfront. "But one of you knows something. If I were you, I would get into a sharing mood."

The shirt smoldered where it made contact. She dragged him forward—despite the fact he towered above her by almost a foot and outweighed her by at least a hundred pounds.

"We have nothing to do with whatever it is you are looking for!"

Elva said from inside the circle, but her voice betrayed her. It was shaky and uncertain.

The Elemental released Alden with a shove that sent him flying back and sliding across the floor like a doll. Alec froze in shock for the space of an entire heartbeat before rushing to help him. After helping his father to his feet, they both turned to watch helplessly as the Elemental moved toward his mother.

"Then why do the winds whisper your name, Elvarosa? They wouldn't be doing that if you weren't involved somehow."

The Elemental's voice was low and throaty. It sounded so wrong. It was too sexy for him to be afraid. And he should be. Even his mother was finally catching up, realization creeping over her face. Then her expression turned stubborn.

Alec knew that look. His mother was exceptional when it came to ignoring unpleasant situations. But this was the wrong time for her to dig in her Manolo's in denial. He stepped closer, determined to do something.

"What have you done, Mother?" he asked quietly.

The Elemental cocked her head again, but she didn't bother to turn around to look at him.

"Tell me about the child," she said.

"Elva? What is she talking about?" his father asked. His mother jerked her head toward the sound of his voice. Alec was only a few feet away now. The Elemental didn't even turn toward him.

Clearly I'm not a threat, he thought, trying not to be insulted.

"It wasn't me! It was nothing!" his mother yelled as the flames flared slightly.

"But you know something," the Elemental said in a singsong voice that should have freaked him out.

But he loved her voice. *Jesus, what is wrong with you?*

"Mother, whatever you know, you have to tell us," Alec said.

Elva turned toward him and the Elemental. "No, it was nothing. Nothing." She was shaking, her eyes clouded and unseeing.

"What was nothing?" the Elemental asked in a cold even tone. She was like the angel that stood at the gates of heaven judging sins and deciding fates.

"They wanted to use one of the houses. That's all!" His mother couldn't seem to control the volume of her voice.

"Who wanted a house? For what purpose? Did they keep Katie there?"

Though her inflection hadn't changed, he was certain the Elemental was furious.

"No! I don't know! There wasn't supposed to be a child there at all!" his mother cried.

The Elemental didn't say anything. She simply let the silence stretch and stretch like a police interrogator would have until Elva broke.

"I didn't know it was a black circle," his mother whispered.

From the corner, his father made an inarticulate choking sound, but Alec didn't look his way.

"We don't traffic with black witches. *We don't!*" his mother cried as she paced in a tiny circle inside the flames. "A friend asked me for a favor, to loan one of our rentals in Dover to some witches she knew. She said the house was in a favorable spot for them to conduct some rituals. I thought it was only basic spells. So did she. But they vacated suddenly and she didn't know where they had gone," Elva said with a wave of her hand that was a little too close to the fire for Alec's peace of mind. "She was annoyed because she couldn't reach them, and she hadn't received the charms she'd been promised."

Inside the ring of fire, his mother crumpled to the floor when she was done explaining.

"What kind of charms?" Alec asked with the sinking feeling that this was simply too much of a coincidence.

A child missing wasn't something out of the ordinary in the human world, but it was in theirs. He remembered the wards on the apartment building where Elias was taken. A skilled witch could have circumvented them.

"Just some beauty related charms, and some listening spells. Nothing big. No black magic."

"But you were concerned enough to check out the house, right?" he asked, causing the Elemental to look over at him and frown.

What? Was she the only one who was supposed to ask any questions?

His mother shuffled inside the ring. "They left so quickly, and Fiona's servants couldn't track them. That in itself was odd. She used a scryer and there was still no sign."

Of course it was Fiona, Sylvan's scheming mother. She was Elva's oldest cohort. They frequently had their little cat fights, but they always forgave each other in drawn out public scenes of reconciliation. They fed off the drama. Alec found it exhausting. But Fiona sometimes displayed some sense. Like using a scryer. The fact the scryer hadn't found anything was telling. Fiona must have really wanted those charms.

"It was too strange that they would disappear like that. Fiona isn't someone you cross. So I went to the house to check things out." His mother seemed to be regaining her composure. Her eyes were focusing now, alternating between him and the Fire Elemental. She sounded relieved to be getting things off her chest. "I found evidence of a black rite. At least, I think it was one. I'm not sure what they look like. Never seen one, don't know what kind of things are used. But the trash left behind, the things scattered around, they weren't *nice* things."

"What about the child?" the Elemental's voice was implacable. "Was there a body?"

"No. But in the one of the bedrooms, there was a blanket and pillow." His mother sucked in a breath. "And some toys. Children's toys."

"Why didn't you say something?" his father said from somewhere behind him.

"Why would I? We did nothing wrong. All I did was lend one of our properties. And maybe the child is fine. It was probably one of their own children. Even a black witch wouldn't harm their own child," his mother burst out, but she didn't sound convinced.

Alec passed both hands roughly over his face. "Is that what you've been telling yourself since you went to the house?" he asked.

His mother knew he was looking into Pedro's son's disappearance. How could she keep this kind of information from him?

"Of course it is. Why would I tell myself anything else?" his mother asked so incredulously he almost laughed in disbelief.

"Where is the house?" the Elemental demanded impatiently.

"Sixteen Citrus in Dover. It's by a stream, but I had it cleaned out the day before yesterday. There won't be anything there."

His mother turned away from all of them, wrapping her arms around herself.

The flames surrounding her died down, and the fire in the fireplace went out at the same time as the electric lights above. The room was thrown into darkness. Alec blinked as his night vision adjusted. His father was standing over his mother, gathering her in his arms.

The Elemental was gone.

6

It could have gone worse, Diana thought bracingly, trying to ignore the tightness in her chest. At least she had some information now—a place to start. She had been hoping to get lucky and find the guilty party among the vampires, but she supposed that would have been too easy.

She should have known this would lead to black magic.

Diana expelled a frustrated breath. She was far from the coven house now. Blocks away. The streets were wet, and the rain was really starting to come down. She should drop by the Elemental's safe house to pick up keys to the bike she kept in this city. They also kept a few cars, which would be better for the rain, but she preferred the bike. It was more maneuverable in tight spaces. And she was too keyed up to be boxed-in right now.

What the hell was up with their son?

In her experience, almost everyone ran like hell when she showed up. But not him. He came right up to her despite the fact she was threatening his parents, the leaders of his coven. Crazy or stupid?

According to what she'd heard about the scion of House Broussard, he was neither. She closed her eyes, and his image snuck into her mind. He was really tall, at least six foot four and muscular. Neither was common for a vampire that age.

Men from that era, especially those born into privilege, were never that well built. Muscles were for the lower classes. His black hair and dark blue eyes were especially striking with those sculpted cheekbones.

If there were real angels, he could pass for one of the fallen. Her mind ground to a halt and she gave herself a small shake.

Enough.

All vampires were handsome. They used their looks to draw in prey, so it wasn't surprising she'd noticed him. But he wasn't involved and was of no further significance to her investigation. Unlike the other Elementals, she was pretty good at detecting deception. She'd had a lot of practice, most of it acquired early in life.

By the time she arrived at the safe house, she was soaking wet. The nice apartment near the waterfront was used by all of them to some degree when they were in the area. They had many like it all over the world. Diana liked to sleep there. Not all of them did. Serin, who was sometimes accompanied by her partner on her missions, usually chose to stay in a hotel when he was with her.

A hotel was an option open to all of them. They had unlimited funds in bank accounts all over the world, established long ago by their predecessors from the gifts of precious metal and jewels the Mother provided. She had wanted them to always be free to do her will. But Diana liked to be surrounded by the clothes and supplies left behind by the others. She felt closer to them that way.

Even though she rarely saw them in person, the other Elementals were her only family. Not that she got to see them that often. In fact, it was forbidden for all of them to be in the same place at the same time, a safeguard the Mother had put in place in the early days when She feared rebellion. Sleeping among the possessions of the others was a poor substitute, but it did make Diana feel better.

Sighing, she took off her jacket and tried to stop feeling sorry for herself. Despite her more recent dissatisfaction, she had a strong purpose in life. But sometimes she couldn't help craving more. Like wishing she could see the others more often, to stay in their homes and eat with their families. Well, Serin and Logan's families. Gia's people were still around, but her immediate family was long gone.

Diana scolded herself. The other girls were always on missions too, and they rarely went home to their families. Really, it was easier for her. And it wasn't as if she couldn't speak to the others. All she had to do was light a candle or small flame. But now was not the time for another group chat. She didn't want to talk to Serin or Gia before she went out to the house in Dover to confirm what Elva had said. No one was going to like the news that a black circle was involved—one they hadn't been aware of before now.

She stripped off the rest of her wet clothes and took a quick shower. Then she fixed a quick meal from the well-stocked kitchen and peeked in the closet in the bedroom. There was a new wool coat hanging on a peg along with several flowing skirts. Serin must have been here last. *Without Jordan?* If he was with her, she would have stayed at a hotel. But the clothes were definitely Serin's style. Logan and Gia dressed more like her, in jeans and leather.

Also, if Logan had been here last, the bed would not have been made.

Diana hurriedly ate her meal. Having a lead for Katie meant pulling double duty here in town, but both cases were important.

Her primary target in Boston was the Denon Corporation. She'd cased her targets there this morning. Corporate jobs required a lot more legwork than her usual cases, but she didn't mind them.

Corporations leveraged ridiculous amounts of power these days and were capable of hurting a lot of people. Especially nameless, face-less, poor people in faraway countries.

The Denon Corporation had exploited many small villages in Africa, coming in and plundering the most valuable resources and leaving the poisonous waste that resulted without any effort to clean it up. She and the others had already decided exposure would serve them best, although her kind of judgement would have been a lot more satisfying.

She had planned on breaking into the Denon Corporation headquarters tonight to try and dig up some evidence on their toxic waste disposal procedures, but now searching the house in Dover was her priority.

Elva said the house had been cleaned, but she should still be able to find some signs. Black magic always left its mark. It just wasn't always visible.

LATER THAT NIGHT, Diana was in back of sixteen Citrus in Dover. The drive was less than an hour from the coven house, but the contrast between that place and this neighborhood couldn't have been more pronounced.

The house was in an isolated part of town in a wooded area. It was a tall elegant two-story structure with wooden shutters and a mansard roof, giving it an elegant old world look. However, the house felt much newer to her. Diana guessed that it had been built in the late eighties.

Gia could have pinpointed its exact age. She was capable of feeling the echo of movement in the Earth. It would whisper its secrets to her, like the wind told Logan what she wanted to know, though it didn't speak as often. To some extent, Serin could divine past events from water, but the oceans were vast and sparsely populated, despite the navies and fisheries of the world. And unconnected water, like fire, had no memory.

The stream Elva mentioned was little more than a trickle in the height of summer. But this was still a place of power. Diana could feel it. Here it was possible for a practitioner to connect to the Mother in a tenuous way. The witches called them ley lines. They were conduits of power they could tap into and, with enough skill, use to direct and move energy.

When it came right down to it, that was the basis of all witchcraft, both white and black. The way witches did it wrapped layers of ritual on top of ritual to bring about their desired effect. They weren't dissimilar to the rites the fae used for their magic, and to a smaller extent the shifters and the vampires in their creation ceremonies. However, as each group had evolved, what worked for one group no longer applied to the others. A witch couldn't use fae magic any more than a fae could work a witch charm.

Which was a blessing. Imagine what trouble a faery could cause with a black magic rite. Fae power was centered on life, whereas some witch magic called for death. Which was why the damn witches were so much trouble.

Diana continued walking around the perimeter of the dark house. She had a few more hours till dawn, and she wanted to be back in the safe house by then. The area was totally quiet except for the trickling of the stream. No animal sounds. No insects, for that matter. Like her, they could feel the darkness that had been done here and they avoided the area. The residual black magic permeated the air like smog. She could practically taste it.

Diana went to the back door. She was about to unlock it when it gave under her hand. Scanning the interior with her other sense, she finally realized someone else was there. Irritated that she'd missed the fact that she'd had company the whole time, she stalked through the kitchen and into the adjoining room. Except for the kitchen, the first floor was an open floor plan with a dining room blending into a sitting room and foyer that faced the front of the house. The dining area was next to the kitchen closest to her.

Sitting on the far side of a large oak dining table was the coven leader's son.

7

"What the hell are you doing here?" the Elemental demanded.

"I'm waiting for you," he answered with a little bow of acknowledgment.

The Elemental scowled at him. "Why? Do you have a death wish? If you do, I can provide a handy stake or at least a pencil. . ." She paused. "Since walking into the sun won't work for you."

He froze. Alec was rarely surprised by anything these days, but this tiny redhead had already floored him once and now she was doing it again.

He had stumbled on the first mention of the ritual of Ra when looking into the origins of his kind. But it hadn't worked, no matter how many times he repeated it. In the following decades, he had hunted down rituals written by civilizations both older and far younger than ancient Egypt. As it turned out, there were hundreds of them, all frustratingly inconsistent. It had taken him years to cut through the bull and make the connections between the different rites and rituals. In the end, it had been deceptively simple to call on the magic and ask for the blessing of sunlight.

Well, simple only after all those years of research. It was his greatest accomplishment and most closely guarded secret.

"You can tell? Even my parents can't tell."

"No offense, but your parents aren't exactly rocket scientists."

Even though he'd had that very thought on many occasions, Alec was indignant to have it pointed out by someone else. Especially someone who had only just met them. He frowned and she softened a little. . .very little.

"They're intelligent enough, I suppose," she continued. "But they haven't exactly made the most of their extended lifespans, now, have they? They're content to pass the time enjoying their wealth and doing little else."

"They're not that bad," he protested, aware he was uncomfortably close to lying.

The Elemental raised her brows and looked him up and down. "You still haven't explained why you are here. And I want the real reason," she said, using a delicate white finger to trace a figure eight pattern on the table. The satiny oak surface smoked as the infinity sign burned in deep. "I'll know if you're lying."

Alec's aggressive instincts and indignation rose to the fore. He was the son of a privileged noble house, and no one ever questioned his honesty.

"I came here to see you. I want to help," he bit off with aggravation.

His house had indirectly helped a group of black witches, and he needed to repair the damage. It was his duty.

The Elemental looked at him with a disbelieving expression. "Listen, Team Edward, people don't volunteer to help me. Instead they take great pains to run in the other direction. Those are *smart* people. Why don't you follow their example and take your metrosexual butt back to the coven house."

Team Edward? Who's Edward? "Look, my mother didn't know what she was doing when she lent this house to the witches. I only want to make things right and reaffirm my house's commitment to the covenant. We don't harm children."

She backed away from him slightly, cocking her head to one side and studying his face intently. "No," she said after a moment. "That isn't it. Try again."

Can she read minds too? Fuck. There wasn't anything in the old legends about mind reading.

But those ancient stories fell far short of the reality, didn't they? Probably because most people *did* run in the other direction. When he didn't add anything more, the Elemental waved an irritated hand in front of his face.

"Hello? I don't have time for. . .wherever this is," she said waving her hand in a circle to encompass all of him.

"I simply want to help," he said in a low, even voice. "My house is involved in this, albeit unintentionally. I need to make reparations."

The Elemental continued to give him the stink eye as she leaned across the table to stare him down. She looked like she was seriously considering leaping across it. Unfortunately, it didn't look like she was gearing up to do something truly shocking, like kissing him.

No, she looked lethal. Bracing himself to run, he was surprised when she suddenly smiled.

Oh, wow. Alec's whole body flushed at the sight of that sweet smile. Even if he didn't trust it for a second.

"I know you're hiding something, and I don't give a rat's ass about the vampiric code of chivalry," she said in a voice like sugar. "If you are keeping something from me, I'm going to burn this place to the ground—starting with the floorboards under your feet." She gave him another smile. . .but not the same one.

Okay, back to cold, very cold. Redirect.

"I haven't been in the basement. I think that's where they did their ritual," he said to distract her.

She stopped moving and stared at him, cool and untouchable. The moment stretched, and with an admirable effort at hiding his discomfort, he said, "I can tell that is where they were conducting their rites. I'm sensitive to that kind of vibration. Maybe a little bit how your kind feels. . .what it is that you feel."

The wood under her palm smoldered a bit. "Would you like to know how I feel things?" she asked, suddenly cheeky.

Yes.

"*No,*" he said decisively. The wood was really smoking now.

He continued, "I didn't want to interfere with your process, so I didn't go down there. I didn't want to risk adding my own heat signature on top of whomever else went down there. Not that there's a lot of it, but I am generally a little above room temperature if I've been moving around."

"Hmm. So Alec Broussard's not just a pretty face," the Elemental said sarcastically.

"You know my name," he said quietly, trying not to let on how inordinately pleased he was.

He failed completely.

The Elemental rolled her eyes. Someone had to be really cute to look good doing that… and she was. Although cute didn't cover it. *Hot does, but that's too on the nose.*

"Well now that you've acknowledged that I'm not a complete waste of your time—"

"I don't believe I've acknowledged anything other than a desire to mock you or set you on fire," she said, cutting him off.

He ignored that. "I can tell my mother's servant, Dietrich, was down in the basement last, presumably cleaning up on Mother's orders. He locked it after he left." There was no reaction, but he hadn't spontaneously burst into flames, so he continued. "I think there were at least four witches," he added carefully, watching as she spun around to the basement door.

It was at the half-way mark between the dining area and the living room space. How did she even know where it was? Did she detect the evil or did Mother Nature beam the floor plans directly into her brain like in the Matrix? He decided not to ask. She still looked annoyed.

"If you insist on staying here, don't touch anything," she said repressively.

Putting her hand on the door, she unlocked it with a rush of hot air he could feel from where he was standing.

That is so awesome. Impressed despite his desire to appear cool and composed, Alec stifled his enthusiasm and put on a passive expression. A witch would have needed an incantation spoken aloud to open the door without touching it. He stepped closer to the doorway as she started down the dark staircase.

"Do you need a light?" Alec asked.

She didn't answer as she disappeared from view.

"Yeah, that was probably a stupid question."

DIANA IGNORED the vampire as she made her way down the stairs. Why wouldn't he go away? She had been right. There was something wrong with that one.

Refocusing her attention on the scene in front of her, she could see he'd been right. There were indeed four witches who used this threshold frequently in the past month. And most recently two vampires, one of them Elva and another younger male vampire.

So Alec Broussard *was* a sensitive.

A sensitive vampire would be able to sense the presence of one of his own. If he knew them from before, he could probably identify them. But that wasn't a universal vampire skill like mesmerism or their supernatural stealth and speed. And sensing past visits from the Otherkind? That meant there was some serious talent there. Very rare for a vampire.

But that didn't explain his insistence on 'helping'. Honor wasn't a good enough answer. There was the small possibility he was lying and *was* involved with the witches somehow. But her instinct said he wasn't. Still, she would have to keep an eye on him.

Saving that thought for later, she faced the dark expanse of the room.

Dietrich does fine work, she mused. *How annoying.*

The room was preternaturally clean. The only thing in it was a neatly arranged tool shelf at the back wall. The tools had no energy attached to them at all, meaning they hadn't been used in months. Maybe a year or more. Plus, they were dusty, despite the Spartan cleanliness of the rest of the room. It practically sparkled.

Diana closed her eyes and took a deep breath. In her mind's eye, she could still see the room like a tape playing backwards, the amorphous shapes of the people who had been here. Dietrich's impression was strongest. Diana watched as he cleaned backwards in jerky motions. She couldn't see what he was cleaning. The debris didn't have a heat signature, although she could sense where it had been. Its presence left a dark stain only visible to her.

And maybe the damn vampire upstairs. A sensitive vampire of all things. Did he feel the ley lines? And how did his knowledge manifest? Her ability worked in a way uniquely tied to her fire gift. She could only guess how the vampire sensed what he did.

Diana turned her attention back to the image of Dietrich, annoyed with herself for thinking of the other vampire at all. Dietrich was farther back in time now. He was gathering things—maybe cleaning supplies. A moment later, he was retreating up the stairs. She skipped back to the earlier and fainter heat signatures: Elva and Dietrich coming in, Elva gesturing wildly.

Further back, Diana willed. For a moment, there was nothing, and then the images started, even fainter now.

The shapes were growing less distinct, the heat signatures slowly fading the farther back she went. The muted figures were in a circle around something now, and for a moment she could see it, a metal bowl that heated slightly when they burned something in it. The heat in it flaring and then dissipating as one of the shapes moved their hand, a lit match retreating backward. She needed to find the trash Dietrich threw away.

One of the figures joined late and settled awkwardly at the ring. It was a man, somewhat overweight. The figure who lit the fire was also a man, but the one to the left of him was smaller and slim. A woman. The last was probably a woman, too, judging by the way she moved.

Two men and two women. A balanced black circle. She went further back, studying the forms even as they grew fainter. She couldn't recognize any of the rites from their blurring movements. And they performed more than one. She could just see the bowl flaring intermittently as they lit fires in it, sometimes candles, too, one in front of each member of the circle.

But the figures were too faint now to make out anything that might identify them and eventually the forms faded completely. Diana relaxed her focus. She turned around and headed back up the stairs, expecting to find the vampire waiting in the kitchen, but he wasn't there. Flexing her senses, she spotted the slight heat vamps retained shifting around upstairs.

Diana found him at a doorway at end of the hall on the second floor. She moved toward him, but he didn't turn toward her till she was next to him. His expression was grave. She looked in the room past him and froze. Her insides twisted.

In the corner of the room lay a dirty mattress, with a blanket lying half on the floor. Next to it was a small dirty pink and white sneaker.

Diana's temperature rose, and before the vamp could move, he was on the floor flat on his back, her hand on his neck. His shirtfront smoked slightly under her touch. She shifted her knee to his chest.

"What do you know about this?" She gestured to the mattress.

"Nothing you don't already know," he wheezed out from behind her hand.

"Try again," she hissed, her hand at her side sparking, fire flaring to life.

"Okay! Okay! I came home because I was summoned."

She rolled her eyes and gestured impatiently for more.

"I always keep tabs on the coven's activities when I'm away. My parents lead well enough but they're. . .a little careless. Not always into details. And they don't watch what the younger members are up to unless it benefits them or they become inconvenient in some way. They're better than the other coven leaders I know, but it's still a good idea to check on them," he said, trying to shift her off him, but she didn't move.

Diana extinguished her fire and brought her other hand down to join the first in a tight grip.

"I was back in England, down at Oxford, checking through some of the Bodleian library collections. One of my men back here contacted me. A child had gone missing, a little boy—not a girl. It was the kid of one of our agents, a human servant. His name is Pedro Montes. He has served us faithfully, as did his father before him. He acts as caretaker for several of our properties, including the one he lives in. His son disappeared almost a week ago. Not all vampire houses treat their staff that well, but in our house the loyalty of our servants is rewarded," he said earnestly.

"When the boy was taken, no one saw anything and no one took responsibility. But the building was warded against everyone but humans and members of our house. And the wards hadn't been tripped," Alec added, surreptitiously pushing against her knee.

He looked confused, as if he was trying to figure out why he couldn't budge someone half his size.

"A boy?" Diana asked, her voice distant. The disappearance could be unrelated, but her gut told her otherwise. "How old?"

"Five, almost six."

Same age as Katie.

"That's why I came home. When my man saw the wards were pristine, he realized one had been swapped out. That shouldn't be possible. He questioned Pedro, but by that time he was too far gone."

"Explain," she ordered flatly.

"Pedro barely remembers he had a son. It was as if he'd been wiped clean."

"So it *was* a vampire." *From your house,* she added in her head.

"That is what I thought. It's why I rushed home. But I saw Pedro this morning. Before you came to case the coven house yesterday afternoon."

I knew someone was out there. "And now you don't think it was a vampire." It wasn't a question.

"No. Pedro is still. . .messed up, and it's been over a week. A compulsion would have worn off by now."

"Even if it was a very old vampire? Like your parent's age? How old is Fiona?" she asked, smacking his hand away from her knee when he started to try and wiggle out from under it.

"She's younger than mother but not by that much. And even my father's compulsion would have faded after a few days without reinforcement. My man has been watching Pedro for longer than that. No vampire has come near him in all that time."

"Still could be one of the ancient ones—or a black witch. And we already know black witches are operating in the area and are not afraid to act under your coven's nose. It must have been one of them that took the boy, circumventing the ward in place and compelling the father to hand over his son somehow. That last is worrisome. That kind of compulsion can't be done with a spell. It's a vampire thing. Trying to use another group's brand of magic doesn't work, at least not well," Diana said, thinking aloud.

She relaxed her grip on his throat.

"I don't think it worked well at all. This man, Pedro, he's. . .broken. He is functioning completely on auto-pilot. He gets up every morning, showers, and goes to work. He does his job but he can't engage anymore. It's like his personality was wiped away. And he's not getting better. Even a compulsion done by an ancient one would fade, although I've only met a few, and they're not exactly open about the strength of their abilities." Alec paused and then asked politely, "Do you think you could let me up?"

Diana looked down at him. She pursed her lips and waited a full minute before shifting off him, rising in a fluid motion. By comparison, the vampire rose awkwardly, probably a first for him.

"I need to see him. And this Fiona, too. Where does Pedro live?" Diana would find him tomorrow after she slept.

"I can bring Pedro to you. Fiona will have gone to ground after tonight. She was in the ballroom when you. . .dropped by."

"I don't need help finding Fiona. If she was there, she can't hide from me. And I don't want Pedro removed from his home. I want to see him there, just tell me where it is."

"My man, Daniel, is still with Pedro. I really think you should let me introduce you two. Pedro isn't reacting well to strangers right now. But he's gotten used to having Daniel around. And well. . .you will scare the shit out of Daniel unless I'm there. Remember the whole smart people running thing?" he asked as he straightened his clothes fussily.

Diana lifted an eyebrow before turning and headed to the stairs. "I always catch them, don't worry your pretty little head about that," she called behind her as she went down the stairs.

"I can find out where Fiona is, too," he offered a little too eagerly as he followed her. Maybe she shouldn't have called him pretty.

"Don't bother. As far as I'm concerned, she trafficked with black witches. I'll find her myself and will deal with her without your counsel."

Or your interference, Diana tacked on mentally.

Alec hurried down the stairs after her. "I realize it looks bad, but my mother is most likely right on this one. Fiona probably didn't do anything wrong intentionally. My mother likes having her around because she can basically look down on her intellectually. She is the kind of vampire who's all glitter and pomp. Her daughter's a little brighter, but both of them are too self-involved for anything like this."

"If she hasn't done anything wrong, I'll know, and she'll be fine. But you have no place shielding the guilty. If you really want to help, you tell me where the trash from the basement is."

Alec thought for a moment. "Dietrich wouldn't have left it in a bin nearby. It's possible he burned it or something. He wouldn't know to throw it in the sea to let the saltwater purify it."

No longer surprised that he knew so much about witch magic, Diana gave the vampire another assessing look. *Doesn't make him useful, just more suspicious.* But if he was hiding some evil seed, it was buried way down deep because she couldn't sense it.

"Let me guess, you want to offer to check with Dietrich and get the stuff if he hasn't gotten rid of it?"

Alec nodded. "I can get in touch with him as soon as I leave here. I don't get a great signal close to the house." He fingered what was presumably a cell phone in his breast pocket.

No, you wouldn't. The electromagnetic nature of ley lines disrupted cell and radio signals.

She wanted to sigh in frustration. He would think he was entitled to some quid pro quo if she took him up on his offer to act as a go-between between her and members of his coven. He would do his best to shield them from her. She didn't need that kind of help.

But she was technically in Boston to deal with the Denon Corporation. Now she had to set that aside because this situation was too important.

Diana mulled it over. She knew her sisters would support any action she chose to take. One of them would even come to back her up if she asked. But all three of them were in far-flung corners of the world right now, dealing with their own investigations, and she didn't want to bother them. If she needed backup, maybe she could do worse than Alec Broussard.

What are you thinking? She inwardly berated herself. Diana didn't need help from a vampire whose only concern was to cover his coven's ass. *Just get the stuff from him and let him introduce you to his man and then you can finish with him.*

"If he still has the trash, bring it to the meet with Pedro," she said. "We'll meet at two PM. I assume you will want to meet in daylight?"

The better to hide your activities from your house.

"Yes, I think that would be best," Alec said.

"Fine." Diana swung around and walked to the back door. She was out of it and halfway to her bike when he called out from behind her.

"Don't you need the address? Should I text it to you?"

"I don't use phones. If you're there, I will find you. So be there," she ordered, climbing on her bike.

"Well, that went well," Alec said aloud to the trees as she drove away.

8

Diana returned to the safe house shortly before dawn, where she briefly lit a candle and, after confirming that her sisters weren't communing, let it flare high and hot for several heartbeats. Then she let it burn out.

The unnaturally high heat she'd generated would serve as a calling card for her sisters when they next checked in. It was just as well. She didn't want to go into everything tonight.

Her thoughts wandered to Alec. She should feel guilty for terrifying him. It shouldn't be funny—the face he made when she had flipped him like a doll.

His kind weren't used to being outmatched. And he was at the top of the heap when it came to strength and power. Few other vampires could match him, even those older than him. But he was either very brave or very stupid if he continued to insist on tagging along during her investigation.

She lay down on the bed and punched the pillow into shape.

Vampire chivalry. Blech.

AT NOON THE NEXT DAY, Alec still had men scrambling to find Dietrich's dumpsite. He hadn't learned where Fiona was hiding, but he had gotten a hold of Dietrich before dawn.

He'd cornered him as they prepared for the daylight rest and learned both the approximate location of the trash as well as the state in which Dietrich found the items the witches had left behind.

Dietrich hadn't burned the things after all, but he'd probably done worse by tossing them in a random dumpster without noting where he was. It took a good twenty minutes for Dietrich to even pinpoint the neighborhood on a map. After that, Alec only had enough time to call his men and start the search before he pretended to prepare for slumber with the rest of his house. When Alec had finally been assured that the human servants were off on their own business, he'd hurriedly dressed and slipped back out of the house.

After watching his men crawl through two dumpsters in Somerville with no luck, Alec accepted that Dietrich's usual precision was absent when it came to giving directions. That or he'd been too rattled by recent events. If he'd seen Diana in action, that was probably the case. So far, all of his men had found were a lot of empty pizza boxes and other way more disgusting discards.

I'm going to have a lot of dry cleaning bills to comp, he thought, making a mental note to look into it. His staff would never bother him with such trivial matters, but the situation with Pedro had highlighted his attitude toward the people who served him.

A signal came from one of his men near the fourth dumpster his men had searched. One of them hustled over with partially filled black trash bag. He looked inside and saw a discarded bowl and an assortment of half burned herbs stained with a sticky brown substance on top of a lot of other more mysterious items.

He threw the bag in the back of the car, relieved he hadn't needed to make a trip to the city dump. A city this big probably had more than one. He'd honestly never thought about it before.

DIANA WOKE near noon with a start. She was sure she'd been dreaming, but it wasn't the typical nightmare she'd had back when she was in the juvenile ward. All she remembered was that she had been lying next to someone, deep in conversation. But it was already too faded for her to hold onto to the images.

She never recalled her dreams unless it had been a particularly vivid nightmare. Shaking off the weird feeling, Diana showered and got in touch with her sisters.

"A black circle, you're sure?" Gia asked. "What did you find exactly?"

Diana filled them in on the details, skipping over Alec's involvement for the moment. "I believe the circle has been active for some time. They may be involving children in their rites. I don't know if the children are being sacrificed. No one died in the basement, or any other part of the house, but they could be working up to it. Two children have gone missing in suspicious circumstances. One is a Broussard servant's son. The other is the little girl, Katie. They're probably moving around a lot, trying to shield themselves from detection with spells and by using houses not tied to them in some way, properties favorable to conducting magic." Diana held her breath, waiting for the others to confirm what she suspected.

"Something is wrong, very wrong with the Mother. . .or with us," Serin said, her mental voice near a whisper.

"Agreed," Gia said slowly. "If Diana is right, and I've never known her to be wrong, then these witches are acting outside natural law in such a way that She must be unaware of them. While we couldn't find a child victim of a human predator so quickly, we should have been aware of a black circle forming much earlier."

Worry flooded through Diana at Gia's words. She had suspected the same thing, but acknowledging it openly made it feel real.

"Wait," Logan broke in anxiously. "Wouldn't we have felt a shift in the balance ourselves even if the Mother wasn't aware of it? Aren't we her first line of defense? She created us as guardians and wardens. Don't we feel the shifts in the balance without her knowledge?"

"Sometimes," Gia answered with an unhappy sigh. "We should feel the shift if we are near enough, but sometimes the Mother feels it first and then relays it to us. It's actually simply based on proximity. There isn't a great difference between the two in terms of time and our perception. But it's clear that none of us felt the shift in the balance that should have occurred when the circle first formed."

"Are we broken?" Logan asked, her young voice sounding desolate.

Diana scowled. "I don't feel any different. I'm just frustrated that I can't detect the circle. My gifts are working the same way they always have," she said. "My gut says there's something about these witches. Something different. They are somehow shielding their activities from us. Maybe they've found a new way to hide from the Mother as well."

She related what she'd learned about Pedro and the strange nature of his compulsion.

"That might be true," Gia said. "We don't feel a shift until the damage has been done in the non-magic cases. It takes so much more for us to become aware of them. We've attributed that to the overall increase in violence in the human world. But there is another possibility. Perhaps She is going to sleep again."

Diana sincerely hoped not. The times in their history when the Mother slept had been troubled for all magical and non-magical beings alike.

"Do you need help on this, Di?" Serin asked. "I can shuffle some things and be on my way there the day after tomorrow. With this and the Denon case, you might need backup."

"No, you have your hands full in Mexico. Besides I. . .I may already have some help."

There was absolute silence for a long moment.

"Who is it?" Serin asked.

"The vampire leader's son offered to make reparations for his families involvement," Diana said flatly.

"Alec Broussard!" Logan gushed. "Isn't he that super hot, most eligible bachelor vamp? He's like their equivalent of Prince William or JFK Jr. Wait...I thought he was in Europe or something?"

Diana frowned at Logan's reaction. Was she following gossip on Alec like some kind of fangirl?

"He was keeping tabs on his parents," she explained. "Apparently he doesn't trust them to stay out of trouble. When one of their servant's sons went missing, he came home to investigate." She didn't offer an opinion on how atypical that was.

"How exactly is he helping?" Serin asked, suspicion threading her voice.

"He brought the second missing child to my attention and is having one of his men care for the father. It sounds like this Pedro's memory was tampered with enough to do some serious damage. The vamp is also tracking down the trash the witches left behind in the house that his mother's servant got rid of. . .and he's a Daywalker. Also a sensitive, it seems."

Someone whistled.

"Interesting," Logan said.

Serin seconded the sentiment.

"And you're all right with this?" Gia asked, her voice doubtful.

"After tonight, I'll be done with him," Diana said. "His stupid vampire honor will be satisfied, and I won't have him underfoot."

"*O-kay*," Serin said, drawing out the syllables. "Well, just be careful around him."

"Careful my bodacious booty!" Logan chimed in. "You should keep that tasty piece around for as long as possible."

"That's not going to happen," Diana said, rolling her eyes. "Both of these cases are too important to bring in an outsider for long."

"Yeah, okay, but it would be nice for you to have some form of support. . .on this case," Logan replied a little too enthusiastically.

Diana sincerely hoped Logan wasn't working up to a lecture about mixing with others again. She knew the Air Elemental loved her unreservedly, but it wasn't the first time she'd tweaked Diana about her loner status.

Logan was always encouraging her to blow off some steam with a guy or make friends outside their circle. It was a teensy bit hypocritical, considering she didn't do either of those things herself. But Logan had her mother's family to lean on. They had long ties to the various Elemental lineages, and more than one had come from their bloodline.

As for men, Logan was a shameless flirt, but she took her legacy seriously. She pushed away the men who flocked to her when they got too close, saying she couldn't afford a real diversion, but that didn't mean she couldn't have a little fun.

"Don't worry about me—I have all of you," Diana said, the last bit tongue and cheek.

They did have each other, just not in person. Not all at once anyways.

"If you do need more help, I can be there in four days," Gia said.

Diana smiled, touched at their concern. "I hope this will be over by then. Don't worry. I'm a multitasking machine," she assured them. "I've got some background research to do on the Denon case, and then I'm meeting the vamp and the father of the missing boy."

"Okay, but if this goes south, make sure to keep us informed and one of us will be there," Serin said.

Logan and Gia echoed Serin's words, and all three withdrew from the conversation.

DIANA TRACKED the vampire to Pedro's building a half hour ahead of schedule.

The apartment building in Brookline was in a nice and quiet residential neighborhood. According to her research, the Broussard's owned hundreds of these all over the state, under different names and shell corporations. They also owned warehouses and office buildings up and down the east coast. Their nearly limitless funds were a major source of contention for her.

Diana had money now, but she vividly remembered what it was like not to have it. Her resentment of the vampires who hoarded it was instinctive.

Technically, plenty of rich humans did the same thing, and she felt the same things about them when she witnessed their excesses on television or saw it in person. But it was the vampires she remembered to hate long after she forgot about whatever rich human asshole had pissed her off. At least the humans occasionally used their obscene wealth for good.

There were a number of good Samaritans out there that did their best to help move humanity forward. A lot of them did good work, but there wasn't a single vampire among them. Since their kind considered themselves not only outside, but also above humanity, it wasn't really surprising there wasn't a great philanthropic spirit in their ranks.

Pedro's building didn't have a whole lot of security in human terms. There was a security door and bars on the first floor windows, but that was about it. In supernatural terms, however, the building was on par with a bank. It was heavily warded against anyone not in the Broussard clan and the humans who lived there.

That level of security was unusual for a mere rental property, one far from the main coven house. Perhaps a member lived here part time.

No. It wasn't glamorous enough. Her senses told her a vampire had come and gone regularly in the recent past, but probably not with enough frequency to be a resident. *I doubt they send one of their own kind to collect the rent.*

It was Alec's signature, but that meant he'd been here fairly frequently in the past week. More often than she would have suspected.

She made her way into the building, the security door and wards inconsequential. The wards didn't even register her presence. She may as well have been a ghost. The apartment she sought was on a third floor, at one end of the hallway. After confirming that the inhabitants were well away from the door, she slipped inside.

It was quite nice inside, light and airy with hardwood floors that were worn but well kept. The furniture was also worn, but the scarred surfaces were polished and a cushion on the couch had been carefully mended.

Voices came from the back corner of the apartment, but she wasn't concerned with the vamp and his servant right now. Turning away from the voices she crossed the central living area. Instinct guided her to the room at the end of the hallway off the living room. The door swung wide on silent hinges.

Toys were neatly arranged in shelves, and unlike the furniture in the living room, most of it looked fairly new. The bed had sheets with the *Cars* characters.

It was the room of a happy and well-loved little boy. Diana sat on the bed and closed her eyes, holding a stuffed cartoon turtle. She focused her mind, searching through the signatures of the people who'd been in this room. Alec and a human who was probably his servant were the last. Farther back in time there was another human man. Presumably Pedro, the father. She went further back, trying to find the last time the boy was in this room.

There you are. And not alone. A woman had been in this room. This was where the boy had been taken from. Was it a babysitter? She didn't think so. The boy didn't seem to know this woman. She could see the scene playing in reverse as the woman knelt by the bed, trying to coax the little boy-shape into taking her hand.

Diana went back as far as she could to see if the woman had been there before, but whatever images she could retrieve were too unclear. She turned toward the door, not really surprised to find Alec standing there.

"What is the boy's name?" she asked.

"Elias," he said evenly, pronouncing it with a Mexican accent. "When did you get here? I didn't hear you come in."

But you still knew I was here. Hmm.

She shrugged. "I came early. I wanted to see his room alone. How is the father?" she asked, rising from the bed.

"The same, I think. He recognizes me now. But he still doesn't respond well to strangers," Alec said by way of warning. "Do you want me to bring him in here?"

"No. This may be too much for him," she said, gesturing to the room.

"Can you use any of the little boy's possessions to find him? I had a witch scry with some of his toys as aids, but they didn't get anything," he said.

"No. It doesn't work that way. Children aren't traceable. The innocent aren't. Is the father in the kitchen?"

"Yes. We sometimes have to remind him to eat. He's...not improving."

"Let's go," she said, waving him in front of her.

She followed him out through the bright sunny living room, its warm and inviting atmosphere striking a discordant note to the grim mood.

Alec pushed open a cream-colored swinging door, revealing an equally pleasant sunlit kitchen. It was cheerful and welcoming despite the second-hand furniture and chipped paint on the windowsill. Inside was a short and stocky muscular man wearing a tracksuit. He was in his late thirties or early forties with salt and pepper hair. Daniel, presumably.

He was leaning over a dark little man with a heavily lined face and vacant expression sitting at the kitchen table. Daniel looked up as they entered and shifted to one side to give them room. He wasn't what she expected.

Most vampires picked their human servants for their looks, and they almost always dressed nearly as well as their employers. It was a point of pride with vamps. Their servants were a reflection of themselves, and image was everything. She would bet good money that his mother's servant Dietrich wouldn't be caught dead in a tracksuit.

Diana turned her attention to the room and the man who had so clearly loved his son. There were signs of the boy here, too. Child-sized cups and plates with cartoon designs. But they were dirty and shoved to the side of the counter. The regular plates were clean and put away, but a cartoon cup was lying on the floor in the corner unnoticed. The rest of the room was clean. Only the things that had belonged to his son were soiled. It was like Pedro couldn't see them anymore. She was glad Daniel had been wise enough to leave things be.

It had to be a black spell. Only strong black magic would be able to wipe a person from another's memory. The effort to wipe a child from his father's mind had to be herculean. Parental bonds were usually the strongest, though there were always exceptions.

Alec stepped toward Pedro. He leaned down, placing a reassuring hand on the unresponsive man's shoulder. "I have a visitor for you, Pedro." He gestured to Diana standing behind him. "Her name is. . ."

She scowled at him, but Alec didn't blink.

"It's Diana," she said grudgingly.

He rewarded her with a dazzling smile and turned to Pedro. "Pedro, this is Diana. She's here to help," he said confidently.

"Wait outside," she said, piqued that he'd gotten her name out of her.

Alec gave her a resigned look but left with Daniel without protest. Diana knelt at Pedro's side. He didn't turn to look at her. Reaching out, she took his hand. He turned in her direction with eyes that couldn't focus.

Then he started to scream.

9

Alec and Daniel rushed back into the room, but Diana waved them away. She caught Pedro's flailing hands with one of hers and used the other to tilt Pedro's head toward her, forcing eye contact.

The second his bloodshot brown eyes met her clear green ones, he stopped struggling and quieted down. From the corner of her eye, she saw Alec and Daniel exchanging a look, but she ignored them and waited until they slipped back out of the kitchen before closing her eyes, focusing on the spell surrounding Pedro.

It was like an octopus—its sticky tendrils threaded in and out of Pedro's aura with a tenacious hold. It wasn't strictly a witch's spell. Traces of something else were weaved into the fabric. She'd never seen anything like it.

It was clear that the spell was failing, too. From what she could tell, it was supposed to remove specific memories and nothing more. But it was killing Pedro, cracking his aura like weeds could break up concrete. Or it would if she didn't remove it.

With a deep breath that did nothing to relieve the weight on her shoulders, she took hold of the spell and started peeling it back from his body, slowly working each individual tentacle away as carefully as she could. She didn't want to damage what was left of Pedro's aura.

It took a long time.

When she was done, she gathered the remnants of the spell in her hands, pulling it up and away from Pedro. He slumped over slightly as he was released, and she stood, staring down at her hands for a second. A black oily substance covered them, one that a normal person couldn't see. It squirmed and stretched toward her like a living thing trying to find a new host. But she was outside its reach. Unnerved, she called the fire and burned it away.

"Was that it? The black spell?" Alec was in the doorway again.

So much for Elementals and witches being the only ones to sense spells. . .

"Do you actually see it or simply feel it?" he asked, the curiosity clear in his voice.

"Do *you* see it or just feel it?" she countered, not really comfortable revealing any details about herself.

"I. . .feel spells. But not the way you seem to. Not as a tangible thing I can hold or touch," Alec replied.

Well, so much for keeping secrets around observant bloodsuckers.

When she didn't elaborate, he gave up on an answer and instead asked, "Will he be better now?"

Pedro was unconscious now, slumped in his chair with most of his weight on the table.

"I'm not a healer, Alec," Diana replied as she checked Pedro's vital signs. "The spell was killing him. I had to remove it. But he won't be the same. The damage to his psyche was extensive. He will start remembering what he lost. But probably not everything."

For a long moment, Alec looked at her.

"What?" she asked stiffly. The way he stared at her was really starting to get on her nerves.

"Thanks for doing whatever you could," he said simply.

She ignored him and turned to Pedro. "He'll sleep for hours."

"Daniel will stay with him," he said.

She simply humphed in response, but couldn't help thinking that any normal vamp would wash their hands of it now, reparations made. Most would weasel their way out of anything that smacked of responsibility.

Daniel came back from the living room and walked to Pedro, who was now sprawled across the table. He checked for a pulse. Diana gave him a reproving look, and the stocky man grinned at her sheepishly, revealing several good teeth and a few gold ones.

Weird ass choice for a vampire servant. Daniel picked up Pedro easily and walked back out of the kitchen.

"Where did you find Daniel?" she asked, curiosity getting the better of her.

"He's from Brooklyn, a former mobster but pretty low level," Alec said.

Diana lifted an eyebrow.

"He was too decent to get very far up in the organization. I gave him a better alternative," Alec said, answering her unasked question.

Diana pursed her lips and cocked a hip. "Do your parents know about him?"

Alec smiled slightly and said, "I think you already know the answer. He doesn't fit with the general image of a coven's *servus*. But he is loyal, and I have several servants outside the coven hierarchy. It's not uncommon."

Diana's only response was to lift the other eyebrow for a moment before her face turned serious. "I'll be back tomorrow to talk with Pedro once he's rested. You don't need to be here if Daniel agrees to watch him. Consider your debt paid."

Alex stiffened. "My house's debt will not be paid until the children are found." His voice was firm. "Even if they are no longer among the living. I will help you search for them."

It sounded more like a command than an offer.

Diana bristled. "That's taking your responsibility a bit far. And we don't let outsiders into our investigations," she said in a cold, flat voice.

He gave her a little smile. "You sound like a soldier," he replied in a softer voice.

"I *am* a soldier."

"Well, I'm a scholar of some renown. I've done a lot of research on black rites. I could be helpful," Alec added.

Diana narrowed her eyes, shifting her body weight so that her position was a touch more menacing. "And just why do you know so much about black magic?"

"It's not what you think. I've studied black circles because I've run into them before. Well, truthfully, it was one wannabe circle and a genuine one. But afterwards I worked up a summary of them, something akin to an anthropological study," he continued. "You've already noted that this circle seems to operate outside normal bounds. I could offer some useful insights."

Diana tried to take the offer seriously. She knew plenty about the top magic families. Probably a lot more than he did, but they weren't dealing with someone familiar. Which meant her target hadn't grown up in one of the families trained in the history and proper use of magic.

Someone who had grown up with that background wouldn't have done that to Pedro. The spell was powerful but clumsy. It only partly worked because of the raw power behind it—not the finesse and skill with which it had been applied.

The spellcaster could be someone who had been banished from one of the family circles early in their training. Or it could be a remnant—one of those humans who was spontaneously able to work magic. They were usually so distantly related to a magical line that the family itself was unaware of the connection. Otherwise they were required to monitor them according to the rules of the covenant. One of those remnants could have pieced together some twisted version of spell craft through trial and error. There were enough books filled with half-truths about magic that had leaked into the human world.

"A wannabe circle?" she asked eventually.

Alec took the chair Pedro had just vacated, while Diana leaned on the counter, arms crossed below her chest.

"It was the first one, close to two centuries ago. The village elders of this little town in southern England had acquired these fake spell books. They thought they could summon a demon to do their bidding and give them riches."

"What did you do?" Diana asked.

"I. . .um. . .I pretended to be the demon," he said, grimacing minutely.

Diana burst out laughing before she could stop herself. The vampire blushed. A real honest-to-god blush.

"I know it was pretty silly. I was still relatively young, on the Grand Tour with some friends. I stumbled across this group by chance and decided to teach them a lesson," he said, sitting up a little straighter.

"How?" she asked, still amused but trying to hide it.

"Scared them straight basically. I made them do silly rituals involving nudity. They were all middle-aged and rather portly. They ran around in the woods naked to commune with the dark forces. I also made them give away their money to the poor."

"Wasn't that supposed to be the other way around?"

"Yes, but I convinced them that the spirits would multiply a thousand fold whatever they gave away. None of the poor children in that town starved that year." His smile faded slightly. "I learned a few had died the year before. The crops were blighted. And those rich bastards let them go hungry."

Alec's expression became grim and forbidding, and for the first time, she could see him for the truly powerful vampire scion that he was.

"So what did you do to them in the end?" Diana was careful to keep an even expression to avoid betraying her curiosity.

"I bankrupted them. I tricked and threatened, and they did as my demon alter ego demanded. Then I exposed them to the town as devil worshipers by pretending to be the devil myself. One of my friends helped me with a costume and some special effects," he said, his eyes lightening in remembrance. "After that, we got the hell out of there, with the only genuine spell book they had. I didn't think they deserved to keep it. It's still part of my collection. No one has ever tried to claim it," he said.

"And the genuine circle?" she asked.

His expression shifted from serious to apprehensive. "That was almost a hundred years later. And it wasn't an accident that I found it. I met a warlock, a scholar in Prague with whom I had a lot in common. He must have known I was a vampire. I thought he was simply a normal warlock at first. My radar has gotten a lot better since then. It took me months of correspondence and a few meetings before I realized he was a black magic practitioner."

"How did you find out?"

"I had begun to suspect he was hiding something, but I didn't know what it was. I had traveled to visit him that winter. He was excited to have another scholar visit. He welcomed me into his home, and at the end of my stay, he invited me to observe a secret rite, unbeknownst to the rest of his circle. I hid in the upper story of this old manor house at the edge of town until the members of the circle came in and did their rite. That's when I realized what he was."

"What did you think of him before that?" she asked, curious about his impression of the man before he revealed his dark secret.

He pursed his lips and lifted a shoulder. "He was my friend, a fellow scholar. But what I saw that night changed everything. I cut off contact and left town. I was still trying to decide what to do when I got word that he and his circle had been killed in a terrible storm."

Ah yes. The previous Air Elemental's handiwork.

Alec gave her a steady look. "That's when I found out that your kind wasn't a myth."

"Is that right?" Her tone made it clear that it wasn't a question.

He nodded. "I had to go back and find out what happened—if the circle had done something that caused a major accident or if they were taken out by something worse. Everyone knew the myths about your kind. I needed to know if their deaths were of their own doing or. . .an execution."

Diana stared at him impassively.

"It wasn't you, was it? With the storm. I figured it was an Air Elemental," he said, leaning forward slightly.

"That was a billion years ago. How old do you think I am?" Diana said with a frown.

But it wasn't because she was insulted. It was because Alec knew too much. Elementals were not immortal. It was one reason their enemies found the courage to sometimes defy them. But what wasn't commonly known was that they could be very long lived. As long as they were in service to the Mother, they didn't age. When they were ready to move on or settle down aging resumed and they lived far quieter lives. Most. . .not all.

In any case, Diana was only a decade off her age in appearance. Vampires also enjoyed a suspended period of aging but after eight or so centuries they aged slowly but steadily. Some even made it to a millennium.

"You look very young, but that means little. Take myself for example. Do I look two hundred and fifty-six years old?" he asked with a wave at himself.

"Yes," she said simply.

Alec paused, his face falling a little.

"*Oh.*"

She couldn't help but smile at his disappointment. "I'm an Elemental in service to the Mother. I can tell how old a vampire is. Part of the job," she said matter-of-factly.

"Of course it is. . .that makes sense. You would totally be able to do that," he said, clearing his throat as he rose.

"And no, it wasn't me in Prague. Or any of the current Elementals. Just in case you were itching to avenge your friend," Diana warned quietly.

Alec scowled, offended. "I wouldn't do that. I know what he was and what he was doing. Avenging someone like him would be wrong." He walked to the swinging door to the living room and pushed it open. "And I still want to help you."

She followed him out of the kitchen, trying to decide what to do with him. For a vampire, he wasn't so bad. But there were aspects of this case she needed to handle on her own.

"Maybe sometime. . .in the next century," Diana said with what was, for her, surprising diplomacy before heading for the door.

If she needed a hand, she could ask for it later—in the aforementioned next century.

"I can help you find Fiona," he said as she took hold of the doorknob.

"Already found her," she called back, letting the door swing shut behind her.

10

Diana wasn't kidding. Tracking Fiona had been child's play. It was similar to a witch's locator spell, but Elementals didn't need any sort of ritual to do it.

She could track any supernatural she'd seen recently enough, which at that moment included everyone at that party. The trace wouldn't last, but her biggest problem was usually identification of her prey, not how to find them. In this case, Diana's job was made a little simpler by her knowledge of the vamp in question. She just set course for the signature of a female vampire near Elva's age that had bolted from town at top speed.

Fiona was hiding out in the Hamptons. Not at the lavish three-story home Gia said she owned. The vampire was also staying far from any of the coven's properties. They had several mansions in the area Fiona could have used, but she'd borrowed one from another wealthy vampire of her acquaintance who had chosen to summer in Europe. That last she had found out from Logan, who had gotten in touch after her meeting with Pedro.

I can't put off my break-in to the Denon headquarters much longer, Diana thought as she rode out to Fiona's bolt-hole. Granted, the damage done in that case wasn't going to get much worse in the near future, but she had a beef with those corporate assholes. Of course, she had a grudge against most everyone she was sent after.

It was dark by the time Diana parked her bike up the beach from where Fiona was staying. For a second, she toyed with the idea of simply parking out front and mowing down the security guards walking the perimeter, but she opted for stealth instead.

Getting past any guards the vampires had posted wouldn't have been a problem, but she was curious about who else might be watching Fiona, so she needed to check out the house first. If Diana were a member of this black circle, she would be watching the vampires to see if retribution was coming their way for using their properties for black rites, making fools of them in the process.

Avoiding the guards did serve another purpose. If she fought them, she might end up killing one, and then she'd never hear the end of it from Serin. Not to mention she might end up tipping the balance to the black herself unnecessarily.

The beach was dark with very little moonlight. Diana preferred it that way, given the superiority of her night vision. A vampire couldn't see as well as an Elemental, although a Were probably could.

Was the ocean always this loud? She hadn't spent much time on a lot of beaches as part of her job. Ignoring the wistful tightening in her chest, she walked closer to the mansion, wishing she could linger to enjoy the rumble of the surf. Maybe with someone.

Not a vampire, she told herself as she walked up the beach.

Diana was close to the house when she sensed the hidden ward. It was buried in a sand dune facing the house's back entrance. More than likely, there was a similar one on each side of the house.

Diana focused her energy on the ward, neutralizing its energy without deactivating it so she could lift it instead of slipping past it. It wasn't the kind vampires typically had fashioned for themselves. This was a black stone with woven reeds tied around it. She turned it over in her hand. The reeds were knotted intricately, making an occult pattern similar to others she had seen in past investigations. But this one was covered with black wax, a novel detail. It was vaguely like a witch's ward to keep out intruders from their own homes. Only it had been modified to spy and leave a trace on any who passed it.

Smart, Diana admitted.

It was definitely not a standard witch ward, though it borrowed heavily from their tradition. No, whoever had made this baby was definitely an innovator. And not exactly well-versed in standard witchcraft. A highly trained witch could have accomplished something similar by spelling a simple stone. It was more complicated to create, but safer.

As it was, this group risked a lot by leaving such an obvious ward where the vampires could have found it. And she was willing to bet one of these was sitting in front of every vampire-owned mansion in the Hamptons. The Broussard coven would retaliate against anyone who spied on them, but perhaps the circle didn't care because they weren't planning on staying in the area.

With that disheartening thought, Diana put back the ward without deactivating it. It wouldn't leave a trace on her. There was no need to tip her hand to the black circle by removing it. And if it were found, it wasn't likely the vampires would move against the circle now. They wouldn't risk getting in her way.

Well, most of them wouldn't.

The vampire's standard ward against intruders didn't react to Diana's entrance, either. She walked in through the back door into a darkened parlor like an invited guest. The spacious room was adorned in the latest style. Or what she assumed was the latest style. Interior decorating wasn't exactly something she cared enough about to keep up with. She preferred the safe houses, which were conveniently pre-decorated. Serin or Gia always took care of that sort of thing. Their places always ended up in in warm earth tones or cool soothing colors that reminded Diana of the ocean and Atlantis.

Walking down a darkened hallway, Diana sensed another guard doing an internal patrol around the corner. Blending into the shadows, she masked her presence.

A sensitive like Alec might have been able to detect her, but in her experience, such people were too valuable to work as guards—unless you had money to burn. She waited until the man had passed and continued deeper into the darkened house.

Fiona was definitely keeping a low profile. No party to hide in the crowd, which she had half-expected. No, her quarry was definitely shaken up and hiding quietly. Scanning upstairs, Diana found three people in the master bedroom. One was Fiona, the other was probably the daughter Alec had mentioned, and either the father or a servant. . .

Well, only one way to find out.

Diana walked upstairs to the second story bedroom the women were in and waltzed inside. The bedroom was decorated in the same clean modern style as the downstairs rooms. In contrast, the stunned vampires looked anachronistic—like they were dressed in period costume even though there wasn't anything terribly old-fashioned about their clothing.

Just overdressed for the occasion, as usual.

Diana turned her attention to the older woman in the room. Yes, she'd caught a glimpse of her in the ballroom at the coven house. And one of the busty blonde shrinking into the corner. The daughter, of course. What did Alec call her? Ah yes, Sylvan.

The last must be a servant after all. He was a monstrously huge man, like a rugby player that had been turned. Very recently from the looks of it. He was young enough to lack a healthy fear of her. He was almost dancing on his feet, clearly trying to decide whether or not to charge her.

When the guard remained twitching in indecision, Fiona burst into speech. "Oh, stand down, Geoffrey! You can't possibly win. And she's not going to kill us. She is after the witches," she said, sitting down at the vanity with a little harrumph.

"There, was that so hard?" Diana asked no one in particular.

This happened a little too frequently. Someone she needed to talk to would bolt, forcing her to chase them down, and then once found they would immediately crumble. It was *so* annoying.

Neither the servant nor the pile of silicone in the corner responded to Fiona's words. *Are those breasts even real? Do vampires get plastic surgery? Would it keep?*

Suddenly Diana was inexplicably angry. Alec probably got an eyeful of those idiotic things on a regular basis. He probably expected that all the women in his sphere to display such cleavage. She pushed that thought out of her mind and refocused on Fiona.

"I'm waiting," Diana said a little more forcefully than she'd intended.

"I didn't know they were black witches. I didn't really know them at all." Fiona's voice held a distinct whine to it.

Diana wrinkled her nose. "Yet you lent them coven property. Not exactly something a vamp does for a near stranger, is it?"

Fiona wrung her hands. "I didn't know them! I never even met them in person. But I knew the person who asked for the loan of the house. It was the owner of that club downtown, the new Underlife one." She gestured at Sylvan who looked perplexed for a second.

"Whore? That one?" Sylvan asked.

"Seriously? A club named Whore?" Diana was briefly incensed on behalf of womankind. The older woman just shrugged. "And you know this man well enough that you lent him your coven leader's house without a second thought?" she asked, shaking her head.

"He said they promised me some beauty charms and a love spell. . .a. . .a permanent one."

"A permanent love spell? For whom?"

Short-term love spells were hard to come by. A permanent one would be worth more than most countries domestic GDP.

"For my daughter, of course, so that she will marry well," Fiona answered, smoothing the skirt of her dress fastidiously.

Diana looked over at Miss Silicone in genuine bewilderment. "You think *those* will have a problem attracting a suitor?"

The servant made a choking sound as he stifled a laugh. And then she realized exactly whom the pair had in their sights.

Of course, the rich future head of the coven might need a little push to choose someone like Sylvan as a mate. A scholar like him might need more than those double D's as temptation.

Diana started to feel a little better about Alec. If they felt they needed a love potion to secure him, then he must be a more discerning man than she gave him credit for.

"When did the club owner approach you, and what is his name?" she asked, moving her arms behind her back to appear less threatening.

Fiona fiddled with the large diamond pendant on the necklace she was wearing. "It was two weeks ago on Saturday, and I don't know the club owner's true name."

She turned to her daughter, but Sylvan shook her head. "Everyone calls him J," Sylvan said.

"That is all we know, I swear!" Fiona said in a rush. "We had no idea they were using children, I mean, why would they?"

Diana studied the two women intently. Her built-in lie detector wasn't going off. These two were pawns. And she would bet good money that they had no idea which black rites would require children. They probably didn't know much about the craft at all; they simply bought the charms and wards like the other vamps and shifters with enough money.

Diana sighed. "I'm of a mind to strip you of your power and leave you human just for your stupidity."

Both women shrank back from her. A pale and distraught Fiona whispered, "But we didn't know!"

"Exactly my point. Next time you traffic with witches, know who you are dealing with," Diana said disgustedly. She turned for the door, their guard scrambling out of the way. She grabbed the handle, and then turned back. "Oh, and if I hear about either of you being in the market for another love spell, I will hunt the both of you down and strip away everything you hold dear. The coven will turn you out, and you will have to start husband-hunting all over again. . .in the human world."

Certain she'd spelled out their worst nightmare, she left.

Diana walked back up the beach, annoyed that her lead was a

lateral move. Instead of being one step closer to the circle, she had to go and question yet another intermediary.

Well, this one better know something or she was going to get angry. *And they won't like it when I get angry.* Diana snorted to herself. She had to stop letting Logan talk her into watching all those terrible comic book movies.

She climbed the last sand dune before the sidewalk where she had parked her bike. Alec Broussard was standing next to it, waiting for her. Again. He was staring at the bike as she approached.

"You drive a Suzuki Hayabusa," he said in a faraway voice.

He reached out to touch the matte black finish.

Diana quickened her step. "Hey, are those clean?" she asked, slapping his hand away from her beloved bike.

"I always wanted a bike like this," he said distantly.

"I imagine you can afford one," she said wryly, wondering what the hell he was doing there.

"Yeah, it's just. . ." He trailed off and gestured vaguely.

"It would mess up your hair?"

Alec broke from his bike-induced reverie and looked at her with a slight scowl. "I don't care about my *hair*. It's simply more convenient to be driven. It gives me more time to read."

She gave him a sad little shake of her head. "God, you're a total nerd, aren't you?"

"No, I'm not," he shot back through a stiff jaw before making a visible effort to relax. "Are the Corsairs still vampires?"

"Fiona and Sylvan Corsairs? Is that seriously their name? Why do all vampire names sound like they're out of a bad regency novel?"

Alec frowned at her. It felt like being scolded by your substitute teacher. She huffed, blowing a strand of red hair out of her eyes.

"Yes, they're fine."

"And did they tell you where to find the witches?"

"I have a lead," she said in an oppressive tone, trying to discourage his prying. "But you should take heart. They won't be looking for another witch to whip up a love spell for you anytime soon."

She climbed onto her bike and started the engine before he could ask her anything else. But the engine wasn't loud enough to drown out the guttural groan he let out as her words finally registered.

"*Oh, God.*"

Diana couldn't hold back the grin that covered her face as she drove off.

11

Five hours later, Diana was back in the safe house apartment. In the end, she hadn't had enough time to hit the club or to sneak into the Denon headquarters. Dawn was too close, and it was a long bike ride to and from the Hamptons. She should have taken the car, but she hated being surrounded by a box when she was upset. She'd had quite enough of that during her childhood.

In her mind, there was a tug along the aether. She sat cross-legged on the bed and lit the candle wick with her mind.

"Di?" Logan asked. "How did it go?"

"Another lead, but technically no closer. I have to interrogate the owner of an Underlife club next," she said, the distaste in her voice clear.

"Which one?"

"Whore."

"Oh, god, even I won't go to that one," Logan said contemptuously.

Logan and Diana were technically both young enough to enjoy clubbing every night, but Diana hated crowds and the Underlife scene. Logan did the rounds but preferred dancing in the human clubs more, and always referred to the Underlife clubs as work.

"It's the principle of the thing," Logan continued. "Whoever named that club should get knocked into next week."

"Well, I may get that chance," Diana said, tugging off her boots.

"And was loverboy there?" Logan asked.

"When did Broussard become loverboy?" Diana asked, perplexed.

"Well, it's been a few days now, and you haven't fried him like an egg yet. . .right? I'm right, aren't I? Or do we need to send a delegation to his coven expressing our condolences?"

"No, not yet. But give me time," Diana replied dryly.

"Oh, come on, I think you like him just a little bit," Logan said suggestively before lapsing into an expectant silence.

"He's okay," Diana finally said grudgingly, because she would never outright lie to Logan. "For a vampire."

"Well, look who's making progress in the whole human interaction thing."

"I wouldn't go that far," Diana said as she flopped onto the bed still fully clothed, "and I would like to point out that there are no humans involved."

"Well, I've been doing a little digging on him," Logan informed her. "Our dear friend, the crown prince of darkness, went through a wild period in his sixties clear on through to his early hundreds, but soon after settled down into more scholarly pursuits. He's been making the rounds through all the ancient collections. He started by trying to divine the true origin of vampires and spent years looking all over the world tying together the threads. . .only to give up in frustration."

Diana smiled. Logan sounded like a teenager gossiping on the phone.

That's because she is a teenager.

"Yeah, well that gobbledygook would drive a saint mad if he took it seriously. And he obviously got something out of it. He solved the riddle of the Daywalker. Although now he thinks it's a big secret he has to keep. He doesn't get the true nature of the ritual. I think he thinks anyone can do it," Diana said, tugging off her pants with one hand.

"He told you that?" Logan asked in surprise.

"No, but it's kind of obvious from the way he's hiding it from the coven. He doesn't trust his own parents."

"He shouldn't. They're total narcissists," Logan said. "Anywho, loverboy got real interested in us after this thing in Prague."

"Yeah, he mentioned Prague," Diana said, stretching out on the bed.

"Yes ma'am, my illustrious predecessor did a number on some black witches. Loverboy got the Elemental bug after that, and he has spent a considerable amount of time since devoted to the study and search of little old us. . .in between other supernatural studies."

"He left that part out," Diana said, unsure how she felt about this new information.

"Oh, lots of scholars of the supernatural get the bug," Logan dismissed. "Some chase us around for a time, but they all give up eventually. Not the healthiest of pastimes, but Alec seems all right to me. He's not a fanatic or anything. Just someone in search of answers. Like a lot of people. You should give him a chance."

Diana frowned. "To do what exactly?"

"Oh, I think you know," Logan said coyly. "But back to the business at hand. What are you going to do now?"

"I've been putting off the Denon Corporation recon for too long, but my nights are going to be full of this circle investigation for the near future. I need an in during the daytime. I've been thinking of arranging for a little sick leave for one of the head honcho's secretaries. What do think would be a good way to go about that?"

Logan was good at the more subtle and devious ways of getting things done. Gia and Serin weren't nearly as talented at that sort of thing. They were a little too honorable and set in their ways. Logan, on the other hand, was a devilish mastermind.

"Oh, I have an idea!" she said. "Okay here's what you do. . ."

Logan really was an evil genius.

It's a good thing she uses her powers for good, Diana reflected as she sat in the office of one of the senior VP's.

She had to wait until lunchtime to put her plan into effect, but once she had, infiltrating the upper echelons of the Denon headquarters was child's play. She felt a little bad about slipping the stomach irritant into the secretary's food, but not enough to find another way. It would only last a few hours, in any case. The woman would be fine tomorrow.

If Diana needed to get into Denon again, she would find another way. She always did. In the meantime, her in was as a temp for the secretary. It wasn't that hard. Her typing skills were good enough to pass muster, but she *hated* the clothes. The skirt of her wool suit was itchy, and the heels were killing her.

Gritting her teeth, she carried on while the senior personnel director explained the computer and gave her an account with limited access to the company's central server. In no time, she would soon expand that limited access using one of Gia's computer tricks.

Diana settled into her emergency temp position with ease. She had learned how to be a chameleon early on in her childhood while in foster care, although she had failed to fit in towards the end.

"Miss Hope," the incredibly officious voice of Keith McMillan came from behind her. "I'll need you to type these up before three," he said, dropping a pile of letters on her desk.

Looking up at McMillan's round pudgy face, Diana faked a smile. She had hated him on sight. And with good reason.

Yup, this one is a definite suspect. Her instincts were all at attention. Unfortunately, her instincts weren't enough to justify a fireball. Not even a little one.

"No problem, Mister McMillan. Will you need any dictation for the meeting Missus Ford mentioned?"

"No," he said abruptly and walked straight back into his office.

Okay. Maybe she should pay extra close attention to this meeting. It might be worth her while to plant a listening stone in the conference room. Like in a potted plant or something. Didn't big corporations had those sitting around everywhere?

A quick trip to the bathroom, conveniently located past the conference room, confirmed the sad lack of a potted plant. A quick crawl through the ventilation vents would have to do if they were large enough.

It was too bad she couldn't use her power the same way Logan could use air to position the stone. People would freak out if they smelled fire and the whole place would evacuate if she tried it.

Disgruntled, she sighed over the limitations of her craft and went to go type the letters.

A few minutes before the meeting started, Diana had stripped off her skirt and was crawling through the dusty air vents leading to the conference room. The spelled stone she carried in her hand would record all sound in the conference until it was retrieved. She just had to get it in place without alerting anyone to her presence.

Ahead the vent got very narrow at the turn. Twisting like a pretzel, she shimmied past the constriction. Slipping the stone in place, she crawled back to the bathroom. After making sure no one was around, she dropped down into the stall where she'd hidden her skirt. Dusting off her tights she pulled on the hated piece of clothing once again.

Skirt surreptitiously twisted back into place, she went back to her temporary desk, deciding to take advantage of the meeting to dig into the mainframe computer while all of the senior heads were busy. They had been joined by a small group of men who had flown specifically for the meeting. All were definitely cut from the same cloth as McMillan.

And not a single secretary to take notes. She didn't know much about corporate practices, so maybe that wasn't atypical. The stone would make sure she didn't miss anything. But it definitely wasn't as satisfying as setting fire to the place. Sighing, Diana began her computer search of the archives.

An hour later, she was ready to kick the computer into the wall. There was a ton of information, layers and layers of bureaucracy. Some of it might well be evidence, but the sheer volume was daunting.

Maybe access from her terminal wasn't what she needed. She was not very good at digging through piles of information. Maybe she could ask Gia to work up a little short cut. Something like a listening stone but for the computer mainframe. It would certainly make her job easier.

Diana finished her day without making any serious inroads in the search. McMillan certainly kept his secretaries busy. Even the temps not trusted with full access were run ragged. But at least she managed to finish the workday without going thermonuclear on anyone.

Feet aching from the heels she detested, Diana walked out of the elevator and into the lobby only to find Alec Brossard waiting for her.

Damn it to hell. How does he do that?

12

"Hello sweetheart," Alec said with a wide grin as he came up to give her a peck on the forehead, the part he could most easily reach given the difference in their heights.

He winked at the receptionist, who was staring at him almost open-mouthed.

For Pete's sake. The woman was at least twenty years older than Alec appeared. Did she have to gawk that way?

"I've made dinner reservations, darling," Alec continued, playing the affectionate boyfriend to the hilt.

Deciding to avoid a scene, Diana let him sweep out the door and toward a luxury car where a burly driver was waiting. She almost waved to the servant when closer examination revealed it wasn't Daniel, but a look-alike. The original must still be taking care of Pedro.

She paused short of the car, prepared to dig in her heels. She wasn't prepared to answer any questions about her *other* investigation. Knowing Alec, he'd volunteer to help with that, too.

"Oh, come on," he coaxed when she didn't get into the waiting car, "You've got to eat. And I wanted to give you an update on Pedro."

She wanted to ask him how he had tracked her down but didn't want to let on that he'd surprised her. And she would eat with him, but only because she was hungry. . .

Sitting down at the Ten Tables near Harvard Square, Diana fidgeted in her seat. Being driven by a private chauffeur to an exclusive restaurant was a surreal experience. She didn't really go out to eat in restaurants. None of the nice ones anyway. She was a diner kind of girl.

A well-dressed waiter handed her a menu before slipping away to get the wine Alec requested. From the waiter's impressed reaction, he'd ordered an excellent vintage of something pricy.

"So, what has the Denon Corporation done to attract the wrath of an Elemental?" he asked without preamble.

"The wrath of the Mother," Diana corrected. "I am merely her servant."

Alec paused, and he gave her a little smile that she found unnerving. "Oh, I think a little of your wrath is mixed in there a little bit," he said. "I'm sorry for surprising you. I saw you going inside at lunchtime and got curious."

Diana's internal sensor buzzed a high alert. "I know you're lying. How did you track me?" she asked bluntly, wondering if she would have to shift to a secondary safe house.

If Alec had found out where she'd been staying, she would have to. Even if she didn't find him to be much of a threat, she simply couldn't afford to leave her sisters exposed.

"I got lucky," he insisted. "I went to check on Pedro earlier and was thinking of you and the situation. Then I saw you in town while I was running an errand."

Mostly true. But Diana could tell he was still holding something back. She pursed her lips, trying to decide exactly how upset she should be.

"I didn't realize your kind targeted corporations for reprisal, but it makes perfect sense," he continued, interrupting her train of thought. "They certainly have a lot of power these days with little accountability. But they don't have a lot of magic to strip, I'm guessing. Do you simply kill the wrongdoers?" he asked while pouring her a generous amount of wine.

"No," she said without elaborating.

The waiter returned to take their orders. Picking the first things that caught her eye, she asked for the veal meatball entree and the pasta special while Alec ordered the vegetarian option. Diana looked at him pointedly as the waiter went away, her left eyebrow at attention.

"I'm not a vegetarian. I've already eaten, but it would look odd if I didn't order anything," he said with a pointed look.

"Sorry I asked," Diana murmured under her breath.

And she really meant it—she definitely didn't want to think about what he had eaten. There were several minutes of silence where Alec just stared at her. But Diana refused to make small talk and eventually the waiter returned with their appetizers.

Well, it beats Chef Boyardee, she thought, looking down at the tempting dish. Maybe she should treat herself to a restaurant meal every once in a while. Some nicer places must let you take-away.

"With the whole infiltration of Denon, you must have something big planned. You're not about to claim that you have a day job, right?" he asked in a pleasant and inviting tone. When she didn't reply, he continued undaunted, "It's some type of set-up or exposure scenario. Maybe I could help. Are you gathering evidence? Or setting someone up for a fall? I employ excellent hackers. Alternatively, I could pose as a potential investor. I've already got a few aliases set up that would be appropriate."

Diana paused with the fork halfway to her mouth. "Do you now?"

Alec shrugged. "It's standard operating procedure for our kind. When one does business in the human world and one doesn't age, it's best to have a few possible identities in your back pocket for whatever comes up."

That could be useful. Diana always made sure she had no identity. No way to trace her real name back to when she was in the system. Not that she had to worry about still being in the social services records.

Gia had seen to that. And no one was better at that sort of thing than the Earth Elemental. When the computer age arrived, Gia had jumped in with both feet. Of course, her talent was computer friendly. Gia could make those infuriating little boxes of metal and glass sing for her.

"How do you know it's not my day job?" Diana asked, giving Alec her full attention.

"Because the Mother has rewarded you for your service, you and your forebears. That is common to many of the legends about your kind among many different cultures. You must be free to do her will. It would be counterproductive if you had to earn a living as well," he said.

She narrowed her eyes at him. "Exactly how much time have you devoted to studying us?"

He paused for a sip before answering. "A lot over the years, but it's only one of the many legends I've studied."

Diana considered his offer seriously for a few seconds before shaking her head. Something Gia whipped up would be more effective.

"No thanks. I have a plan and would not be pleased if you interfered," she lied smoothly. She *would* have her plan in place once Gia created the new toy she needed. "What about Pedro? How is he? Does he remember anything else?"

She intended to drop by on him later, but hadn't wanted to jump all over the poor man right away. He had to get past the initial blow that the memory spell had delayed. The first few days would be painful; the realization that his son had been taken from him would hit him hard once his memory returned.

Alec frowned and poured himself more of the wine. "Not much yet. He's only now realizing that his son is gone. But it's coming back in bits and pieces. The memory spell really did a number on him. But the fact that it was cast in the first place means Pedro must know something about the circle."

Diana sighed. It wouldn't kill her to throw him the occasional bone and discuss the case with him.

"Or they just think he does," she volunteered. "Or maybe they just wanted to do it to see if they could remove his memory. It could have easily been the act of a new practitioner flexing his muscles."

She had seen that kind of thing before.

"What if they've been cast out of one of the families instead?" he asked, perking up.

"The families know it's their responsibility to keep watch on their banished ones, and most of them have had run-ins with one of us at one time or another. Enough to know what is expected. And banishment doesn't extend to the next generation. Offspring are brought back into the fold so they can learn the craft. We keep track of some outcasts ourselves. Those that need watching. A surprising number don't."

"Why not?" Alec asked with a little frown. "Aren't most of the cast-offs dangerous?"

She shook her head. "It's not usually magical misuse that leads to banishment, but normal family drama. And the real asshole to watch isn't usually the banished one in those cases," she said, looking around the restaurant abstractedly.

"Fiona told me you need to see the owner of Whore," he said, wincing slightly. "I, uh, called her after I saw you last night. She answered this time, assuming the worst is over."

"You didn't see her in person?" Diana asked with a little smile, knowing full well he would be staying far away from the two women for a long time.

"No," he answered shortly with a betraying little hand gesture. "I wondered if you wanted an introduction to the club owner. You know, if you wanted a. . .softer approach. You're welcome to crash the club, of course. It's effective. But I imagine the rumors and storm of gossip your appearance at the coven house caused is making the rounds and the ones involved in the circle are underground now. J is probably hiding out somewhere out of town."

Diana ignored the implied criticism. Going in soft wasn't usually an option for her. "Do you know him?"

She wouldn't have pegged him for a frequenter of Underlife clubs.

"No. I think he's a shaman of some kind. He wasn't around before I left, but to be frank, the Broussards know everyone. Even people we've never met know us. That's simply the way it is," he said in a matter-of-fact tone.

Diana leaned back in her chair. Getting someone to give up the shaman might not be necessary. Tracking was central to an Elemental's ability. Like some witches, her kind had the ability to track from an object, provided it was something of value to the person in question. It was a rare gift, even among the witches. If this J person had left something personal behind, she could find him, even if she'd never met him. But Diana didn't feel comfortable sharing that with Alec.

Alec took another sip of his wine. "I don't expect him to be at the club, but someone there should know where he is. Someone will talk —especially if they think they can gain favor with the Broussard house."

"Ah, to be rich and influential," Diana said with a smile, but Alec didn't exactly look pleased by the status quo. More like resigned. "Fine. I'll go with you," she said abruptly, surprising herself a little.

It wouldn't hurt to go in a little quieter after the entrance she had made at the coven house. Bringing Alec along would make the other Supernaturals more talkative. It would save her the trouble of having to chase them down. And really, was there anything she hated more?

Alec looked more surprised than Diana felt. "That's great. We should go tonight. You don't have Denon strongholds to pillage tonight, do you?"

Despite her effort to stay aloof, Diana let a tiny smile play on her lips, but she dropped it right away when he grinned back.

"Storming the castle can wait," she said deadpan, before returning to her meal.

In fact, it *had* to wait. She wanted to give Gia time to cook something up that would speed her search of the Denon database.

Normal spells didn't usually work on such intricate human technology but Gia's ability was able to defy that usual limitation of witchcraft. Logan, the only other Elemental with an aptitude for computers, wasn't as skilled, but she also might have some useful tips.

Serin, like Diana, didn't have a talent compatible with computers—quite the contrary—which was why neither owned one.

Diana enjoyed the rest of her dinner. She was surprised to find Alec a good conversationalist. Especially since she didn't contribute much. But he didn't seem to let that bother him. Instead, he launched into anecdote after anecdote, occasionally asking her a question in an effort to draw her into a conversation. Efforts she mostly ignored.

Alec was well read and seemed to be up on current events, something atypical for a vampire his age. He also didn't bother to hide his interest in her and her kind. Despite how comfortable she was getting with him, Diana didn't like his enthusiasm for what she was. It didn't feel like a strictly academic interest, despite his attempt to play it off as one. He was simply too earnest.

"Dessert?" he asked when Diana had finished her meal.

He'd eaten only a small fraction of his meal, but it was more than she would have guessed. She'd never thought much about a vampire's basic biology.

Was he going to have to run to the little vampire's room before they left? She didn't think it was polite to ask after such a nice meal.

"No, thanks," she replied. "There's something I want to do before tonight, so why don't we meet at the club after midnight."

Most Underlife clubs didn't get busy till one AM at the earliest.

"Can your errand wait? There is something I'd like to show you, and it's nearby," Alec said in a hopeful tone.

"What?" she asked, drawing away from him as they stood up and walked to the door.

"It's something very old. Ancient, in fact," he said, opening the door for her with an elegant gesture. "Do you like museums?"

13

"Who gave you keys to a Harvard museum?" Diana asked, her brows drawn down in a little V as Alec ushered her through the basement door of the Peabody museum.

He glanced behind him to meet her eyes briefly. "In addition to being a consulting archaeologist, I'm an excellent donor. A set of keys to the basement entrance isn't too hard to come by when you ask the right person the right way."

"You're obviously very familiar with this place," she said as he made his way through the Peabody's basement like an employee.

"I've spent a fair amount of time here in the past," he said as he led her through a series of darkened rooms. "I raided it for knowledge of my kind as soon as it was established. There was nothing here related to vampires, of course, but I started to come here a lot to do unrelated research. Once I began traveling, I sent some things here from my personal excavations."

"So this thing you want to show me is something you found your-self?" she asked when he stopped outside an exhibit in the upper story.

"Yes, in an excavation in Veracruz about fifty years ago or so. I sent it here because I don't believe in maintaining a personal collection."

"Not very vampiric of you," Diana pointed out.

"I guess I think more like an academic. I want to share the things I find and get the interpretation of others about my findings."

Diana stopped short and waited until he turned to face her. "Have you published your theories about these artifacts?"

"I couldn't consult without a proven publication record," he said frankly. "I simply change my pseudonym periodically. And avoid conferences."

"Humph," Diana grunted.

Like so many other things about him, she was ambivalent about his chosen career. She thought better of him for having one, but if his research was centered on Elementals then she wasn't thrilled his finds were displayed publicly.

I doubt he would be so open about vampiric artifacts, she thought, following him into one of the larger display rooms.

Inside, glass cases holding an assortment of Mesoamerican relics were lit with a subtle glow, even though the overhead lights were off. Wondering if they did that for the guards, she followed Alec farther inside.

She had only taken a few steps when a weird buzzing filled her head. It was faint, kind of like when your ears started to ring, but in this case between her eyes.

"Here is what I wanted to show you," Alec, gesturing to a stela covered with glyphs the same way a game show hostess presented a new car.

Was it Mayan? Aztec? Curious, Diana walked toward it. When she did, the buzzing in her brain grew fainter, as if she was walking away from its source. She frowned and turned away from the stela to glance around the room. Nothing stood out.

"Is something wrong?" Alec asked.

Diana shrugged and turned her attention back to the stela. She gestured toward the glyphs. "Can you read it?"

"Yes," he said with a smile before pointing to a central set of characters. "This set here is you," he said proudly.

Diana leaned in to study the glyphs. The pictograph didn't even resemble a human, let alone a woman.

"It's *me?*" she asked.

"It's the fire goddess for a small tribe, an offshoot of the Olmecs. By my estimate, this representation is from around eleven hundred BCE. It's the oldest evidence of the existence of Elementals. That I know of anyway," he finished self-deprecatingly.

He was actually pretty close, but it wasn't the oldest artifact that she knew of. Serin's people had artifacts that old or slightly older in their island's repository.

Diana had never really dived into Elemental ancient history and hadn't ever entered the crypt Serin's community guarded, where the bodies of Elementals of their line were kept. It was also where they kept their most sacred documents and ancient artifacts. Personally, she found the idea of the place macabre and hadn't bothered with the dusty and earnest scholars who'd followed her around the one time she visited the island.

Alec would probably give his left nut for access to that crypt. Maybe someday, she thought. If he proved reliable in the long run. *And if he doesn't insist on publishing a paper on it.*

"You're sure it's a Fire Elemental?" she asked aloud, making a face. "Lots of civilizations have fire gods in their mythos. Especially if there are volcanoes nearby or if the area is prone to wildfires."

"I know, I thought of that. It took some time for me to be sure, but some of the neighboring tribes also had a fire goddess legend, and some of those mentioned a sister goddess of the river. That is the most reliable pattern. One village would receive a visitation and then one nearby would years later. Sometimes it was the goddess of the streams and lakes, sometimes of the ocean itself, sometimes the wind or the soil," Alec said animatedly, using his hands for emphasis.

It was just one piece of the puzzle. The legends appeared across so many of the major ancient civilizations. It proved to be a more interesting subject of study than that of my own people." He rocked on his heels and got what Diana was beginning to recognize as his crafty look. "So, do you think there are older records than this still out there in the world, or can I retire now?"

Well, that wasn't exactly subtle. "I've never concerned myself with our ancient history, and I know little about the artifacts related to us," she answered with a half-truth.

"Is that because you can speak directly to the Mother and she tells you whatever you need to know?" he asked earnestly.

I walked into that one. "That's not really how it works," she said wryly.

Communicating directly with the Mother was difficult at the best of times. And it didn't involve *talking.*

Alec paused long enough for Diana to think she'd adequately discouraged him, but he screwed up his courage enough to ask, "So, how does it work?"

"I could tell you, but then I'd have to kill you." Diana sighed half-heartedly, fingering the stela despite the sign prohibiting touching the artifacts.

She had to nip this line of questioning in the bud before he whipped out a recorder and started to interview her like the classic anthropologists whose work was all around them. Turning her back, she walked toward the display cases nearest the door.

The buzzing she felt earlier had subsided quite a bit next to the stela in the far corner, but near the entrance it increased again. It was like walking toward one of those irritating alarms that buzzed instead of wailed. It set her teeth on edge, but she didn't see anything significant in the nearby cases, nothing that could be causing it.

Diana exited the room and checked the nearest display case outside. The buzzing intensified, coming off in waves from part of a stone artifact with a fragment of a design made up of curving lines. It was too incomplete to make out much of the original pattern. The sign under said: Fragment of Olmec figurine or totem, period unknown. She looked up to find Alec also staring down at the piece of stone.

She may as well use his expertise. "Do you know anything about this?" she asked him.

"Yes, but not much. There isn't a whole lot known actually. It was found in a major Olmec excavation and couldn't be dated properly. I don't think anything else was found near it that resembled it. Whatever it was, that's all that survived," he replied. "Why? Do you sense something from it? Is it magical?"

She answered his question with another question. "How about you? Do you sense anything from it?"

He should. He'd already admitted to being sensitive, but this wasn't a ward. She didn't know what it was.

"No, it's not giving me anything. What is it you're feeling?"

"Irritated."

"*Oh*," he said with a crestfallen look.

She caught his expression and shook her head. "I'm irritated by that," she pointed to the stone. "It's buzzing. Like a giant mosquito."

"Really?" he asked with a sniff. "I wouldn't have guessed that it was of any significance."

He didn't sound upset, but his face was a little tight.

Diana fought the urge to roll her eyes. "Are you seriously that annoyed that you didn't realize it was different before I did?"

"Of course not," he said dismissively. His face cleared as his mood shifted back to academic curiosity. "I think it's interesting you can feel it. Your sensitivity must be off the charts. All part of the package, I guess."

Stepping back, Diana made her second spontaneous decision of the evening. "Will you do me a favor and look into it some more? Maybe the records the museum keeps have some more details. I don't need you to fly to Mexico or anything."

Alec lit up like a campfire. "Of course. I know the archaeologist who found it, and good news, he's still alive. I can speak to him and pump him for information."

Diana nodded absently. "This thing is giving me a headache. I'm going to leave now. I'll meet you outside the club at one sharp," she said, turning away.

He shifted, blocking her path. "I think it might be a good idea if you came with me," he said, his expression growing less confident as he took in her growing scowl.

Diana did not like being stopped in the middle of stalking out of a room. "I had Daniel get you a few different choices for outfits. You know, like a disguise. . ." he trailed off as her face grew darker.

"I don't do disguises," she said flatly and continued out the door.

He followed close on her heels. "It's only that your description is pretty widespread in the local Underlife, and you agreed it was a good idea to go in quietly."

"You are way fucking braver than you look," she returned with a bite as she exited the building and he locked up behind them. "I'm not going to dress up like one of your blood sluts."

The temperature around Alec dropped by several degrees. "I don't like that term," he said, his tone suddenly sharp as he grabbed her arm in one swift motion.

Diana gave the restraining hand a pointed look before slowly raising her eyes to meet his own. He faltered slightly when he met her eyes, which were no longer green. His hands dropped to sides, but he kept on.

"A blood donor should be given the utmost respect," he added with a careful measured tone. "A vampire should always be grateful for their gift. I don't like when others use that term—even one of my own kind. And yes, I know they use it a lot."

There was a trace of an apology in his tone by the end of his little speech, but she ignored it and walked away.

"Are we still on for tonight?" he asked. She was halfway down the block before he tried again. "Diana?"

"One AM in the back of the club," she called back before disappearing from his sight.

"He's a total nerd and a self-righteous prig," Diana told Logan through the aether. She was actually feeling guilty for using the term blood slut but wasn't about to admit it. "And insane. He actually had his servant get me disguises—a trampy vampire groupie outfit I bet," she huffed.

"Well, he does have a point about not wearing your uniform."

Taken aback, Diana looked down at her black cargo pants and tank. "It's a *good* uniform."

"If you don't want to be recognized immediately, changing it would be a good idea. And the winds are whispering about you. The description circulating through the local Underlife is not too far off. Why don't you borrow something of mine from the closet? I left a plain black corset and leather pants in there. That'll be perfect and not so far from your usual clothes. Although the combat boots have got to go. . ."

"No way." Diana was aghast. "The boots are non-negotiable."

"Okay, well, I have some other boots in there, I think." Logan was unfazed.

"You know I can't wear anything with heels." Diana was close to whining, and she hated herself for it.

"I think those are Serin's. I left some that are like knee high riding boots. Those are perfectly okay, and you know it."

"*Fine,*" Diana grumbled, aware she hadn't put up much of a fight.

She had long ago realized arguing with Logan was pointless. The girl was relentless till she got her way. It would be annoying if she wasn't so damn lovable.

Digging around the walk-in closet for the boots, Diana filled Logan in on the rest, including dinner and the visit to the museum. She mentioned the weird buzzing artifact.

"I don't think I've ever experienced that sort of thing before," Logan sounded intrigued.

"Not even in the mausoleum on Serin's island?" she asked.

Diana had refused to get anywhere near it, but it hadn't bothered Logan much. She said it had been like visiting the catacombs in Rome.

"No, but I didn't really check out the artifacts," Logan replied. "I mostly skimmed the written records. But those old guys get pretty huffy if you want to actually touch their stuff, so I didn't stay long."

"What about all that crap about preserving the record for future generations that they always go on and on about when they chase you around for interviews?" Diana asked with frustration.

"Well, I've decided it means future generations of scholars, not actual Elementals who inherit the gift," Logan said.

"Figures. . .They're all eagerness and sunshine till you try and make them useful," Diana grumbled as she pulled the corset from the closet.

Am I seriously going to wear this? It has embroidery. "How do you tie this thing up if it laces in the back?"

"Those are just for show. That one has clips in the front."

Diana signed loudly. "This is stupid. I don't know why I'm bothering. We don't have to hide what we are. . .I can track down this club owner without getting all girlied up."

"But it might be faster to do it Alec's way. Especially if your mark has already left town. I know you will track him down eventually, but first you need to find something deeply personal, and he might have cleared all that stuff out. Or he could be another dead end, and you'll have to find the circle another way. The Supes will want to talk to Alec. He's their Prince William with a better hairline, even among the non-vamps. If there were more Supes in the world, he would get mobbed all the time. They'll bend over backward to get on his good side."

"Yeah, well, I don't think he likes that," she confided.

"Rough to be a celebrity," Logan said authoritatively. She had met several of the Hollywood variety in the human clubs she frequented. "So, what do you really think of him now?"

Still a little annoyed that she felt guilty for the verbal insults she'd been slinging, Diana said, "Surprisingly prudish for a vampire. . .but if he acted like a typical one I'd already have set him on fire."

Logan practically squealed, "Aw! I'm glad you like him."

"Not what I was trying to imply but whatever. . ." Diana grunted while squeezing into the leathers to see if they fit.

She wondered if they were supposed to coordinate with the corset because they had lacing up the side too.

"When do you have time to go shopping for this stuff?"

"I bet it only takes slightly longer than your clothes shopping does."

"Since I order in bulk online and deliver it to a safe house, I'm going to call you on that one," Diana said, squeezing into the skintight leathers with a pant.

"Fine. I like to shop, and I like to dance. Doesn't make me less effective at what we do." Logan sounded a little wounded, and Diana felt guilty for a whole other reason.

"Of course it doesn't," she quickly agreed. "It just makes you more interesting than the rest of us."

"I wouldn't go that far. And I think the vampire prince finds you plenty interesting." Logan was back to normal.

"Maybe," Diana said. "But not in the way you think. He is more interested in learning all he can about us. He'd write a paper—or several—on us if we let him. And I don't plan on letting him."

"Are you sure that's all he's interested in?" Logan sounded disappointed.

"What more could there be?" Diana asked, though she knew perfectly well what Logan was getting at.

"I know you never believe me when I say this, but you are drop dead kill-for gorgeous. Any heterosexual male would give his right testicle for a chance with you. Men would give up their fortunes, leave their wives, and possibly sell their souls."

"All right, enough," she laughed. "I'm not ugly, I get it. But you mention another distinct possibility. What if Alec isn't hetero? I mean, he hasn't been linked with women since his wild youth. Maybe he's not into girls," she added, sounding satisfied with that explanation even though she knew it wasn't right.

Alec watched her in that non-platonic way men did when they were interested. She just didn't know what to do with that interest. He wasn't the jerk she'd assumed he was. But she didn't have male friends. Could she be friends with Alec? She could email him from the road maybe.

What am I thinking? Pen pals, seriously?

"Well, I forgot to add that one to my diatribe—gay men would switch for you." Logan was unfazed.

Diana rolled her eyes at her reflection. "Okay, stop."

A pretty face wasn't important. Look where her mother's attractiveness had gotten her. The other Elementals were better looking than her anyway. If they had been friends and not Elementals, their collective beauty would worry her. A lot. That kind of loveliness tended to attract the wrong kind of attention.

"Will you ask Gia if there's anything she can do to speed up my search at the Denon headquarters? If you talk to her before I do, that is? And if you can put your ear to the ground about Brenda, Katie's mom. See if you can get a bead on her location," Diana said while adjusting the borrowed corset.

"I will. But do both of us a favor and try to have some fun with Alec tonight. He sounds like a decent guy with varied interests. Even if one includes bloodsucking. He doesn't have to take a personal interest in this, but he wants to help you 'cause he takes care of his people. You read people better than anyone. If your gut says he's trustworthy, take the leap and let him stick around. There's nothing wrong with being cautious, but eventually you have to take a chance and let someone into your life. Be friends." Logan's voice took on a teasing note. "Maybe you can be more someday. But at least let him be a friend now."

Diana thought for a moment. "I will do what is best for all of us, not just me. I am not going to let anyone near us if he has any ulterior motives. And we already know how important Alec's studies are to him. We can't have an outsider revealing our secrets to the world."

"I'm sure he wouldn't do that," Logan protested.

"You don't know that, and neither do I. So far as I can tell, he's thrilled to learn about us. He's not stupid; he knows we'll kill him if we consider him a threat. But that doesn't mean he doesn't intend to study us and continue to publish what he can get away with. His work is really important to him. His friendly helpfulness may ultimately just be a means to an end."

"I still say it pays to give people the benefit of the doubt. Don't prejudge," Logan said with obstinate cheerfulness.

"And is this attitude serving you well? Found anyone special yourself?" Diana asked even though she knew the answer already.

Logan had lots of male friends in the human world. She said they were good practice. But she hadn't taken that extra step and gotten seriously involved with any of them. When Diana had pointed out the hypocrisy of Logan's frequent suggestions to take a lover, Logan simply pointed out their age difference and the amount of time spent in service to the Mother.

It was one of the drawbacks of having a substantially younger best friend. They didn't have to practice what they preached.

"Not quite yet, but I'm starting to look around. I'm thinking of having a fling with an actor. Maybe Michel. Sort of a practice run," Logan confided.

"Eww. Can't you pick someone less likely to have an STD?" Diana asked, wrinkling her nose as she tugged the boots up her calves.

She was not a fan of the french actor.

"It's only an idea. And there isn't a drop of magic in him or anywhere in his lineage," Logan said enthusiastically.

"I don't get how that's a plus. It's not a guarantee they won't hurt you. Emotionally at least. And you won't have carte blanche to put the guy through the wall when and if he does."

"Pessimist."

"Always," Diana said, frowning at herself in the mirror. "How many times have we had this argument?"

"Too many, but now there are real guys to argue about, so in a way, it's a totally new argument," the Air Elemental replied cheerfully. "How does everything fit?"

"Okay, I guess. Since I'm a little taller, there's more skin than what you probably intended with this outfit. I am showing way more cleavage than I am comfortable with," Diana said, looking at herself in the mirror in dismay.

"Well, considering that you never show any, that is a step in the right direction. It will help you fit in as Alec's companion."

"I may be too subdued for that, actually," Diana reflected aloud, remembering the glittery and revealing clothes the women had worn the night she'd crashed the coven's party.

And my boobs are nowhere near as big as Sylvan's.

"With your hair, you can't do subdued. Actually, you might want to darken it with a charm if you're trying for incognito."

"I'm going to leave it wet and slicked back with something. It will look darker."

She didn't want to actually color her hair and prove to Alec she'd taken his suggestion to heart.

Logan said, "Won't even throw him a crumb, will you?"

Diana smiled. "I'm going to make everything as hard for him as possible."

"My guess is you already have," Logan said suggestively, jumping to the innuendo Diana hadn't even realized she'd set herself up for.

She sighed. "Goodnight, Logan."

14

Alec was waiting when Diana pulled to the back of the club. From the front, it looked like every other night spot, except it didn't display its name for obvious reasons. It had the requisite line of young and nubile people waiting to be let in. The plain vanilla humans always had to wait unless they came with a Supernatural. Most of those didn't know about the true nature of the other patrons.

He rushed to help Diana off the bike. Noting his eagerness, Diana lifted a brow. "Were you that unsure I'd show up?"

"I want to apologize about earlier. About using the term 'blood-slut'," he began, and she recognized the signs of a rehearsed speech. "I've often wished attitudes were different among my kind with regard to our blood donors. I hate it when they say that word, but they do so regularly regardless. In any case, I can't expect you to meet expectations they don't, especially when you're not a fan of my kind to begin with," he finished in a resigned voice.

Though it had made her feel guilty, she'd respected him for standing up to her. Diana felt genuinely terrible now, but you couldn't tell from her tone of voice.

She crossed her arms. "You can stand your ground, old man. I won't hold it against you."

Pursing his very young-looking lips, the vampire moved back. Diana took off her leather jacket and handed it to him. Getting his first good look at her outfit, Alec's face lost all expression.

His voice was extremely level when he said, "You look. . .nice. You should fit in perfectly."

"Good. This thing pinches. I can't wait to take it off," she said as she adjusted the side of the corset.

Alec's eyes followed her motion with a slightly dazed expression. Wondering what was wrong with him, Diana started for the back door. He caught up with her and offered his arm.

"It might be a good idea if you let me do the talking in the public rooms. If you're recognized, there's going to be a stampede, and we don't want that." He gave her a pointed look until she finally took his arm.

"Fine," she grumbled.

They reached the back door, and it opened automatically as if they had been watched the whole time. No one stood behind it, but at the end of the hallway, there was a young woman, dressed to the Gothic nines ready to greet the VIP. She managed to smile while simultaneously breathing in deeply to stick out her chest as much as possible.

The woman waited until they reached her before extending a manicured hand to Diana. It wasn't a typical greeting for a vampire. Diana looked at her closely. The hostess was mostly human, with some magical sensitivity, but not enough to be a practitioner.

"Greetings, Doctor Broussard. Welcome to Whore," the hostess said with a welcoming gesture before standing aside. It would have been impolite to touch a vampire without invitation. "You and your guest have been set up with complimentary beverages in our most exclusive VIP suite at the front of the club. If you'll follow me, I'll take you there."

"The front?" Alec asked as they walked behind her.

"Our guests enjoy being seen but can still enjoy their privacy in our VIP suites," the hostess said, angling her bosom into his view a little more.

It was quite an accomplishment given that she was ahead of them. The hostess led them down a brightly lit corridor with white walls and a red tile floor that led to a busy kitchen and farther down into the club.

The music wasn't the hard, driving beat Diana associated with clubs on television, but it was still danceable. The hostess swung open the inner club door open to reveal a futuristic vision.

The walls were a matte white plastic with lights inside that changed colors slowly. Red melded into orange and then into yellow before skipping through the rest of the spectrum. The light flattered and flirted with the crowd, reflecting off the white leather furniture in cool patterns. Diana liked the effect even if she hated the name of the club and by extension its owner.

They were led through the well-dressed crowd toward the front. Most of the heads in the room turned to follow them. Diana was apprehensive, envisioning the crowd turning to her en-masse and charging. Visions of her having to fight her way out of the club faded as she registered that no one was looking at her. All eyes were on Alec. Logan was apparently right about his celebrity status.

They were ushered up a grand staircase made out of a clear plastic of some kind. The effect was like walking on ice. The owner may be a misogynistic piece of shit, but he had a definite sense of style. Not a good style, but style nonetheless.

Their hostess opened a set of ornate carved white double doors at the head of the stairs, revealing a moderately sized room with more leather and lights. The couches were black leather here and the lights were a darker color than the rest of the club. The hostess briefly explained the other amenities of the room, including the glass top coffee table that was actually a touch screen computer. After some more preening and deep breathing, she left, visibly disappointed at Alec's lack of interest.

"It's not what I was expecting. The name doesn't match. I was expecting it to look like a high profile bordello," Alec observed.

"Yeah, like the coven house," Diana said absently, fingering the table to explore the display.

He let out a choked laugh. "Don't say that around my mother's decorator. They spend a fortune to update the look every decade. Funny thing is that it never seems to change much."

"Sorry. You don't actually like that look, do you?" Diana asked almost apologetically, dropping her hostility for the time being.

It was starting to take too much effort.

Alec smiled thoughtfully. "You don't spend a lot of time around people, do you? It seems odd, since men must trip all over themselves to meet you."

Diana frowned. "What does that mean?"

"I was only thinking that you probably spend more time interrogating people than actually talking to them."

Annoyed at his perception, she ignored the comment, sitting next to him and crossing her legs.

The vampire proved exactly how intelligent he was by moving on. "I've been pretty antisocial myself for the last fifty or sixty years. But I wasn't righting grievous wrongs, simply poring through dusty books and scrolls."

His tone was commiserating, and she decided to let it go.

"Is your doctorate in archeology?"

"One of them is," he said, smiling again. "I've had a considerable amount of time to accumulate degrees, but they're all in related fields. I would have loved to get a medical degree, but for obvious reasons that one was out of my reach."

Diana studied him in amused disbelief. "You are the weirdest vampire I've ever met."

"Thanks," he said, looking pleased. "Knowing how you feel about my kind, I'm going to take that as a compliment."

He glanced at the display. It had a list of events for the club and a menu. Pretty banal stuff. Until he hit the VIP icon. Then a menu of another sort was displayed, one that catered specifically to a vampire and his entourage. And it was clear that more than blood was on offer.

"Well, now we know why they call it Whore," Diana said flatly.

Alec wrinkled his nose. "At least they don't actually send the girl, or boy if you swing that way, up here like they do in Europe. Over there, it's considered a matter of etiquette to sample what is offered. In private of course."

It was Diana's turn to make a face. "You don't even get a choice? Bite the merchandise or you've violated the vampire version of Emily Post?"

He gave her a quick resigned smile. "I stopped visiting the noble houses and Underlife clubs after a while because of it. The blood exchange shouldn't be trivialized."

Diana tried to picture being bitten. There wasn't a scenario she could think of where she didn't set the biter on fire.

"They should be sending up the owner to greet me soon if he's here. If he's not, then the person the next rung down on the ladder," Alec explained without a shred of conceit.

He extended a glass of champagne from the complimentary setup at the bar. The lights changed to a soothing blue.

"No, thanks. I don't like the bubbles," Diana said, refusing the glass.

"No bubbles at all? No soda or beer?" he asked, surprised.

"Yeah," she said, stopping to think about it. "Why? Is that weird?"

She sounded unsure. Nobody had ever questioned her preferences. Not even Logan.

"No, it's uncommon but not enough to be weird," he reassured her, and Diana found herself incrementally relaxing.

She walked around the room, examining the luxury items laid out for the VIP. There were high-end cut crystal glasses for whiskey and champagne on the bar. Some nice looking plates with gourmet treats. Vampires usually traveled with more non-vamps than not in their entourage so there was a wide selection. Foie Gras on toast, figs stuffed with some sort of cream and drizzled with honey, and some other cheese with a sun-dried tomato spread on a soft white bread. Diana had eaten her fill, but these looked good so she sampled a few. Alec shifted behind the bar and served her a glass of something else.

"It's a sweet dessert wine. It's French, Pineau de Charentes," he said with flawless pronunciation.

Diana sampled it while she helped herself to more of the hors d'oeuvres. It was good, sweet, but not overwhelming. There were other toys, stuff that looked like it came out of the one percenter's version of the Skymall catalogue. She leaned over to examine them more closely. Diana never bought anything that wasn't functional since she had to travel light. In other circumstances, she would have liked to play with them.

"You should have the best of everything," Alec said quietly without preamble as if listening to her thoughts.

Her lips twisted. "I have the best of everything," she said and meant it.

"We have differing opinions of what everything means, I think," he said.

She could feel his intent gaze even though she wasn't facing him. An unfamiliar tension filled her, and atmosphere became thick. Racking her mind for something, she grew irritated when she couldn't think of anything to say. Thankfully a knock at the double doors saved her from replying.

The door swung open, and an elegantly dressed man came in with a flourish. He stopped short when he saw Diana. Fear flashed in his eyes, and he backed away.

Guess my description has made the rounds.

She resisted the urge to rush forward to grab the man. For one, he looked too sweaty. And she had agreed Alec should take the lead.

Their guest was about to bolt back out the door when Alec gestured to him and said in a commanding tone, "Come, sit."

The man twitched but sat slowly on the couch while Alec sat at the armchair. Diana chose to stand.

"Are you the owner?" Alec asked.

"I'm Carter, the manager. I'm at your service," he finished nervously as he eyed the door longingly.

"Where is the owner?" Diana asked. Carter jerked his gaze her way, avoiding direct eye contact.

"Gone," he said. "He needed a vacation."

"Gone where?"

"Not sure. Miami or the Hamptons. Maybe Manhattan? Wherever the hot spots are now. He scouts the latest places to scope out the competition. Doesn't specify where he goes. He just takes off," he said, diligently avoiding eye contact with Diana.

"What is your employer's full name?" Alec asked.

"He only goes by J. No one knows his full name."

Diana could see the magic entwined in the man's aura. "What spells have you been using, Carter?"

He cleared his throat. "None, I simply activated some protection charms."

"Did they work?" she asked mockingly, guessing that they were meant to keep her out.

He looked away. "Don't know. They are meant to keep black witches out."

"Sure they are," she said, knowing full well this guy was on the gray end of the spectrum. She leaned in close and spoke in a low voice. "Now tell me where J is."

Carter gulped. "He didn't say, he just took off."

"And do you know why?" Alec asked.

"No," he said.

Another lie.

Diana leaned in closer to Carter's ear. "I can tell when people are lying. So start telling me what you *do* know. The sooner you talk, the sooner we leave."

Carter looked to Alec for help, but all he found was an unyielding and unsympathetic stone sitting there watching him. "He brought in a group one night to his office. I wasn't sure why, but I don't interfere with the boss's business. I'd never seen them before. It was a strange group. Two men and two women. I got a bad vibe from them."

Alec gestured for more. "Can you describe them? Did you catch any names?"

"No names. And I only caught a glimpse of them before I had to go check on a mess in the kitchen," he said, still only looking at Alec despite Diana's menacing presence hovering over him.

Alec gave Carter a pointed look, raising one fine black brow. "Describe what you can."

"One man was a little older than the rest. He was the only one I got a look at. He looked dignified and powerful. I don't know if he was the one in charge, but that's what I thought at the time. He had close-cropped grey hair, like a military cut, but his outfit was like dark bohemian, if that's a thing. That's all I know. Can I go now?" Carter looked ready to bolt out of that chair.

"After you show us your boss's office," Diana added, going to the door and gesturing for him to follow her.

Carter started and made eye contact with her for the first time. "J doesn't let anyone in there without his permission. I don't have the key."

"Don't worry about it," she said.

He rose to his feet and edged around her, then led them out of the VIP room. They walked along the upper story balcony and looked down onto the dance floor. The club was going strong now. The well-dressed masses writhed on the floor below them with the vibrant red light shifting underneath.

The club's main office was directly opposite. Carter shifted to one side of the double doors, looking around as if expecting his employer to appear from thin air to give him hell. Diana moved to the lock, and immediately Alec moved to hide her from view.

There was a simple keypad coupled to a standard locking mechanism. She covered each with her hand and fried the connection between them. More direct heat, and the tumblers of the lock shifted and the doors swung open. Carter looked surprised, as if he had expected her to whip out some sort of lock picking set.

Diana decided it was time for him to go. "Your help is no longer required. You may return to your duties."

Carter practically ran away as she and Alec moved inside, pulling the door shut behind them. The noise from the club ceased. It was more than soundproof; a spell muted the noise absolutely.

"What are you looking for? I doubt he kept a record of his meetings or anything to identify the witches," Alec said, walking slowly around the room.

"I just need something of his, or theirs, that's special enough to them, and then I can track the object back to the person," Diana replied as she examined their surroundings.

If he was going to insist on tagging along, he would figure that out on his own soon anyway.

"Really, like a witch scries?" he asked, intrigued.

Some skilled witches could track in that fashion, but the gift was rare, especially if they hadn't met the person. Vampires could track their blood donors if they had given them their own blood. Unlike the fiction in the movies, tracking was the only purpose for a vampire giving blood most of the time, since most of their donors didn't have the innate ability to be turned.

"We are not entirely dissimilar," Diana admitted reluctantly as she searched the desk.

"But you didn't need anything of Fiona's to find her."

Perceptive bastard.

"No. She was at the coven house. I didn't need anything else after I'd been in her presence. I'm wired to track Supes."

"Oh," Alec said quietly. "But you need something if you haven't been around them before?"

"Or if enough time has passed since I've seen them," Diana shared before deciding it was high time to shut up.

Alec searched the desk for an object of sufficient personal value. He picked up and examined a paperweight while she looked for a hidden safe.

There was no obvious safe in the wall, but a guy who ran a club had to have one. Turning her attention to the floor, she searched for irregularities and soon hit pay dirt. A small Brown model safe was installed under the desk's seating area. Rather than waste time trying to reason out the combination, she sent a blast of heat to fuse the mechanism before wrenching the handle open. The whole door came off in her hand with a protesting shriek of metal.

Alec raised a brow but kept silent as she tossed the door aside and crouched down next to the open safe. Inside were a large gun and a lot of cash, but nothing related to witchcraft or something that resonated with J's specific vibration.

Annoyed, she stood, spinning around to examine the rest of the room. Unlike the others in the club, this part of the building wasn't outfitted with glowing walls and floors. It was painted a deep dark green, a shade close to black. Sleek and expensive lamps lit the room. On the right side of the room stood a tall cabinet made out of a deep reddish wood. Its shelves were littered with small objects, a collection of baubles and curiosities that must have taken years to accumulate.

Diana leaned in closer to run a finger over a delicate glass globe. There was something odd about it. It was out of place next to the other objects, which were more of the weapon or totem variety.

She picked it up. Inside it, a light flared briefly. It was a spell, contained in a glass globe. There were particles shifting inside, not exactly glitter, more like dirt in red clay tones. It was perfectly sealed round globe, rather unusual for a spell. More unusual was that its power had been muted until she touched it. Usually she could see spells like beacons in the night, but this one only had a dull glow.

Enclosing a spell in a glass globe wasn't a practice of the various witch covens. They might use a stoppered vial, but nothing like this. It was something a new practitioner, untrained in the craft, but with talent to spare, might make to house spells with a kind of flourish. A unique touch to impress other practitioners and consumers of spells.

She held it up to Alec. "This was made by them but wasn't for them. It must have been commissioned by J."

"Can you trace them directly now?"

"No. It wasn't theirs to begin with. It was always meant for someone else. I can't trace J with it either because he didn't have it long enough to make it his." She expelled a harsh breath, frustrated. "We will have to track J first after all."

"We?" Alec smile peeking out. He didn't wait for an answer. "Do we know what type of spell it is? Or do you have to break it to activate it?"

"No to the last. Hold on," she said and picked up a cut crystal paperweight from the desk.

She melted a layer of glass onto her hand and placed it over the globe. As the surfaces made contact, she melted the inner layer of glass and for a minute she touched the spell. Technically the second layer was unnecessary but it was added protection, in case the spell was lethal.

It probably wouldn't have hurt her, but Alec might be vulnerable, although there weren't many spells that could affect a vampire. To some degree, vampires were impermeable to most forms of magic, but there were always exceptions to the rule.

"It's a confusion spell. It would muddle memories in normal humans and susceptible Supernaturals. A useful tool in certain situations. Not exactly endorsed by our kind, but this one is a low-level spell. J probably took the stronger ones with him," she said.

A flame flared inside the globe and the materials suspended inside burned to nothing. A puff of smoke and the entire globe was gone. She turned her attention back to the other items on the shelf, as did Alec. There were empty spaces. As suspected, J had taken most of the objects of value.

"What about this?" Alec asked, pulling out an elaborately engraved dagger.

She took it from him. "No," she shook her head. "It was probably a gift he left out for display."

She rounded the desk and sat in J's leather chair so she could examine the shelf from his normal vantage point. From here, there were a few objects closer to the eye level. One of these was far more likely to be an object of personal value, even if J himself wasn't aware of it.

"Hand me that figurine. The fertility totem," she said, gesturing to one of the lower shelves.

Alec gave it to her, and she instantly felt the connection. The totem was a focusing tool used by practitioners, an object with a long history. It was the type of thing passed down in a family. But not J's family. His possession was an interruption of its path. However, he valued it highly, more than he knew, probably because he'd stolen or cheated someone out of it. Now it was tied to him with enough force that it had become his.

"This will work," she said, throwing a smile in Alec's direction.

Flushing slightly, he asked, "Do you know where he is?"

She turned her gaze inward, focusing on nothing, reaching for the threads that tied the object to J. "South. Quite a ways south. Took a car. He probably thought it would be harder to track. It's actually easier."

"When do we leave?"

She looked up at him, weighing her decision to take him along. If she didn't, he would just end up following her. It was probably better to keep him with her than have him nipping at her heels, interfering with her investigation in ways she couldn't anticipate.

"You're absolutely committed to this search?" She narrowed her eyes at him. "Even if we end up in Cuba?"

"Absolutely."

"Fine. But if you get in my way or get all bitey on me, I will set your ass on fire and won't even feel bad about it."

He smiled. "I think I can promise I won't bite. Not unless you want me to. . ."

She made a face. "Is that vampire flirting? 'Cause. . .eww."

Alec snorted but made no reply as they walked out of the manager's office and back into the noisy club.

For a second, Diana felt the wild impulse to turn around and torch the expensive furnishings. But she resisted the urge and faced Alec instead. The deep bass of the current song made it hard to hear anything, so she gestured that they should leave. They were heading to the stairs when a sudden and very sharp shift in the balance hit her.

It was like a sudden drop in the barometric pressure, but its source was localized to someone in the crowd.

Somewhere in shifting mass of dancers, a murderer had chosen his next victim.

15

"What is it?" Alec asked. She had stopped so suddenly he'd almost crashed into her.

"Shh," she said, turning her attention to the left corner of the dance floor.

Placing both hands on the rail in front of her, she let her vision unfocus. The disturbance and the person causing it became clearer. It was a man of average height and looks. But she could see the aura that was undetectable to others, and it was swirling violently.

Her quarry was focused on a small brunette who was happily dancing with a group of women. She looked completely oblivious to the men in the room.

It was obviously a girls' night out. All the women were technically ignoring men, but this one didn't even see them, not on this night. And that was probably the lure.

She turned to Alec. "I have some things to take care of before we go. Things not related to this case. Let's split up now and meet at dawn."

"Do you need back up?"

Hating she was that obvious, she turned away. She had to

remember to put on a better front when she didn't want him taking an interest in all of her activities.

"Diana?" he wasn't going to let up.

"Not necessary," she assured him.

"If you're sure," he said slowly. "I have a small plane I can pilot myself. Not one of the coven's jets. I can fly us south. Can you track from the air?"

"That shouldn't be a problem. Where will we meet?"

He gave her the address of a small private airfield. "The coven doesn't know about this plane. It's not a fancy jet or anything. Just good for getting around without anyone knowing."

She nodded. "Okay, I'll see you at dawn." She started for the stairs, then stopped short. "Hey, will you pack a lunch? Maybe some more of those fig things?"

Alec smiled. "Of course."

He headed for the club's kitchen and she headed for her new mark.

Diana blended in with the crowd near the bar, sipping a twenty-year-old scotch. She picked a dark corner and settled down to watch her prey stalk his.

By this point, the pretty girl was drinking and laughing with a group of men who had stopped by to chat with the women. None flirted with the brunette, but at least two eyed her with interest.

Diana checked on the mark, to see how he was taking the new development. She never knew what would make a killer lose interest. Sometimes her talking to another man was enough to cause a murderer to choose someone else. Sometimes it was why she was chosen.

The mark was angry. It had been fine when she ignored all the other men. Seeing her smile at one enraged him. In his mind, she was already his.

And you're mine, asshole.

An hour later, the girls' night out was breaking up. The pretty brunette got her wrap from the coat check and walked to her car with one of the other women. Carpooling complicated the murderer's plan, but he wasn't dissuaded. He got into his car and tailed both girls.

Diana followed at a distance on her bike, ducking behind cars to make sure her mark did not spot her. She needn't have bothered; the murderer was too focused on not being seen by the women to notice her.

They arrived at a small two-story house on a quiet part of an otherwise busy street. After sliding into a resident's-only parking space, they got out of the car, chatting animatedly. The mark idled just out of their eyesight long enough to register where the girls lived and then drove away.

The murder was not going to happen tonight. Diana started her bike and followed at safe distance.

Mister Average lived in a three-floor walkup in a large apartment complex built in the seventies. It was clean and functional, but not especially nice. Diana trailed him to his door, making sure she wasn't seen. She was able to watch his door from underneath the stairwell leading to the floor above.

There was still a lot of noise in the building. She would have to wait till the building's occupants had settled for the night. Once she was sure, she would enter the mark's apartment and take him out quietly.

He would make history, another bizarre case of spontaneous combustion. It was an explanation few people truly believed, but given the lack of evidence she and others of her kind left behind, one that was accepted as an infrequent oddity. Most of the kills she made left no evidence, but she was in a hurry and didn't have time to stage an accident that would explain why this man died and why the fire didn't spread to the other units of the building.

Hours passed, and the mark's neighbors were still going strong. Damn college kids, she grumbled to herself.

She was considering taking out the building's electrical system when the door suddenly opened and her target came out. Ducking back into the shadows, she watched as he quietly made his way down the stairs.

It was past three in the morning. Perhaps he'd decided to go after the girls tonight after all. She followed him like a ghost, her Elemental nature masking the noise she would have otherwise made.

Her mark went back to his car and took off in the direction opposite his future victim. Diana was starting to get really annoyed with this guy. He wasn't heading in the direction of a potential victim, unless he was working off a list. And he was in a reminiscing mood, apparently; satisfaction came off of him in waves.

Diana followed him for another ten minutes before he stopped at a self-storage place. She squinted at the location. It was fairly isolated and next to a highway. The perfect spot for a trophy room. Or a kill room.

The self-storage place was locked tight for the night, but that didn't matter to the mark. He wandered to the left side of the lot, where chain link fence had been cut. The location of the opening was shielded from the street. After rolling back enough of the fence to crawl inside, he took the time to fix it so that it looked intact.

The mark disappeared around the corner, and Diana followed after him. She paused at the corner as he headed for the second row. As quietly as he could, he opened a door, but the mechanism needed oil. The grating metal sound made him look around nervously, but the area was completely dead at this hour.

A quick scan confirmed there were no security cameras. It was probably one of the reasons this particular storage place was chosen. She turned back to the man. He'd lifted the door only part way and had ducked inside.

Closing her hand into a fist, Diana followed him.

INSIDE THE UNIT, Sam Levin turned on a small table lamp that ran on batteries. He had a chair and table there—a place where he could take out his trophies and relive how he'd gotten them. Not the most ideal spot, but he couldn't afford better for the moment. Soon, though. He was saving.

Eventually he would buy his own house, far from other people. The long drive to work would be worth it for the solitude he would gain. Where he could be alone with his treasures.

He always took something different. The thing he associated with them the most. Usually their hair. Sometimes their beautiful eyes, which he would put in a jar. His forever.

The girl tonight was so pretty. And she'd had eyes only for him. He would take that hair and those eyes and put them here with the rest.

Once I'm done, those eyes wouldn't look at anyone else, he thought happily.

A noise startled him out of his reverie. He turned around, surprised to see a beautiful girl with dark red hair in black leather standing near his shelf of keepsakes. She picked up one of his prize jars.

"Do you always keep their eyes?" she asked, her husky voice sending a frisson of sensation down his spine.

"Eyes are the window to the soul," he said feeling slightly dazed. The night had grown very warm all of sudden.

"Kind of cheesy for last words," the redhead said.

"What?" he asked, confused, just before he started screaming.

DIANA CALLED THE FIRE, like she had thousands of times before, creating a ring of it around her mark. She made sure it consumed his lungs first, so he couldn't cry out for long.

The fire cascaded down his throat, and he burned until there was nothing but ashes.

Her intense satisfaction ebbed slowly away as the fire died. It was nothing but a greasy stain when Alec spoke from behind her.

"Are you going to burn down the rest?"

She swung around, surprised. "How long have you been following me? Christ, you're not supposed to be here!"

Alec looked uncomfortable, but he stood his ground. "I had a feeling about what you might need to take care of at the club. The way you zoomed in on that guy. I didn't want you to go in without back-up."

"I don't need back-up." Diana gestured to the pile of ash and grease, exasperated.

Alec put his hands up. "I know you don't, believe me. I just. . ."

"Just what?"

"I don't want you to have to do this alone," he said quietly.

Diana chest tightened, but she ignored it and sighed loudly. "I've been doing this alone for a long time. And this thing," she said, pointing to the greasy ashes, "had it coming."

"That's kind of obvious," Alec said, glancing at the grisly objects in the room. "I'm not here to defend him or to criticize what you do. I only wanted to make sure no one surprised you or something. I'm sure you can take down entire armies, but that doesn't mean I'm not going to worry about you."

Diana shifted her weight, hands on hips, staring Alec down. "What the hell am I supposed to do with that?"

He smiled that little boy smile. "Accept it and let me be your back-up."

Diana gave him an incredulous and puzzled look. "I don't need your help. We don't have back-up. None of us do, and Serin has a full-time man. He doesn't tag along after her, worrying about her and getting in her way."

"Then he must not love her," Alec said slowly.

"Of course he does," she snapped, but for a second, doubt crossed her mind.

She had wondered that herself. "Anyway, this isn't about them."

And it certainly wasn't about love. "We need to get out of here. It's almost dawn," she said ducking out of the storage unit.

He followed her, noting that she didn't bother to close the door. "You're going to leave everything here?" he asked, looking back at the gaping door and ashes on the floor.

"The police will be notified sooner this way," she said, leading him away from the grisly little gallery.

"And you're simply going to let them find everything?"

He frowned in the direction of the now-distant storage unit as they reached the fence and climbed outside.

"Yeah, maybe there will be enough to tie his victims to him. The families might get some closure. If the victims have been missed that is. Not everyone is."

"I don't know that finding out what really happened to them would be a comfort. Especially if they never really connect the ashes to him and no one realizes he's dead," Alec said.

"It's the best we can do. The job is simply to restore the balance, nothing more," she said.

"Sorry," he said with feeling in his voice as he trailed her to her bike.

"Why? Even if I wanted to, I couldn't spend all the time it would take to check on each and every victim's family. We have to be satisfied with the fact that there will be fewer victims in the future," she said, echoing Gia and Serin more than herself.

"I'm still sorry. It's not easy, what you do. It must be emotionally draining."

He reached out as if to take her arm but stopped himself before making contact.

Diana shrugged. "Sometimes it is, other times it's. . .energizing."

Before he'd shown up, she'd still been riding that high. Although now his presence was starting to make her wonder about things she hadn't really thought about before. Like how an outsider would feel about her job. She had a hard enough time deciphering her own feelings sometimes.

"I can see that. You get to turn monsters into toast. It must be satisfying. I simply think you could use some help is all."

Diana climbed onto her bike. "I did let you help. You got more of those fig things, didn't you?" she asked in a chipper tone, wondering why his solicitude was sweet now, instead of aggravating.

"Of course I did. You really liked them," he said, as if no other outcome was possible.

"Then stop with the Boy Wonder act and follow me to the airfield," she said, pulling on her helmet and starting her bike.

"Sure thing, Batman," he said, heading for his car.

16

Alec arrived at the airfield in record time—mainly because he was trying not to lose Diana in front of him.

She drove like a maniac. Another reason to fear for her safety, even if she *was* fireproof. Would it make a difference if she hit the pavement? Maybe she could make a cushion from a fire's drafts. It was the first thing he asked her when he finally caught up with her at the edge of the airfield.

"Is this the way you always are?" Diana asked with a furrowed brow.

"What way is that?" he asked, exasperated.

Being so concerned for someone else was tiring, and the fact she didn't need or appreciate that concern was starting to grate on his nerves.

"So geeky and analytical. Kind of doesn't go with the whole crown prince of darkness image," she said with genuine curiosity.

"Well. . .I don't mind the last part much. And yes. I'm a scholar. I ask questions," he said with the tiniest hint of pride.

"So I've gathered," Diana said drily. "Well, Boy Wonder, which one is your plane?"

"It's in the private hangar on the left," he said, trying not to be annoyed at being reduced to sidekick status.

When Diana saw the plane, she rounded on him. "I thought you said this thing was small!"

"It's the smallest Gulfstream that can still fly long distance, and it's been modified for a single pilot. Go ahead and get comfortable. I have to log a flight plan and make sure we're fueled up."

"We don't really know where we're going yet," Diana said.

"I did a little more digging before I found you tonight. I have a pretty good idea of where we should be heading, a suspicion you'll need to confirm once we are in the air." He pulled the ladder up to the door and then hurried away.

When Alec got back from the hangar office, he found Diana inside the jet, peeking into the cockpit and examining the comfortable leather chairs.

"Have you ever been in a private jet?" he asked, watching her open and close drawers.

"A charter here and there, but not a nice one like this," she said, poking around the well-stocked bar cabinet next to his seat. "It's usually easier to get a lift from Logan than to get on a plane."

"Logan?"

"The Air Elemental," she said.

"Oh," Alec said, skipping a beat. "You can travel in another Elemental's medium? That's fascinating," he said, downplaying his reaction as he sat to wait for the pilot.

He wanted to ask a million more questions, but there were only so many he could safely ask before Diana clammed up. But if he was patient…

"Yeah, but it's not always convenient since we are sent in different directions most of the time," she said finally, and Alec resisted the urge to punch the air in celebration before Diana continued. "Logan can cover a lot of ground, so I ask her for a lift every once in a while." She waved toward the cockpit with a frown. "I hope you can make sense of all those little buttons and levers."

"I decided to contact a private pilot from an agency to fly us down.

We haven't gotten a whole lot of rest lately, and I personally don't want to fly the plane tired. I took the liberty of filing a flight plan under a pseudonym." He paused, working up the courage to drop another little bomb. "I told the agency they were flying a Mister and Missus Collins to New Orleans for a little R&R."

"Okay," Diana murmured as she finally sat.

"*What?*" he asked, stunned.

An easy acquiescence wasn't what he'd been expecting.

"I said that's okay. Pseudonyms are a good idea. And we could pass for a married couple if I'm a much younger trophy wife," she teased unexpectedly. "Although we lack luggage."

"We don't need it. Part of our cover states we have a house there. I can send out for anything we need."

"Do you have a house there? Is that why you picked New Orleans for a starting point?"

"The coven has one, although they haven't used it since those Anne Rice books got popular. Too cliché for them now. They rent it out. But since the staff would recognize me—and probably you by now, given how the grapevine works—I don't think we should stay there. I actually have reason to believe J may be down there."

"Is he part of the supernatural bandwagon since the town got an image makeover?"

"No, I think he might have been born there," Alec said, crossing his legs.

"Damn, I wanted to call him out for being a trend-following douchebag as well as an asshole."

Alec smiled. "You can go ahead regardless of what I think. You should kick the crap out of him simply for the name of his club."

"That was already my plan," Diana finished as the pilot walked in. "I promised Logan."

The pilot greeted them very professionally and went to the cockpit. Within twenty minutes, they were underway. Alec let them climb to their cruising altitude before he resumed the subject of J again.

"J is a mysterious character. I had Daniel dig up whatever he could on him. It wasn't easy. J doesn't let on about his origins at all, not even to his closest underlings. They've only known him for the past ten years or so. And he's tight-lipped about his past. My hypothesis is that he works at maintaining a shady reputation intentionally. You know, cultivating a mystique to draw in customers of our kind. Or he really is a dark one, which is less likely or you would have known about him sooner."

Diana nodded. "So how did you come up with New Orleans?" she asked with a little yawn.

He watched her get comfortable in her seat. "I followed the money. Tends to be the most reliable method of hunting people down, provided they have some, that is."

"A lot of the people I have to look for don't." She gestured to the cockpit. "Getting the pilot was a good idea," she added in a sleepier tone. "I've been running on empty all today."

She shifted her seat to a nearly reclining position. Without a word, he handed her Tupperware, the requisitions from the club. When Diana opened it and revealed those figs, she let out a tiny little squeal before abruptly cutting it off. Alec hid his answering smile. She gobbled down most of the figs as well as some of the other choice tidbits in the box and fell asleep with the last fig in hand.

From across the aisle, Alec watched Diana sleep. She was curled up in the large leather chair like a child. He wanted to take the fig before she smeared it all over herself but instead waited till she dropped it on the floor before he bent to pick it up.

You don't suddenly wake someone armed with a flamethrower, he thought dryly before reaching for his bag and pulling out his computer. Sleep would be a good idea, but the side effect of the day-walking ritual was an unfortunate state of wakefulness. He could keep going for days but still became tired.

Although tired was not the right term for it exactly. It was more like being in Technicolor and then slowly fading into black and white. Determined to test his limits, he once went as long as a week before he'd started to feel thin and stretched. The feeling had been so unnerving that he'd terminated his little self-experimentation after that.

Potentially, he could go longer than a week. If things kept up like they were, he might make it past that.

He looked back up at Diana. She was sound asleep. While they were on a case, it would probably be best to stay awake when she was asleep. Someone had to watch over her. Even if she was the last person who needed it.

THE FLIGHT WAS TOO short to get a real restful sleep, but Diana still felt loads better when she woke during the landing at yet another private airfield.

"Sorry, I should have woken you earlier to make sure we were headed in the right direction," Alec said from across the aisle.

"It's okay. We're close," Diana replied in a slightly hoarse sleepy voice. "He's in this city somewhere or just outside of it."

She fingered the totem in her pocket. It was pulsing in waves, connecting to the animal part in the back of her brain, giving her a direction to follow. According to Gia, their parietal cortex was unique, enhanced, and likely responsible for their tracking ability. Magic and biology intertwined. In normal humans, that part of the brain was responsible for a sense of direction, or the lack of one.

They disembarked to find a town car waiting for them. "All this luxurious leather, and the polished wood accents do not go well with my badass image," Diana announced as they settled inside, snuggling in the plush seat in spite of herself.

Alec chuckled, seemingly delighted with her unexpected frankness.

"Are you sure it's wise to be laughing at me?" she asked with raised red eyebrow.

"Of course not. That would be extremely stupid," he said still smiling before lifting two drinks in her direction, one a cold gourmet coffee beverage and the other a bottled water. "If you're still tired, we can head to a hotel. Or we can start our search now."

"It's better to follow the trail while it's hot or he may move on. I don't want to have to chase him to another town and waste more time not hunting the circle directly." She yawned and reached for the coffee.

"Then where to, Batman?" he asked, pulling out a bottle of something dark.

Probably blood, she thought wrinkling her nose.

For his kind, bottled wasn't the preferred way to drink, but it would do in a pinch. Someone of Alec's status would have fresh daily, delivered in the form of a young and attractive woman.

Diana felt her goodwill travel south several notches at the thought, so she shifted to professional mode. She pulled out J's totem and focused her energy on it, pushing the vibrations that were J's imprint and turning them outward, into a direction. She could feel the echo of a response from where J was hiding.

"South of here, and a little east, Boy Wonder."

Alec's lips flattened, but he didn't say anything about her continued use of the nickname before relaying the directions to the chauffeur on the other side of the raised partition via an internal intercom system.

The sun was rising in the sky as they pulled away and headed toward the city.

17

The Faubourg Marigny neighborhood hadn't suffered as bad as some other neighborhoods in New Orleans after Katrina, but the house J was hiding in hadn't been favorably situated. It was a shotgun row house with gingerbread molding in desperate need of a paint job. From the looks of it, the house had been affected by the storm more severely than others around it, or at least they had been repaired better.

Alec peeked at the house from their position half a block down. "Not what I expected a successful club owner would choose as a hideout."

"You'd be surprised at how often someone being chased will go home," Diana replied as she unbuckled her seatbelt and exited the car.

He followed her out. "Any plan?"

"Yeah, stay out of the way," she called behind her.

Alec gritted his teeth as he followed. Playing second fiddle was frustrating. A vampire of his age and social standing wasn't accustomed to being a mere observer. In any other situation, he would have been heading this investigation, calling all the shots.

But then you wouldn't be with her. And he was wearing her down.

Diana was getting accustomed to his presence, warming to him.

He almost snorted aloud at that last thought, but she was getting farther ahead of him and he didn't want her walking into that house alone because, as he could see from the street, she didn't bother knocking on the door.

She probably never does. Just walks right in like she owns the place, be it a palace or a shack. In seconds, Diana had the door opened. She moved inside, Alec hot on her heels.

J had clearly not been expecting them because he didn't even try to hide when they came inside.

He was taller and more muscular than Alec had been expecting. Muscles bulged from behind a skintight designer t-shirt and loose shorts. He cast a surreptitious glance at Diana, to see if she was impressed with the overt display of masculinity, but he needn't have bothered.

She had stopped short a few feet of the frozen man and paused to examine her surroundings. The interior of the house had been completely redone. It didn't reflect the worn look of the exterior.

Diana spun in a circle, examining the costly furnishings before running a white hand over a teak end table. Unlike the table in the Dover house, this one escaped getting a brand burned into its surface.

J still hadn't moved. Apparently, he'd decided on the 'no sudden movement' method of dealing with her.

"Nice place, J. A little nicer than your club actually. Who lives here now?" she asked, lifting a picture frame from a nearby table. The photo was of a much younger J and an older woman with grey hair. "Your grandmother?"

J turned to Alec, presumably for help. Alec rolled his eyes. Were they all going to do that?

J finally turned to Diana. And unwisely chose to change the subject. "I don't believe you are who you say you are."

"I don't believe I've had the pleasure of meeting you before, and therefore haven't claimed to be anyone in particular," she said, moving her hands to her hips.

"They say you're one of them. One of those freaky Elementals."

"Ooh, that makes me sound scary," Diana said in a reasonable tone, cocking her head slightly in Alec's direction.

J continued his downward slide along the IQ ladder by choosing belligerence. "I don't believe it. I don't have to talk to you," he hissed, his eyes darting to the side, eyeing the door before turning back to Diana and stepping close to tower over her and sneer.

Alec waited to see what Diana would do. He was a little startled when she gave J a dazzling smile and lifted her hand, as if to stroke him lovingly. With her index finger, she drew a letter J on the center of his chest. The sizzling flesh that resulted was rather disconcerting, as was the faint, cooked pork smell.

Ouch, he thought as J wised up and scrambled as far away from Diana as he could.

"Now do you really want me to torch grandma's house to prove you wrong?" she asked pleasantly.

Wincing, J gave Diana a wide berth as he sat in the dining room that shared the living room area.

"What do you want?" he asked grimacing, his hand hovering over the burn on his chest.

Diana tuned briefly to Alec, who'd found a convenient wall to lean against, before answering him.

"You already know that or you wouldn't have run," she said.

J shifted in his seat. He still seemed to be weighing his options when he suddenly bolted and threw a glass globe at her—a smaller version of the one from his shelf. It shattered against her chest, the contents splashing over her tank top.

Whatever was inside, it didn't activate like its creator intended. Instead, it just boiled away like water against a hot frying pan.

By the time Diana looked up, J had reached the doorway at the far end of the room, but she didn't move to race after him. Alec was about to go after him himself when J opened the door, only to be blasted back by the backdraft of a huge fire.

Fire that then started walking toward them.

CHANNELING her energy in a specific pattern, Diana gave the flames form. It was the massive shape of a huge animal, something like a lion. She'd latched onto the image by instinct, but past experience had taught her that her instinct was preternatural. The form was governed by the fears of her opponent.

In this case, J seemed to harbor a fear of big cats. The lion-like fire creature padded toward J, forcing him back into to the room, leaving fiery footprints in its wake.

"I knew that last fire was shaped like a snake! The one at the coven house that you wrapped around you," Alec burst out as he left his place at the wall and crept closer to the fiery lion, making Diana sigh aloud.

"No self-preservation instincts whatsoever," she said, sadly shaking her head.

Alec looked up at her, his smile irrepressible. "It's so cool."

Diana smiled back at him resignedly and waved him back as the lion circled J until the man scrambled up onto the couch. He climbed as far away from the beast as he could, his breath escaping in rapid short pants.

"Now why would you do something stupid like trying to run, making me mess up your grandma's nice house?" she asked him with annoyance. She turned to Alec. "I hate doing that to an innocent bystander's house. Unless she *isn't* innocent," she said, directing the last back to J. "Someone taught you the craft. Maybe Grandma taught you that questionable judgment as well. The one that said dealing with a black circle was a good idea." She leaned against the dining room table, crossing her legs in a relaxed pose to give her words added menace.

J shook his head. "My grandmother is a practitioner. A medium," he said. "A real one."

Hmm. That was interesting. Charlatans were common as grass. A true medium was rare. But J registered as a shaman to her senses, so that had to come from somewhere.

"And no, Nona is a white witch, mostly," J said, flinching away from the lion as it moved in to sniff him.

"Mostly?" Diana asked pointedly, that red eyebrow working overtime.

"So she was a little grey on occasion," J said defensively. "Times were tough here growing up. And after the storm. But Nona would never countenance any association with a black practitioner, let alone a black circle. She's a descendant of Marie Laveau. She does right by people, even at her own expense. But walking the righteous path doesn't always pay the bills. Even before Katrina. I hustled, walked the line. Crossed it on occasion. And I did right by the woman who raised me. She wants for nothing now," he finished with an emphatic sweep of his arm, which he immediately regretted as it stretched the burned skin on his chest.

"At whose expense?" Alec asked with a scowl.

"I don't do anything that keeps me up at night," J spat.

"Well, that's the problem with sociopaths. Most of them sleep real well," Diana replied.

J's aura indicated that he was definitely in a downward slide to the black. But he wasn't there yet. She might be back in a year or two to strip him of his magic, but that wouldn't stop him from buying the spells of others. Either he went straight now or he was going to be a problem that got fixed in a more permanent way.

"You're straying, J. Soon you won't be salvageable. Then grandma will be all alone. Tell me what I want to know and turn over each and every one of your contraband spells. I have bigger fish to fry than you, and I'll be pissed if you make me come find you again after this."

J stopped trying to climb the wall as she called the lion to her side. She stroked its fiery surface with a sedate little smile, the way someone would pet a housecat. J looked down at the letter burned into his chest and started talking.

"I don't know where they are. They have enough connections now to have heard they were of interest to someone dangerous. They'll have gone underground."

"Are you sure they haven't gone to another property you arranged for them through my kind or another Supe?" Alec interrupted.

"That was a one-time thing. That Fiona owed me. Racked up big bills in the club, her and her girl, that they had no intention of paying. I forgave the debt in exchange for use of a property. One that suited the needs of my newest vendor."

"And how did that start?" Diana asked.

"A young woman came to see me a few months ago. She said she was going into business with her circle. They would be selling new versions of class A spells and a few new inventions they'd come up with themselves. She left a sample, a top-notch appearance spell. Lasted several hours. Not like the common ones that are only good for a few minutes. And it was tight. More like a Fae's glamour. It was impressive," J said, his enthusiasm getting the better of his sense.

He was practically glowing until he noticed both of them frowning ferociously at him.

"And so you decided to become a customer," Diana said, motioning him to get on with it.

"Hell, yeah. It was good for business. That glamour spell alone was worth the price of admission. It was the kind of thing I could offer to VIPs of the club and their rich friends. I had access to the market they wanted access to—the richest Supes in North America. In return for opening that market to them, I got a taste. And a break on the price for whatever I chose to purchase from them for personal use."

"But you *did* meet the other members of the circle?" Diana asked.

This is what she needed. A real starting point for her search.

"Only once, but that won't help you."

Shit, Diana thought. "They were using their own glamour spell."

"Yeah. I could tell that much," J said a nod.

Diana looked to Alec for confirmation he was following, but he was still staring at the lion as it rubbed up against Diana's leg. Lost in thought, it took a snap of her fingers inches from Alec's eyes to bring him back to reality.

"Care to join me here?" Diana asked, sarcasm bleeding into her voice.

"Sorry. . .snakes. . .and lions. Um, what did I miss?"

"The circle members always use their own glamour spells to disguise their appearance when dealing with outsiders." J recapped with a shake of his head. "I thought it was a little weird, but everyone has a thing."

Diana rubbed her temple, annoyed. Being constantly under a glamour was unusual outside of the fae, some of whom had the power of disguise innately. But for a witch, the amount of effort required to create those spells was considerable. Making sure they lasted longer than a few hours took painstaking effort. Using them to mix with a buyer spoke of a considerable amount of paranoia. . .or the intention to get away with something very dark.

"Was there anything identifiable about their speech?" she asked. "Any accents or unique vocal patterns? Do they tend to dress in the same style every time you see them?"

"Like I said, I only saw one of them more than once. The youngest woman. At least she sounded young. I don't know how dramatically the glamour changed her look. I'm not good with accents. I did my best to get rid of mine. And none of them had an obvious one, but the one I think is the oldest man sounded educated, like he went to school someplace fancy. Pretentious. Didn't mind rubbing the fifty-cent words in your face. Their girl rep doesn't sound the same. Not stupid, but flaky. Always mentioning energy and magical currents. Not trained proper. The other two didn't talk at all. And their clothes during the meet were nice but hippie-like or new-agey. Youngest called herself Sarah and oldest Tom. They just referred to the others as brother or sister, like cult members do." He looked up at Diana and made direct eye contact. "That's it. There's nothing else. They never left anything behind. Not even a stray hair."

"No jewelry? Sarah sounds like the crystal type," Alec asked.

J frowned, wrinkling his chin in thought. "No crystals. . ." He shifted in his seat, the chest burn obviously painful. "The girl who did the talking. She had this thing, like an insect. An insect pin thing." He pointed to his chest above his heart.

"An insect shaped brooch? What kind of insect?" Diana asked.

"More like a bee than anything, I guess. It was in the fancy old style my grandma likes."

"What style is that?" Alec asked.

"Like that," J said, pointing to a vase that vaguely resembled the Chrysler building.

"The art deco style," Alec said.

"Yeah, and it looked real. Like a genuine antique. Real stones."

Well, it's better than nothing. But not much better.

"And that's it?" Alec asked. "You don't know where they are? Haven't heard any rumors that might help?"

"I already said no." J's nostrils flared. "Are we done now? I want to go get Nona. I checked her into a hotel last night. Told her it was for the spa."

"You may want to have the floors redone first," Alec said, shaking his head at the charred paw prints.

"Yeah. . .right," J said slowly, taking a good look at the fire cat sitting at her feet.

"We're not done yet," Diana said. "Where are the spells?"

"I left the last one I had in Boston," he said, waving a hand dismissively.

"*No.* You brought several with you. Or have you forgotten why there are scorch marks on your floor?"

"That was the only one. A defensive spell."

Diana sighed. "I figured you'd want to do this the hard way," she muttered with a little eye roll, igniting her hands.

J jumped up and out of the way, but Diana didn't follow him. Instead she held out her arms at her sides and walked around the room.

Alec followed her, fascinated as she headed toward the back of the room and out the door. They continued into the kitchen. Diana turned in a wide circle, looking for likely hiding places. She discarded the possibilities in the cabinets and focused on the refrigerator.

It was an old-fashioned Frigidaire, a massive number that probably took two people to move. A tell-tale shimmer came from underneath it. She took hold of the side.

"Do you need help with—" Alec began. "Never mind," he muttered as she shoved it aside with one hand.

Stooping down, Diana lifted a false floorboard and found the stash of vials and glass globes.

She turned to Alec. "I think you should stand back. Or better yet, go watch J, make sure he's not doing something sneaky."

Alec frowned. "Fine," he agreed before heading back to the other room.

As soon as he was gone, Diana torched the vials, enveloping them completely in fire before she broke the structural integrity of the glass. Normal fire wouldn't destroy a spell without disastrous consequences, but the fire Diana called was from the center of the Earth, the core at the heart of the planet and closest to the Mother. Nothing could survive, except another Elemental or their mates.

There was no blowback, just complete disintegration of the spells inside. She could tell what most of them did, but at least one in the bunch was ambiguous. She'd never encountered that particular configuration of ingredients. All she knew for sure was that it was pretty nasty. And new.

What are you guys up to? And why do you need two children?

She didn't know what was going on, but none of the possibilities involved rainbows and candy. Truly exhausted now, she went back to Alec and J, hiding her fatigue.

Alec, the big softie, had found some burn cream from god knows where, and was watching J apply it to his chest. The lion had disappeared as soon as she'd willed it to leave.

"We'll be leaving now. . .but I'm pretty sure I'll be seeing you again," Diana said with crossed arms. "You keep fucking with the black, and I'll return to make sure it fucks you back, you got me?"

"Yeah, I get you," a subdued but still defiant J muttered.

"You better, if you want to keep the patronage of the Eastern Coven," Alec added.

"I said I get it," a significantly more respectful J reiterated.

Making enemies with the most powerful vampire coven in the Americas would not be a good move for a businessman. Or one interested in the whole breathing thing.

"Come on," Alec said to Diana. "Let's leave J to clean up." He paused. "What does the J stand for by the way?"

"It really is Jay, but it doesn't pay to let people know that," he said, backing up from them.

"Hold on," Diana said.

She walked over to Jay and punched him hard in the face.

"What the fuck!" Jay said, nose spurting blood as he backed away. He covered his face with his hands but the blood still dripped on the floor.

"Stop being so dramatic. I pulled that punch," she said flatly, brows drawn down. "I promised the others I would do that, for calling your club Whore."

"Fuck, it's just a name," Jay mumbled behind his bloody hand.

"Names are important," Diana replied with an icy glance before walking to the door. "And clean that blood up before you pick up your Nona!" she called behind her.

When Alec finally joined her in the back of the car, she was raiding the minibar. She dug around until she found another gourmet coffee drink and popped it open.

"Did you kiss his boo-boo and make it all better?" she asked, fighting a grin.

"No," he said, a touch acidly. "I was simply explaining a few of the ways the coven could hurt his bottom line."

She rolled her eyes, but she had to acknowledge it was an effective tactic. "It might actually make a difference, your threat. Sometimes moral incentives don't cut it. Even when someone knows his or her life might be at stake. They just keep on doing whatever it takes to get money or power. But if they potentially risk losing business, then they might think twice about it," she said with some annoyance.

"Glad I might be of some use," Alec replied wryly. "Look, I have a plan. Our best move may not be to go back to Boston right away. I think it might be a good idea if we check into a hotel and regroup. Put out feelers to our contacts to see if they can track that insect pin or have heard anything new. Get some real rest. By the time we leave tonight, we should have a better plan of action. The circle may have bolted to a place far from here."

Diana thought about it. "All right, but if there's not a good reason to search elsewhere, we go back to Boston. I have another case to wrap up there."

"Is there a lot of collateral damage being accumulated by a delay on the Denon case?" Alec asked, leaning over to buckle her seat belt when she didn't do it herself.

"Not in the short term. It's a slow burner," Diana said absently, too tired to complain about the liberty he had just taken.

The sleep on the plane hadn't been enough. She nestled into the leather upholstery and closed her eyes.

ALEC SMILED at Diana's absent use of fire metaphors. Before she drifted off completely, he picked up the phone and made reservations at the Hotel Maison de Ville. Once he was done, he found Diana wide awake, staring at him expectantly.

"I've never actually stayed there," he said. "I usually go to the Ritz when in town. It's a famous landmark. Tennessee Williams wrote *A Streetcar Named Desire* there."

"Finished it there anyway," she said, surprising him. "It's okay with me. Staying there. But I'll pay for my room. I'm well provided for."

"And yet you don't treat yourself enough," he said, running his eyes over the long length of her legs. "Tonight after we've done our research, we are going to indulge in the best cuisine New Orleans has to offer. It's too good an opportunity to pass up," he said. "This case is going to take its toll. It's important to take some downtime."

Diana gave him an openly skeptical look. "Will *you* sleep this time?"

Alec paused. "You know I didn't sleep? On the plane?"

"Yeah, of course," she said as if it were obvious. "Is it a side-effect of being a Daywalker?"

Damn, she was good. He nodded. "I can forego sleep for a long period. Up to a week maybe. But I am hard to wake up when I do go down."

"I think you should sleep, and I'll wake you for dinner. Don't start racking up a deficit, just in case."

Alec smiled. "It may not be easy. I sleep like the dead, pun intended."

Diana cocked her head, considered him silently. "May I be blunt? And slightly terrifying?"

"Of course," he replied, enjoying her quirky and rare flashes of humor.

"When I'm standing above a vampire about to torch him, they *always* wake up first. Waking you up isn't gonna to be a problem."

"Ah. . .all right. Well, in that case, I'll get some shut eye," Alec said, his voice pinched.

They arrived at the hotel a little later. After Alec flashed his black card, they were checked in at speed by the efficient smiling staff. They ended up in two of the four historic Audubon Cottages. Alec saw Diana to her door before going inside his room. Grateful for the good Wi-Fi, he started making inquiries right away, searching for the antique bee pin or any insect pins that resembled bees. He also checked in with Daniel for a report on Pedro.

Pacing the length of his room, he listened to Daniel's deep gravel voice run down Pedro's progress. It was times like this he was grateful that he'd added Daniel to his staff. The man was a fount of information, and what he didn't know he soon found out.

Alec also put Daniel on the trail of the bee pin and asked him to scour the club scene for other witnesses who might have seen the members of the circle. Maybe they could get a better description of the clothes and basics about their stature and weight. Alec was pretty sure a spell couldn't disguise the body's basic height and weight. The image had to conform to the laws of physics.

After informing Daniel that he should offer a reward for information on the circle, he hung up.

He checked in with some of his other contacts and spread the same information among them and then followed up with his lawyers and business interests. After contemplating what Diana might like best for dinner, he made a final call before lying down on the bed.

For a long time, Alec stared at the ceiling, trying to decide whether or not to sleep. The idea of being woken up by Diana had definite pros and cons. If he did sleep, she might change her mind about their temporary alliance and leave town without him. It would be a challenge to find her again, but he was getting pretty good at that.

It still felt weird, lying out in the open in an unsecured room. But, somehow, knowing Diana was in the next room made him safe.

Oh, I'm in deep shit.

Pushing away the impending sense of doom, he shut his eyes.

18

Diana walked into the guest cottage and marveled at her surroundings. The place wasn't big, but it was a decent size and had some lovely old furniture. Their safe houses had nice furnishings and probably some real antiques but those were mostly of the weapon variety. None of the buildings were historical. Even in Europe, they shifted to newer buildings with higher security as a precaution. It would take an army to take down a single Elemental, but it had happened before, if their history was to be believed.

This place was cozy, and the huge four-poster bed looked inviting. Maybe they could shift a few safe houses back to old buildings and retrofit the security. It might be worth it in a few cases, she mused, stripping down for a shower.

Even the bathroom was charming, Diana decided.

This town was an interesting contradiction. She'd passed through before but hadn't spent a lot of time here. Despite what people thought, this place wasn't all that different from any other in magical terms.

It was her theory that people confused a pleasant historical atmosphere with a magical one. It made no difference to an Elemental, but most Supernaturals and even some humans swore that New Orleans was special. A place where magic was closer to the surface.

Well, it did have a good vibe—even if she didn't feel a closer connection to the Mother here. And really, she was already as close as she wanted to be.

Diana put her pack down and pulled out a candle. She felt Gia's presence across the connection and no other. Secretly relieved she wouldn't be forced to dish for Logan, she called out.

"Diana? Is everything okay?" Gia asked concerned, more adept at feeling emotion across their connection.

"Yeah, I'm just processing a lot. I'm in New Orleans with the vampire," she said.

Though Logan was the most open and tolerant of other Supes, Gia had more rational insight into their natures. She knew a lot about the major families and their scions and probably knew more about Alec than Logan, whose only information was based on gossip.

"And how is that going? Are you two working well together?"

"Well, he hasn't gotten in the way. And I'm not being *that much* nicer."

"Not nicer how exactly?" Gia asked.

"As in not pulling any punches with the people I'm trailing and questioning. Not with this last one anyway, the club owner who was trafficking black spells on behalf of his VIPs. Or so he claimed."

"What did you do?"

"Called forth a lion and gave the ass a permanent brand," Diana said.

The Earth Elemental laughed. "A brand? Couldn't you just burn his house down?"

Gia sincerely believed in the destruction of property over people.

"It was his grandmother's house, and I get the sense she is good people. And at least I did his initial and not mine," Diana reasoned.

"And how did the vampire take that? They do tend to be more flammable than the average Supe. Did he run from the flames?" Gia asked.

"Didn't seem to bother him at all."

"Really? That's certainly. . .refreshing."

"No, it's not. There are no self-preservation instincts in that sucker at all." Diana sighed.

"And you think that's because he's an academic first and vampire second?" Gia asked, a smile in her voice.

"Yeah, I do," she said, mulling over her impressions. "I also think being friends with one of us is a goal for him, probably has been for a long time."

"Do you really think he doesn't like you for you?" Gia's voice was gentle.

"More like he'd probably be predisposed to like any of us. Like a kid hanging out with celebrities, only not that bad. He's. . .trying to be useful."

"Which is extremely high praise for you," Gia admitted. "Do you think you can trust him?"

"I think so, but actually doing it is difficult," Diana spit out grudgingly.

She didn't like addressing her trust issues with Gia. Mostly because the Earth Elemental understood her better than the others, how Diana had been abandoned by a mother on the run and left in foster care and what a disaster that ended up being. It was also why when it came to this situation it was Gia's opinion she trusted the most.

"You have to take the leap sometime, and I honestly don't think you could choose a better man than Alec Broussard for it. Or vampire in this case. I've done some homework on him since his name came up," Gia informed her. "He's genuine."

"Just *friends*," Diana said emphatically.

"Of course," Gia replied though the smile was back in her voice. "You know, if you feel comfortable and he reciprocates, you should share some personal details of your life. It's normal to confide in your friends."

"You want me to tell him about my childhood?" Diana asked, slightly sick to her stomach.

"Only if you want. If you get to the point where you trust him.

Friends confide in each other. Real ones anyway." Gia was firm. "He's your first potential friend outside our group. It's always a risk taking someone into your confidence, but it can be a rewarding one. I think it's time you took that step."

"You really sound like a therapist," Diana grumbled.

"I'm sorry. I'm just excited for you," Gia said, with genuine enthusiasm.

Diana decided to broach the subject now that it had come up. "You know, you could find someone to confide in, too. I don't want to sound like Logan, but it's been a long time since. . .well, you know. You should find someone for yourself. It's not like you're, well, *me*."

Gia paused before answering. "I'm keeping an open mind. I may not be actively looking, but I'm not against meeting someone new anymore. I think when I meet someone worth it, I will be all right. . .with being friends."

"That's good. That's real good. Um, did Logan mention that I wanted an assist with the Denon situation? A bit of your special computer voodoo," Diana said, eager to change the subject.

"Yup, and I cooked up something special and sent it to the safe house in Boston. You're going to love it. All you have to do is plant it. I tried looking from the outside, but their secure servers are in-house only. But this thing is thorough. It should get everything you need with a minimum of face-time. And your listening stone is still active. I checked. I suspect it got some interesting stuff."

"I hope so. I've definitely been neglecting that case," Diana said, shifting uneasily on the bed.

"A delay there won't have much effect at this point. You're right to focus on the circle. We know what's at stake."

"Gia, what if they're already dead?" Diana voiced her worst fear for the children the circle had taken.

"Then we avenge them, and make sure no others are taken," Gia said in a soft steady voice.

It may have sounded cold to someone who didn't know her, but the Earth Elemental had been around the longest. She had seen a lot of messed up shit in her time and accepted what she couldn't change.

Of course, some of what was happening now could have been avoided. "Regardless of the outcome, I think we should take a vote," Diana said, deciding. "Whether or not. . .to make an example and extend punishment outside the immediate circle. I think they are getting help from someone who knows better."

For a long moment, Gia was silent. "We haven't done that for years."

"And the supernatural community is slipping away—especially if we are right that this black circle is led by a witch descended from one of the major families. And someone this talented *has* to be from one of the big seven," Diana said.

"If it's another Delavordo, I'm going to bust someone up. *Bad,*" Gia said with a rare show of irritability.

"I know they're at the top of the list of usual suspects, but enough black has come from the other six to avoid jumping to conclusions," Diana said reasonably. "Besides, the Delavordos keep track of their remnant talent a lot better these days. They've kept a fairly low profile for decades now."

"Only because they don't want us coming down on them as hard as we did the last time. And because being shunned by the supernatural community does limit your social options." Gia sniffed before returning to her old reasonable self. "We should discuss this with the others. It would be the first time for you and Logan, and it will depend on what you find when you catch up with the circle."

"I know, but if it's the worst, then we should be prepared," Diana said, reaching out to touch the candle flame with her finger.

"Agreed. And you're right. An example outside the first degree of culpability hasn't been made for so long. The vampires would remember, I guess, but most of the current gen of witches and Weres weren't around the last time," Gia pointed out. "Memories like those fade into myth fast because people who don't witness it firsthand don't believe it happened in the first place. And those that did deny their involvement. Maybe it is time for a refresher."

"Yeah," Diana agreed. "Oh, hey, can you look into something else for me?" she said, remembering the bee brooch. "Someone in the circle has an antique pin thing, a bee or something like it. Art Deco period. Can you see if there's a vibration for something like that?

"If the stones in it are real, then maybe. I'll see what I can do," Gia promised. "I'll mention it to Logan as well."

Diana said goodbye and blew out the candle. She peeked in the direction of Alec's cottage. No man shaped heat signature was stirring. Closing the curtain, she pulled back the covers on the luxurious bed, sinking down into the mattress with a satisfied wiggle.

It was kind of nice knowing that when she woke, Alec would be there. Of course, she would set fire to a whole block before admitting that she liked having him around.

19

Hours later, Diana was standing over a slumbering Alec. He was *out*. He hadn't stirred at all when she'd come inside his room. Not even his chest was moving, but that was probably because of the whole being dead thing.

It was actually a very nice chest, not unlike the kind Abercrombie used to have standing outside their stores. She'd never been this close to one actually.

Alec had also stripped down to his shorts, a silky looking boxer brief thing that hugged his hips. The sheet was thrown carelessly over the good parts. She decided to wake him up before she got tempted to move the fine Egyptian cotton away.

With a regretful sigh, Diana put her hand on Alec's bare arm. He woke with a start, sitting bolt upright with vampiric speed.

"Told you it would work," she said, averting her eyes from his chest now that he was conscious. "Sorry, I had to give you a little jolt."

"You mean an *electric* jolt? Is that part of the fire gift?" he asked blinking rapidly before getting up and pulling on his pants.

Diana shrugged. "It's one way to start a fire."

Alec's eyes widened. "Do you shoot electricity out like Zeus?"

"Not exactly, although there was at least one past Fire Elemental who developed that skill," she said, peeking in the mirror as he put on a fresh shirt.

It was a *very* nice chest. It could be tanner, but vampires, even the Daywalkers apparently, didn't spend a lot of time sunbathing. Diana couldn't really complain, though. Redheads didn't tan, either.

"Can you develop different aspects of your talent and not others?" he asked as he finished putting on his shoes.

"Sort of," she said, turning back around now that he seemed to be fully dressed. She squinted, trying to crush the mental image of that chest hidden underneath pristine white cloth. "Did you get in touch with your people?"

"Yes. They'll be looking for anything on the whereabouts of the circle and on that brooch. It would help if we found someone more observant that took a good look at that pin. Then we could get a sketch made to pass around to some jewelers. I've got Daniel on that," he said, wrapping a fresh tie around his neck.

"Sounds good. I've got Earth and Air checking in with their sources, too," she said.

"Sources?"

"Their element," Diana replied, wondering how much she could trust him.

"How does that work?" he asked.

With a sigh, she decided to take the leap. He was too intelligent to share their secrets with the wrong people or in some wordy monograph. And Gia was right. She could use a friend.

"They listen to their element. Air hears the things whispered on the wind. And Earth can. . .well, it's like she can hear the echoes in the earth. Like memories. Neither is truly reliable, but a surprising amount of information can be found that way," Diana said.

She didn't mention communing directly with the Mother. It was a difficult and potentially damaging thing to attempt, and so far Gia was the only one who'd successfully done it.

"Can you do that?" he asked.

"No. Fire has no memory," she said simply, waiting as he pulled out a jacket.

"Oh. Well, I guess that makes sense since it's ephemeral. Except maybe at volcanoes. Are you immune to lava?"

Diana laughed. "Since I've never jumped into a volcano, I don't actually know. Believe it or not, it's never come up before. Where are we going for dinner? I've had some good take-out in this town."

"No, no, no!" Alec said loudly, startling her. "Fine dining in New Orleans is beyond. . .well, it's simply beyond. There is no excuse for eating take-out here as a visitor. It should only be a restaurant or star-vation," he said, arms wide for emphasis.

"You're a vampire. You barely eat," she said in an incredulous tone.

"Which is why my word on this should be highly valued. If you can only consume a little bit at a time, it damn well better be good," he said with a warm smile.

"Fine. So what's for dinner?"

He stopped short. "There's a restaurant called Broussard's here, but since you haven't been out to dinner here before, I opted for a classic, Antoine's."

"I think I've heard of it," Diana replied as they made their way into the courtyard.

"Yeah, it's always mentioned in books about New Orleans and highlighted on tourist websites," Alec said. "We could go someplace else if you like."

"No, it's okay if we can get in. But we could try the Broussard place too if you want. Are they related in some way?"

"Yes, but they don't know it. It's a branch of the family where the ability to turn died out ages ago. We don't keep in touch. Family, even distant family, outside the community is too tricky to deal with since we can't be honest with them about what we are," he said.

"Yeah, I guess that would be problematic."

Guess there are advantages to not having a family.

Alec ushered her toward the luxury car he had waiting for them. This one was a shiny black Ferrari convertible he chose to drive himself.

"Little mid-life crisis, isn't it?" she asked trying not to laugh, even though she really liked the 458 Spider in this color.

"Says the woman with a Suzuki Hayabusa," he teased.

"Hey, that's for speed," she said, wrinkling her nose as she climbed into the car.

"So is this," Alec argued as he revved the engine, making her laugh out loud.

By the time they arrived at the restaurant, Alec had covered the history of the Broussard's in New Orleans and had gone into the history of Antoine's restaurant. As she'd come to expect, they were ushered inside to a prime table as soon as they arrived.

"This is the Mystery room," he explained to Diana as he handed her a glass of wine. "I believe there is a hidden door in a ladies room somewhere that led to this space. People would get served alcohol in coffee cups here during prohibition."

Diana's interest was immediately caught. "I like movies about that era, about Gangsters. I don't like them in real life, of course, but as fiction, they're okay."

"Me, too. I met Capone once."

"*Really?*" It was her turn to be fascinated. "What was he like?"

"He was charming and utterly ruthless. It was at a party in Chicago. There were a number of colorful characters wandering around in those days. I was attracted to the atmosphere, people partying despite the blue laws. Those little illicit rebellions." He shook his head and smiled. "The little rebellions are so much more enjoyable than the big ones," he finished, his gaze growing distant and unfocused.

Determined to keep it light, Diana narrowed her eyes. "Were you studying them like an anthropologist?"

"In a way, I suppose," he admitted ruefully as he focused on her again. "But I did partake in the parties myself. A real anthropologist wouldn't get involved in that way."

"I don't think that was always true," she said.

"It was for me when I was working," he said with a smile. "I knew some of those other types. Men who staged fake rituals among primitive peoples so they could write about them. I did not approve."

"Staged rituals like Krippendorf's tribe type stuff?"

"Yes, only worse. Not exactly the right note for dinner conversation, though," Alec said, turning the conversation to New Orleans history and legends of the supernatural tied to the city. He was one of those who maintained that the city was special.

"I feel different here," he confessed.

Diana pursed her lips. "Our kind feels the same everywhere. New Orleans is a nice place but not extraordinary to us, because we feel her magic everywhere."

It was almost the complete truth.

"And you don't feel even a special tingle here? Or Stonehenge? The Pyramids?" He prodded as he poured her more wine.

"Not really. Some awe, of course. A sense of history. I like ancient ruins. To some extent, we can superimpose our own history over some of those sites. But I don't often get a chance to do that kind of thing. No time to stop and smell the roses."

He nodded. "I imagine you are kept busy. What happens after?"

"What do you mean?" she asked, swirling her wine the way she had seen him do before sipping it.

"After your service to Her ends?" he asked.

The question caught Diana off guard. She knew what happened in most cases. . .but didn't think it applied to her. Thankfully the arrival of the waiter saved her from answering.

"You have to have the Oysters Rockefeller. It was invented here," Alec suggested.

"I was thinking shrimp remoulade. Why don't you get the Oysters?" Diana asked.

"I decided on the alligator soup," he said absently as he studied the menu.

"Oh, so it's like that," she whispered with a little head nod.

"Like what?" he said, putting the menu down to look her in the eyes.

"Predator eats predator. Dog eat dog," Diana teased cheekily, resting her chin on her hands. "In a fight between you and the movie Predator, who would win?"

"Why don't you bring us the shrimp remoulade and the oysters," Alec said dryly to their waiter, who rushed away to fill their order.

"I agree. Predator would totally kick your ass," she said, leaning back and nodding sagely.

"Don't think I don't know you're avoiding my question," he replied, shaking out his napkin with a snap and laying it in his lap with a flourish.

"And I'm going to keep avoiding it," she agreed with a cheerful nod, reaching for her wine.

Diana continued evading talk of the future well into her main entree, fried crabs with almonds. It was delicious, once she figured out the best way to eat it. Seafood was not as common in take-out form, and she was enjoying the novelty.

Thank god for a Fire Elemental's metabolism or she'd be hard pressed to squeeze into her leathers at this rate.

They were both eating the cinnamon and raisin bread pudding before Alec managed to return to the topic of life after service. "You do get to stop sometime, don't you? I mean, you guys age out eventually?"

She took a deep breath and thought about what to say. "This isn't going in some manuscript, is it?"

Alec frowned and leaned closer. "I may ask questions like I'm interviewing you, but you know I'm not, right? It's not about that. Your kind. . .you're the answer to a lot of questions I've had my whole life. But our friendship means more to me than getting those answers. If you want me to stop asking you things about the Elementals, I'll stop, all right? Just say the word."

Diana thought about it. He sounded so earnest, and she knew he was telling the truth. And he was already claiming friendship so easily, like it was a normal thing.

Maybe it is normal.

She leaned back in her chair. "We don't age out exactly. While we serve, everything slows down. You pretty much stay the same until you decide to leave her service. Then another is called. You can spend years or centuries doing her work. It's up to you."

Alec's eagerness was palpable. "How long have you been in service?"

"About a decade."

"Oh. That would mean you're roughly late twenties. Okay. I'm only two hundred years older. There's nothing creepy or weird about that," he said, tugging on his tie a little too hard.

Enjoying his discomfort, she added, "It's more like two hundred and thirty years. How many generations is that? If I'm gen Y does that make you generation A? Or did they use something before letters? Roman numerals maybe? Are you generation XXII?"

Picking up the gauntlet, he took a big sip of wine before asking, "Why do most Elementals leave the service? It's a great honor, after all. Is it simply too exhausting? Do you burn out?"

"Good fire pun," she acknowledged with a snort. "Sometimes we do. Or Elementals leave when they want to settle down. They decide to start families or they meet someone. . ."

"Does the meeting someone not usually happen first?" he asked.

Diana pursed her lips and rested an elbow on the table. "Elemental lines are matrilineal. And the women who inherit are. . .strong," she said euphemistically. "They don't always feel the need to include a father in the picture. Making sure the line continues is important. It's not always a direct line of inheritance, but the gift frequently circles back when it strays. And some lines just die out and others are born. Like the vamps and the witches."

"But only one inherits a specific Element at a time? Why? Does the Mother worry you all wield too much power?" he asked, waving a hovering waiter away with an elegant gesture.

Startled at his perception but refusing to show it, she avoided his eyes. "There are probably various reasons that are equally valid. Too much firepower at one time in the same family would be a disaster waiting to happen."

"But your families are still practitioners, right? They still have magic?"

Diana expelled her breath loudly, rubbing her temple. She was taking a lot on faith, but she did eventually answer. "Some do, not all, and not the same brand of magic as everyone else. More tied to nature. But most know and feel a connection to the Mother. The history gets passed down pretty succinctly in most cases."

"In most cases. Did it get passed down your family?"

"No," she said curtly and looked away.

Alec apparently saw the flashing warning lights ahead and veered away. He gestured to her now empty dish. "Are you through?"

"Yeah, let's get out of here. I'm kind of talked out," she said, fighting to maintain a tranquil expression.

Wordlessly, they exited the restaurant and walked out into the night air. The French Quarter was busy at all hours. Though she didn't feel that mystical pull others felt here, she acknowledged that this place was unique. It had a little something extra. What did they call it? *Lagniappe.* No city she'd visited in Europe had this feel—light and dark blending with music and spice. It had a look and feel that was not European, and definitely not American.

"You do like this place, don't you?" Alec asked, watching her face closely as they walked along the cobblestone streets.

"It has its charms," she said noncommittally.

"Well, I'm glad you enjoyed dinner. I did, what I could finish anyway." He sighed wistfully. "I miss food. It's not fashionable to admit, but I do. I tried a stint in a cordon bleu academy in France fifty or so years ago. I thought the next best thing to getting to eat it would be to prepare it," he said, falling into step beside her, his hands in his pockets.

"You do seem very enthusiastic about food, considering your primary source of nutrition," she said wryly.

"You would be enthusiastic, too, if you couldn't eat any solid foods for decades after you were turned," Alec replied in complete seriousness.

"Yeah, I heard that's what happens. Most of your kind don't bother to go back to solids from what I hear."

"Oh, that's only vampire image hype," he said dismissively. "All of us eventually start eating again. We miss the sensory experience of chewing too much. You simply don't get to enjoy full and robust meals anymore. Just little tastes."

"Don't you need blood soon?" she asked, trying to hide her discomfort at having to ask and failing utterly.

"I'll make arrangements for that before we leave town," he said, looking up at the wrought-iron balconies of the French Quarter, the ones that always ended up on postcards, before changing the topic to Mardi Gras.

As they strolled the cobblestone streets, Alec talked about the celebrations he'd seen in Rio and Quebec. Diana had been hunting a rogue werewolf in Rio during Mardi Gras once but hadn't paid much attention to the festivities.

He peppered her with questions about her hunt as they walked, while she absorbed the festive and open atmosphere of the Quarter. Eventually, they wandered to the French Market, where Alec badgered and wheedled until she agreed to have beignets from the Cafe du Monde. He nibbled one as well while Diana inhaled the rest, washing it down with a cafe au lait.

"It's a good thing I literally burn calories, you fat enabler," Diana said half-grumpily when she'd finished.

Alec was still laughing when his phone rang. He moved away and began talking animatedly. Diana watched him from a distance. It was probably his go-to man, Daniel, on the other end of the line judging from the way he was interacting on his end.

She liked his laugh. She did *not like* the fact he had to drink blood.

From across the way, Alec gave her a thumbs up. He hung up the phone and came back to their table. "I got a better description of the insect pin. It's not a bee. It's a beetle with red and orange enamel. Daniel's sending a picture of the sketch he had worked up."

"He talked to more people at the club?"

"Yes. The staff as well. The bathroom attendant got a good look at the brooch when our mystery woman decided to use the facilities. Do you have a cell? I can send the picture to you."

"I don't use one. Just show it to me," she said, reaching for his phone to examine the drawing.

"Who would choose a beetle?" Alec asked with a frown as she studied his screen. "Other than Haldane?"

"Who?" Diana asked absently.

"J.B.S. Haldane. A naturalist. He once said something to the effect that God, if he exists, has an inordinate fondness for beetles."

Nerd. "Well, I doubt we're looking for a beetle biologist. Hopefully it's a family heirloom or something traceable."

The brooch was an elaborate piece. Probably an antique from the looks of it. The pin certainly didn't look modern. Diana turned away, lit a match, and blew it out. She sent the mental image of the brooch into the aether, knowing one of the others would eventually receive it when they next communed with their element.

"Did I just witness Elemental email?" Alec asked.

"I guess that's one way to describe it. Any reason to stay in New Orleans?"

"No, unfortunately."

"You really like those oysters, don't you?"

"I do, but we might as well head back to Boston since you have other things to take care of. I'll call for the plane."

They headed back to the hotel, and Alec picked up his bag while Diana grabbed her pack. She headed outside and breathed in the night air, wondering how long it would take to track down the beetle pin woman.

A few minutes later, Alec came out of his room, and they were on the road to the airport.

An hour later, they were back in the air. Diana slouched in the comfortable leather chair, surreptitiously watching Alec. He was on the phone again while messing with his tablet. From the sound of things, he was wheeling and dealing, making what were probably multi-million dollar deals.

He'd already checked on Pedro and had seemed genuinely concerned for the man. Diana was even ready to admit that it wasn't an act for her benefit. There was no pretense or deceit in his manner. He was just being himself.

And she'd spent a little too long staring at him. When Alec looked over at her, she quickly averted her gaze and contemplated the interior of the plane.

I wonder how Logan would react to being inside a plane. The Air Elemental had never flown in one. She'd never had to. Diana made a mental note to ask. She'd sent her a message to check out Katie's mother Brenda, but Logan hadn't heard anything about the woman's whereabouts yet.

It was so frustrating not being able to track humans. The non-serial killer ones anyway. She closed her eyes for a minute only to be startled by the smell of fresh beignets. Alec had stopped working and was waving one under her nose. She breathed in a little powdered sugar and sneezed on his hand for his efforts.

"Here, have a fresh one," he said, laughing and extending the bag to her.

Diana didn't argue, taking a beignet from the bag and eating it. For the rest of the trip, she created little fireballs in her hands. She really needed to get one of those e-readers or a tablet if she was going to continue to be driven and flown around by Alec. Then she could read. Or play Angry Birds or Candy Crush.

"Why don't you have a phone? Or a computer?" Alec asked, clearly honing his mind-reading skills.

"Don't need it to get in touch with the others most of the time. And computer hardware doesn't have a long shelf life around me. Water has the same problem. Air and Earth, especially Earth, do a lot better with electronics. There are laptops in every safe house. I try not to stay on them too long. Shortens their lifespan."

"Which means unless we find you an extremely heat tolerant phone, we should stick together for the duration of this investigation. . ." he suggested with a smile.

"Nice try. I have some stuff I need to do solo in Boston. I can pick up a burner phone. We keep several in each stash and replenish them often," Diana said, one of the corners of her mouth turning up.

"Yeah, that one was a long shot." Alec murmured before adding in a louder voice, "of course. I'll do my thing and get in touch with any news. If you need a hand with your Denon case, I would be happy to pitch in."

"I think I've got it covered," Diana said, rubbing her neck.

"I also give great massages," Alec drawled, with more suggestion in his voice than he'd allowed around her before.

"I'm fine, thanks," she told him flatly. "We're not exactly in coach here, but I'm not used to sitting so much."

She punctuated her statement by reclining her chair to its horizontal position and closing her eyes. Once he resumed typing she peeked at him from behind her lashes, interested in the way his hands moved over his tablet.

20

After they landed, Diana and Alec split up. She rode her bike out to the safe house and left messages on the aether for Logan about Katie's mom and checked in with the other two.

After showering, she turned her attention back to the Denon Corporation. She still had to gather evidence of their systematic abuses during their mining operations. Digging into the box Gia had sent, she pulled out the Earth Elemental's latest creation.

It looked like an innocuous fuse, something she could easily plant on the internal network's power source. From there, the little gem would copy all of the information in a completely untraceable manner. It circumvented the need to access the server room itself, which was accessible only by key card. She had planned on stealing one, but now she wouldn't have to.

Too bad. This meant that she would have to get back in there with her temp disguise. Maybe another secretary would have car trouble this time. It was kinder than the food poisoning.

She looked through the company's internal directory for a secretary on the right floor. A few more of Gia's tricks, and she found a home address and made sure she was at the top of the temp roster.

She went to sleep after going over the electrical plans for Denon headquarters.

The secretary Diana had targeted for car trouble was a particularly well paid one in the upper echelons of the Denon Corporation. She worked for one of the senior vice-presidents, Donald Price.

Diana hated having to target the little guy when doing these large corporation cases, but it was for the greater good.

At seven AM the following day, she waited patiently under an elm tree for Ms. Ellison to leave for work. In a few minutes, the older woman came out of her suburban home, coffee in hand. She started the car, and in another minute, her repeated attempts only resulted in a lot of smoke pouring from under the hood.

Across the street, Diana controlled the small fire she'd set in the engine block, making sure it looked alarming enough for Ms. Ellison to call in absent to work. Luckily, the woman did not appear to live with someone she could ask for help, nor did she have a second car. When she saw Ms. Ellison get on her cell phone and start making call after call, Diana slipped away and went to a gas station to change into her temp disguise.

She planted Gia's bug around lunchtime when the building was more empty than usual. It took only moments, but if all went well, it would bring down a company for over forty years of flagrant malfeasance overseas.

Satisfied, Diana went back to Ms. Ellison's desk and ate the tuna sandwich she'd packed for her lunch. She chewed with some dissatisfaction as she remembered eating out with Alec.

Damn. Her sad little sandwich paled in comparison to all of those gourmet meals. And she used to love tuna fish. She'd gotten spoiled, a side effect of befriending a man with an unlimited income and refined taste.

Just before quitting time, she checked on her listening stone in the air duct. Using a partner stone, she did the magical equivalent of downloading the information recorded. There was quite a lot of it. The higher-ups had been doing a serious amount of chatting lately. There was enough data to suggest that some of the recordings were made after hours. Maybe they had realized they were under investigation. She knew she hadn't tipped them off. Perhaps some government agency had finally gotten off their butts and started their own investigation into the company's practices.

Before she was able to leave for the day, Diana had an unpleasant visit from Matt Archer, a lecherous junior vice president who'd been overly friendly to her the one other day she had worked here.

"Hi, gorgeous," Matt said, sauntering up to her desk and sitting on the corner.

"Do you do that when Miss Ellison is here?" Diana asked caustically.

Matt gave her his most charming smile. "The dragon would staple my ass to her desk if I tried."

"If you don't have any business for Mister Price, I need to get back to work," Diana said in her most business-like voice.

Hurt flashed across his face. "I just wanted to invite you to drinks. A bunch of us are going after work."

She wanted to snort, but she bit her tongue instead. He was lying. The slight flush and increased heart rate was enough to convince her of that.

Now I remember why I hate these corporate jobs. This sort of thing happened every time she went undercover.

"No, thanks, I'm having dinner with my husband tonight. It's date night," Diana lied smoothly.

More smoothly than him.

His face fell. "Oh, I didn't know you were married. You don't wear a ring."

"I can't wear jewelry. Sensitive skin goes with the red hair," she lied again. She actually had a few piercings, just not visible ones.

"Well, you should call him and invite him," he said. "It'll be fun."

Liar, liar pants on fire. Literally, if you don't go away.

"Sorry, we have plans," Diana finished with a polite and distant smile. A deflated Matt slunk back to his desk.

"You were right to reject him, but if you come back to temp here, it won't matter that you're married," a voice off to her left said. "He'll definitely try again."

Diana turned to find Erika, another secretary on the floor, waiting with an interested expression on her face. She was a friendly and overly gossipy young woman, not quite attractive enough to have to worry about the Matts of the world. But she was nice and genuine. Diana liked her.

"That would be unwise," she said, completely honest for once.

"You just defined Matt. He pushed and pushed until he got a junior exec's secretary to see him. She was married, too. Ruined her marriage, and then he dumped her and got her fired. He's a jerk," Erika said, sitting on the same spot Matt had been occupying.

"Yeah, that was clear, but thanks for the info," Diana said. He wasn't bad enough for her to deal with officially, but maybe there was something she could do about Mr. Archer. She gestured to the packet of papers Erika was holding. "Are those for Mister Price?"

"Yes, he needs to sign these today." Erika handed over some of the papers and headed back to her desk.

Diana did not escape the rest of working day entirely unscathed. A few minutes before quitting time, Mr. Price came over to suggest he could get her a permanent position with the company if she played her cards right. She resisted the urge to roll her eyes.

I should cut my hair or something. Maybe die it brown or shave it off. Her built-in jerk magnet was clearly working too well. Maybe if she got a little uglier, she'd have less asshole face time.

"I prefer the flexibility of temping," Diana replied with a stiff, plastic smile.

When the governing board goes down, I will make sure you go down with them.

"You should think about the advantages of a permanent position. More job security and better pay. And a lot of new friends."

His emphasis made it clear what kind of friend he wanted to be with her. Apparently, he preferred the image of her at the desk outside his office than the uber-efficient Ms. Ellison.

Ugh. Two in a row. "I don't think it's for me," she said politely.

Mr. Price's smile turned a touch more brittle. "Well, if you ever change your mind, you know where to reach me."

"Of course I do," she said with another one of those distant and polite smiles.

She was getting too good at those. The demise of the Denon corporation couldn't come soon enough.

21

Diana was counting the minutes till she could leave Denon headquarters. The minute the clock hit five PM, she was half-way to the elevator, but that still wasn't fast enough.

Both Archer and Price were following close at her heels, and despite the fact they entered the elevator after her, they moved behind her so they could check out her ass the whole way down. They weren't even subtle about it. Teeth gritted, she kept her hands clenched at her sides so she wouldn't give in to temptation.

Mysterious elevator fires were a thing, weren't they?

This time Diana wasn't the least bit surprised to find Alec waiting outside the main entrance. What was surprising was that she was actually glad to see him. He was lounging against a shiny black town car, some sort of Bentley this time. Her relief at seeing him must have been clear on her face because he sprang up and was at her side in seconds.

Side benefit—his imposing presence, including the proprietary arm he put around her, stopped Archer and Price dead in their tracks.

Noting their interest, Alec gave her a warm hug and whispered in her ear, "I hope you mentioned a boyfriend to those two. They seem overly interested in you."

"You mean in you and your shiny car," Diana replied quietly. "And I didn't mention a boyfriend. I mentioned a husband." Alec froze when she stood on her tip-toes to kiss him on the cheek. "So, hi honey, how was your day?" she asked in a louder voice.

Alec's eyes flared, going from dark chocolate brown to a shade of light honey as they heated, along with the rest of his body. He blew right past the two men trying to casually catch their attention, handing her into the car with a flourish before he followed her into the backseat.

As soon as the car door closed, enclosing them behind a tinted window screen of privacy, Diana relaxed her guard.

"Ugh," she shuddered and shook out her hands before taking a deep breath. "I was this close to torching something," she said, holding her fingers a millimeter apart.

Alec laughed, despite his obvious disappointment that her warm welcoming act was over. "Well, given how your admirers are practically licking the windows to get at you, I must applaud your will power. Go ahead, Daniel," he directed his driver. "Before we need to get the car washed."

The two men were still standing nearby on the sidewalk. Both were frowning as they realized the occupants of the car were not going to get out to talk to them, as was their due given their position at Denon. Their displeasure at being ignored was all over their faces as the car pulled away.

Sighing, Diana leaned back. In a perfect world, she could deep-fry the chauvinists or at least singe them, but honestly, they hadn't done anything bad enough to deserve it. She got that sort of shit all the time. The small pleasure of snubbing them was going to have to do.

"Who's watching Pedro?" she asked with a nod to the track-suited Daniel behind the wheel.

"His assistant," Alec said.

Diana smiled. Of course Daniel had an assistant. Being Alec's right hand was a full-time job and then some.

"It's a bit early for dinner," Alec began, "but I thought we could check out a few jewelry stores and antique shops that sell jewelry. We could show them the sketch we got from the bathroom attendant unless you have an errand. Do you want to get dropped off to change? That skirt looks itchy," he said, handing her a printed list of stores and addresses.

Diana frowned. "It *is* itchy. How did you know?"

"I know fabrics. Kind of unavoidable in the coven. Vampires tend to be clotheshorses."

"I knew that already," she said, eyeing his fine tailored suit sideways. "But this outfit works for something else I have in mind. Will you drop me off at this address?" she asked, handing over a slip of paper from her purse.

"Of course. Would you like some company?"

"Since you insist on stalking me, do I have a choice?" she asked, unable to work up any genuine irritation this time.

"No, not really," he admitted comfortably. "Where are we going?"

She pursed her lips. "That's the address where Katie lived. I haven't seen her mother since I brought Katie home last year, and now they're both gone."

"Brought her home? You knew the little girl already?" Alec asked, his brows drawing down.

Diana gauged Alec's reaction. He was upset, indignant. But not with her.

"She was taken by a child molester last year. I brought her home before he did any permanent damage. Many others weren't so lucky..." She looked out the window, watching the streets pass as they made their way across town.

Reluctantly, she continued. "I may have made a mistake when I brought her back," she confessed, shoulders tight. "Her mother *seemed* relieved. I didn't suspect anything might be wrong. But now Katie's missing again, and so is her mother. So maybe there was something I should have seen back then that I missed." She shook her head. "Brenda was just so terribly emotional. I couldn't wait to get out of there."

"Wait, the mother is missing, too?" he asked, confused. "Can't you track her like you did Fiona or Jay?"

"It doesn't really work that way for humans. Not unless they've done something bad enough to move the needle for one of us. And that takes a lot these days. It's getting harder to track humans who do wrong. There are just so many more than there used to be. Their signal gets lost in the noise. Even if Brenda's shady, I probably can't find her as easily as I could find the circle. Which isn't turning out to be easy at all. They're masking themselves somehow, or we would have been aware when they started creating those black spells."

"And now you suspect this Brenda woman is involved with the circle? You said she's only a human. It could be a coincidence."

Diana stared at him. "Maybe. . .but her sister, Katie's aunt, was there, and she was uncomfortable. *Really* uncomfortable. I didn't think anything of it at the time. Lots of people clam up when you flash a badge. But there could have been something there. Her name was Catherine." Diana rubbed her temple.

"Brenda and Catherine. I can get my men on looking for traces of them if you think they're involved," he said. "People are easier to find these days. Just takes some old fashioned police work."

"I tried that already. We have access to the human databases. Nothing's turned up."

"Well, a little more legwork couldn't hurt," he said. "I could put some private detectives on it. There are a few I use regularly that have done good work for me in the past."

Something in Diana balked at the thought. She wasn't used to getting outside help. There had never been a need. But she had to think about what was best for the children.

"Okay. Why not," she said, exhaling deeply.

She almost changed her mind, but stifled the urge to take it back.

"Look, I need to talk to you about something." She hesitated before pushing her shoulders back and continuing. "When I catch up with the circle, it won't be pretty. When I find them, they will be punished. Harshly. I'm going to do things to them you may not be able to live with. You may not want to stick around for that part."

Alec frowned. "I know it will be harsh. And if they've harmed the children, they deserve it. If they have broken the covenant, then their lives are forfeit. I may be a boring academic, but I'm still a vampire of house Broussard."

"I wish everyone felt the same way about the covenant. Even humans no longer follow her ways—and most of the rules of the covenant were put in place to protect them. There's too many of them, and they have no respect for the Mother, for the earth, or for themselves. They take each other's lives and the lives of their children. Even the witches are not so callous and bloodthirsty. We're losing them." She sighed, covering her eyes briefly.

"A witch circle took the children. Not a human," Alec said.

"It doesn't matter. The witch in charge, the one with the real magic, was raised outside the magical families, among humans like I was," she said. "Otherwise they might know better."

"I didn't know that you grew up among humans," Alec said carefully.

Diana waited for him to start pushing for answers, but he just watched her, his big brown eyes filled with patient understanding.

She took a deep breath. "My mother was from an Elemental line long forgotten. She was murdered when I was four by a serial killer, one fond of strangling pretty young women. Even if they have little children."

Alec's mouth dropped open. "How did an Elemental get killed that way?"

Diana met his eyes, "I didn't say she was an Elemental. She was just a woman. The line of inheritance is not always direct."

"Oh, yes, of course. What about your father?" he asked a little hoarsely.

"Never knew him. I think he was in the army."

"Is he still alive?"

Diana shrugged. She didn't know and didn't care.

"Did you ever try to find out more about him or your mother's family?" he asked.

"Her family was pretty much all gone. And no. I didn't try to find out more about my father's family. The inheritance is matrilineal. The

Elemental scholars don't keep track of the fathers unless the relationships are long-term. And the boys don't inherit."

"You didn't try to find out on your own?"

His voice was soft with sympathy. It was making her skin crawl.

"No," she said pointedly. "There was no reason to." She looked out the window with relief. "We're here."

They were outside of a seventies industrial-looking apartment building. It was next to others of similar design in a cheerless and drab neighborhood. Diana got out of the car first, eager to escape the small enclosed space. Alec followed her out a little more slowly, probably processing everything she'd told him.

Not waiting for him she climbed up the stairs to the apartment the little girl had shared with her mother. Assuming that there would be new tenants, she reached into her bag for her fake FBI badge, ready to flash it when the door opened, but a minute passed, and the door remained closed. After more knocking and waiting, she put her hand on the door and closed her eyes. There was no warmth in the rooms behind.

"No one home," she murmured to Alec.

"You can feel heat like those infrared cameras can see through walls, can't you?"

The quiet reticence that had come when he learned her secret had lasted the length of time it took him to climb the stairs. Her geek was back.

Diana didn't bother to answer his question. Instead, she took the doorknob in hand and moved the tumblers with her heat. A chain stopped the door short, but she could see inside clearly. There was no end table in view, no furniture at all. She reached up and melted the chain with one hand, pushing the door wide with her hip.

"That is so badass," Alec said in an undertone.

Diana shot him a look. "You're a *vampire*. Try to at least act a little cool," she said pushing the door wide with her hip.

"I am cool," he said in an injured tone. "I got voted one of the supernatural world's most eligible bachelors for Pete's sake. Not that I care about that," he said as Diana started to choke back her laughter. "But they did. They make a list every twenty years or so…"

"Well, all right then," she said, no longer bothering to hide her laughter. "Consider me chastised. Why don't you stay here in the doorway, 'cause I don't want all this eligible bachelor hotness," she moved her hands up and down to encompass all of him, "to interfere with reading the room. That okay with you playboy?"

Alec closed his eyes. "Carry on. If you're done mocking me, that is."

Moving inside, Diana giggled. "Not even close, stud." She circled the room, and her laughter subsided. The room was totally empty. There wasn't even any trash. "If I didn't know better, I would say Dietrich had been here."

She had expected new people to have taken up residence, but apparently the landlord wasn't in a hurry. It was off-putting to see it so empty. Closing her eyes, she scanned the heat signatures but gave up quickly. She shook her head resignedly, and Alec came inside.

"Humans. They don't leave much behind."

Alec frowned. "Why would a mother move house when her child is missing?" he asked, rubbing his chin. "Shouldn't she be waiting in the home her child knew and remembered in case she came back? Unless she thought to search on her own and couldn't afford to keep the place while she went looking…"

"I don't know." Diana fingered the layer of dust on the shelves and counter, trying to decide how long this place had been empty. "She fell apart the first time Katie went missing. Or at least it looked that way. I can't imagine that she'd be all that capable of striking out on her own to look for her, but like I said, I think I missed something there."

"We should check with the super. Someone renting this place would've wanted their deposit back."

The super was no help. Brenda had a month-to-month lease and had been a good tenant. When she suddenly gave notice and moved out, the guy hadn't begrudged her the deposit. He knew Katie had gone missing, but handing over the cash without argument had been the extent of his concern.

From the general condition of the common spaces, and the lack of lighting and broken fixtures, the landlord didn't use any of the rent to keep up the place.

And in addition to being a slacker, he had no compunction about leering, despite the presence of the very large and aggressive male with her. Tired of being ogled, Diana was tempted to punch him in the face, but she restrained herself when Alec gave her a little warning shake of his head.

"Let me," he whispered. Turning to the lumpy excuse for a man, he said in a clear commanding tone, "Tomorrow I want you to come in to work and fix all of the things you've been neglecting for months. Wear those jeans you have on right now, the ones that ride low. And underneath them, you're going to wear some *clean* underwear. Not like the ones you have on now. And they're going to be lacy women's panties all right? Something pink... a thong."

Irritation completely gone, Diana left the office laughing.

22

Diana had Daniel drive them to the safe house so she could change. She was no longer concerned with Alec knowing the location. After pulling on clean cargo pants, she joined him in the living room to search for her boots while he wandered around, checking out the various knick-knacks and weapons displayed. He'd already been through all the swords and crossbows in the gym and had even tested one of the maces.

He was fingering a fourteenth century Japanese Koto when she finally found her left boot.

He turned to her, shock lining his features. "This is from the Kamakura period. It's spectacular. And priceless in certain circles."

"Yeah, I know," Diana said with genuine nonchalance, bending down to tie her shoelace.

"But this thing is not only for display. You. . .you've been using it."

"It's a weapon," she said dryly. "It's common for a soldier to train with a variety of them."

Alec stared, mouth slightly open. "It's worth thousands, maybe hundreds of thousands of dollars. I can't believe you practice with this as if it's any old sword," he said, taking it in hand and turning to display it to her, as though he was trying to make her see it clearly.

Suppressing a smile, Diana took the sword from him and put it back in its holder. "All of the weapons you see here are used. We train with them throughout our lives. We have to be ready to use whatever comes to hand. It all depends on the situation. We hone our skills with these as well as our Elemental abilities. Sometimes it's better not to have to start a fire."

"But this sword," he said pointing, "it's meant to be used from horseback."

"I know that," Diana said with a laugh.

"You've trained with it on horseback?"

"Well, actually, I used my bike most of the time." She turned to grab her jacket. "Horses don't like fire."

"And the other times?"

She paused. "Well, you remember the lion?"

Alec stopped short. "You can ride your element like a. . .a. . ."

"Yes," she said pointedly, cutting him off before the mental imagery became too colorful. "I left a message for the girls while I was changing. They will look into Brenda's whereabouts if she left a trail. If she's dead, the Mother will know."

"And She'll tell you that? Speak to you directly?"

Diana looked up at him and decided to be honest. He was a sensitive. He might be capable of sensing it anyway, but might not know how to put it into words.

"Maybe, and maybe not in a timely fashion. She's. . .grown quieter in the last decades. Especially where humans are concerned. Earth will try to commune with her since the rest of us haven't had much luck at it. The Earth Elemental is closest to her by design."

"Is that normal? For Her to be quieter sometimes?"

"There have been periods when She has fallen silent," she admitted. "Those were bad times for everyone, Supes and humans alike. As for now, She hasn't withdrawn yet. She's just slow to respond. A strong sensitive might be affected—have a sense that something is not right. There are probably some worried witches out there right now."

"Are you saying that if I were stronger I could sense this withdrawal? Because I've never felt her presence at all."

"I think you have. But maybe you didn't know what you were feeling. Have you felt a. . .greater sense of dissatisfaction lately?"

He sat on a leather chair with a thump. "Yes, but I'm not sure that's a huge change," he said honestly.

"Oh." She decided to change the subject. "I'm hungry. Have you made arrangements to. . .to feed?"

Why did I go for feeding? Couldn't I have asked about cars or something?

Alec paused. "I'm having some bags sent from our private blood bank later tonight. Do you want to get dinner now?"

She nodded and bit the bullet before heading for the exit. "I thought live blood was better," she said, holding the door open for him so she could lock up.

"It's more pleasant that way," he said carefully. "From a blood bag, it's more like eating tofu and rice cakes, or drinking plain water when all you want is a coke or a good pinot noir."

He stopped at the landing at the next security camera. He'd already commented on the infrared sensors and the thickness of the doors.

"Do you have access to these feeds?" he asked.

"Not supposed to, they're part of the normal building's security. But we hacked into it. We made our own additions as well."

"Right," he said, turning away from the camera and heading down the stairs. "No doubt you have your own wards and spell traps. You could withstand a siege from this place."

"That's the idea," she murmured.

"Expecting an army to attack at dawn?" he joked.

Diana turned and shrugged.

"It's happened before," she said indifferently before going out the building entrance.

23

Dinner was delicious as always. Alec had opted to have one of his favorite restaurants prepare a selection of their best meals in advance so Diana could simply choose what she liked without having to wait.

He encouraged her to try a bit of each dish. She was pleased with the selection, but she didn't feel good about the waste.

"It's fine, take what you want. The rest will be packed off and taken to a homeless shelter nearby later tonight."

"You always think ahead, don't you?" she mused, trying a mushroom risotto that was to die for.

Alec took a bite of Foie Gras poêlé with a fruit compote.

"I try. All the time and as hard as I can."

"Me too. But sometimes I feel like I'm just playing catch-up. Punishing the bad guys after the fact has lost something. They keep multiplying. You knock one down and two more spring up in their place."

"You're talking about humans now, aren't you? The supernatural crime rate is fairly steady, isn't it? It's the human crime rate that keeps exploding."

"Yeah. There's. . .just too many of them. They used to kill each other in wars, used to invade and rape and pillage," she said, running a hand through her hair. "But that was the part of the process, the mysterious way the Mother worked. Sometimes it's the little deaths that move the world forward. Or send it reeling back. But more and more, we don't feel the shift in the balance until the crimes are well beyond the pale," she said, putting a hand up. "Like I said before, the signal is getting lost in the noise. And it's going to get worse. The further humans get from nature and the Mother, the less we are able to detect and intervene. They're slipping away," Diana finished in a whisper.

"It's too much," Alec said almost distantly, like he was thinking of something else.

She took a deep breath and shook off her melancholy. "It's a burden, but we handle it. It's just hard sometimes," she said with a roll of her shoulders. "So many innocents die before we get the call. We don't get to save very many. I've been frustrated lately."

"You probably save many more people than you realize. The crimes you prevent must number in the thousands. Not to mention the pain you spare the families of potential victims," he said, leaning back in his chair. "But it's the emotional burden on you I'm concerned about. The weight on your shoulders and the others is simply insane. You're not superwoman."

Diana looked up with a *well, actually* expression.

"Well, all right, I guess you kind of are. But that doesn't mean that the emotional burden isn't intense. . .I think you need something. Someone to help you out, to do recon or research. Even Batman has Alfred."

"I don't need an Alfred," Diana replied, aware of what he was offering.

"Every Batman needs an Alfred. They're awfully handy. That's why I have a Daniel. Probably more handy than an Alfred, actually."

Diana snorted, but her heart wasn't in it. "Alfreds have high overhead, and I travel light. Always on the move. I bet Alfred would hate that," Diana said pointedly.

"Not if Alfred was used to being on the move. I bet there's some that could adapt," he added in a neutral tone.

But Diana didn't want to picture life with Alec on the road. It was a tempting image, but it would never work out. She and her sisters lived a solitary existence for a reason.

"Alec, you'll get bored—or frustrated. In no time, you'd want to go back to your books and scrolls. This life is hard," she said, her brows drawn together. "Much harder than you think. You haven't seen anything yet. You haven't been sent to catch a killer but not known who he was until he killed again. You haven't been there *literally* seconds too late. Sometimes we have to let people die. Wars happen, and we can't stop them. They are part of our nature and Hers. And to be frank, I'm not Doctor Who and you aren't, by even the most generous standards, companion material," she said, throwing down her napkin.

Alec narrowed his eyes. "You don't know what I can or can't handle. I've been around for a long time, Diana. I've seen a lot of things in some pretty twisted corners of the world. I'm not only about books and scrolls—although a lot of useful information can be gleaned from those. Besides, I prefer to think of myself as an Alfred-Boy Wonder hybrid. I can handle your lifestyle, and I want to help you. I've been helpful on this case, haven't I? And given your caseload, couldn't you use the help?"

Diana ran her eyes over him. She had seen this coming but still didn't know what to do.

"Getting used to a companion, even in the short-term, is a little too much. Being here with you now is weird enough. Besides, you're the heir to the most powerful coven in North America. Someday you will have to actually settle down and run it."

Alec leaned in quickly. "I don't have any plans to run the coven. I never have. It's starting to sink in with my father that it's not going to happen. The leadership isn't necessarily a hereditary position. There is precedent for declaring a non-familial heir. And you're starting to like having me around, aren't you?" he finished, giving her his most charming smile.

She angled her head and looked at him sideways. "Look, you're already on this case even though I *never* work with anyone. And the fact that you're not even a little bit singed is enough of a miracle. Let's just focus on finding those kids, okay?"

"You're right," he said, resigned. "One thing at a time. We can start with the list of jewelry stores that carry antique pins."

"All of those places will be closed by now."

Alec smiled at her. "For the right price, any store is open."

"You can't throw money at everything, you know. It won't always work."

"I know it won't. Usually when it matters the most. I learned that a long time ago. But it certainly makes the everyday stuff go far more smoothly."

Diana sniffed. "We have money, but we don't use it like that. We have our own way."

"And I'm a fan. All that violence really does it for me," he teased. "But sometimes money greases the wheel, and given the nature of this case, that can't hurt. Why don't we get going? Are you planning on any Denon-related espionage tonight?"

"No need," she said, ignoring the innuendo.

"All right, then, let's knock off a few of these jewelers and antique dealers. I had the sketch faxed to similar places up and down the coast, and we can expand that if we don't get any leads."

"Okay," she grumbled. "It's not like I have anything better to do."

"Thanks. That is so sweet," he said wryly.

Hours later, after posing as newlyweds for five different jewelers and antique dealers, Diana was looking for any way to escape. Not only was the search fruitless, but pretending to be part of a happy couple with Alec was disconcerting.

Diana would have set a building on fire before admitting that playing Alec's other half felt completely natural. There hadn't been a trace of awkwardness as they chatted about fictional wedding plans and Art Deco rings and brooches. None of the dealers had heard of the beetle brooch, which Diana said was a family heirloom that had been stolen from her. Her fake groom's evident wealth ensured helpful answers from the dealers. She hadn't been able to detect any subterfuge.

They gave up soon after the last antique shop, where the motherly dealer started naming their future children. Alec dropped Diana off after that. She entered the apartment alone, emotionally drained. After showering, she went to bed without checking her messages and slept like a rock.

The next morning, Diana woke up with a renewed sense of purpose. She gave herself a pep talk, one that dealt mostly with Alec. And she told herself in no uncertain terms that they would find the missing children.

She checked for messages, hoping for good news. Unfortunately, there was nothing from Logan and only a worried message from Gia saying the Mother had remained silent.

The last message filled Diana with anxiety. Was the Mother going to sleep again? If so, it would be the start of a period of strife and turmoil for all of her children.

Or maybe it's us? Are we being punished? Have we not served her as well as others in the past?

Diana silently admitted that she hadn't, not really. This was her case, but she hadn't tried to contact the Mother herself because she had been afraid of failing. It was cowardly.

On impulse, she turned on the television and scanned all the news channels. It didn't take long to find what she was looking for. A large wildfire was currently burning in Colorado. In the height of summer, it was common enough, though she felt more than a twinge of guilt for being happy about it.

The buzzer distracted her from making plans. The doorman had a package for her. A few minutes later, she was opening a large box marked with the distinctive Broussard crest. Two smaller boxes were inside. Opening the larger of the two, she was greeted by the smell of fresh warm bagels.

Taking them out of the box, she found an assortment, including her favorite, poppy seed. While she toasted it, she pulled out a bag that held several types of schmear. Humming a random tune, she picked a salmon one and applied a generous amount on her bagel.

Nibbling on her treat, she pulled out the smaller box. Inside, she found a phone—a weird industrial looking one. She had just pulled it out to take a closer look when it started ringing in her hand.

"Err, hello, Morpheus?"

"I was going for that!" Alec said, laughing. "Did I time it right?"

"Yeah, you did. But you shouldn't be giving me a phone unless you are prepared to send it to that big electronics graveyard in the sky. And why is it so bulky? Are you recycling your old phones? Is this from the eighties?"

"No, it's not." She could hear the smile in his voice. "I was checking with my contacts in the defense industry. This is the latest prototype they are developing for generals deployed to the Middle East. It's been adapted for the heat of the desert. It should last you a bit longer than those portables you've been burning through. All my contact numbers are pre-programmed for your convenience. There's also a special app that features a list of top rated restaurants, and it's global. It even has a search feature for places that do take-out."

"According to you, every place does take-out," she said, rolling her eyes.

"For the right incentive, they do," he insisted. "You should try it sometime."

"Throwing money at something is your thing. I'll leave it to you," she said, taking a bite of her bagel.

He laughed. "Knowing when and where to throw it is a skill I've honed over the years," he said before getting serious. "Besides, the police do it all the time in smaller amounts."

"Because they have to. We do things differently," she reminded him.

"I'm sure your ways are best, but we shouldn't leave any stone unturned while we lack leads."

"You mean while my tracking ability keeps failing." Diana said in a self-recriminatory tone.

"*No*," he said forcefully. "You can't blame yourself. These guys have found some way to evade your ability." He paused. "It's time to try something else. Think outside the box. Any ideas, chief?"

"I have one. It's time to do something I've been avoiding. I shouldn't have let Gia make the attempt to contact with the Mother without trying myself."

"You're going to contact her? How?"

"I'm going to start a fire. A big one."

"How big a fire?" he asked.

"Big. And I'll need enough fuel to keep it going for a while." She was silent for a moment and then spoke before she could change her mind. "You can help. You can keep it going long enough to complete the ceremony."

She decided not to spring the other details on him until it was time.

"There's a ceremony?" Alec asked excitedly.

"I'll tell you all about it later. Right now, I need to find a place with a fire pit or a really big fireplace. Bigger than the one here," she said.

"Well. . .there is a rather large one in the coven house. We used to observe the tradition of burning a Yule log, a custom from the old country," he offered.

Diana's insides curdled. "That sounds like a terrible idea. I don't think I'm a welcome guest there right now. Have you even told your parents you're working with me?" she asked, trying to hide her horrified reaction.

"Not exactly," he admitted. "Being over two centuries old means I don't have to check in with my parents all the time. I told them I was working on the children's disappearances and not much more. Going into detail is generally unproductive when dealing with members of my house. It slows things down. And I think we should go in daylight. I keep track of the day servants' movements pretty closely. I've got tracking devices on all of them."

"You did *what?*" she said, genuinely surprised. "How politically incorrect of you."

"I'm actually lucky that I thought of it first," Alec said wryly.

"Everyone spies on everyone else in the coven. But most of the coven isn't well versed in technology, so I'm still managing to stay ahead of the curve. I can ensure the staff stays away by asking for a lot of errands. How long do you need?"

"That's not really up to me." Diana pursed her lips. "It could take hours. Do you still want to try it there?"

"Is there a better option? Do you know of a nearby hotel with a really big fireplace we can rent for the day?"

"No. Do you?" she asked.

"Not offhand. Do you want me to start looking for one?"

Diana was conflicted. It wasn't like she was afraid of going back to the coven house. But going back there after she had terrorized his parents made her feel guilty. That feeling was a first for her, and she blamed Alec. If she hadn't gotten to like him as a friend, then she wouldn't care if his parents were afraid of her. But they were likely to be asleep the whole time, unless her attempt took too long. In which case a confrontation was inevitable.

"No," she said finally. "The coven house is fine, but if it takes a while then your parents are going to wake up to the bogeyman."

"They don't think of you as the bogeyman anymore. These days it's more like Godzilla terrorizing Tokyo."

"*Great.* Serin's going to give me a really long lecture about diplomacy again."

"Tell her not to bother. My parents haven't been able to see past their own interests for a long while. I actually think meeting you has been good for them. It's shaken them out of their complacency. Maybe they'll pay greater attention to what the coven members are doing from now on."

"Well, I'll tell Serin you said that. She takes diplomacy very seriously."

"Do that," Alec murmured huskily before pausing. In the distance a door closed. "Listen, I'm going to send the servants off and get back to you when it's all clear. We should start sooner rather than later."

"What if you get caught being up during daylight hours?"

"The oldest among us can stay awake, but they have to stay indoors. If we're disturbed I'll lie and say I've gained that ability. I've always been advanced," he said without a shred of humility.

Amused by his arrogance, she told him to go ahead and make his plans.

24

Diana arrived at the coven house within the hour, careful to park her bike out of sight. She walked to the side of the building, puzzling over a Yule log tradition that required the construction of a fireplace larger than her. Especially one built by a group that was so flammable.

It takes all kinds, she thought, knocking on a side door. It swung open to reveal Alec waiting inside.

"Did you get rid of the servants?" she asked.

He nodded. "They are currently running around town trying to find some information on the beetle pin or the woman who wore it. I told them you would come back if they didn't find it," he added with a grin. "I thought multitasking would be the most efficient way to go about this. Come on in."

With a smirk, Diana stepped inside. The irony of being invited inside by a vampire was not lost on her.

Alec led her through a hallway that opened onto a grand foyer in dark wood tones, with lots of genuine antiques and expensive-looking paintings scattered about. She stopped to peer at a landscape in a vaguely familiar style.

He stopped, too. "It's a Monet," he said, pointing to the signature.

"One unknown to the public. He painted it on commission for the coven."

"Why doesn't that surprise me?" she murmured.

"The coven makes it their business to find future acclaimed artists when they're still up and coming. They commission private works that others aren't allowed to see. There's actually quite a number of works from artists that did not stand up to the test of time up in the attic."

"Seems like a waste," she said, following him.

He turned back. "Well, some of the ones of middling value may have been donated to certain charities," he said in an innocent tone. "Anonymously, of course."

Her lips twitched. "How generous of your parents."

"Yes, well, sometimes they are so generous they can't keep track of their donations."

This time she did smile as they walked past the grand staircase and took the corridor leading to other ground floor rooms. From the hallway, she could see a bit of each richly appointed chamber. They were furnished with Persian rugs and antiques from all over the world, although there was a strong preference for Europe.

The Broussards were clearly sentimental about the old country, and they chose to surround themselves with only the best from home.

Alec led her into a large parlor that adjoined the ballroom where she'd made her grand entrance. It ran down the entire length of the neighboring room, but was only a quarter of its width.

Silk and velvet covered armchairs and sofas were scattered in regular intervals. Figurines in jade and onyx, as well as several framed pictures, decorated the tops of delicate tables, the kind with spindly legs that didn't look strong enough to support them. In the central portion of the room, there was a massive fireplace running along the back wall. A huge set of double doors were meant to open onto the ballroom so the guests could see the blaze.

Diana's attention was caught by one of the pictures. Picking up the heavy gilt frame, a corner of her mouth turned up as she examined the image.

It was a Victorian-era daguerreotype with an upside down vamp hanging from a chandelier like it was a trapeze. There were others of the same vamp posing in his finest clothing on top of the Egyptian pyramids. The one on the side table in front of the fireplace pictured an unknown male vampire in full formal dress on one of those eagle gargoyles on the Chrysler building. He was balanced on one hand, tipping his hat.

"The pictures are part of a long-running joke," Alec said, noting her interest. "The old wives' tale about vampires not having a reflection is partly true. We don't have a reflection in daylight, as you know, only at night. That's one of the mysteries of our kind I wanted to solve and never could. But we can be photographed, day or night as long as there is no flash to blind us. When this was discovered, there was an explosion of vampire photography. It was a huge fad for a while."

"That is both weird and amusing. Mostly weird," she said, studying the picture. A thought occurred to her. "Do you have a reflection now? In the daytime?" she asked, studying the other photographs.

Alec was arranging the kindling in the fireplace. He hadn't been kidding. It was massive and would suit her needs nicely.

"Yes, I do. I didn't know the ritual would have that side effect. It was never mentioned in any of the records I found on past Daywalkers. Maybe because there weren't as many mirrors in homes back then and it wasn't as much of an issue. But it is now. If there's any light outside, any at all, I have to stay far away from mirrors if there is even a small chance another Supe is around. Or anyone who might recognize me," he finished in a half-hearted grumble.

He was about to strike a match when she stopped him with a hand on his shoulder. "No need."

"Of course," he said, backing away. "Why exactly did we need so much fuel? It didn't occur to me earlier when we talked but can't you sustain a fire indefinitely?"

Definitely a very smart man.

"Yeah, about that. See, I need you to keep the fire going while I'm gone."

"Gone? Where are you going? Are you missing something you need for your ceremony?"

Diana turned away from the fireplace. "No. I meant I am going away. I'm going to use this fire to transport myself to a bigger one. There's a pretty big wildfire in Colorado right now. I saw it on the news. If the Mother is looking anywhere, then that's where her attention will be turned."

She paused. "It's kind of a big *if*," she admitted. "If the Mother is falling asleep, then there's not much that will rouse her. I need you to keep the fire burning on this end so I can get back. It won't sustain itself once I leave. Which is why you need to keep it burning here."

Alec's eyes were wide and he stared at her with a starry eyed expression before blinking rapidly.

"You can do that? Use the fire like a Star Trek transporter?"

"Yeah, nerd. But not as reliably, I'm afraid. Fire has no memory, no consciousness. I can use it to get someplace, but I can't see who might be there. I could travel to a wildfire but might end up surprising some firefighters. And our anonymity is too important to mess with. If I am seen by an outsider, or caught on film, then there would be hell to pay."

"And the others can do something similar?"

"Yeah, but Earth and Water can't go very large distances without taxing themselves too greatly. There are limits."

"But Air can travel long distances?"

She nodded. "It's a big advantage for the Air Elemental. Sometimes I get a lift from her when we're close enough to each other."

"And you're sure it's safe? Going out to the fire? You would be concerned about being seen if this fire wasn't already massive and out of control. What if a tree falls on you? The ground gets unstable. Are you sure it's a good idea? And why would the Mother have an eye on this fire? Don't they stem from Her inattention, not Her focus? She doesn't start fires, does She?"

Diana sucked in a breath. "It's more like She doesn't stop them."

"Oh." Alec looked rather crestfallen.

She knew how he felt. Mother Nature could be a bitch. "Look.

These fires are part of a greater whole. There are cycles she set in motion when the Earth was new. It's all a part of the process. It's better if you don't think about it."

"Does She know about the people who make their home in the fire's paths?"

"She knows. Or at least we think She does." Diana's voice was gentle.

"And She doesn't care?"

Diana moved in front of him. "Honestly, I'm not sure. But I don't think She can change the way things are now. I like to think She would if She could."

"I see. Right," he said, going back to stacking wood.

"Sometimes being privy to the secrets of the gods just. . .sucks," she commiserated before glancing at the fireplace. "I'll try not to be too long, but I'm not actually sure how much time I'll need. If you run out of fuel, it's okay. I'll make my own way back."

His lips firmed. "I will keep it burning as long as it takes," Alec said. He removed a tarp from a pile of wood next to the fireplace. "I had Daniel get an entire truck of the stuff. It's pulled around back."

"If vampires could join the Boy Scouts, there'd be a joke here."

"The Boy Scouts are a little after my time." He sighed. "Please be careful. I'm serious about the falling trees."

"I know. Here, take this," she said, handing him her new phone. "I know it's desert-proof, but I don't think it's going to survive what's coming."

He nodded as he took the phone, and she turned to the fireplace. With the flick of her hand, she sent the fire to the kindling Alec had arranged so carefully. An inferno roared to life with a great whoosh, the flames taking on the bluish-purple tint that they always did around her.

Taking one last look at Alec, Diana walked into the blaze.

25

The fire swirled, blazing hotter and higher until it covered Diana. It curled around her like a living thing.

Alec could see why primitive man had created the myths of fire gods and goddesses. Diana in all her glory was an awesome sight—but before he could blink, she was gone.

He glanced at the pile of firewood. *Better to be safe than sorry.* Using vampiric speed, he went outside to bring more wood from the truck.

Alec's tension and excitement dissipated as the minutes stretched into an hour. On impulse, he searched for news coverage on the fire on his tablet. Given the scale of the fire, there was a lot to choose from. He scanned the various media outlets for signs that Diana hadn't been discovered doing whatever it was she was doing.

Or that the body of small redhead hadn't been found buried under a fallen pine tree.

Shut up, he told himself sternly before tossing a few more logs onto the fire, wishing he could have gone with her. But that would have been suicide. On impulse, he called his man at Defense. He was in luck. A government satellite was monitoring the fire.

Once the feeds were forwarded to him, Alec sat down in front of the fire to look for signs of unusual activity. After several minutes, he noticed a small disturbance in one of the feeds.

Alec peered at his screen. The video was live. It looked like a satellite image of a hurricane...except it was made of fire. Enthralled, he watched as the edges seemed to draw in and the center got denser.

What was Diana doing? Building up a tower of fire? One that could be seen from space? It looked small on his screen but in reality it was probably massive.

The firestorm was localized to one small valley. Passing a hand over his face, he sincerely hoped no one else was watching. It wasn't likely anyone would be able to get close enough on the ground to spot Diana, but he still worried about her.

Alec knew that was ridiculous. She could take care of herself. But the feeling remained. It was second nature now. Diana had swiftly become the most important person in his life. And if that wasn't a kick in the pants, he didn't know what was.

The fire in front of him was getting lower. Kneeling closer, he placed two more logs inside and studied the strange fire. The flames still had Diana's signature color, but otherwise, they behaved like a normal fire with no intelligence or form. Which probably meant he was sitting too close to it, but he didn't care. It warmed the coldness inside him. Maybe that was why he wanted to be around Diana so much. Even though he could walk under the sun now, he was still cold inside—except when he was with her.

A loud popping sound shook him from his reverie as the fire snapped and the logs shifted. Instinctively, he reared back, but not fast enough. A large spark flew out and caught him on the hand.

For a second panic flared but before he could react, the ember died out on his skin. Bewildered, he rubbed the spot. It didn't hurt at all.

What the hell?

Senses on high alert, Alec stared at the fire before slowly reaching out to take hold of a glowing ember from the bottom of the fireplace. Picking it up, he held it in front of him until the glow faded and he was holding a bit of charcoal. There was no pain.

By rights, as a vampire, he should have been fiercely burned, but he had felt nothing at all.

He dropped the charcoal and studied his fingers. There was nothing, no redness or swelling. No burn marks of any kind. How was that even possible? At the very least he should have smoldered a bit.

Could it be? Alec shifted his eyes to the flames and tentatively reached out until the fire enveloped his hand.

"What are you doing awake?" his father asked from behind him.

Alec snatched his unburned hand out of the fire and spun around. He had been so engrossed he hadn't heard his father come in. Standing up, he hoped Alden hadn't seen what he'd been doing.

"Hello father," he said formally, inclining his head in a gesture of respect.

It wasn't strictly necessary since the head of his house happened to be his parent, but he did it nevertheless.

"What are you doing?" Alden asked, taking in the piled wood and the fire.

Caught red-handed, he decided not to lie. "I'm helping Diana with a small matter."

"What?" Alden was confused. "Who's Diana? You aren't referring to the Elemental, are you?"

Alec didn't answer.

"You are joking, aren't you?" His father's eyes were wide, his face twisted as if he was smelling something unpleasant.

"No. I'm helping her. Or rather, she's helping me restore the honor of this house," he said, annoyed. "We're conducting an investigation into the disappearance of those children. We're looking for them together," he said, picking up the poker and stirring the fire with a rough slashing movement.

"There is no reason for you to be involved!"

Unbelievable. "A child of one of our retainers was also taken by the circle, in case you've forgotten. I'm going to get him back or kill the circle trying."

His father rubbed his face with both hands. "You should leave it to that. . .thing. The Elemental is involved now. You don't have to help her. She can manage on her own. You've done enough."

"Honor won't be satisfied until those children are returned and the circle is dismantled or destroyed," he said from behind gritted fangs.

His father sneered. "That's not the way these things work. You can't honestly tell me the Elemental even wants you around. She probably doesn't appreciate your interference. Just leave things well enough alone. You should be focusing on this coven for a change, and your place in it. You have neglected your duties too long," he said, drawing himself up to his full height.

Since Alec was a little taller, it didn't intimidate him. . .anymore.

"Whether you like it or not, I *am* fulfilling my duties," he ground out, repressing an urge to roll his eyes. "The ones *I* value most. I know you don't agree, but seeing to it that our family's retainers aren't used or abused is my highest priority."

"Pretty words when you neglect everything else," his father said.

Alec rubbed his temple above his left eye, which was starting to twitch. "I'm not going to have this argument with you again. I have more impor—"

A *whoosh* from the fireplace distracted him mid-sentence. The flames flared high and coalesced into a form. Shaking embers from her long red hair, Diana stepped out of the flames, and Alec sagged in relief. So much so that he forgot the presence of his father.

He moved close to her and put his arms on her shoulders before drawing back to check her up and down. She wasn't even dirty. Not even a speck of soot. The tight worry he'd had at his core since she'd left relaxed.

"Are you all right? Did it work?" he asked.

She ignored him and looked over his shoulder with a carefully blank expression.

He turned back to see his father was watching Diana with a look somewhere between distaste and fear. It was, however, carefully controlled into a rigid mask.

ALDEN WAS STARING a hole through her.

"Diana, you remember my father?" Alec asked as if they were in a polite drawing room a hundred years ago.

Blergh. She put her hands behind her back.

"Yes, of course. How do you do, Mister Broussard? I trust you and your wife are well," Diana said with studious politeness.

Serin would have been proud of that delivery.

"We're as well as can be expected given the circumstances," Alden said with equal formality.

Diana kept a neutral expression as she looked to Alec for a little guidance. What was she supposed to do now? Talk about the weather? Thank him for his son's help?

Well, why the hell not?

"Your son has been very helpful in my inquiries. I'm satisfied your house was not responsible for the disappearance of the children."

"Good. I trust this matter will be resolved quickly, and my son will be able to resume his duties here soon," Alden said, doing his best impression of someone with a broomstick up their ass.

What duties? She and Alec exchanged a look. One Alden did not miss. He glared at the way Alec's right hand still held her shoulder securely, which made her realize it was still there, too. And she hadn't pushed it off yet.

Ignoring the hand, Diana smiled at Alden.

"I'm sure he'll be free to go on his way soon," she replied evenly with the faintest stress on the *his*.

Alden scowled. "Good," he said before stalking out.

"That went well," Diana said in a perfectly serious tone. "I think he's warming up."

Smiling faintly, Alec turned to her. "Sorry about that. His age allows him to wake several hours before sunset, but he can't go outside in actual sunlight."

"How did you explain being awake at this hour?"

"I didn't," Alec said, bending to clean up some stray logs.

"Well, that's one way to avoid an awkward discussion. Ignore it."

He dismissed her comment with a wave. "Were you successful? Did you get anything useful?"

"I don't know. Nothing was clear. It was all very confusing. And I have a raging headache now. Why don't we get out of here before we have to have a real show and tell for the rest of the coven."

She rubbed her head, and his face creased with concern. He put his arm around her shoulders.

"All right, let's go."

26

A little later, Diana was on the computer in the apartment she shared with the other girls, flipping through images of pastoral scenes. Her headache was gone, and she was starving, so Alec had called his men to bring some take out to the safe house after Diana admitted that she did not cook—she only reheated.

"What are you looking for?" Alec asked.

He'd been prowling the apartment restlessly since his run in with his father. She'd already had to scold him for using the Koto sword as a light saber.

"I'm not sure exactly," she admitted. "Trying to commune with the Mother is kind of like trying to mind-meld with a giant sperm whale, only the whale is all knowing and probably the size of a small city."

"*Really?* No wonder you had a headache," he said, taken slightly aback as he sat next to her.

Diana could practically see the wheels turning in his head as he digested this new bit of information. Personally, she didn't care about the pain because she had successfully made contact with the Mother in the fire. Sort of.

As she'd built the flames high into a tower, a sensation of intense pressure had overtaken her. It was like being squeezed all over. And then her head had split wide open. Or at least it had felt that way. A roaring sound that had nothing to do with the wildfire burning around her had filled her head. It was soon followed by a flood of memories and images so vast it had threatened to burn her brain out.

It had been hard to make anything out of the data dump. The few images she had seen had burned behind her eyes before she'd fallen out of the stream, coming back to herself as the flames around her died down. A little dizzy, she'd walked back into what was left, trying to be happy she had made some form of contact.

It was more than Gia had gotten the last time she tried, but not much more.

"I did see a few images I think She intended me to see. Enough to know who I'm dealing with but not where they are. The witch responsible is a Burgess by blood. But they weren't raised on the inside. I got snippets of Hillard Burgess with one of his mistresses. The child is theirs. When the relationship ended, it was messy and the kid and mother were cut off. I didn't see anything else about the child, not enough to even know what sex we're dealing with. I'm lucky I saw anything at all," she said, massaging her temples.

The headache was gone, but its memory lived on.

"Shouldn't one of the big seven have been monitoring their own so something like this wouldn't happen?"

The Burgess was one of the oldest lines of practitioners. Unlike the Delavordos, they had a much more upstanding reputation. For witches anyway...

"In a perfect world, yes. But it happens more and more these days. The Supes are splitting up, getting divorces, too. Not as often as humans but still. The kids that are the products of these unions sometimes fall through the cracks. We try to make sure it doesn't happen but you can't fight the future. And marriage is going the same way as the bees and the environment."

"All right. How are we going to find them?"

"It's a muddle, but I think I saw a location. It's not very helpful. Just a few images of a rundown farmhouse in the countryside," she said, lapsing into silence while continuing to scan pictures on the laptop.

Alec started wandering around the apartment again, fingering weapons and examining figurines. "These pieces are museum quality and then some. It's an amazing collection. Do you have any old manuscripts by chance?"

"Not here. Serin's people have scanned some of the old stories, though. Stuff they think is important, but they don't give access to outsiders."

"Oh. Well, maybe they'll not consider me one in time," Alec said.

Diana grinned at his wistful tone, but she didn't turn away from the images on the computer screen.

"I don't think your father is going to be okay with any further involvement with Elementals after this case is over."

Alec frowned. "That's not up to him. I've been leading my own life for a few centuries now."

Diana considered his determined expression before replying. "He expects you to lead the coven," she said, giving him a sideways glance while twisting a lock of her hair around her finger.

"He knows better." Alec walked toward her until she was forced to meet his eyes. "And honestly, my father has no plans to step down in the future. It's only that he believes, like all good dynasties, the heir should be visible to its subjects. He knows I've always had other plans for my life, Diana. Your presence in it hasn't changed that."

Not convinced, she raised her brows. "You might have a change of heart about that in the coming years. The head of the Eastern coven had a lot of pull and a lot of influence. There's a lot you could do in that position," she said, trying to be practical.

Alec rubbed the back of his neck. "How many times do I have to tell you that heading the coven is not something I want? I have never wanted to follow the path my parents laid out for me. It's not even a remote possibility. I can't stomach the empty gossip and backstabbing that passes for vampire politics."

"Never say never. And circumstances might change. What if they really need you someday? Would you be able to turn your back on them? Because if the Mother is falling asleep, then hard days are ahead for everyone."

He digested that in silence for a while. "It would have to be pretty extreme circumstances. And, honestly, there are some capable people in the coven despite their outward frivolity," he said waving her concern away. "Any luck with the image search?"

"Not exactly. There were some mountains in the background and the feel of the place was familiar, but there wasn't enough for a definitive location." She sighed. "I don't think flipping through pictures is the most productive way to do this. I would have to have the angles right in order to really recognize it from that. I need to narrow it down. Those mountains could be anywhere."

"Can you draw?"

"Not even a little bit," she said, wrinkling her nose.

"Well, I'm a fairly good artist. I had to learn to sketch reasonably well to document my artifacts, although I use a camera these days. Maybe you could describe the scenes you remember to me, and we can get close to what you saw. Then we can scan it and use an image search to find similar, and hopefully, documented photographs."

"It beats flipping through pictures aimlessly like this," she said, putting the computer on the coffee table before stretching out on the couch.

Alec grabbed a few pens and one of the large notepads Gia kept around to sketch before sitting in an adjoining armchair. They must have resembled a therapist and his patient as Diana proceeded to detail the scene as best she could.

It went terribly for a good hour.

"I can't do this. I just don't have the ability to describe what's in my head!" she finally said exasperated before throwing a pillow in Alec's general direction. He snatched it out of the air without looking up with those freaky vampire reflexes.

"It's all right," he assured her. "I think we're getting closer. I know you can't draw, but why don't you try and do a rudimentary sketch and then flip through some of these pastoral art books, and tell me what scenes look similar. Maybe you could draw the plant life in a little greater detail, or I could have some botany books delivered."

Diana pulled at the threads of the last pillow left on the couch. "I guess I could try to draw some of the flowers. And Gia is not that into landscapes so maybe you should have some books sent."

He sat up straighter. "We can't give up. If this works out, we don't have to keep hammering the beetle pin lead. It's too tenuous to rely upon."

"I know," she grumbled before grabbing the notepad and pencils from his hand.

It took another three hours, including two deliveries from Daniel, one for books and one for dinner. The latter was ignored while they flipped through large books of landscapes, and Diana sketched the ugliest flowers anyone had ever seen.

"Don't feel bad," he said with a grin when she torched one of her less-than-successful efforts. "I'm personally rather relieved to find something I can do better than you."

He missed the pillow she threw at his head that time.

When they were finally done, Diana was nearly ready to pull out all of her hair, but at least they had a reasonable facsimile of the exterior of the farmhouse.

"It is a little vague still, but the feel is European, isn't it?" Alec mused as he turned and bent the sketch to view at different angles.

Diana shrugged. "Could be. Could be anywhere."

"You mentioned the Burgess family. We should start by looking at their English holdings. Maybe we'll get lucky and find a match. If any of them are near mountains, we might have a starting point."

"I don't know." Diana was skeptical. "From what I saw, this guy has been raised outside the family and isn't likely to be on good terms with them. Not enough to be staying at their country house, if you know what I mean," she said, continuing to flip through pictures.

"True enough, but I've run into a lot of outcasts in my time," he said, putting down one volume and picking up another. "I know you have, too, but I imagine the circumstances were different. Less screaming and running away in my case. Actually, I've known a few personally as friends. And while most have claimed to care less about what their family thinks of them, every last one would have done anything to be accepted and respected by them. They emulate them, buy the things they have, live in equally fine homes if they have the means. Finer if they can manage it. And when the family is doing worse than them financially, more than one has bought their ancestral home and edged their family members out. I think we should look at properties the Burgess family used to own. Farms in the European countryside, specifically."

"Well, we don't have any better leads. Go nuts," she said, waving him on.

His eyes twinkled. "I'll put my people on finding out anything about any Burgess remnants and have my bankers run down any associated properties."

"Bankers?"

"Like I said before, it usually pays off to follow the money. I'll tell them to go back a few hundred years."

"Witches don't live as long as vampires. Don't you think one century is enough?" Diana asked.

"We'll start with the most recent records. Why don't you let me do the search while you heat up the food Daniel brought?"

"Okay, but I should warn you that if the head of the Burgess clan is unaware he has another heir, it's not very likely you'll find a trace of one yourself," she said, getting up and heading to the kitchen.

Feeling weirdly domestic, Diana started pulling out plates and opening containers. Daniel had brought an assortment of Thai dishes, including Pad Thai, eggplant with chicken, and duck in a cracked black pepper sauce.

She opened the sweet sticky rice and mango desserts and almost squealed with delight. It wasn't as decadent as other meals Alec had arranged, but it was a feast of favorites for her.

Damn, that man is a freaking mind reader.

She peeked over at him tapping with vampiric speed on a shiny laptop he'd brought with him.

Okay, so not exactly a man.

She finished setting out small plates with a little bit of everything and heated it all up with little controlled blasts of heat. There was no dining table, just the coffee table and the bar, so she set the plates out on the coffee table and threw pillows at Alec till he stopped typing.

Smiling good-naturedly, he set down the computer and they ate, him a little and her a lot. He pretended to fight with her over the last piece of mango, but in the end he let her have it.

Alec's phone rang as they were clearing the plates. He picked it up and spoke for a few moments.

"Good, email me the list." To Diana, he said, "We have leads, with pictures in some cases, on their way."

"That was fast," she said, throwing herself on the couch next to the sketch Alec had made. "You know, this makes me think of France more than England," she said, studying the drawing.

"The Burgess family has holdings all over Europe, including some in France and Spain. I'll start with the French Alps," Alec said, leaning forward to look at her over the couch.

Diana nodded and dug out the laptop that belonged to the safe house to do her own image search. Ten minutes later, she almost flung it out the window with a panoramic view of the city.

"It's not the Alps! It's the Pyrenees!"

She ran out of the room to grab one of their old topological maps.

When she came back carrying it, Alec put his hands in his pockets and said wryly, "You know, you could find one of those online, like on the computer you just threw across the room."

"It wasn't across the room, only to that armchair. . .which is some-what soft and fluffy," she said defensively.

"I'm starting to think that heat may not be the only problem your electronics have with you."

"It's *fine*," she huffed "And an electronic map will not show ley line hotspots or other points of magical convergence," she added instructively, tossing the empty takeout containers into the fireplace and lighting them before rolling the map out on the space she'd cleared on the coffee table.

"What do you mean by other kinds of magical convergences?" Alec asked, leaning in.

"Like portals or time slips and loops. Stuff like that," she murmured, only half paying attention as she smoothed out the thick oily paper.

"Portals to *where?*" he asked.

When she didn't answer, he traced a ley line on the map with his finger. "Are all of these still active? I thought most ley lines drained and dissipated over time only to be replaced by new ones somewhere else."

"Most of them are like that, transient. But not all of them disappear. The bigger ones can last decades or even a few centuries. Some only appear to dissipate, but in reality they shift along a certain geographic range. It's kind of like magnetic fields, but ley lines are more affected by the topography of the region they are found in," she said, poring over the map.

"I always figured it was something like that," Alec mused aloud, and Diana wondered if she should be grateful that vampires couldn't tap into ley lines.

"How often do you update these?" he asked.

"We inform each other about changes as we find them."

"But this looks old, and there are no corrections," he said.

Diana tapped on the map. It went from featuring Western Europe to focusing on the south of France.

"This is charmed. It updates if we will it to do so," she said, flattening out the area she wanted to focus on more closely.

Alec let out an impressed whistle. "Now I know how you managed to survive without a computer. This is remarkable. Aren't you afraid of it falling into the wrong hands?"

She gave a dismissive wave. "The people who would be the biggest problem are sensitive enough to detect major ley lines on their own. The witch clans keep their own maps. A ley line in of itself is not a problem. The practitioner is." She pointed to an area outside of the city of Toulouse. "We need to look around here. There's a major point of convergence at the base of the Pyrenees, but it's been a while since we've been in that area. It's probably shifted around since we were there last. It has a history of moving around. I'm going to get in touch with Logan. She spends more time in southern France than the rest of us."

"Why?" Alec asked, but his phone rang. "Sorry. I have to take this. It's Daniel."

He went to the other room to take the call. When he came back, his face was drawn and pale.

He started gathering his things. "There's a problem with Pedro. Daniel is not sure, but it's possible he tried to commit suicide. I need to go see him."

Their pleasant dinner turned into a rock in her stomach.

"What happened?" she asked.

"He drank something toxic from under the sink," Alec said. "Daniel isn't sure if it was intentional or not, but Pedro served himself some bleach with dinner."

"I should go with you. But. . .we need to get to France. I need to update the others and get some gear together."

"I understand. And you said you're not a healer, so you're not going to do him any good. I'll go alone and call in a healer I know to look in on Pedro. One with a record for reliability. Maybe they can do something. I'll get the plane ready unless you want to try and find a fire that is capable of transporting you," he said, pausing to look expectantly at her.

His concern that she would go without him was written all over his face.

"There aren't any in that region right now that are big enough to ensure I wouldn't be seen," Diana reassured him. "There are always campfires and fireplaces but those generally have people around. The last thing we need is for me to end up on YouTube. I can't tell if there's someone on the other side, so I usually don't travel that way unless it's prearranged with one of the other girls. Exposure has to be avoided at all costs."

"Makes sense," Alec said distractedly as he put on his coat.

His gaze was distant as he kissed her on the forehead before hurrying out the door.

Diana stood frozen in front of the closed door. She didn't think

Alec was aware of what he had done. He'd been a little disoriented, which was disturbing in its own way, too.

And she hadn't even thrown a fireball at him in response. Had the same thing happened a week ago the vampire would have gone up like a Roman candle. But she didn't do anything right now because she liked him.

Maybe more than like.

"Are you in love with him?" Logan asked excitedly. Diana jumped.

"For the love of the Mother, Logan! How many times have I asked you not to do that?"

"If you don't want me dropping in, you should have closed the window in the library," Logan replied reasonably, tucking her shoulder length black hair behind her ears.

The Air Elemental was dressed the way she preferred to dress when traveling the air currents: in a form-fitting mock turtleneck, dark jeans, and biker boots. She teased Diana about her 'uniform' but when it came right down to it, all of the girls dressed similarly when they worked. Form-fitting clothes and tied back hair were require-ments for fighters—although Serin often did her best work in a bikini. Regardless, giving your opponent something to grab onto was a bad idea.

"How long ago did you get here?" Diana asked in a resigned tone.

"Only a few minutes. I was dying to meet tall dark and deadly, but he seemed a tad distressed, so I thought it could wait," she said before smiling wickedly. "It also gave me a chance to spy and see if you would send him off with a kiss. And you did!" she crowed. "Well, almost..."

"Are you six years old or something? We are working this case together. At most, we are friends. That last thing was a weird anom-aly. He was totally distracted by some bad news," Diana said, motioning Logan to the map. "I have a lead. I connected with the Mother. Kind of. It wasn't like Gia described."

"How was it different?"

Diana rubbed her head, remembering the pain. "It was a flood of images like she said. That much was the same. But there were so many, I could barely distinguish one from the next. It was like being in whitewater rapids and then being dashed against the shore. I could only grab a few images before I got spit back out again."

"That sounds exactly like what Gia described."

"Yeah. . .but she said she could feel the Mother's presence. Her awareness of Gia's attempt to communicate. Gia *felt* her guidance. I didn't feel that. I didn't feel another's presence at all. But it happened so fast. Maybe I just didn't have enough skill to hang on long enough. It felt like my brain was being fried."

Diana put her hands on her head and propped her elbows on her lap.

Logan sat down next to her with a thump. "Wow. I wondered what you had got up to when I felt that spike coming from your direction. What did you do? Set Boston Harbor on fire?"

Diana smirked. "I decided the Colorado fire was big enough to passage to. I used the big fireplace in the coven house to get there."

"And there was nothing useful?"

"I wouldn't say that. I saw a connection to the Burgess family. The witch we are looking for is Hillard's illegitimate son or daughter. Not the one here in the states. I doubt Gerald is even aware of this one's existence," she said.

Gerald Burgess was the current patriarch of the Burgess family. None of the Elementals particularly liked him, but they didn't like any witches. And Gerald had kept the covenant. To their knowledge, he had never before failed to keep track of any of his heirs before. Even the illegitimate ones had his support.

Logan frowned and reached for one of the full take-out containers still on the table. "That family hasn't had this kind of trouble for centuries. They have a reputation for staying on the straight and narrow. I guess it makes sense the current generation has forgotten our warnings to keep track of their own."

"Yeah, but there wasn't an image of who the child is now. I don't know what they look like. I couldn't even tell what gender it was. In the present day, I got a quick flash of a farmhouse. I'm hoping that's where the kids are. The vamp and I spent the last few hours trying to define the location from the snippet I saw of the surroundings. We think it's in southern France, somewhere near the base of the Pyrenees," she said, moving to smooth the map again.

"You can call him Alec. I know he's your new BFF. No need to pretend with me," Logan said.

"I'm not pretending anything. We're partners on this case. *Possibly* friends. That's it," she lied.

She *was* trying to distance herself from Alec in front of Logan. But she had gotten pretty soft about him and felt the need to backtrack now.

"Suit yourself," Logan said. "Well, I'm not sure if it's relevant anymore, but I have a lead on your insect pin lady. The wind whispered a location, nothing more. And it's not in France."

"Where is it?"

"Salem."

"Of course it is." Diana groaned. "If a wannabe witch or outcast wants to play at witchcraft they always end up in Salem."

Few genuine talents called Salem, Massachusetts home these days. Today it wasn't any richer in ley lines than any other part of the state. But at the time of the Salem witch trials, a large unstable line had run through that region and some genuine practitioners had lived in the area.

One of them, a Delavordo descendant, started a whole heap of trouble that resulted in the deaths of as many as two dozen people. It was considered bad luck to live in the area if you were a Supernatural —something that became a lasting legend about the area even after everyone had long forgotten the details of what happened.

"I can give you a lift to Salem right now."

"Thanks. Let me grab some stuff. I can text Alec to meet me there. And then we need to get to France. He's getting his jet ready," she said, pulling out Alec's gift.

Logan hopped closer. "Since when do you have a phone?" she asked, plucking it out of Diana's hand. She whistled. "What kind is this? It's huge."

"It's the most heatproof one Alec could find," Diana said with a little smile she couldn't seem to hide.

She took back the phone and finished her text, ignoring Logan's smug expression.

"I would take you to France, too, but I've got a pressing thing in Mexico City," Logan said apologetically while peeking over her shoulder to read the text.

"That's fine. Alec's jet is a fast one. Maybe you can manipulate the currents to give us a little push. Also, I don't know how the children of the night feel about taking to the air for that long a trip," Diana finished with a shrug.

"Well, some of them can fly short distances. I'm sure he would make it in one piece. . .probably," Logan added before pursing her lips. "If he's your mate, he should survive."

Diana rolled her eyes. "He's *not* my mate. And even if he was, only *your* mate would be adept in *your* medium."

An Elemental's mate was partially immune to her ability. With practice, he would be able to travel with her through her medium, but only if the Elemental was highly skilled. Logan was.

"Yeah. We'll see," the Air Elemental replied, swinging her foot.

The phone chimed with a text message, and Diana read it as she started gathering her things.

I would rather you waited for me but will of course do as you ask. I'm sending the plane ahead to a private airfield outside Salem. Pedro will be all right. I think it was an accident. He doesn't seem to be aware of what he did.

"Okay, I'm ready to go," Diana said, grabbing her coat and slipping a pair of leather gloves into her back pocket.

She carefully folded the ley line map and put it in her pack.

They shifted to the library, and Diana took Logan's hand. Her body shuddered, and she transitioned the same way she would have while traveling through fire, but the sensation stopped short of completion as the air current picked her up and carried her along for the ride.

27

Ten minutes later, Diana was dropped into the Burying Point Cemetery. The wind rushed over her as Logan made her way to her engagement in Mexico. She took a moment to whisper a prayer to the Mother for the safety of her sister and then took a good look around.

All was quiet. It was one of the many advantages of the Air Elemental. Logan could see and feel the area she was passing over and avoid the locations where people were present.

Diana's ability didn't work that way. She couldn't differentiate from the heat of the fire and the body heat of people around the fire in question. Occasionally, one of the other girls could start a fire and open a secure gateway for her, but they were usually nowhere near where she needed to be.

The historic cemetery was deserted at this hour. Closer to Halloween there probably would have been tourists or wannabe practitioners wandering about. If she remembered correctly, one of the judges that had sent so many to hang was buried here. Though she knew that one of the Delavordos had started the frenzy, she sincerely hoped the old bastard of a judge was not enjoying eternal rest. Too much innocent blood was on his hands.

Wishing she had her bike, Diana walked along trying to pinpoint a location. Reaching out with her other sense, she searched for recent disruptions in the balance.

There.

A ripple signaled a disturbance somewhere to the east. It didn't look like she would have far to walk. She turned away from Salem Common, away from the waterfront, and headed deeper into town.

The streets were also deserted at this hour. The night tours were long over, and no enterprising tourist crossed her path, although the occasional car passed in the surrounding streets. Passing various cafes and shops that played up the town's association with witchcraft, she pulled out her new phone and texted Alec her current location and where the disturbance would likely be.

She followed Logan's directions, trying to decipher the signals she was receiving, anything that would explain why the winds were calling out this location, but there was little she could be sure about. There was a vague swirling in the aether, localized a few blocks away. As she got closer, for a split second, there was the signature of violence, but in the next blink, it was gone.

"Of course," Diana muttered as she reached her destination.

It wasn't the site where the witches had hung as she'd initially suspected, but was an old building dating from that time. The sign outside declared it the 'Witch House'. It wasn't actually associated with the trials themselves except for the fact one of the judges had lived here at the time. But it was one of the few buildings still standing from that time in Salem proper. More were located in nearby Danvers, which was originally called Salem Village, the true origin of the hysteria.

The Witch House served as a museum these days. It was a dark, multi-gabled structure that managed to look both pious and sinister at the same time. Slipping into the shadows, Diana reached out with her senses, looking for the presence of another person inside the building. There was nothing except the fading heat signatures of the museum's daily visitors. No listening spells or trespassing wards were discernible, either. She walked around the perimeter to be sure, but there was nothing to find.

Releasing a pent-up breath, she narrowed her eyes at the house. If there was a person inside, or a body, it was masked somehow. Getting closer, she found an unlocked window. She passed unnoticed by the alarm system, slipping inside the building with supernatural stealth.

The room had an old-fashioned hearth and table set up to display what life was like at the time of the trials. Stepping deeper into the interior, she scanned the darkness, alert and ready for battle. Despite what her senses were telling her, she wasn't confident there was no one else here.

Diana systematically searched the ground floor of the house, sorting through the mishmash of heat signatures for anything that would explain why the winds were whispering about this place. Finding nothing, she made her way upstairs, looking through darkened room after darkened room.

The body was upstairs. It was a young woman laid out in the middle of a pentagram, her throat cut. She was dressed in a long flowing skirt and a revealing peasant blouse—clothes far less conservative than those Diana had seen the one time they'd met. It was Catherine, Brenda's sister. The beetle brooch was pinned over her heart.

Diana stood by quietly, the sinking feeling in her stomach solidifying into anger. Was Brenda in the circle? It looked a lot more likely now. She could be the second woman in J's club, selling their illegal spells.

But that didn't make sense. Neither woman had a speck of magical ability in them. If they did, it was so negligible that it didn't register. Perhaps Catherine had simply been a groupie who'd then been recruited as a salesperson. Swearing to herself, she knelt down to examine the body.

Even this close, she couldn't sense any heat emanating from it, not even the work of decomposing bacteria. There was simply nothing for her to find.

Suspicious now, she reached a hand out to touch the body on the arm. For a moment, she felt the resistance of an unseen barrier. It wasn't very dense. It dissipated as she pushed through it, breaking the spell the way a kid would smash through a sand castle that had hardened in the sun.

When it was gone, Diana could smell and feel the decay that had been completely obscured only moments before. She searched the air for the heat signature of the murderer, but there wasn't one. It was possible that Catherine had been killed elsewhere and dumped, but she still should have seen the signature of the one who did the dumping.

Except this hadn't been a simple body dump. According to the amount of blood, she'd been killed in this room. Could the spell of concealment have masked the signatures of the murderers? It shouldn't be possible, but little about this case was in line with her past experiences.

She had a hard time believing the body lying in front of her was Katie's aunt. Whoever was in charge of the circle could have found another person with actual magical ability far more easily. There were a few spells to mask abilities, but none that could have fooled an Elemental and certainly not one that would work on the dead. And there wasn't another spell active on the body.

Perhaps Diana was leaping to the conclusion she was meant to. Someone in the circle could have learned that someone was looking for a woman with a bee pin. It could have been placed there to implicate Catherine and Brenda both. Brenda could be lying dead somewhere, too, masked by a similar spell.

She scanned, but found nothing on or around the body that would explain the masking spell. Which meant there had to be something under her. She fished out the leather gloves from her back pocket and put them on, then lifted the right leg near the booted foot, looking for symbols drawn underneath. But the floor was bare. She put the leg down and then noticed the stickiness of her glove. It was tacky with drying blood.

She picked up the leg again and checked the underside. Even

though the pool of blood didn't reach down past her waist, the entire calf was coated with blood.

Pulling back the cloth took some effort. It was stuck to the skin, but once she'd separated it, the carving was clear. An unfamiliar rune had been cut into the skin behind the back of the ankle.

Well, that was overkill. A carving in the wood would have sufficed. Diana seriously doubted it was a case of them not knowing any better. Whoever cast this spell had enjoyed inflicting the maximum amount of damage possible.

There were more symbols carved in other parts of the body, on each arm and leg and on the back of the head. Diana made sure the body's limbs were exactly as she found them, but the puddle of blood had been disturbed. She debated leaving it, but in the end, she used a fraction of her power to warm the blood so that it settled around the body once more.

Cleaning her hands with a quick burst of flame, she circled the body, examining the rest of the room around it. There wasn't much in the way of furniture, and there were no signs of a struggle. Even the dust around the body was mostly intact. Catherine probably hadn't seen her death coming. She had either trusted the person with her or was caught completely unaware.

Diana turned away and closed the door behind her, leaving it unlocked. It was time someone found Catherine. Perhaps the rest of the circle was waiting for that to happen, but the lack of wards suggested they didn't care. The masking spell was probably to buy time for them to get away.

When she shimmied back out the window, Alec was waiting for her. She kept to the shadows, but needn't have bothered since he had chosen to park directly in front of the building.

At least he didn't park it under a streetlight. Suppressing a groan, Diana slipped into the backseat with him, prepared to rip him a new one.

"Did you find something?" he asked.

She hesitated. Alec looked mussed and so uncharacteristically grave that she couldn't give him a hard time for his choice of parking spots.

Nodding, she buckled up. "I found Catherine, Brenda's sister. Her throat was slit. She was wearing the beetle pin."

"Well, hell. Are we after her sister or is she dead somewhere, too?"

"That's what I've been asking myself since I found her," Diana said, running a hand through her hair. "Both are real possibilities until we know more."

"Did you burn the body?"

"No."

"Are you going to leave it for the authorities to find again?" he asked, surprised. "Even in this case?"

"Sometimes that's best. It looks like some black magic ritual. She had symbols carved into her body that masked her from me until I was on top of her. The police will draw the same basic conclusion and chalk it up to a psycho."

"Are you sure that's wise? What if they come up with a suspect?"

Diana frowned. "I doubt they will. And if there's someone with the same m.o. then they deserve to be caught. But I doubt that will happen. The authorities might make anti-Wicca noises, but these days the only witches they know about are pretty tree-huggy. There shouldn't be any repercussions to that group. The only likely side effect is a probable rise in tourism. Human nature will take over." She sighed and sank back into the seat.

"Why would the circle leave the body like that? Undetectable unless you come across it?"

"My guess is they wanted it found but not right away. The spell was probably good for a week. It masked both heat and scent."

Alec shifted restlessly. "Is their circle incomplete now? Or was she collateral damage?"

"Don't know. If she was in the circle, triads have certain advantages or maybe they plan on recruiting. Catherine had no real magical ability. They might have found someone with actual talent and decided to get rid of her so they could take on someone else. Or she was never one of the real members in the first place. We won't know until we find them."

"What a mess," he said slowly before giving himself a little shake. "The airport is five minutes away. I'll call ahead and make sure we are ready for takeoff."

Alec was still obviously upset by what had happened with his servant. A little voice in her head that sounded remarkably like Gia was telling her to comfort him somehow. Should she hug him or something? The very idea made her tense up. But she couldn't leave him hanging.

"Tell me about Pedro," she said softly.

Alec's broad shoulders slumped. "I thought he was getting better, and then this happened. He seems more aware of himself these days, but this incident with the bleach is worrisome. Daniel will stay with him," he said. "I tried to be honest with him. I told him I wasn't sure if his son was still alive or not. But I promised to bring back the heads of the people who hurt him."

Wide-eyed, Diana stared at Alec. "A little bloodthirsty for you," she said surprised. "Definitely not scholarly."

He met her eyes with a resigned expression. "I may be a stuffy scholar, but I am also a vampire on the Ruling Council. These witches have broken the covenant and taken the child of one of my house's retainers. I need to make sure no others follow in their footsteps. You're going to kill them anyway. I want their heads as a message that they cannot cross my house and harm one of our own. Even the children of our servants are off limits."

"That was always your plan, wasn't it?" Diana asked. She wasn't judging. It was what she would have done in his place. "With or without my involvement..."

"It's my responsibility. But I may not find them without you."

Drumming her fingers on the seat, she frowned. "Even with me you may not find them," Diana reminded him stiffly. "You didn't mention being on the Ruling Council."

Despite her attempt to soften her words, it came out as an accusation.

"I know. I'll get to that, but we're here now," he said, gesturing to their surroundings.

They'd arrived at the airfield. She waited till they boarded and had taken off before she started on him again.

"I'm waiting for an explanation, Alec," she said, arms crossed. The temperature around her grew several degrees hotter.

He closed his eyes briefly. "I accepted a position on the Council decades ago."

Diana opened her mouth to throw out another accusation, but he forestalled her with a hand.

"It's not like being the head of the house," he assured her. "Vampire covens operate independently for the most part. But in times of crisis, they defer to the Council's edicts. If they know what's good for them, that is. I thought it was important to have a voice, so I chose to serve when I was asked. But I act independently of them if I don't believe it serves the greater good. Most council members do the same, but for different reasons. Which is why little is accomplished unless something big happens."

Diana didn't like the sound of the 'greater good'. "How often do you and the council have to make these monumental decisions?"

Alec drummed his fingers on the armrest. "Whenever something sufficiently disruptive happens. Something that might affect us. Last time we met was 9-11. We decided to let things run their course geopolitically but moved things around financially when there were concerns shared across houses." Diana lifted a brow and he gave her a weak smile. "Like you, we don't interfere when it comes to big political movements, but we do protect our own interests."

"Of course you do," she muttered. "And do you plan on continuing your involvement with the council indefinitely?"

Even if he decided to chase her around the world? Or had he changed his mind about that? She ignored the pang of discomfort that last thought caused.

He nodded. "It really has nothing to do with ruling a house or over other vampires. It was decided long ago that the head of a house was disqualified from serving on the Council. It's more like the Supreme

Court, only the decisions are few and far between. The positions are for life, such as it is. . ."

Diana mulled that over. It made sense that he'd hold such an exalted position, but knowing he was on the Council made her uncomfortable. She knew enough about it to know he was being truthful about how the Council worked.

Mostly truthful anyway.

But she decided to let the matter drop. They had bigger fish to fry. Together.

She got up to get a drink from the bar. "Okay, well, let's make Toulouse our base of operations. We should rent a flat or get hotel suites near their Natural History museum."

Alec frowned, shifting in his seat. "Is there some research we need to do there?"

"Not exactly. Natural history museums are great places to steal raw materials for spells. This one even has a botanical garden attached if memory serves. Museums are like Wal-Mart for spellcasters."

"Well again, that makes sense," he said loosening his tie and tossing it away. "I never even realized. Stupid of me."

"Not stupid. It takes a witch and a thief to make the connection," Diana said with a curl of her lip. "Try not to beat yourself up for having too much moral fiber."

Smirking briefly, he started making calls, finding a place for them to stay and getting special access to the museum.

While he was busy, Diana pored over the old ley line map she'd tucked into her bag at the safe house. She cross-referenced it with what she knew about the shifts of magnetic fields in the area, marking likely search areas.

Hopefully they would find something at the museum or through one of their sources that might narrow down the possibilities. After a while, she put away the maps and settled down to sleep. It was a good idea to conserve energy for what was coming.

She slept the rest of the way to France, aware on some level of Alec's watchful gaze on her for the duration of the flight.

28

Toulouse was known as the pink city because of the brickwork on the old buildings in town and along the river that flowed through it, the Garonne. Diana had zipped through it on her way to the nearby cities of Barcelona and Bordeaux. They had a safe house in Provence that Logan especially liked, but Diana hadn't spent any real time in Toulouse before.

She had a basic idea about the layout of the center of town. The natural history museum was attached to a complex of public gardens near the Palais de Justice, the city's courthouse. Alec had rented a recently renovated eighteenth-century house near the gardens to use as their base of operations. The three-story building was meant for multiple families, but Alec had rented the entire thing to make sure they had complete privacy.

Diana put her pack in the bedroom. From the window, she could see part of the public gardens. It was not quite dark yet, and there were still people milling about, enjoying the late light despite the humidity in the air. After fishing her super phone from her pack, she made a call to arrange for one of her bikes to be delivered before dark fell.

She and her sisters had resources in every country in the world, and it was a good idea to avoid being restricted by a car in this town. Europe's small and narrow streets were difficult to navigate, and she didn't know where this search was going to take her.

Us.

Having second thoughts, she called back her service and had one of her spare bikes delivered as well. One for her and one for Alec. She couldn't leave him behind at this point.

Besides, he had a definite knack for tracking her down. Which was weird. Elementals had evolved to be difficult—nearly impossible—to trace. Except by their own kind. . .and their mates.

SUMMER HEAT generally meant shorter hours at the municipal buildings of the city, but it also meant longer days with people lingering in the park as it cooled off. It was late evening before it was empty enough to enter the area surrounding the museum and its small botanical garden. Diana led Alec around to one side near the greenhouses where she jumped the fence in one smooth motion.

"You know, we could have had the museum's curator lead us around," Alec said, looking askance at the fence and then down at his designer suit. "It wouldn't have been a problem."

"And we tell him what? That we're looking for signs you've been robbed by a bunch of witches?" Diana said from the other side of the fence, hands on her hips.

"Fine," he muttered, jumping over the railing at human speed.

Using his vampire grace, he avoided snagging his suit, but he landed in a particularly muddy spot. He shot her a look, shaking the mud off his shoes.

"Seriously? Why did you wear those anyway?" she asked, gesturing to his feet. "They must cost like thousands of dollars. Those are not caper shoes."

He grinned at her. "This is a caper?"

"Close enough. Come on. Let's take a look and see if any plants have been lifted from the garden," she replied, rounding the greenhouse.

"Okay, I'm going to ask. How can you tell normal gardening activity from outright theft?" he asked and then stopped short, looking at a small hole in the dirt where a plant had been clearly ripped out by the roots.

"Yeah. Not exactly subtle. They'll want to keep the plants as fresh as possible for as long as possible so they take the whole thing, roots and all. I think this one was betel nut," she said, bending to examine the labels fixed to little sticks in the grounds. "Look for more."

They split up and found an additional four more stolen plants.

"Three of the usual suspects: henbane, belladonna, and anise seed. And that last one, *alihotsy*, is pretty rare. It had been used in some dark spells in the past," Diana said as he knelt in front of a particularly large hole in the ground. "The circle has definitely been here."

Alec straightened up. "I thought *alihotsy* was fictional."

"Most people do. You know it as *asafoetida* but it's a specific subspecies that only grows in a specific corner of Eastern Europe. . .and museum collections."

"Interesting. Do you think we need to look inside?"

"Definitely. We need to pay special attention to their gem and fossil collections," Diana said, leading him toward the back doors.

No cameras were apparent on the exterior of the building. The doors, however, were sure to be wired. She had bent over the back door and was starting to tap into the electrical system when Alec tugged on her shirt. He whipped out a key from his suit pocket and nudged her toward another door.

"How much did you pay for that?" she asked with a knowing smile.

"Actually, I called in a favor. No silver crossed any palms. Honest," he said, taking the lead as they moved into the darkened interior of the museum.

Left of the door, there were a number of skeletons set into the wall of windows between two panes of glass. It was a striking effect, but most of the skeletal remains were plastic reconstructions, so they moved on. They quickly glanced over the rest of the fossil collection and concluded that none of the genuine ones were missing. The ground up powder of human and animal bones was a common base in dark spells.

Unfortunately, their luck didn't hold. Diana knew there was trouble when they stepped into the gemstone and mineral exhibits.

"It's the fucking meteorites."

Alec frowned. "They're still here," he said, pointing at the stones in their display case.

"No, they're not," she replied, rubbing her forehead at the hairline. "These are definitely common earth rocks, not meteorites."

"How can you tell without looking at them microscopically? Do you have a geology degree that I don't know about?"

"I can tell when something is not from here. Something not of the Mother. And these are just rocks," Diana said, turning to meet his eyes. "This is not good. If I'd known they had meteorites here, I wouldn't have waited till night to take a look around."

"What can they do with them? I know they are prized as materials for weapons, but what can they do in spells? Magic is centered around the natural world, isn't it?" he asked, frowning at the display.

"That's exactly why they're so useful in weapons. If the forger knows what he's doing, they can break through any sort of protection spell. Fortunately most don't. The circle shouldn't be able to use them in spells properly, but they've been able to innovate in unexpected ways. Maybe they think they've found a way to use them in their magic," Diana mused, biting her lip.

"Or they're going to try and use them to forge weapons to use against you," he added in a worried tone.

"I doubt they know what I am. Besides, we wield weapons like that sometimes and spar against each other. We're not immune to the effects, but they can't undo our magic. Our abilities are a facet of the Mother and don't require spells to use. Not something undone so easily. These stones haven't been missing for long. Judging from the state of the garden, the theft happened within the last few days. It would take a master much longer to forge a weapon."

"And if they can find a way to work them into their spell-craft instead of using them to forge weapons?"

"Ve vill burn that bridge vhen ve come to it," she said in a terrible Transylvanian accent, and he broke into a grin.

"Don't make me smile. This is serious," he said, forcing a scowl over his handsome features.

"I can't help being hilarious," she said with a perfectly straight face, making him laugh outright before leading the way deeper into the museum.

They checked the other gem and mineral cases, but nothing else was missing despite the presence of several minerals useful in spell craft.

"They left some valuable things behind," Alec said. "Maybe they didn't want to get greedy and alert the museum's security to the thefts. It looks like they took only what they really needed."

"Or they didn't know the value of the other things in here. My gut still says untrained in traditional spellcraft. Do the most common spell books, the kind outsiders can get their hands on, mention the healing properties of jade? Or the energizing boosts from amethysts? Only trained witches learn how to use them in their spells. These guys might have had no idea," she said, heading toward the exit.

"Maybe. Maybe not. But too many things missing would alert the authorities. And they might want to blend right now and not call attention to the theft," Alec pointed out as they went out the door and back into the garden.

"Doesn't matter. We need to start looking for that farmhouse. They might not be there anymore, but it's got to be a better lead than this. Meteorites can't be traced—at least not from a distance. They are not of the Mother and so are outside of our ability to track. But they sometimes buzz like hell when we are close."

Alec harrumphed. After waiting for some late-night passersby to leave the park entrance clear, they jumped the fence. They slipped across the street unnoticed by others still walking about.

"But if you were near a meteorite-based weapon, you could sense them right? I thought you could tell what wasn't of the Mother as readily as what was?"

"When it has a heartbeat and is making trouble yes, but when it's inanimate, what doesn't belong isn't easy to find from a distance. It doesn't vibrate on the same frequency that earthly things do—and it's not apparent till you're close to it. If it's terrestrial and significant, the Earth Elemental could connect to it to track it down, provided we could narrow the search enough to differentiate it from others of its kind. But not something extraterrestrial in origin," she said. "It's not a viable lead. What have your men done to find the farmhouse?"

"They are out looking at likely properties based on matching descriptions from tax records and the like. They eliminated a few possibilities, but they aren't capable of detecting ley lines, and I haven't found a ley line witch nearby yet. We should get out there ourselves," he said.

"My thoughts exactly," Diana murmured, heading to the garage.

She was pleased to see that their MTT turbine bikes had been delivered, along with a matching set of leathers for Alec.

"Why are there two? I ordered a car to take us to start searching in the areas you pointed out. It's a long ride to get out there on a bike."

Diana beamed. "Not at the speeds these two are capable of. The black Turbine is mine and the blue is yours. These two bikes are literally the fastest and second-fastest in the world," she said, gesturing to each bike in turn. "They've been specially modded by specialists I found in Tokyo. . .and a little juice courtesy of Gia. With the mods, they leave the Dodge Tomahawk in the dust," she said, stroking the black bike lovingly. "Technically, these two clock out at the same speed but the black one is faster on the curves."

"Err, I haven't ridden one of these in a while," he said, looking down at the leathers and helmet with less than his usual confidence.

Diana waved off his concern. "With your supernatural reflexes, I'm sure you'll do fine," she said before heading for the staircase to get her pack from her room,

She waited till he was out of sight to grin. The vampire had actually gone pale. That had to be a real achievement. When she returned with her pack, Alec tried to convince her to take the car again, but she wouldn't hear of it.

"These bikes are more flexible on all terrain than your stretched out sedans or SUVs. Come on, it'll be fine. Plus this way, we can split up to cover more territory in the hot spots," she said as she climbed onto her bike. "Oh, and Alec?"

"Yeah?"

"If you scratch my baby, I'll kick your ass into next week," she said with a sweet smile as she started the bike.

"Right," Alec said, looking down at the bike in a sour look of dismay as he pulled on his helmet.

She pulled out of the garage and waited on the drive until he reluctantly mounted his. Minutes later, he was following her out of town on the world's second-fastest bike.

29

They were running out of paved roads in the rural countryside surrounding Toulouse. Their bikes were pretty quiet on the road, quieter than occasional cars that passed.

They'd hit the largest hotspots near town already, and Alec's men had been making a sweep at the far end of the range they'd defined. They were looking to match the rough farmhouse drawing Alec had made. At the rate they were going, the two groups would meet in the middle by dawn.

Diana stopped her bike under a tree and waited for Alec to pull up alongside her.

"Did we miss a ley line?" he asked.

"I think so. There used to be a major point of convergence near here at the base of these hills. It shifted away from the stream in this area," she said, scanning the darkness, her night vision giving her a clearer view than his.

"Wouldn't it shift closer to the water?" he asked.

"I don't think so. Too many people have moved close to the stream. They build their houses near them as long as the law allows. The manipulation of energy and water to converge in one place, namely a house's electricity and plumbing, forces ley lines farther away. The point of convergence was strong but unstable. I think we should head into the hills in the east, away from the water and the houses in this area. If there are any old homesteads in your records that wouldn't have electricity or running water, we should start there."

He nodded and made the call to his staff, trying to find farmhouses in the area they were headed to.

According to their research, there were two possibilities. He relayed GPS coordinates to Diana, and they were on their way.

THE SPEED at which they drove in the darkness made Alec distinctly nervous for Diana. He knew she would be all right if they crashed, but her delicate build and fragile features put his protective instincts into overdrive.

To make things worse, she had opted to leave the lights turned off on their bikes, another detail that made him extremely anxious.

He followed the other bike as closely as he could. His senses were also in overdrive from all of the adrenaline. He was able to smell the night air, the greenery and warmth radiating off the soil despite the speed at which they were traveling.

Ahead of him, Diana crested a hill in the dark and paused. She waited for him to catch up and then lifted her visor. "This is the wrong way. I don't feel any ley lines this way. Let's turn around and head down west," she said, gesturing to another road in the distance.

"There won't be any houses down that way at all according to the records," he added.

"They're just spread farther apart, which is what we're looking for. And there is a greater likelihood of finding their hiding place near a convergence point," she said, dropping her visor and heading off to find the start of the road in the distance.

It took another half hour before they found the leyline and the abandoned farmhouse Diana had seen in the Mother's memory. Wordlessly, they stopped some distance away, parking the bikes behind a stand of trees. They were too far away to see if the house was occupied or not.

Diana took off her helmet and paused in a break in the trees. Taking his own helmet off, he moved to stand next to her. Unsure what to do, he studied her taught profile. Tension was coming off her in waves.

"Whatever we find, we are here to make this right," he said firmly.

"Yeah," Diana said, sucking in a deep breath before starting toward the house.

As they crept closer to the structure, they could see the old place looked better from a distance. Up close, the house was a ramshackle. The left side of the roof was missing, as well as part of the wall closest to them. A crumbling barn was moldering on their right.

Diana paused catty-corner from the house, looking for signs of other people in the vicinity. "No heat signatures that aren't animal-sized. No child-sized ones either," she finally said, her voice heavy.

"Let's take a closer look. They might have left something behind."

"Like a body under a concealment spell," she muttered, running over the elephant in the room with a truck.

"Yeah, something like that," he said softly before subsiding as they approached the house.

Diana didn't bother with the door; using instead a gap in the wall into what ended up being a ruined kitchen. Moonlight filtered through the holes in the ceiling, revealing a wooden table on its side. All the chairs were gone, but in the corner, a broken down china cabinet with no glass still stood. A lone stirring spoon was its only occupant.

Turning in a slow circle, she examined the residual heat signatures in the room. People had passed through it in the last week, but the forms were too degraded to see clearly. The ambient heat in the room contributed to the weakness of the signal.

She motioned to Alec who was waiting outside the hole in the wall.

"There are no clear signatures. Only adult-sized people were in this room. No one *appears* to have been here recently," she said.

As Diana made her way through the empty front rooms, Alec ducked inside through the gap, letting her look for signs of the children without adding his own slight heat to the mix.

The living room was completely devoid of furniture. "It looks like this room was cleared out recently. Some adult-sized signatures are present. If children had passed through the front door, it was way before these adults. Unlike the cooler environment of the basement in Dover, the ambient temperature of these rooms is significantly higher. It's swamping out all but the most recent movements," she said.

"It will be worse upstairs," Alec warned, gesturing for her to precede him up the mostly intact stairs.

The second story was in far better shape than the first. The floors were complete and relatively clean, as if someone had swept them recently. The upper story was divided into more rooms than the first, as if it had been added decades later for a larger family.

Diana nodded at Alec, and they took opposite sides of the hallway, opening the closed doors and checking the rooms inside. She turned away from one bare room to look into the one Alec had opened last. This one had a bed and couch, both new, although there were no linens on the bed.

Walking closer, she said, "Someone stayed here a while, an adult. Nothing else is clear." She gestured to the last room on the right. "That one should match the vantage point I saw."

When she didn't move, Alec put his hand on her back and gently pushed her toward it.

The view from the window confirmed that this was the room from the Mother's memory. The children had spent a lot of time here, enough to leave faint echoes in a few places. She nodded, knowing Alec would understand.

Unlike the room in Dover, the circle took everything this time. The room was completely bare.

Then she looked out the window into the wood surrounding the farmhouse and saw it.

Alec let out a frustrated breath "We're too late," he said from behind her.

"Yeah. We are," she whispered, staring at the newly overturned earth at the tree line.

30

The grave was small, the warmth from the decomposing body close to the surface.

Alec had called in his men to remove the body. He hadn't wanted her to dig it up herself. She'd seen worse, a lot worse, but when she pointed that out, he only seemed to get more upset. He was determined to shield her as best he could, and in the end it was easier to let him have his way. And though she didn't say so, she was grateful.

It was always different when little kids were involved.

"Can you tell which child it is?" Alec asked, his voice distant and flat.

He seemed to be taking it better than she was, but she knew better. Alec was as crushed as she was.

"No," she said, leaning on a tree while they waited. "From here I can tell that there is only one body, not two. And I think the kids were roughly the same height as far as I know."

The last was said in an absent, far-away voice. If Alec hadn't been here—hadn't insisted on calling his men—she would be digging up that grave alone right now. She'd had to deal with the bodies of innocents before, but not children this small. She was glad he was there with her.

Diana was past anger. Her grimness was edged in despair, the kind that sneaks in between disasters. She remembered the bitter feeling well from back when her mom had died. You could put away the emotions when the next hurdle loomed, but they always snuck back in when things went quiet again.

"You know," he said suddenly. "I thought we would make it. I thought together we would stop them."

She nodded. "I wouldn't have thought so before. This job teaches you not to expect a happy ending. But somehow having a partner made it seem possible," she said, giving him a ghost of a smile. "But this is what it's like, you know. . .this job. Sometimes. Too often."

"Which is why the thought of you having to do this by yourself drives me fucking crazy," he returned hoarsely.

No other words were spoken as two cars drove up the lane, bringing Alec's men and their shovels.

Diana decided to wait by her bike during the exhumation. Alec had ex-Sûreté on his European staff as well as former Interpol. Proper forensic technique would be observed. Diana doubted it would make any difference. The body had been hidden, but not that well. The chances anything would be found were slim.

A warm wind whipped around them, and Diana heard the wind whisper something to her. She normally didn't hear it unless it was something Logan had passed on, but there were always exceptions. Turning to look into the wooded area behind them, she scanned the area with her extra sense. Without a word, she walked into the woods and towards one of those tiny heat sources, which was surrounded by the faint and fading signature of a slightly larger one.

It was smaller than an adult's. Alec followed silently behind her.

Crouching near a tree, Diana brushed leaves and dirt away, uncovering a small item that had been buried. It was one of those novelty rubber duckies, the kind with the little devil horns. When squeezed, it lit up. The faint light inside accounted for the faint heat source she had seen.

"This was Katie's. She buried it here. She remembered."

"Remembered what?" Alec frowned. "And how do you know it's hers?"

She looked up at him before straightening up. "Because I gave it to her."

DIANA ONLY HAD her bike when she'd rescued Katie from her captor's hideaway. She'd carried the pale and silent little girl in front of her till they'd reached the nearest town where she'd rented a car.

The little shop next to the car rental place had had the novelty duck display. Diana hadn't seen them around in years, but Katie had stopped to look at them. It was the first thing she'd reacted to with any interest, and Diana had immediately bought her one.

The first words Katie had spoken were after she'd received the duck. The little girl hadn't looked directly at her when she'd said in a matter-of-fact tone, "You killed him."

Diana had contemplated lying, but she'd said *Yes* before she could stop herself.

"That's good," Katie had said quietly, looking her in the face for the first time.

Diana hadn't known what to say, so she'd settled for the truth, "It's what I do. Come on. Let's get you back to your mom."

USING a pristine white handkerchief Alec took the duck and brushed the dirt off, careful not to touch it, before handing it back to her. Putting it in her pocket, Diana inhaled deeply and walked back to the burial site. She had to know if it was Katie's body they had found.

Alec's men had set up a perimeter around the now empty grave. The body had been moved; it was covered in white sheets on a gurney that had already been loaded onto the back of a van. It looked very small on the adult-sized gurney.

Alec's men whispered to him, telling him what, or who, it was that they'd found, but she didn't hear a thing. Her ears were filled with the sound of a roaring fire as she pulled down the sheet.

She had never seen the little boy, but he'd been small for his age. His clothes were simple but of good quality, and his shoes were new. Scanning the body carefully with all her senses, she searched for clues, but there were none to find. Her enemy was too careful.

"Nothing?" Alec asked, coming up to the open end of the van.

"No," she said, turning to him.

He was stiff and ice-cold, the area around him cooler by at least ten degrees.

"I'm sorry," she whispered.

In a way, Elias and his father were his people. At least that's the way he saw it, and she had grown to respect him for it.

"The little girl isn't near here, is she?" he said, scanning the dark woods for another small grave.

Diana thought back to the child-size form she saw in the heat signature around where they found the duck. "I think she's still alive. I think she's hoping to be rescued." She held up the duck. "By me."

He nodded, his eyes glowing with anger. "Then let's find her. Can you track her with that? It must be a prized possession."

Diana took a moment before she answered, "I don't know. It's not the same for children. You know that."

"You have to try," he said.

"I've *been* trying," she said, rubbing her temple with her palm. "The connection is tenuous at best. It flickers in and out. I'm not getting a direction like I would if she was an adult who'd shifted the balance. And probably the only reason I can feel it at all is because I gave this to her."

"Well, don't let go," he said, taking her elbow and practically dragging her back to their bikes.

Diana looked up at his face and decided not to blast him with a little fireball for manhandling her. It didn't seem wise to argue with him when he had that expression. This was worse for him. The little boy had been his responsibility.

"Are we heading back to town?" she asked.

"I don't think they would be hiding here in the middle of nowhere. This guy, the leader, he wants luxury and convenience. Even if they did have the kids here, I would bet money that the leader never stayed here. He'll be in town, if he's still here at all."

She hoped he was right.

31

As soon as she and Alec had gotten back to their safe house, shortly before dawn, he had mobilized his men to search for the rest of the circle in town. It wasn't as large as most American cities, and they had a good chance of finding them the old-fashioned way as long as their quarry hadn't moved on to a bigger place like Paris or London.

And perhaps they had, but Katie was still here in Toulouse. Or at least that's the sense Diana got whenever she tried to pinpoint the little girl's location. She'd showered and changed, but neither she nor Alec tried to sleep. They were close to the end, and she could feel time running out.

She was still pacing the room, fingering the toy duck in her hand, when Alec knocked.

"Any luck?" he asked, sitting on the bed with a handful of papers.

"She's still here, somewhere in town. Not sure where. It's like I can feel her nearby, but without a fixed direction, so it's like she's everywhere. And nowhere. The feeling is faint and blinks out. I'm starting to get a headache," she said, rubbing her forehead again.

"Well, I might have a few leads. They'll want a base of operations similar to ours but more private if possible. I think we can safely restrict things to the higher end of the price range. This is a list of some recent high end rentals that might be where they are holed up," he said, extending a sheet of paper with some addresses. "I've got men watching them all. Fortunately, this town isn't that big. Unfortunately, it's a vacation spot for Brits and other refugees from the cold, so there are a lot of rentals to check out."

"Well, I'm still not sure about the specifics, but I'll go with your gut on this one," she mumbled as she scanned the addresses. "We don't have much else to go on."

"*Thanks?*" Alec asked with pursed lips.

She threw him an apologetic glance before turning back to the list. "Most of these are pretty close by," she said after a minute, handing the papers back.

"If my people spot any likely candidates coming in or out, they'll call us immediately. We should rest while we can," he said, standing. "I'm having a tray sent up, a cold repast you can eat at your leisure. In the meantime, I think we should rest, or you can talk to the other Elementals again. . ."

"I'm not sure that would help. If they knew something, they would have gotten in touch. It's just us now. Look, I'm going to take a walk and pass by some of these places. I might be able to get something by proximity," she said, grabbing her jacket and her phone.

"Do you want me to come with you?" he asked, rising from the bed.

"No," she said, turning to him and screwing one eye closed. "I want to be able to focus, and having you around is a little distracting."

"Is that a bad thing?" he asked with a hint of a smile, his first since earlier that evening.

Diana paused in the act of putting on her jacket. "I don't know," she said honestly before walking away.

Toulouse was a livable city. Paris was nice to visit, but living there would be harder. More isolating and anonymous. Toulouse was smaller, with a welcoming, open vibe, at least on the surface.

Diana didn't ever *live* in any of the cities she visited. Maybe if she and Alec really tried to partner up, then she would pick one to stay in, kind of like a home base.

No, that wouldn't work. Serin was obligated to try because of her situation, but it wasn't practical for the rest of them. They moved around too much. Diana had never once thought about it before she met Alec. She didn't want to question why she was thinking about it now.

She walked through Carmes, one of the oldest quarters in the city. The area boasted a number of historical apartment buildings and probably the highest concentration of restaurants and bars from the looks of it. Alec probably knew which ones were the best.

Sighing, Diana passed several high-end patisseries. Distractedly, she cut through a parking structure and was surprised to find herself in a gourmet market. The parking level's were restricted to the upper stories, but the ground floor was filled with shoppers browsing stalls and deli cases.

Putting in her earphones to discourage conversations, she took a good look around. She had stumbled on a Marché that sold every-thing from gourmet meat and seafood to fruits and nuts and oils. Rabbits were laid out alongside ducks and pots of Foie Gras. Turning left, she found a high-end cheese counter laden with things she couldn't identify or pronounce. Behind it, a counter sold bottles of wine.

Diana made a complete circuit of the market, discreetly checking out what few little girls were present with adults. Most of the people didn't have kids. This was a place for chic couples to shop, not so much a place to grab mac and cheese for little ones. If the French ate mac and cheese…

She headed out the other exit of the market, past more fruit stalls and some sort of modern art/flower shop. Blending into the crowded cobblestone street on the right, she let herself be propelled past full bars and cafes that catered to the well-dressed and attractive natives. The town definitely had an above average percentage of good-looking people compared to other places she had been. Alec fit right in.

As Diana wandered through narrow cobblestone streets interspersed with broader paved avenues, she studied every face that passed. It seemed too early for the density of the crowd, until she stopped in front of a jewelry store with watches in the window and realized it was almost noon. And it was a Saturday. People were taking advantage of the good weather to shop for things they weren't able to get during the workweek and wouldn't be able to get on Sunday when most of the shops were closed.

She skirted to the edge of the crowds and ended up on the boulevard running alongside the Garonne. Stopping to sit on a low stone wall with a view of the Pont Neuf, the oldest bridge in town, Diana let her mind go blank while fixing her gaze on the arches and the vaguely lion-like cutouts in the stonework.

It was a trick she'd learned during her training when she'd initially had trouble tracking a perpetrator. Smaller shifts in the balance were easier to detect when her mind was silent and she was staring off into space.

It had become unnecessary after the first few months. With practice, her skill set had sharpened rapidly, and she was now considered the best tracker of the four Elementals. But nothing of this case had been typical, so she reached into her reserves for the focus needed to quiet her mind.

She was still watching the slow water flow toward her through the arches under the bridge a half hour later when she felt something. Closing her eyes again, she reached out with the extra sense to a familiar signature.

Katie. She could feel the little girl somewhere nearby. But there was something off. Since she wasn't supposed to be feeling Katie at all given her youth, Diana couldn't pinpoint what was different.

Scrambling off the wall, she walked towards the crowds moving to the center of town. The crowd thickened at Quai de la Dauraude, where the concrete banked down to a picnic area and a playground set crawling with children. She took a good long look at every little girl below, but Katie wasn't there.

The tug she felt on her senses began to fade. Maybe Katie was somewhere in the shifting crowd and was being led away. On alert, Diana picked the most likely direction and followed it like a predator who'd scented prey.

In a few streets, she was completely lost. She could barely feel anything anymore. A crushing sense of disappointment descended. Whirling around, she tried to get her bearings, but her pulse was racing and she couldn't calm down

Dammit, I lost it!

Walking in a wide circle, she tried in vain to recapture the signal. Tired and frustrated, she stopped short in front a brick wall. Backing away to figure out where she was, Diana found herself looking up at a huge brick Gothic church.

Les Jacobins was built in the thirteenth century by a group of Dominican brethren, according to the poster at the door. It also housed the remains of Thomas Aquinas under the altar in the center of the church.

The energy coming from the building itself confused her senses, increasing the buzzing in the back of her brain like static. Some places with a lot of history tended to do that. The best option was to absorb it and let her senses adjust to the level of background noise, much the same way a person's hearing acclimated to a noisy restaurant.

The church was mostly empty space with a very high ceiling held up by large pillars. At the base of one of the pillars was a rounded wooden platform with a mirror, so visitor's necks wouldn't cramp when looking at the palm-shaped vaulted ceiling high above. She walked around it, avoiding eye contact with the few tourists milling nearby.

Diana stilled, ignoring her surroundings as she let her mind empty again. Most of the tourists wandered away, except for one young man opposite her across the mirrored base. He appeared lost in thought and was too well-dressed to be a tourist. His suit was new and fit like a glove.

The stranger looked like a model. That wasn't actually that unusual for Toulouse. Diana refocused and tried a little harder to shut him out when she realized something. She didn't have to expend any effort to ignore his presence…because he wasn't there.

Her heart raced. Adrenaline surged, quickening to anger as reality settled in. The man wasn't there to her Elemental senses because he was masked by a spell similar to the one concealing Catherine's body. But he was visible to her human eyes, as solid as the other people around him. Except there was nothing real about the man she was seeing. The handsome face was a glamour. This was a member of the circle.

Even ghosts, or those echoes of energy people called ghosts, had a signature she could detect. But this man didn't. Averting her gaze, Diana pretended to be lost in thought as she contemplated her own image and the ceiling above.

She was taxing her control, making sure she didn't show any signs of recognition. As a redhead with a temper to match, she had spent quite a long time learning to master her facial expressions, first in foster care and then well into her training. Now, if she chose, her discipline was on par with her supernatural abilities. She no longer betrayed her every emotion with a flush of anger, but it was a near thing this time. Tamping down the swirl of violence inside her, she took a deep, steadying breath.

The young man kept shifting his body weight until she looked up at him. When she made eye contact, he gave her a flirtatious smile and then wandered away to look at the rest of the church. He turned back to glance at her several times.

Great. The pattern holds.

If any predator in a ten-mile radius got a good look at her, then her job was half done. But in this case, she couldn't afford to lure this guy to a dark and eventually *very hot* alleyway. Not until she'd found Katie. Her best shot would be to follow him.

Avoiding further eye contact, she willed him to give up trying to get her attention and go home. It would be a piece of work to blend in now that he'd noticed her, but she had to try. The other option was to make nice with the piece of shit in the hopes he would lead her to Katie.

Hopefully this was faster, with the added bonus that she wouldn't lose her cool and toast the freaky little fucker too soon.

Diana turned her back on the guy to examine the rest of the church, but it was a little empty and bare compared to some of its counterparts in town. After a few temper-releasing deep breaths, she walked past the man that wasn't there without a glance. He waited a minute before following her out, but she'd taken the opportunity his hesitation provided to hide behind a crowd of teenage school kids outside. After a few minutes of looking for her, he gave up and took a left towards Rue Pargaminières.

Diana followed her mark in and out of the shifting crowds as he arrived at the Capitole, the central square in town adjoining city hall. The main plaza was surrounded by city hall on one side and shops, hotels, and restaurants on the other three. In good weather, it was always crowded. Today there was a farmer's market and there were people handing out pamphlets under red tents.

The well-dressed man cut across the square and through the walkway that led through the city hall's courtyard and out the other side. It exited next to the old Donjon, which now served as the town's tourism office instead of a dungeon.

The building was practically vibrating with the residual energy of former residents, enough to catch the attention of her mark. He stared at the building for a long moment, confirming her suspicion that he was a real practitioner. For anyone with a moderate amount of talent, that building would be screaming at them.

The mark made his way back into the heart of Carmes, away from the Capitole down the Rue Alsace Lorraine. Chic shops lined both sides of the street, but he didn't stop at any of the high-end men's stores. He kept on going until he came to a large brick building, something that was probably once a cathedral. Moving inside, Diana followed unobtrusively, that little something extra she used to shield herself from notice working overtime.

A desk and a list of prices and hours made the new purpose of the building clear. It was a museum, Le Musee d'Augustins. She stayed behind the mark, who didn't turn around as he made his way through the galleries and into a central cloister. A columned arcade with a low border surrounded a sunlit inner courtyard garden. One side of the covered walk was lined with gargoyles. He spent the largest amount of time there, loitering in the hot summer sun of the courtyard while the covered walkways around it were in shadow that seemed to deepen the longer he loitered.

What are you up to?

Diana stood behind a glass gallery door that separated the courtyard from an inner gallery. This place housed many historical artifacts as well as some paintings. But the mark didn't seem to be casing the place for a theft. He was sitting in the courtyard, staring aimlessly.

She leaned closer. His lips were moving. He was casting a spell.

A normal bystander wouldn't notice how much deeper the shadows were around the gargoyles, how much substance it seemed to have. They would attribute the hazy darkness to the contrast created by the bright sunlight. But it was different to her eyes, creeping from statue to statue like fog, pulsing as though it had a heartbeat.

"What the hell is he doing?" Alec said from somewhere behind her.

She jumped and turned around. It shouldn't have surprised her that he'd found her again, but she'd been focused on her mark.

"I think he's impressing himself with his new skills. And he's getting ready for something later."

"He's definitely one of the circle?"

"Yeah."

"How are you sure?"

"Because he's not there."

Alec turned to her, wrinkling his brow and then turned back to the man himself. The confusion fell away as recognition dawned. "You're right. I should be able to hear his heartbeat or breathing from here. There's nothing."

"It's the best masking spell I've ever seen on a practitioner. It doesn't just cloak their magic, their very presence is undetectable.

They could break into all sorts of places with that. All they have to do is add a block to being recorded on security cameras and avoid any guards," she continued, moving away from the glass doors as she saw the mark shift toward them.

With studied casualness, she wandered to a display at the far end of the room, Alec at her heels. He leaned in closer to her ear. "Why not go completely invisible?"

Diana narrowed her eyes and considered. "Might be too costly in terms of spell power. Plus then he'd have to keep dodging everyone in the street, and they're crowded these days."

She glanced over their shoulder. "Don't engage and don't let him know you looked outside in time to see the fog," she added in a low voice.

The mark entered the room. His eyes lit up when he saw her, but they dimmed almost immediately when the tall and well-built vampire moved next to her.

Alec's presence was imposing. He almost crackled with a power, and he wasn't bothering to try and hide it. If anything, he was doing his best to throw his weight around.

In fact, he might be trying to look taller.

The nothing man had enough talent to perceive Alec's true nature, despite the fact the sun was still high in the sky. He also didn't miss the possessive hand Alec put on her waist. His eyes still passed covetously over Diana, but a little dismissively now, probably guessing she was a blood concubine—one that belonged to a powerful enough vampire to put her out of his reach. He wandered about the room a bit longer, making sure they didn't get near the courtyard door while his spell was active. Eventually, with more than one envious glance at Diana, he left.

She started to follow him when Alec stopped her with a restraining hand.

"Let my men follow him. You'll not be able to blend in. He's already taken too much notice of you. Not that I blame him," he said, looking her up and down.

Diana's scowl was fierce. "He won't see me," she hissed, watching her mark disappear around the corner.

"Or he will, and he'll wonder what is going on. If he suspects what you are, he'll bolt. It's bad enough that he saw you with me. We're lucky that he didn't seem to recognize me."

"Fine," she said through gritted teeth. "But don't let them lose him," she ordered. "He'll be hell to track down again."

Alec got on the phone to his men, who'd been waiting outside. He described the mark's clothing and finished with, "Let Dmitri take the lead. He'll be able to spot him by what's not there, no breath, heartbeat, or smell. Keep him in visual at all times but make sure he doesn't catch on to you." He hung up and turned to Diana.

"Is Dmitri a local vamp?" she asked, wiping her hands on her shirt.

"A Were actually. Keeps a place here. He's Russian born and for hire to the right people," he said.

One red eyebrow twitched. "And he's willing to work for you?"

"He's more friend than employee, though I will be compensating him for his time."

This time, Diana's eyebrow went up all the way. Weres were notoriously anti-vamp and vice versa. Communications between the two groups only occurred at the highest levels—through ruling councils. They did not work together unless major apocalyptic events were going down.

And individuals from the two races were not friends. *Ever.*

"A Daywalker who's friends with Weres. . ." Diana said. "You sure as hell don't want to be like all the other good little children of the night."

Alec ducked his head, turning away to hide a wry smile. "I don't dislike Weres. There are a few in academia with whom I've corresponded with over work."

"I guess a liberal education breaks down more barriers than anyone realizes. But this Dmitri doesn't sound like a scholar."

"He's not one. He has the mind for it, but not the patience. His is a colorful story. Maybe he'll tell it to you one day," he said, stopping short.

They had moved back across the room to the glass doors. The pulsing fog had dissipated, but not in the way Diana had expected.

"It's gone," Alec frowned.

"No, it isn't," she replied, taking his hand and allowing him to *see*.

Below them, the vapor had seeped into the ground, becoming a network of threaded goo. Passersby did not notice anything as they walked over it. Diana and Alec moved outside to take a closer look.

"I can see it," he whispered, amazed.

"Unless I let go of your hand," she said in a flat tone—though she was secretly pleased by his delight.

"This is incredible. Do your sisters have this ability to share what they see too?"

Only with very specific people.

"Sometimes," she answered noncommittally.

He squatted to get a better look, holding tight to her hand. "It looks like a slime mold. A huge one."

"A what?" Diana asked.

"It's a microorganism that can grow quite large. Like a fungus. They often look like this, but smaller. Some even move and pulse like that," he continued, pointing to a nearby section which appeared to be throbbing as it crawled deeper into the soil.

"Eww."

Slime and mold were not her department. That was Gia's thing. The Earth Elemental would have known all about slime molds. She loved all sorts of gross earth-related crawly things from rhizobia to centipedes.

"Don't touch it," Diana told Alec as he shifted closer to one of the edges creeping toward them in the courtyard.

"Don't you want to take a sample?" he asked.

She wrinkled her nose at his irrepressible curiosity. "I'm not a scientist. And I don't want that shit to know we noticed it. It may have a memory, so don't touch. It looks like a distorted lattice charm," she said, edging them both away from it.

"If it's a lattice charm, why does it look like this?" he asked.

A normal lattice charm was a protection spell practitioners cast over an area to watch who came and went without the limitation posed by a physical ward. When done properly, it could be quite sophisticated. Lattice spells required great talent and were frequently used to spy. More than one shady government contracted with practitioners skilled in latticework to spy on their enemies. But this one was different, more advanced and yet crude at the same time.

"A real lattice spell wouldn't look like this. It's been modified," she said.

"It's working itself into the ground," he noted.

"Yeah. It'll be gone from view soon. It probably doubles as a *paratus* charm," she said.

He looked up at her. "What is that?"

"Some major magic requires a foundation—especially if it's not a place of power. "

She scanned around the gargoyle-lined courtyard. "They're planning something here. Something big. The museum isn't far from a small ley line, and its artifacts make it an attractive place to cast spells. But it's not a true place of strength. It only looks like one. They're enhancing the location for a larger spell to be cast here later. That's probably why he was checking out the church earlier, too. I found him at Les Jacobins. He was probably finalizing a location. And this one would have more Gothic appeal to a new practitioner." She gestured to the gargoyles.

"How many parts can a spell have?" he asked.

"Infinite, if you were inclined to waste all of your time on it," she said.

"Hmm," he murmured as he returned his gaze to the swiftly disappearing network.

Diana tugged on his collar. "People are starting to stare," she whispered.

"Oh, of course," he said, rising slowly and brushing off his pants. "I clearly have more research to do. I don't know enough about this type of spell."

She adjusted his shirt collar back into place. "I'd be pretty surprised if you did," she said, murmuring quietly as tourists passed them. "Those types of multi-part spells are the most closely guarded magic. They're complicated for a reason. I don't know what they plan on doing, but it's big. Only the most senior members of the seven families should even know about them, let alone be able to work them. Someone in this group has learned enough to innovate, but without out all the restrictions being raised in the family would impose."

"And you think a family member was helping them in some way?" Alec asked perceptively.

She cocked her head to the side. "It makes sense. They have too much knowledge and not enough at the same time. Someone, and not necessarily a member of the *same* family, is feeding him or her information. Enough to do some serious damage, but without the training to know the rules or the finesse to pull some of these off the normal way." She gestured to the distorted threads at their feet.

Alec's phone rang, and he whipped it out quickly for an update "My men have followed our suspect to an apartment building nearby. Looks expensive, and there are wards all over it."

"Did they find Katie?" she asked hopefully.

"There's no sign of her yet. They're still watching. What do you want to do?"

Diana paced. "I want to watch him, but I get the feeling this is where we need to be. The energy here is darkening. It's only a matter of time before the circle comes back to finish what they started. Just make sure your men call out right away if they find a little girl."

Alec nodded and went off to relay those instructions while Diana set up her own spells, taking the time to make sure they were undetectable to anyone but her own kind, at least under normal circumstances.

She could only hope the circle wasn't as skilled at detecting spells as they were in casting them. The witches would be paying close attention when they returned, so she left intact the spell the mark had cast. No doubt they would set more when the entire circle arrived.

By the time Diana was done, the museum was empty and it was almost closing time. They vacated with the last stragglers and settled into an old fashioned stakeout. Alec had a van waiting around a corner and a shifting supply of men watching the different entrances to the building.

It was only their constant updates that kept Diana in her seat, eating a cold crepe.

"This is not the way I do things," she muttered between bites.

Alec threw her a commiserating glance. "I know you're used to a little more action, but you know why you can't do things the usual way."

"Yeah, I know. I just. . .hate this. I hate it a lot," she said, shifting her booted feet up to the dash.

"I'm right there with you," he said, voice grim as he checked for texts from his men.

In between, he took surreptitious glances at the long length of her legs, which were stretched out next to him.

Diana swallowed her mounting sense of frustration and began to prepare. She lit a small flame and held the fire in her hands, trusting the tint in the windows to keep it hidden.

She sent another message into the aether, telling the others what was happening and where. Then she let the flame go out.

32

It was after two in the morning. A prolonged shower and thunderstorm had emptied the streets. Diana usually loved the smell after rain, but this time she was insensible to anything but the cold center of anger in her core.

The museum—a former Gothic convent—took up an entire city block along the usually busy Rue de Metz. The original compound around it had probably been much larger, but the encroaching city had cut it down to its central buildings. Apartments and shops had sprung up on all sides, making the museum an anachronism among its newer, less stately neighbors.

Alec and Diana waited a few blocks down the street next to the van. They were parked next to the river, next to the Pont Neuf bridge while they waited for the circle to appear. Alec's men had staked out all the entrances and were updating him every few minutes.

Diana chafed at the wait. She'd never had to work with a team before. The few occasions she'd pulled a job with one of the other girls, they had done little beyond support, both technical and logistical. None of them had ever needed any real backup. When push came to shove, each Elemental had little need for additional muscle.

Alec's phone rang. "They're in," he said. "We needn't have bothered staking out all the entrances. They walked in through the front door. Let's get ready."

She nodded as a tall handsome man sidled up to them. His tell-tale heat signature identified him as a Were. Next to Alec's coolness, he was practically a walking furnace.

With the build of an Olympic swimmer, he was as tall as Alec but broader in the chest with defined muscular arms. His light brown hair was streaked with gold, a sunny contrast to Alec's darkness. Like most Werewolves, his chest tapered a little dramatically to a narrow waist over legs that were also corded with muscle. He was still leaner than a lot of gym rats she had seen, but the power of a Were's muscles was in their density.

Clapping Alec on the back, he exchanged a muted greeting with his old friend. Then his eyes lit on her and his hard stoic face changed. His eyes heated, and he gave her a toothy grin.

"Mmm, hello gorgeous," he growled as he stepped closer. "You must be Diana. I'm Dmitri." He paused to give her a sweeping bow before straightening in a way that emphasized the muscled expanse of his upper body. "When we're done here, why don't we go to this charming little after hours place—"

Alec moved between them. "Don't even think about it."

Diana rolled her eyes and walked away toward the museum without answering, leaving the two no choice but to trail behind her.

The Were lowered his voice conspiratorially, but Diana could still hear him thanks to her enhanced hearing.

"She's not yours yet," Dmitri was saying. "I can tell. Your scent is on her, but it's not strong enough for a mated pair."

"Stop smelling her, you dick." Alec huffed, and Dmitri chuckled a little too heartily.

"The Professor has a crush. And not just any crush. A crush on an Elemental. A *Fire* Elemental, judging from her scent. You are either the luckiest sod alive or the stupidest," Dmitri whispered. "Better make sure she really likes you before you start anything. You are extremely flammable, my friend."

Diana spun around. "You can smell what kind of Elemental I am?"

she asked from what would have been well out of earshot for a normal human.

"And she has super hearing. . .I am in love," Dmitri murmured. He raised his voice. "And yes, I can smell your talent. It's like a wood fire in winter, love. Absolutely delicious," he said, inhaling deeply as they caught up to her.

Diana ignored his flirting with a shake of her head. "Did your men spot a child in the group?"

"None walked in with them, but they were carrying several large parcels. . .one could've been a sleeping child," Dmitri said, instantly serious.

Or a dead one, Diana thought, refusing to voice the possibility aloud.

"She's alive. Right now she has to be for any of their rituals to work," Alec said quietly, doing his damned mind-reading trick again.

Dmitri nodded, puffing up in anticipation.

Two heroes, she thought, almost sentimentally. It had taken longer to see that selfless quality in Alec that was so readily apparent in his Were friend, but that was only due to her own stubborn prejudice. She knew that now.

"Yeah, of course" she finally lied in a reassuring tone, though in her mind, she could think of a few spells that would work regardless.

But she wasn't about to tell that to the two hopeful men. She could break their hearts later. Or never, if all went well.

A minute later, they reached the museum. There was a little playground and a sculpture garden in between the main entrance and a long wing that jutted out onto the street. Diana led them to one of the sculptures underneath some trees.

The small group of commandos Alec had organized had been instructed to wait for her signal before entering to avoid alerting those inside. A few were stationed in the sewers under the museum, prepared to enter through the basement and up through a grate into one of the galleries nearest the entrance. More men were on the Rue Alsace-Lorraine, the large street full of shops that ran parallel on the left side of the museum complex. At least one barred door was on that side, waiting to be broken into once they were given an all clear. More men were ahead on Rue de Metz, prepared to scale the shortest wall of the complex.

"We go in only when I say. Are your men ready?" she asked in an undertone.

"Yes," Alec answered in a harsh tone.

His normally calm and collected demeanor was shifting. He drew himself up taller, and his expression was ice cold.

"Remember. Your men are here to make sure the circle doesn't escape, not to engage. Without warded armor, they're too vulnerable. And make sure they stay out of my way," she said, taking off her leather jacket as she moved to the entrance.

Diana opened the front door silently, but stayed on the threshold, examining the new spells the circle had cast.

Focusing her energy, she concentrated on the network of threads beyond the door, disabling them with a quick incantation. Pressed for time, she didn't undo them outright. Instead, she placed a stronger charm over the room, effectively smothering whatever was underneath, closing the door when she was done.

"Aren't we going in?" Dmitri whispered.

"Not this way, but that should clear the path for your men. Follow me."

Walking silently, she headed around the right side of the building along the Rue des Arts.

"Oh, this is. . .convenient," Alec said, examining the brickwork on the right side of the building complex.

In three different places, a protrusion of bricks formed a ladder-like trail straight up the side of the building. The farthest one ran along the tower that overlooked the entire complex. Several walls must have been removed during the city's evolution to make room for the street on the right side.

She headed for the last one, testing for spells of contact first, but the circle had chosen not to ward the whole building. If they had, any drunk coming to pee or puke at the wall would have set them off.

Diana quickly scaled the bricks. Some of them crunched slightly under her fingers due to age. At the top, she stretched her leg, and in one fluid motion, crossed to the right, turning the corner of the rectangular tower and shifting onto the terracotta tiled roof of the building above the courtyard. Not a sound was made when Alec joined her.

Silent as the grave, she smirked to herself, then frowned when a crack sounded behind them. Breathing audibly, the heavier werewolf climbed up beside them. Diana turned to give him a dirty look, and he shot one back that clearly apologized.

"Don't move," she mouthed at him with a scowl before turning away.

She crept closer to the inner courtyard, carefully staying in the shadow of the tower.

The scene in the inner courtyard was like something out of a movie, one about black magic and death. Four robed figures were setting up a ritual altar lit by torchlight. In front of it, they'd drawn a sacred circle with what could only be blood. She hoped it was animal blood, but at this distance, couldn't be sure.

The only thing missing was the bleating goat tied to a stake, ready to be sacrificed. Spurred by the thought, Diana scanned for other heat signatures. Out of sight, in a room across the courtyard, there was another person.

A small one.

Still alive. Diana breathed a sigh of relief.

"She's there," she whispered to the two men.

"Where? I can't smell a blasted thing beyond that crap those gits are spreading around," Dmitri whispered.

"In the room behind them. Let's go," she said, raising her hand to signal the waiting men before jumping.

Diana landed in the courtyard in front of the circle with the softest of thuds. None of the four robed figures reacted right away, but the louder twin cracks behind her were harder to ignore. One by one, the circle members noticed they weren't alone. Diana faced them, flanked by the larger men.

"None of them have heartbeats," Alec said, speaking first as he studied the tableau of frozen witches in front of them.

"You!" A hooded figure pointed to Alec. "I knew it was a mistake! I knew you saw something!"

The nothing man threw back his hood, his handsome face twisted in anger. For a moment, it flickered as his rage weakened the glamour, revealing the falseness of the face he was wearing.

The other three figures had taken down their hoods as well. There were two woman, a brunette and a blonde, and a tall black-haired man in addition to the nothing man. All three looked like they fell off magazine covers, but one wasn't using a glamour charm.

No Brenda, Diana realized as she quickly scanned the others. Even with the glamour charm, she would have known her by her heat signature. And all of these people were true talents, unlike the humans they used to cover their tracks. Two of the others were also staring at Alec. But one wasn't.

One was looking directly at her.

"You," Diana said, pointing at the blonde woman with delicate features and wide green eyes that fell shy of true beauty. "You're the leader."

"No, she's not!" The nothing man shouted. "I am!" He moved in front of the slim blonde, shielding her from view.

She didn't buy that for a second. It didn't feel right.

"Is that really what you think?" she asked, shifting slightly to see the blonde again, who hadn't moved. "Did she tell you that? Did she tell you she *needed* you? Did she tell you were special. . .*necessary*?" A slight mocking colored her tone now.

"Shut up," he said, sneering. "You're just a blood whore. Does he tell you you're *special* to him?"

"He doesn't have to," Diana said honestly. "But you're not in charge here. Why don't you let your leader speak?"

Nearly apoplectic with rage, the nothing man's glamour fell away completely. In real life, he was a slightly overweight twenty-some-thing with greasy brown hair and the pallor of a gamer.

"I am in charge here!" he shouted again, spittle flying.

Inflexible, she shook her head. "No, you're not. And do you know how I can tell?" she asked, never taking her eyes off the woman behind him. "I know because of all of you, she's the only one who knows who the real threat here is. So why don't you back off so the grownups can speak?"

Without warning, the blonde woman hurled a cursed spell ball at Diana. Judging from how closely it passed the nothing man's head, it was clear she didn't care if she hit him or not.

Worried the curse might hit Alec, Diana didn't dodge it. Instead, she deflected it with a blast of heated air, causing it to crash harmlessly in front of her.

Truly pissed now, she smiled coldly at the surprise and shock of the circle members. It was harder to see on the blonde's face than on the others, but it was there. And Diana's actions had finally moved her to speak.

"What are you?" the blonde asked, suspicion and wariness on her almost-pretty face.

The enemy's features were familiar. She had a narrow patrician nose and eyes set a little too close together. Her high sculpted cheekbones and pale skin were set against brows darker than her hair made for a combination Diana had seen before.

"You know you look like him," she said, stalling for time as she worked silently to disable the spell traps set in the courtyard.

"Who?" the woman spat.

"Your father, of course. You're a Burgess remnant. . .Hillard's bastard to be precise. He's the only one stupid enough not to take an illegitimate child in hand."

And his brother and sister were either too decent or too boring to have affairs.

The other three members of the circle stared at them. The other woman, an attractive brunette with an ugly expression, hissed. "Ignore her, Sage. Just kill them and let's finish this."

Diana ignored the interruption. "If you had been born legitimate to the Burgess clan, or had your father seen fit to inform the old man —your grandfather's name is Gerald, by the way—that he'd had a child out of wedlock, you would know *what* I am. And you would know that there are consequences to those who fuel their magic with death. That's when you get to meet someone like me, Sage."

The nothing man stepped in front of Sage. Pointing to Alec, he said, "That is her master. We kill him, and they're finished."

Sage flashed him a look of contempt. "Shut up, Chase. That *thing* has no master."

Diana smiled. "Actually, I do. But my master doesn't walk on two legs. Doesn't walk anywhere, actually. Not in this neighborhood anyway," she said, gesturing around her.

"Are you saying you answer to *God*?" Sage laughed, a true witch's cackle.

"Never seen one of those, although there are number of winged things around that call themselves angels," she said, engaging and distracting the circle while she put her right hand behind her back, signaling to the mercs that all the spell traps were down.

Men poured into the courtyard, and the circle members started running. The brunette screamed as a soldier cut her off.

"The wards are down!" the nothing man yelled as all four regrouped and took defensive positions. Sage threw down her robe as the other three started throwing spell bombs and curses.

Alec waved his men back behind the stone wall of the arcade. "Behind the wall and the columns. Don't let them leave!" he shouted as he whipped in front of one of his men at vampiric speed. Snatching a glass vial out of the air, he hurled it back at the witch who had thrown it.

A scream filled the air as pandemonium broke out. The courtyard filled with smoke.

"Get the girl!" Diana shouted to Dmitri.

She knew Alec wouldn't leave his men while the circle was throwing spells. The Were ran to the right, dodging balls of red and blue light. A spell blasted Diana's front, a black and green sticky mass that swept over her searching for a weak spot to latch onto. She ran a hand down the mass, burning it away.

"Okay, now I'm mad," she hissed, holding out her hands and igniting them into twin torches before heading into the heart of the battle.

33

Alec was in front of his soldiers when he lost Diana in the haze of green-blue light and smoke. A few seconds later, an unnatural fog rolled in around him up to the waist. It washed over the men concealed behind the wall, obscuring his sight and muffling his hearing. A flurry of spells and curses followed the fog. Streaks of light and glowing balls fell like a rain of arrows all around him.

Batting one of the red balls of light away from the head of a crouched soldier, he yelled, "Don't let them hit you!" but his voice didn't carry farther than few feet.

Shit. He had to get to the witches. Springing forward, he plunged into the ever-thickening haze. Behind him, fire devils sprang up, neutralizing spells before they could hit him and his men. A whirling mass of fire danced in front of him, burning away the cloying vapor. Suddenly, the courtyard blazed with light and smoke, as a wall of purple-tinted fire rose between the soldiers and the witches. Nearly blinded by the brightness, he covered his sensitive eyes.

Fuck it. He closed his eyes and focused on listening to his enemy. Over the booms and cracks of falling spells, he trained his supernatural ears on the more subtle sounds of human movement—the pounding hearts and rushing blood.

Ahead of him was a fast moving heartbeat. He opened his eyes, but the smoke still obscured his vision, until a stray fireball caught a man's lank brown hair in the light. Alec raced to catch the nothing man, eager to inflict some damage on the guy who'd visibly lusted after his mate.

Despite the fact they were mid-battle, the nothing man had tried to restore his glamour, but it was on the fritz. It blinked in and out like a strobe light as he shed the robe impeding his movement.

Whipping forward, Alec grabbed the guy by the collar. He pulled him in, but the piece of shit twisted like a snake. His arm drew back, and he somehow managed to hit Alec point blank on the chest with a blast that slammed him against a statue, one of the howling gargoyles lining the passage closest to the entrance.

Winded, Alec brushed his hand across his front. There was a layer of burned skin under a hole in his shirt the size of a softball. Luckily, the damage was superficial and already healing.

Scrambling up, he scanned for his enemy. The little prick had taken the opportunity to run toward the west building—the one where the little girl was.

Dmitri better have her.

Alec grimaced as he got up and ran after the warlock. He shot in front of him and grabbed him before he could escape. Swinging the man like a rag doll, Alec pulled him down toward his sharp teeth. Blood singing in his ears, he bit down as the witch screamed and kicked.

Inside of him, the heart that barely beat began to race as live blood poured like ecstasy through his body. It would only last as long as his food still breathed.

Determined to make that as short as possible, Alec started to drain the witch. But before he could finish him, a massive blast of spell light and fire made him stop and turn.

On the ground lay the male witch with black hair, taken down by bullets from Alec's men. A smoldering pile indicated another was gone by Diana's hand. Directly behind their bodies was a scene straight out of his worst nightmare.

Diana was in the center of the courtyard. The blonde witch, Sage, was in front of her, holding a large knife by the hilt. The blade was buried in Diana's stomach.

A huge roar filled Alec's ears. It was an inarticulate sound of rage and pain that seemed to stop everything around him, and he was making it. Despite the bleeding wound at his neck, the witch he was holding laughed delightedly as he caught sight of Sage and the knife. In one motion, Alec snapped the man's neck and tossed him aside to run toward his mate.

Diana fell to her knees in front of him. Blood seeped through her shirt as she grabbed the blade just below the handle.

The hilt began to glow red-hot. Sage let go with a yelp and turned to Alec as he charged toward her. The witch recoiled as she took in his murderous expression. He fell on her, swinging her up to tear her throat out. A blast from her fists, wedged between them, sent him flying back.

He landed on the other side of the courtyard but in a flash was on his feet, ready to rush her again. Sage tore open a satchel he hadn't noticed around her neck. From it, she drew two spell stones and hurled one at him. It missed and hit one of the columns holding the roof of the walkway behind him, completely leveling it.

Men scrambled out of the way. An unlucky few were buried underneath and more ran to help them.

The distraction gave Sage enough time to spell the second stone before she threw it at him. Alec dodged, but the damn thing changed course with him. He darted in the opposite direction. It followed him with increasing speed. Feinting right, he realized it was too fast as it corrected like a heat seeking missile.

The spelled stone was seconds away from hitting him when the air around him shifted. A young woman coalesced in front of him with a blast that blew down every plant in the courtyard. It happened so fast it looked as if she appeared out of thin air, even to his eyes. The spell stone crashed harmlessly against her, dropping to her small feet with a small burst of air.

"Logan, don't let her go!" Diana gasped from the courtyard's center.

The Air Elemental turned where Diana kneeled with a huge knife sticking out of her stomach. Alec flashed to Diana's side, Logan at his heels.

"Logan! She's getting away!" But Logan ignored her, reaching Diana with a stream of swear words that would make a sailor back away.

"We'll get her later!" Logan yelled.

Alec turned in her direction as he reached out for Diana. All he got was a quick impression of a slim young girl with an Asian cast to her features as she shoved him away.

"*Cut that out.* I'm trying to stop the bleeding." He crowded back over Diana, his hands on her shoulders.

"How?" Logan asked, clenching her fists.

Alec closed his eyes. "I'm calling the blood. Making it slow down." His hands crackled with magical energy, but he couldn't feel the connection that he felt when he fed or when he tried to heal one of his own.

"That won't work on us," Logan said, elbowing him aside again and crouching near Diana.

"Stop it, you two," Diana wheezed. "What is this thing?" she asked, looking down at the blade hilt sticking out of her.

Alec touched the markings on the hilt, which was made of either silver or platinum. The ancient lettering wasn't legible to him. It was roughly made, unlike the other objects strewn about. The offering bowls and embroidered bags and one or two other ceremonial knives —all of it looked like they ordered it from a catalog. But this thing was old and obviously genuine.

"Can you hear it?" Diana asked.

"Yeah," Logan said, leaning closer with a grimace and gritted teeth. "It makes me want to chop off my ears."

"What?" Alec turned to her, confused. "I can't hear anything."

"Shit!" Dmitri said from behind Logan.

The other Elemental gave him one dismissive glance before turning back to Diana.

"Is Katie okay?" Diana asked the Were.

"The little one is fine. Sleeping spell." He growled. "We'll deal with it later."

"What do you hear?" Alec shouted at Logan, his control splintering the longer he went without an explanation.

"Shouting won't help," Logan yelled back. "That thing is buzzing like a fucking tuning fork."

"Like the Olmec piece in the museum?" Alec asked Diana desperately.

"Yes. But *louder*," she said, her breath hitching.

"I'm calling Gia," Logan said, standing and raising her arms.

"No time," Diana muttered.

With an expression full of pain and anger, she began to pull the knife out.

"*No!*" Logan and Alec shouted in unison.

"Don't worry," Diana gritted out as she continued.

Flames surrounded her hands and started to spread over the rest of her body.

"Are you crazy?" Alec said, grabbing at her hands. "Stop or you'll bleed out."

"Self. . .cauterizing. . .you. . .idiot," Diana said as she continued to pull out the blade. "And this. . .better not. . .be making you. . .hungry."

"How can you joke at a time like this?" Alec asked, terrified for Diana.

She was starting to flicker as if she was made of flame herself.

"Hey, it's a valid concern!" Logan said, pushing him aside again.

Despite the fact he outweighed her by a good eighty pounds, Alec slid away through the muddy courtyard as if he was a sack of potatoes.

"No it's not!" he yelled.

He picked himself up and flashed back to Diana's side. But he refrained from laying hands on the tiny Asian sprite this time. Pissing off the Air Elemental would be counterproductive now.

"What's happening?" Logan asked, putting a hand on Diana's shoulder.

It remained remarkably untouched by the fire that was growing higher and hotter with every beat of her heart.

"Not. . .sure but. . .you. . .should get away," Diana said, the flames surrounding her flaring and becoming denser. "Damn it. . .that. . .bitch is mine. . ." She grunted in between gasping breaths as she finished pulling out the blade and handed it to Logan.

The flames were overwhelming now. Instead of retreating, the soldiers still on their feet crept closer in fascination. Logan tossed the blade away as the flames grew hotter and lighter in color.

"I'm calling Gia," she repeated, the panic in her voice clear.

She extended her arms, but before she could call the winds, the fire in front of her blazed white hot and she decided retreat was a better idea.

Alec started forward, making a move to take hold of Diana.

"Get back!" Logan barked, grabbing him by the collar pulling him with her, away from the blaze that was Diana.

"Let go! She's dying," he yelled in a tortured voice as he struggled against her iron grip, but it was no use.

Logan was a third his size, but ten times stronger. She pulled him behind her, her tiny body between him and Diana.

"I don't think so, but if she is, she won't be happy if she takes you with her," the sprite called back to him. "Now stay behind me, cause I think she's going to—"

Alec didn't find out what Logan thought was going to happen because she was suddenly tackled by something large and furry as a blast rocked the courtyard.

"Get off me, you god-damned furry moron!" Logan shouted as she shoved Dmitri off her. He was in an in-between stage of transformation, still mostly human but with furred claws and feet.

"Well, that's fine, thanks," the angry werewolf bit back at her, his deep voice an octave lower than normal. "I save you from one of you going supernova and. . .what the hell is *that*?"

Craning his neck to see behind them, he looked toward Diana. . .or where she had been.

His mate was gone.

In her place was a figure made of fire. And it wasn't human shaped anymore.

"What the hell?" Alec asked in a dazed voice, as he stepped in front of Logan.

"I didn't know you could do that. That is so cool!" Logan said as the firebird looked at itself in realization.

After a beat, it gave a cry and flew away.

"What the hell just happened?" Alec repeated.

"Diana has a phoenix form!" Logan said with an excited clap of her hands. "I can't wait to tell Gia and Serin!"

"Is she all right? Is she going to change back?" Alec asked worriedly.

Diana wasn't a shifter. None of his studies had mentioned a fire god that was both woman and bird. What if she got stuck that way? Panic started to bubble up his throat. Dmitri and the other men stared at Logan with mystified expressions.

"Um, I think so," she said eventually.

Her tone did not inspire any sort of confidence.

"What do you mean, *you think so*?" Alec shouted, forgetting himself and towering over her with every ounce of aggression he could muster.

Bad idea, he thought as a whirlwind lifted him up and slammed him against one of the stone pillars surrounding the courtyard. Picking himself up with as much dignity as he could muster, Alec stared her down. Instead of being intimidated, Logan looked a little contrite.

"I realize you're a little stressed right now, so I'm going to overlook you getting all up in my grill. *This time*," Logan said with an infuriating amount of attitude. "And Diana should be fine. After she kills the witch. . .I think."

"Explain," he said in a voice bristling with testosterone and dominance.

It was a tone he'd been careful not to use around Diana.

"You know. . .you and Diana make a really cute couple. For ruthless uncompromising bringers of death." Logan smirked with a rueful shake of her head. "You're going to be a lot of fun at the office holiday party."

Behind them, Dmitri snickered.

"*Come on!*" Alec's control was hanging from a thread.

"*All right!*" Logan said, throwing her hands up. "Our legends say the first Elemental wasn't a woman but a firebird. A phoenix. All the Elementals were something more. . .primordial in the beginning. Afterward, when the need to walk among humans became necessary, the Elementals were fashioned into women." Logan shrugged. "I think she will change back. Not practical to stay a bird these days. . ."

The way she trailed off made Alec's skin crawl. He scanned the sky and prayed she was right.

34

T he firebird could smell the witch's blood. The corner of its memory that was still the woman could feel confusion and anger but no fear. Those feelings would be dealt with when it was a woman once more. For now, the bird had a task the woman couldn't complete because the witch had injured her with something alien. . .something wrong.

Once their fight had become physical, her human form had grabbed a hunk of the witch's hair, hard enough to tear it from the roots. Now the phoenix *or* the woman could find the black witch anywhere. There was no hole deep or dark enough to hide. However, a hunt wasn't necessary.

The witch hadn't gotten far.

High in the sky, the bird scanned the wet street below. *Rue de Metz*, the woman's memory provided. The street ran all the way to the river. The witch was headed there, probably reasoning that water would protect her. If the bird could laugh, it would have.

The witch had run fast and far in such a short time. She reached the river and climbed onto a cruising tug, the fastest boat the slow river would afford. Speedboats were not the norm here.

The witch had reached for the boat's controls when the bird plummeted through the wooden roof. Talons of fire grabbed the enemy's shoulders. Sage screamed and struggled to reach for her pockets. She knocked at the bird's slighter body despite her burning skin. The bird shifted forms, slipping away to let the woman emerge.

"Sage, you have committed murder for magical gain," Diana hissed. "You've broken the covenant and forfeited your life. In the name of the Mother, I'm here to claim it."

"I didn't know!" The witch gasped.

"You knew enough. You knew it was wrong. And a little boy is dead. . .not to mention the other murders I can see in your aura," she said.

Diana's hand clenched into a fiery fist. With a sickening crunch of bone, she punched through the witch's ribcage and reached in to pull out her heart. For a moment, she stared at it, almost surprised to see it there, cradled in her hand. She blinked and then ignited it, silently watching it burn to ash.

The rest of the body stood in front of her on its own power for a ridiculously long moment before it, too, was consumed in flame. Unnerved, Diana pushed the witch's body away. It fell against the helm of the boat, spreading the fire.

The conflagration would take the entire boat with it, a fitting funeral pyre for a Burgess witch. Black or white.

Diana jumped out of the boat, belatedly checking for an audience. Satisfied to find herself alone, she watched the fire consume the boat until it began to sink. Once it was gone she started to walk back to the museum.

Or maybe the Phoenix wasn't a one-time thing? Can I fly now?

Taking another furtive look around, she reached for the phoenix. With buzz of pleasure, it came when called.

When the bird returned, Alec was pacing a furrow in the muddy courtyard. It landed with a fiery thump that startled the waiting audience. As the flames receded, the bird shifted into the woman once more.

Diana stood there, swaying slightly, her hand fisted tightly. Logan ran up to her, her hands reaching immediately for Diana's torn shirt.

"The stab wound is completely gone. How cool is that!" she exclaimed before noticing Diana's tightly clenched fist. "What's that?"

Diana stared at her fist. She couldn't remember why she was holding it so tightly. Opening it, a fine ash fell to the ground.

"Is that what's left of the witch?" Dmitri asked as Alec walked closer to Diana.

Her vampire didn't look too steady, either. Whiter than any of his kind should be, he reached for her torn shirt as well. Crowding Logan away, he went down on his knees in front of her, his hands on her stomach.

"Um, yeah," Diana said, uncomfortable with Alec's long-fingered hands on her bare skin in front of everyone.

Even if everyone was just Dmitri and Logan.

"It's gone," he whispered.

"Yeah, I'm fine now. See. . ." Diana said, holding up her shirt higher to show off rock-hard abs that were completely unmarked.

She wiped away the ash on her pants as she pulled her torn tank down and tried to dislodge Alec's hands from her hips, but they wouldn't budge.

"Snap out of it. I'm okay," she hissed with a blush.

He hadn't put his hands on her before, not on her bare skin. It felt intensely private, and they had an audience.

Alec blinked and got up. "Apparently, rebirth as the Phoenix means extreme healing. This is good. Good news," he mumbled, relief making him sound drunk and confused.

"Are you sure 'bout that, mate? They're already nearly bloody invincible," Dmitri said flatly.

Both Elementals turned to frown at him.

"Just saying, hope you always get the right guy is all," he mumbled and turned away rather than meet their eyes.

"Trust me, we don't mistake innocents for the guilty. The stain on their soul is glaring even when their actions aren't dead giveaways," Diana said, gathering herself together after the disorientation that came with changing forms for the first time.

"And we don't *always* kill them," Logan finished cheerfully.

"Hmm," Dmitri said and then cocked his head as if he heard something. "The little one's waking."

Prying Alec's hands off her, Diana tugged him to his feet before rushing off. She ran toward the small heat source inside the building. A soldier was holding the sleepy little girl on his lap. The other guards drifted back when she, Logan, and Alec entered.

"Hi sweetie," Diana said, kneeling in front of the little brown haired girl. Katie's delicate features wrinkled and then smoothed in recognition.

"Yeah, you remember me," Diana said as she ran her hands over Katie's hair. "Are you okay? Does your tummy or head hurt?"

Katie glanced shyly at Logan and Alec behind her. She shook her head.

"It's all right," Diana continued, stroking her hair. "These are my friends."

Katie blinked at them and then looked at Diana directly. "Did you find my mommy?"

Diana looked at the two behind her and caught clear signs of conflict on their face.

"Not yet, honey," Logan said, bending slightly and placing her hands on her knees. "We're still looking for her."

Logan shot a look at Alec as he moved behind Katie's field of view. Diana could tell from Alec's expression that there was trouble.

She turned back to the little girl. "We'll be back soon. We're going to go look for her," she said before letting Alec usher them out.

He led them to the room across the courtyard, his expression grim.

The sight that met her eyes was more of a shock than it should have been. On the floor, in a similar pose to her sister, was Brenda. Spelled stones surrounded her and the same symbols and writing were beneath her, under the spilled blood. It was in chalk this time. The circle hadn't taken the time to carve the symbols into her flesh.

Swearing under her breath, Diana kneeled down. One of the stones around Brenda had been kicked away from the circle, breaking the preservation spell that would've kept her body fresh after the moment of her death. A gash across her neck and chest was the source of all the blood, now barely a trickle.

"You stopped the bleeding." Diana turned to Alec in surprise.

He had called the blood. It was the only reason Brenda was still alive. But postponing the moment of her death was cruel. She couldn't understand why Alec had done it.

"I want to try and turn her," he explained from somewhere behind her, "but your friend here won't let me try."

Her eyes widened in shock. "What? You can't turn her!"

"Why not?" he asked, brow creased. "That little girl needs her mother."

Diana looked down at Brenda and shook her head. "I can see it in her aura. She's responsible."

"What if they tricked her?" he protested. "She could be entirely innocent."

Diana met the desperate woman's eyes. There was no way that could be true, but she knelt anyway. "I think you're too far gone to save, no matter what he wants. But you'll tell me the truth anyway, won't you?"

"She can't answer for Christ's sake. Her throat is cut," Alec said exasperatedly.

Diana ignored him. "Did you know what they were planning with your little girl? Did you know she would die?"

The terrified woman moved her head fractionally to the side, but the change in her body temperature contradicted her despite the blood loss. Diana stood and drew Alec away from the body.

"She's lying."

"How can you be certain? She's lost so much blood. You can't know for sure." He sounded angry with her.

Diana sighed. She had hoped he would handle this kind of thing better. If he didn't, there was no way he could find a place in her world.

"I *am* sure. And if you tried to turn her, you would fail. She isn't a candidate," she said, acknowledging what few vampires would realize.

Only those who could bend magic to some degree could be turned.

It helped if the person doing the turning was powerful. Alec was. . .but there had to be some magical aptitude in the recipient to begin with. And seeing Brenda again only confirmed what she already knew.

Neither Brenda nor her sister Catherine had any talent. How they were drawn into the circle's sphere was still a mystery, but in her world, things rarely got tied up in a neat bow.

Guilt radiated from the dying woman, but Alec was determined. "You can't possibly be certain. I'm stronger than those who made me. I can do it. That little girl—"

Diana cut him off. "Deserves a better mother. This one intentionally put her in harm's way, probably more than once."

"But she wanted her back. When you brought her home the first time—you yourself said she wanted her back."

"She did. But only so she could use her again. I don't know what the circle promised her, but it was enough to trade her little girl's life for it."

"I can't believe that," he said finally. "A mother wouldn't."

"You are not nearly cynical enough for a vampire." Diana said in a low voice, glancing to the doorway where the Were was waiting with a resigned expression.

"You can smell her guilt, can't you?" she asked softly.

"Yeah," Dmitri said as Alec turned to him. "It's a nasty business."

Diana couldn't keep arguing. Brenda's time was running out. "Go ahead and try. I'm sorry it won't work. But if it makes you feel better, go ahead. Try."

Logan gave her a commiserating look as she moved past Dmitri back into the courtyard. Diana followed her.

"He could succeed," Logan suggested as they walked to the center of the courtyard.

"No. She's flat. There's no anchor for the magic," Diana said.

"Well, that's probably for the best. I would offer you a ride, but I'm guessing you're going to take Katie home. Is there any other family? The father?"

"Not that I know of. I have another idea."

"Care to let me in on it?" Logan asked.

Diana hesitated. "I...uh...I thought the little boy's father might be able to look after her," she said, running a hand through her hair.

Logan frowned. "Are you sure? You know they're not exactly interchangeable."

Diana's lips firmed, and Logan shrugged. She unzipped her pack and handed her the jacket she kept in there.

"You should put that on if you're going to take Katie. You're still a little bloody. It doesn't show up that much against the black, but she'll eventually notice if you take her home with you."

"Oh, thanks," Diana said, slipping on the jacket. "And I know my plan isn't perfect. But I have a feeling about this. I think she'll be better off."

"I trust your gut. And I think it's safe to assume all of us will be looking in on Katie whenever we can," Logan said. "By the way, I had to give your boyfriend a little shit for getting all vampy on me."

Diana laughed. "I'm sure he didn't mean anything by it."

"I know. He was just a little stressed out for a minute there. Can't really blame the guy, but you know what they say. Start as you mean to go on...and I can't be the pushover Elemental," Logan said, drawing herself up to her full height, all five feet two inches of it.

"Yeah, I get that. Where are you headed?" Diana asked as they walked to the center of the courtyard, recognizing the way Logan was scanning the sky.

"Budapest. Gotta give some fairies a little fear of the devil."

"All right. Go nuts. Do you think you can drop the blade with Gia or Serin?"

Though Gia was their elder, Serin's people were the ones that kept detailed records on anything supernatural. If an Elemental had encountered anything like the knife or the Olmec artifact, they would know.

"Already packed it," Logan said, gesturing to the bundle tied to her back.

"Safe journey. And thanks for coming," Diana said with gratitude.

"Like I would let you have all the fun." Logan gave her a hug before she pulled away and let the wind take her.

From somewhere behind her, Dmitri gave a low whistle. "Is she single?"

Diana turned around. "Yeah. But she doesn't like Weres," she said, taking in Dmitri's lustful expression.

"Does she not like Weres like you don't like vampires?"

Diana decided to ignore him in favor of rejoining Katie and making travel plans.

35

It was late, and Alec hadn't come back to the house he'd rented for them. Katie was asleep. Telling her that they'd found her mother and that she was gone had been difficult.

But Katie's reaction had been telling. She had not expressed surprise or the hysterical grief that Diana had felt when her own mother had died. She had simply nodded, no tears. All she'd wanted to know was what would happen to her now.

"Do you want me to find your dad?" Diana had asked.

"No. He doesn't want to be a daddy," Katie had said, breaking Diana's heart.

"Then I have an idea. I know of an excellent daddy who is missing his boy a lot right now. Your friend, the one who stayed with you at the farmhouse? He can't go home. You know about that, don't you?"

Katie nodded.

"I think it would be a good thing for you to stay with his daddy, Pedro. It might be hard at first. You would have to start at a new school."

"Do you think he'll want me?" Katie whispered.

"I think he will, but if he doesn't, I will find you another home. A good home," Diana promised.

"I can't stay with you?" Katie whispered, her eyes closed.

"I'm sorry, sweetie. What I do is very dangerous. Not as much for me but a lot for the people around me."

"Even Mister Alec?" Katie asked.

"Er. Well, yes, but only a little. Alec is more like me than he is like you. He can take care of himself. He'll be fine."

"Good. I like him," the little girl said sleepily.

"Yeah. He's very likable," Diana muttered. "Don't worry about anything else tonight. Tomorrow we start looking for a new home for you. But no matter where that turns out to be, I'm going to come visit you when I can. So are my friends. You'll like them."

"Are they like you, too? Do they find bad people?" Katie whispered.

"Yes," Diana said.

"That's good then. I want you to find the bad people." Katie sighed and lay down again.

One of Alec's men had had the foresight to buy a few stuffed animals in case they succeeded.

Diana had tucked them in around Katie. The little girl had chosen a stuffed lion to hug tight and sleep with. Thinking back to the lion she'd chosen to scare J straight, Diana approved of her choice.

***

HOURS LATER, Alec still hadn't returned. Diana knew there was next to no chance that he could have successfully turned Brenda, but he had been gone a long while. A niggling doubt entered her mind.

Vampires as strong as Alec were rare. Though the belief that vampires grew in strength as they aged was largely true, there were some that were simply born stronger than others. He was one of those rare breed. He was also more adept at manipulating magic than any other living vampire. If he hadn't been, then he wouldn't have been able to make the Daywalker ritual work.

A door closed somewhere downstairs, and Diana felt Alec's presence moving below. She debated going to find him, uncertain if he would come to her or not. Deciding it didn't matter, she went downstairs.

He was in the formal parlor, pouring himself a drink from a bar service cart. Reading the failure in his posture, she was sorry for him.

"You know you would have been responsible for her for the rest of her afterlife. It's better this way."

He looked at her beyond his glass and swallowed the entire drink down in a gulp.

"That's no way to savor a thirty-year-old Armagnac," Diana chided gently.

"It's fifty years old," he informed her, pouring another for himself and one for her.

"I'm not a fan," she said but took the glass anyway.

The drink burned on the way down, and she screwed up her face in a scowl.

He smiled at her, and the atmosphere in the room lightened considerably. "You should hold the glass in your hands and warm it. It enhances the flavor. Just try not to heat it so much that you boil the alcohol off."

"You didn't do that," she pointed out, directing a mild heat wave to the glass.

"It's a little hard for me to warm it above room temperature," he noted wryly.

Diana gave him a tiny smile. "It was for the best, you know."

"Yeah. I know."

"If you didn't succeed in turning her, why were you gone so long?"

Alec sat heavily in the padded leather armchair and stared at his glass. "I was making arrangements for the body. And for the repair of the museum. It should be set to rights before the end of the week. I wanted to fix it before the employees came back to work on Monday, but things happen slowly in France. After that, I started trying to track down the little girl's father. He's in jail, however, and there were no other close living relatives, so I contacted child services in Boston instead."

"You did *what?*" Diana froze in anger and shock.

He looked at her strangely. "Did you have something else in mind? You can't care for her. And there isn't a good alternative among my relations."

When she didn't respond, he continued, "It's the best thing for her. They may even find someone she knows to take her in. If not, they are prepared. The system is there for such cases."

Diana's blood boiled.

She closed her eyes and set the glass on an end table. "I'm taking Katie back to Boston. But I'm not turning her over to social services. I'm taking her to Pedro. He will take good care of her."

Alec stood, jaw clenched. "You can't do that. Pedro is not an appropriate choice."

"As opposed to turning her over to the system? Are you crazy?" Diana said, making an effort to keep her voice down despite the blood pounding in her head.

"Pedro is not well. Not yet. Even if he has recovered enough, it's still not a good idea. You can't replace one child with another. That's not how human hearts work."

"Says the vampire," Diana ground out. "I know they aren't interchangeable. But they've both suffered major losses. They can help each other heal. It will work. And if it doesn't, I'll find Katie something else. But I'm not putting her in the system!"

"You act like it's a fate worse than dea—," Alec cut himself off abruptly. "*Oh.* I'm such an idiot. You were in the system. After your mother died."

It wasn't even a question.

The familiar rage and panic rushed, unbidden, up her chest, giving it a good squeeze. Diana turned away and took a few deep breaths before she could speak.

"We're leaving in the morning. Are you going to have the jet ready, or should I call the airlines now?"

"Diana," his voice was soft and gentle, "What happened?"

"Are we taking the jet or not?" Her voice was strained.

She felt his hands on her shoulders, but she shrugged them off and stalked out.

After charging up to her room, she locked the door and went to the fireplace. Calling the fire, she built it high and hot. She sat in front of it for a long time before going to bed.

36

Alec's attempts to engage Diana in conversation the next morning failed spectacularly. She avoided him by fussing over Katie whenever he got too close.

The little girl was adorable and very shy. And she was clearly worried about what was going to happen to her.

Katie asked a few questions about Pedro, and Alec shot Diana a disapproving look before he could stop himself, ratcheting up the tension between them. It got a hundred times worse when she overheard him on the phone, instructing his people to look into other options in vague terms the little one wouldn't understand.

He genuinely didn't know what Diana was thinking, telling Katie that Pedro would take care of her. He'd called his man in Boston and was gratified to hear that Pedro was doing better. But he was still far from well.

Alec kept his mouth shut about it, not wanting to worry the child, despite the fact he was honestly itching for a fight with Diana.

He didn't want to jeopardize his budding relationship with her, but he didn't want to back down on this either. He wasn't Diana's equal in magic or even strength, but he had to be her equal in this. She had to value his opinion and listen to his concerns—even when she didn't agree with him. Otherwise, he was going to be constantly compromising himself and everything he believed in.

Not that he foresaw a lot of conflict. He knew that, for the most part, they would agree on how to get on. And he did see a future for them, even if she wasn't ready to admit it.

Unfortunately, he'd stepped on a land mine he hadn't even known was there. Something awful must have happened to her in foster care. He shuddered when he thought of all the terrible things that could happen to vulnerable little girls.

I am an asshole, he thought suddenly. He hadn't given a second thought to calling child services. *Let humans take care of their own.* It was one of the few rules vampires actually followed. It was relatively easy for them since most didn't care about anyone but themselves.

The situation did not improve in the afternoon when they boarded the jet and flew home. For a Fire Elemental, Diana did a damn good deep freeze.

There were no signs of thawing by the time they landed. She only gave one-word answers to his questions unless they were addressed to Katie as well. Once he'd acknowledged that he was still looking for different housing options for Katie that did not include foster care, it got marginally better. But it wasn't enough to get back to the rapport he'd struggled to achieve with her.

They'd landed in Boston before she spoke a full sentence to him. "I'm going to take Katie with me tonight. I will check things out with Pedro tomorrow."

"Please don't take her until I've seen him," he pleaded. "I need to tell him about his son first. I promised him things that are ash now."

"I guess I should say I'm sorry you don't have a head to deliver, but that would be weird. And I don't think it would have helped him."

He leaned in to whisper. "I disagree, but it can't be helped. There wasn't a better way. More to the point, this thing you propose. . .I don't think it will help him. Or her. Pedro is better, but not well yet. He may not be able to handle the care of another person. I'm going to see him tonight."

He wanted to say more, but he didn't want to get into an all-out battle with Katie watching them with those big brown eyes.

Diana nodded curtly and took the little girl to the waiting car. Passing a hand over his eyes, Alec got in with them.

"I think we should stay in a hotel tonight. The safe house is not a good place for a little girl to wake up in," Diana said quietly after settling Katie inside.

Reflecting on the number of weapons he'd seen there, he quickly agreed and dropped them off at a hotel he owned.

Of course, he hadn't volunteered that last bit of information. Or the fact that that they would be closely monitored in case Diana decided to disappear after she settled Katie somewhere.

That last was a fear he didn't want to dwell on. Diana had opened up to him a little, but there was a lot more to her current behavior. He'd thought her reticence and distance was a result of her mother's death but clearly that wasn't the complete story. And there was a real possibility that she would rather write him off than share her history with him.

Badgering her into confiding in him was not going to work. Even though he was sure he could find her again, he didn't want to spend years chasing her around the world trying to make her accept him in her life. He'd waited so long for someone like her, even if he hadn't known exactly what he'd been looking for. But now that he'd found her, he didn't want to wait a second longer to hold her, to make love to her.

It was burning him up inside. Hiding that level of arousal from her had been a challenge, even for a vampire in complete control of his blood flow.

Alec smiled wryly to himself. He hadn't even desired the company of a woman for decades. Maybe even the last century. He'd thought he was past those basic desires. And now he could barely contain himself. The only thing that sobered him and tamped down his hunger was the task ahead of him: telling Pedro about his son.

He'd given bad news like it before, but it never got any easier.

As for Diana, as much as it went against his every possessive instinct, he would give her time. And if she didn't come to him. . .then he would try a more aggressive tactic.

37

The next day, Diana took Katie to meet Pedro. She left the little girl outside with one of Alec's men while she went to speak with him.

Alec hadn't called her, so she could only assume that either Pedro was better or he wanted her to see for herself how impossible her idea was.

The little man had aged considerably, and he was still a little vacant. He puttered around the apartment cleaning what was already clean and straightening out things that did not need straightening. Diana had serious misgivings, but she couldn't shake the idea that this was the right move. And when all was said and done, she was a creature of instinct.

"Pedro, I want you to know how sorry I am about your son," she said finally.

He looked at her directly then. "I understand that it was you, not the vampire, that killed those responsible."

She was surprised he had been told of Alec's true nature. Only the highest level servants were privy to that sensitive information. She hadn't known he was that high in their servant hierarchy.

"He helped."

A lot.

Pedro nodded.

"He must trust you a lot to tell you what he is," she said softly.

He sat. "It was not him that said what he was," he said, waving that away. "It was the leader, the father. Long ago. Not a bad man. Perhaps not a good one, but not a bad one either." Pedro paused. "I have served the family since I was a boy. When my father died."

"I see," Diana said. "And would your son have served after you?"

If he said yes, there was no way she could leave Katie here.

"No. It was understood. Only my lifetime is expected. There is a choice these days as long as you don't know the secret of what they are. And they keep their word in these matters. It is part of their code."

Diana hesitated, but the sense that this was where Katie belonged remained.

"Okay, then. I know this isn't a good time to ask, but I need a favor."

DIANA LEFT the apartment an hour later convinced things would work out for Katie. Pedro had immediately been taken with the little girl who had known his son. He had made Katie lunch and showed her around the apartment.

Watching her play with his son's toys had made him tear up, and Diana had asked him if he had changed his mind. But he said no. Katie could stay.

Before she had left, Diana had taken Pedro aside and put several unpolished gemstones in his hand. The old man hadn't recognized them for what they were until she told him.

"No, please. I have a good income. I don't need this," he'd said.

"But she might someday. Put them somewhere safe. She might want to go to an expensive university," she'd said, and Pedro had stopped pressing her to take them back.

Diana didn't return to the hotel suite Alec had gotten them. Instead, she made her way to the new safe house.

Gia had decided to move it once Alec had learned its whereabouts. She should have told her not to bother. Alec would find the next one so long as she was there. But Diana hadn't been able to acknowledge to her sisters what Alec was. . .not yet.

How could she when she couldn't even tell him? Or at least confirm what he already seemed to know. Admitting it would require the telling of secrets she'd never spoken aloud, secrets only Gia knew.

Gia kept all of their secrets.

Diana decided to avoid dealing with Alec for the time being. She did have other business in Boston, and it had gone unattended for too long.

When she got to the new safe house, she started going over the building plans for the Denon Corporation once again.

38

I t had been two full days since Alec had seen Diana. He'd stayed busy checking on his business interests and reading reports from his men. One was on the Denon Corporation and several detailed Pedro's progress.

Pedro seemed much better since Katie's arrival. He had even enrolled her in school.

It grated slightly that Diana had been right. Very few people had ever dared to contradict or disagree with him. And even though he had always known Diana was special, he had still expected to be right and her to be wrong.

Well, in this case, he couldn't argue with the symmetry of Diana's plan. Not now that it had worked anyway. Feeling magnanimous in defeat, he decided to set up a trust for Katie's care. He would make sure Pedro had whatever he needed to keep her happy and safe.

Alec had also reluctantly made contact with his parents as well, stopping in briefly to inform them that the issue with the Elemental had been resolved. He also strongly suggested that his mother take greater care in her future dealings with the Otherkind.

They hadn't said much, restricting their complaints to the fact he was now staying at his penthouse at the waterfront instead of the coven house.

By late afternoon on the second day, he was ready to reach out to her. He knew she had another investigation in Boston on the Denon Corporation, and he was sure he could be of use. It was an exciting prospect. The leisurely part of his life, that of travel and academic study, would be too quiet now that he'd met Diana.

Alec was confident he could help her in all of her cases. With his business contacts and corporate ties, he could open doors for her almost anywhere. She would never have to pretend to be a secretary ever again. And when cases involved the supernatural, he thought he'd proven the advantages of having someone there for help and support.

Determined not to wait any longer, Alec got ready to go meet Diana. He turned on the news and business channels in his private office as he put on his tie and cufflinks. He'd opted for more formal business attire in case he had to go to Denon headquarters with Diana later today. But when local news bulletin came on, he realized he was overdressed.

"Shocking revelations regarding a huge environmental disaster that were covered up by the board of the Denon Corporation were revealed today as private internal communiqués were anonymously sent to hundreds of news outlets," said a male reporter standing outside of the now-familiar office building.

Alec sat down with a grunt. "Well, there goes the easy way," he muttered to himself, sitting to watch the news coverage.

He had some idea of what was coming due to his preliminary investigation into the company's dealings, but he hadn't yet discovered what Diana had just made public.

The company had knowingly and systematically been poisoning entire villages with heavy metal waste across the African continent as they mined for precious metals and raw materials for the computer industry.

Most of the major computing companies were in some way tied to the scandal as customers of Denon's various subsidiaries. Their eco-conscious customers were already expressing their outrage on social media. Boycotts were being organized. After strong advisories that children should not watch the broadcast, graphic pictures of villagers who had died from poisoning flashed across the screen.

Despite the sadness of the news, the pang of concern he felt was about Diana. She had moved faster than he'd expected. Now she could leave town whenever she wanted. He wanted to believe she would get in touch with him on her own, but he couldn't take the chance. Worried, he called Daniel first to check on his mate's current whereabouts.

"Do you know where she is?" he asked as soon as he'd reached his man.

"I saw the news. Was about to call you. 'Fraid she gave us the slip. Guess she's going to be moving on soon if she hasn't skipped already. I don't know where she is at this moment, but it looks like her people moved their local base. I've got it narrowed down to two blocks near Chinatown. Should I get more men out here?" Daniel's naturally hoarse voice was a little out of breath, as if he was walking the area on foot instead of by car.

"No, I'll go down myself," Alec said.

He'd been exceptionally lucky at tracking Diana down when he tried. Hopefully, his luck would hold.

Unless she's left town.

Hurrying now, he grabbed his suit jacket and threw it on as he went to the front door.

He stopped short at the sight that greeted him on the other side. Ten men in dark suits with black embroidered insignias over where their hearts no longer beat.

Shit. The Council.

39

Diana was feeling fairly accomplished. She'd managed to send off hundreds of secure emails without frying the safe house computer.

The charms Gia had sent to the apartment had done their job and ensured the emails were untraceable.

Gia's talent was extensive, but she hadn't found a way to safeguard electronics against Diana and Serin's inherent destructive ability. Diana had worked in short speedy bursts, interspersed with frequent long breaks to make sure her talent wouldn't affect the computer too badly.

Consequently, the laptop in their safe house would live to fight another day. In the meantime, she might look into getting one of those rugged laptops used in combat like the phone Alec had given her.

Alec. She looked at the phone lying on the coffee table and tried to work up the courage to call him.

Stop being an ass. You know you want to see him.

Doubt assailed her. What if she was wrong, and he didn't want her after all?

She knew that probably wasn't the case, but she still didn't pick up the phone. If she called him now, it meant she was starting a relationship. There would be someone there to second-guess her decisions. But he would also be there to comfort her when the job started to get to her. Provided it didn't get to him first.

He'll want to know your secrets.

That was the worst part. She knew Alec would never hold her past actions against her. His willingness to cut a bad guy's head off suggested a certain moral flexibility. And he wouldn't turn away from her when her job got ugly. What she wouldn't be able to stand was the forgiveness.

Diana sighed and sunk into the leather couch and stared at the phone a little longer.

"I don't think you can make it ring that way," Logan piped in from somewhere behind her.

Diana turned in surprise. "You're back already. How'd it go? Did you give one of the others the blade?"

"Gia is taking a look at it. She was closer than Serin. She's not sure of its origin yet, but she's working on it. And she attributes the annoying buzz to its material. From a rare asteroid."

Diana lifted her brows. "I was afraid of that."

Logan flopped on the couch next to her. "Do you think it's like our kryptonite?" she said with a wrinkled nose.

"In case you missed it, I'm still alive," Diana said, hitting her with a green throw pillow.

It looked like something Serin picked out. Lots of beads.

"Well, it's definitely not something we've seen before. And the fact the circle had it when most of their other things were new and cheap is. . .disturbing. Gia suggests we send a little message to the old man at the Burgess estate. She supports your idea of making an example of them. Serin and I agree."

"Yeah, I thought it would come to that," Diana said. "I've been looking into the current generation. I have an idea of who might have helped the circle in the first place, but I'm not sure."

"Who do you think it is?"

"Hillard's wife. Maybe. She's been clean all her life, but you know

what they say about the woman scorned. I'm gonna go shake the tree
and see what falls out."

"About that. . .I figured you might want to head over there, but I
think you should let me handle that for you. I need to go back to
Europe anyway. And there is something you need to do here first.
Something more important," Logan said, rising from the couch to
stand in front of her.

"What?" she asked cautiously.

"You need to rescue your boyfriend."

"What? Why?" Diana burst out, incinerating the pillow inad-
vertently.

She threw it in the fireplace and turned back to her sister ques-
tioningly.

Logan glanced at the impromptu bonfire before grimacing. "I
heard whispers on the wind about the vampire Ruling Council. They
know about the two of you. How he helped you. And they figured out
he's a Daywalker. They are going to censure him."

40

This place needs a makeover.

The East coast headquarters of the vampire Council were not what one would expect if they'd ever been a guest of any of the coven houses in U.S. or Europe. Instead of a mansion, the headquarters was a plain stone building hidden in the woods of upstate New York.

There were no sumptuous furnishings or delicate antiques here. Instead, the furniture was massive and heavy, imported from the old country and their earliest days as an organization. The entire place was a throwback. The only concession to comfort was the richness of the rugs on the floor.

Alec studied the imposing and impossibly large dark wood table in the central meeting hall. Even though it was rare for all the members to attend a meeting at the same time, tradition dictated that there be a space for every member of the council.

Meetings were held once every ten years, and many members still didn't bother to show up. Only the weakest and most powerful members attended regularly. It was a pattern that fueled itself. If they were savvy enough, the weak might grow strong based on what happened in that chamber. And the powerful maintained their control by feeding on those that weren't. The only impromptu meetings happened after cataclysmic events in the human world so they could assess how it would impact them.

For the moment, the meeting hall was empty except for Alec and the ten sentries stationed behind him. He recognized all of them. They were the most senior members of the Council guard, the strongest vampire warriors chosen to serve from the lower classes.

As if he needed their presence to convey the seriousness of the situation he now found himself in.

Just what exactly did they find out?

He could only think about Diana. Her strength, her deep green eyes, and the smell of her skin. God, he wanted her. And he should have known his kind wouldn't let him have her.

Maybe he could overwhelm the guards and fight his way out.

He glanced in their direction. Now there were thirteen. All old and strong.

With an inaudible sigh, he sat at his normal position at the council table and waited.

It took over an hour for the Council members to drift inside. And there were a lot of them. He locked eyes with Daviel Saturne, a junior member of the council, and, though Alec normally had many allies here, the only one he considered a true friend.

One look at Daviel's face was enough for him to be sure that his friend didn't know why they had been summoned in such an unprecedented manner. And in such unprecedented numbers.

Good god, even Edenny Stanishlough is here.

The pompous ass had an air of gloating triumph as he walked by to sit opposite of where he normally did at Alec's left. None of the council members took their normal seats, save one.

Socar Diespiter was the oldest vampire in the room. Whether or not he was the strongest was debatable. As a diplomat, he had no equal, though it was the kind of ruthless diplomacy that made as many enemies as it did allies. He was still considered their *de facto* leader because those enemies never had enough impetus to join forces against him. Socar made sure they had more reason to distrust each other too much to consider allying against him. He'd been the council head for the last two centuries, since before Alec had joined.

In all, there were almost two dozen Council members, more than was typical for a council meeting. And they had all seated themselves opposite him, instead of around him as they normally did.

Alec showed no reaction when he saw his father Alden. His father was not a member, but he occasionally attended during those big disastrous events when the Council weighed the concerns of the coven heads as well as their own.

Okay, this is bad.

"Well, I take it there is a problem," Alec said suavely, sitting back in his chair and crossing his legs.

His urbane attitude and tone were flawless. He had done nothing wrong and wanted them to know it.

Socar inclined his head slightly but was obviously annoyed that Alec didn't seem concerned. Though they had butted heads with him before, their interactions had been cordial. Mostly. There was no sign of cordiality now.

"It seems you've been keeping some very unusual company lately," Socar said.

Alec considered his answer carefully. He smiled. "I made a new friend recently. We had a matter of mutual interest to attend to. A matter of honor to my house," he said with a pointed look at his father.

Stanishlough leaned in and sneered. "You don't make friends with an Elemental. They are our mortal enemies."

Socar gave Stanishlough an annoyed glance but didn't contradict him.

"Is that what you believe?" Alec asked with a note of disdain.

There was a general rustle of discontentment among the others. Most did see the Elementals as the enemy, but more of a symbolic one. If vampires had bogeymen. . .But no one in that room would ever admit they feared anyone or anything.

"So this is about my relationship with Diana?"

"She gave you her name?" Socar asked with a lift of his thin grey eyebrow.

"Why wouldn't she?" Alec asked.

He knew some in the room believed Elementals were simply witches with singular gifts. To witches, names had power. Most did not share theirs readily. But Diana was beyond the type of magic Socar was alluding to.

Socar dismissed the issue with a slight movement of his hand. "The witch doesn't matter. What matters is you and the secrets you've been keeping."

Crap.

"And what would those be?"

The Council leader's expression hardened. "Do you dare deny that you found the secret of the Daywalker ritual?"

There was a buzz of astonishment among the rest of the Council, save a few. Only a handful knew why they were here. . .Stanishlough among them.

"Why would I deny it? Most everyone here knew I was searching for the ritual. I actually found many of them scattered among different cultures. Some of those rituals are known to others here. Searching for the true Daywalker ritual is a favorite pastime of our kind. Just because I found something doesn't mean it worked. What makes you think I succeeded where so many others failed?"

"Don't think to make fools of us. You were seen walking in the daylight."

Shit.

He should have been more careful, but he'd been too wrapped up in Diana and the investigation. And now the Council knew, and he only had himself to blame.

"Has the council taken to spying on its own?" he asked evenly.

An outright denial would have been unwise.

Another ripple passed among the council until the rumble of whispers became a roar. Some clearly did not believe what Alec was being accused of. Other members were hissing their disbelief to one another. A few took exception to the implication of spying.

Alec was a respected and powerful member of the council. If he had been spied on, then it was likely they were all subject to the same kind of treatment. And that violated their unspoken code of honor when it came to dealing with their own kind. It was one very few of them adhered to, but all of them pretended. At least openly. An admission of spying in open Council was unprecedented.

"You were seen in New Orleans and again in Toulouse, France. Your association with the Elemental was being closely monitored. It was foolish to think otherwise. When one of their kind shows up, it is always trouble." Socar drummed his fingers on the table in a slow and deliberate movement.

Alec conceded that with a shrug and a hint of a smile despite himself. Diana was trouble. Just not the kind they thought.

"Well, now what?" He sighed, affecting boredom.

Socar bristled with anger. "Now you hand over the details of the Daywalker ritual or you face censure."

Censure.

Alec stifled a shudder. His gut twisted. It was the worst punishment the vampire Council had to offer.

That particular penalty had been carried out only a handful of times in their long history, and all of those times had occurred in distant dark periods no one spoke of.

Censure had destroyed some very powerful members of their kind who'd found themselves at odds with the ruling faction of the council. They had been buried deep underground only to be periodically dug up for systematic torture. Then they were reburied again. The cycle repeated every few years.

The few vampires who had been interred deep under the ground of the vampire council's seat in Europe had long since been dug up. They were put out of their misery sometime during the Enlightenment.

Usually they went mad within the first decade, although one had supposedly kept his mind mostly intact twice that. Maybe he would get lucky and last as long.

"Where the hell do you get off threatening me with censure? There is nothing in our laws that says I have to hand over something as sensitive as the Daywalker ritual to you lot. In fact, it's the last thing I would do."

Stanishlough leaned forward. "How dare you keep something like that to yourself, you selfish bastard! We have been searching for a way to walk under the sun again for as long as we have existed. You have no right to keep the secret to yourself!"

His outburst had an electrifying effect on their audience. The reality that there was a Daywalker in their midst was slowly sinking in. So was the idea that maybe they too could walk in sunlight some-day. The rest of their audience looked confused or apprehensive. Even Daviel was glaring at Alec.

Socar's attitude was calmer however. After Stanishlough's flare-up, he tightened his control.

"Of course, I knew *you* would not hand over that kind of advan-tage to your house without some persuasion. Censure was probably inevitable in this case. You will be buried under this Council house and exhumed once a year until you hand over the secret."

How many years before he went insane? Alec shot a glance at Daviel, who now looked troubled as more security guards filed into the room.

"That's not why I'm not giving you the ritual details. I'm not doing it because I don't want a bunch of irresponsible idiots running around on a power trip swarming the world over in daylight as well as night. That includes the members of my own house," Alec said harshly, meeting Alden's eyes.

His father looked angry but didn't say anything.

"You self-serving sanctimonious little shit!" another member of the council yelled.

"Bury him now!" another shouted.

Alden walked to his side and said, "You've done it now. Just hand it over to them."

"I'm sorry," Alec said sadly. "I'm afraid I can't do that."

He and his father frequently didn't see eye-to-eye, but most of the time it didn't matter. This was different. Like the others here, his father believed they were the superior form of life on Earth. To even share the same air as one of their kind was a privilege.

No wonder Diana hates us.

Diana. He wished he'd had more time with her. She was starting to come around. He was close to convincing her that they belonged together. She simply needed a little more time with him and his more persuasive talents, the ones he'd been too cautious to employ yet.

If he ever got out of this, he wouldn't waste any more time. Whatever was keeping her from being with him was going to be dealt with, whether she liked it or not. If he ever got out of this that is. And since no vampire ever had survived censure *compos mentis* for long, that better be soon.

The guards swarmed around him, waiting for Socar to give them a sign.

"Last chance, Alec," Socar said. "Just tell us what we want to know and you are free to go. For a time, at least."

"For a time?" Alec asked, deadpan.

"We expect your assistance with the ritual should we run into any problems," Socar said with a dismissive hand wave.

Alec drew in a sustaining breath. "I'm not going to help you. You may as well just get on with it," he said at length, sounding and appearing more firm and in control than he felt.

Socar looked simultaneously disappointed and smug. He signaled his men, and two of them went to the marble mantelpiece. Working synchronously, they tugged on the widely spaced circular carvings on either side of the front panel. The small moon shapes were almost obscured by other occult symbols that had been added later.

Before this more technological age where the lights of cities drowned out the stars, the moon was the most revered symbol for the vampires. For a long time, it had been the only light that had guided them.

The entire mantelpiece slipped back and away, revealing a pit with a mechanical lift. Levers on the side walls had to be pulled simultaneously to lower the lift and a huge stone slab down from the ceiling. The thing had been left open since the creation of this place, back when only Native Americans and Supernaturals had walked this continent.

The door opened, and more men wheeled in a huge stone sarcophagus. The top was carved with the symbols of Alec's house.

"Well, clearly you did not have any confidence in your powers of persuasion. This carving work would have taken some time," Alec said in a flat tone.

Socar dismissed that with a languid wave. "One has to be prepared for every eventuality. But you will tell us everything in time. We can afford to be patient," he said, smiling at Alec.

Asshole.

The men who wheeled in the stone sarcophagus stopped in front of the opened pit at the far end of the room. Four more joined them, and together they lifted the lid of the sarcophagus with strained effort. It must have weighed several tons.

Alec's heart sank. Well, that's inconvenient, he thought as the guards dropped the lid on its side. It landed with a resounding thud. He fought the urge to get up and run as the men moved aside to display the open tomb and waiting sarcophagus.

"Last chance," Socar said.

"You already said that. I'm not giving you the ritual details," Alec said disgustedly as the guards moved behind him.

"Then I have no choice. Alec Broussard, I censure you to entombment beneath this hallowed ground for the rest of your life or until you reveal the secret of the Daywalker ritual."

The guards behind him grabbed his arms and were starting to drag him from his seat when a melodic voice interrupted.

"Hallowed ground? Seriously?" Diana said with a little laugh.

The guards in front of the sarcophagus parted like the Red Sea to reveal the Fire Elemental in all her leather-clad glory.

Several members gasped as she walked farther into the room. Except for his father, none of the vampires in this room had attended his mother's soiree. But apparently they had all gotten the description.

The guards backed away like there was a bomb in front of them instead of a five-foot-four-inch woman.

"You know, for a group of *decidedly* flammable individuals, you lot are overly fond of fireplaces," Diana said nonchalantly as she reached the long wooden table.

Without missing a step, she hopped onto its surface and kept walking.

"What the devil is this?" Socar seethed, head drawn back stiffly.

"Your kind is not welcome here!" Stanishlough spit out, his face purple as Diana sauntered over the long table to Alec's side.

The guards behind him started to edge away. When she reached Alec, she smiled down at him. He looked at her in astonishment, and in one fluid movement, she dropped into his lap and sat on it.

"Hey," she said, twisting to look back up at him, giving him another little smile.

He smiled back, momentarily forgetting everyone else in the room.

"Hey, yourself."

They must have smiled at each other a little too long because there was a heavy rap on the table.

"What do you want, Elemental?" Socar asked, his voice deceptively calm.

Diana turned around to glare at him. "I want to know what the hell you think you're doing," she said, annoyance dripping from every syllable.

Socar was surprised into stunned silence. Unfortunately, Stanishlough wasn't. "This is Council business, and you have no place here! You pollute this sacred place with your presence! You're forbidden from interfering with our affairs!"

Diana's face hardened. She put both hands on the table and slowly leaned forward from her seat in Alec's lap.

"If *I* were you, I'd shut my stupid fucking mouth right now because there is nothing forbidden to one of my kind. And as for me polluting this place, I will remind you that there is nothing as purifying as a little fire," she hissed before leaning back into his embrace with a relaxed expression.

Alden had remained rather still during Diana's sudden appearance. Now his features were expressionless.

"Is this some sort of declaration?" he asked, his glance flicking back and forth from Diana's face to Alec.

She turned to Alden. "And what sort of declaration would that be?"

"Are you here to tell us that Alec is under your protection for the service he provided you?" he asked, his face carefully neutral.

Diana cocked her head, and seemed to consider her answer.

"I'm here to tell you that if anyone fucks with my mate, I will burn this place to the ground with everyone in it," she said before smiling sweetly at their audience.

41

Behind her Alec tensed, his body heating around her, but she didn't turn to look back at him.

Wordlessly, he took her hand in his and gripped it tightly. while she took in everyone's frozen expression. None of the other vamps made a sound. Seconds stretched to a full minute before anyone stirred.

It was Daviel Saturne, of House Saturne, who finally spoke. "This is unexpected. Are you sure?"

Diana shot him a speaking glance, and he coughed apologetically. "I mean, an Elemental has never taken a vampire for a mate. A Fire Elemental has never. . ."

The poor guy couldn't think of anything else to follow that.

She shrugged. "There's a first time for everything."

Socar took a steadying breath and stood. "Your *association* with Alec is a. . .an honor to his house," he finally said with an acknowledging nod to Alden.

Diana pursed her lips, waiting for more.

"But I'm afraid that the business we have with Alec supersedes any of his other associations," Socar continued. "This Council requires that he hand over information critical to our survival."

Diana rolled her eyes. "I realize you might actually believe that, but your kind has gotten along for a millennium without walking around in daylight, and you can get along without doing it now."

The level of tension in the room jumped up a notch.

"Are you refusing to give us what is our right? What is our due!" Socar's renowned control broke down.

The guards responded by fanning out behind them. But they kept a noticeable gap between them and the chair in which the odd couple sat.

"No, actually," Diana replied without batting an eyelash.

The whirl of confusion that swept over the crowd left several with comical dumbfounded expressions on their faces. Her smile grew wider and Daviel's expression went from confused to besotted as he looked at her. Alec shot him a warning look before turning his attention back to Diana.

"Not that I believe anything of *Alec's* is *your* due," she continued. "He owes you nothing. His discovery was the result of decades of brilliant work, and if he wants to keep it to himself, he can."

"So you don't want me to hand over the ritual?" Alec asked looking down at her, genuinely confused.

"No, you can give it to them," she said gently. She twisted a little on his lap so she could put a hand on his cheek. "The ritual is pointless. It worked for you because it was *you*. It won't work for them." She paused to make sure he was taking it in. "It's simply a tool, a way to focus what magic there is in this world on you. If you are worthy and have the skill, it changes you. If you're not, you stay the way you are. There is usually only one of your kind in a millennium that can pull it off. . .if that."

Diana's explanation was met with complete and utter silence. Alec looked simultaneously relieved and disappointed. She continued to stroke his cheek.

Stanishlough laughed. "She's lying!"

For people who didn't need to breathe much, the shocked intake of breath coming from multiple vampires around the table was very loud. Even some of the guards behind them broke their stoic silence to gasp aloud.

Insulting the bogeyman in their midst was suicide.

"I'm going to pretend I didn't hear that," Diana said, fighting the urge to laugh. "But only because your scintillating company is starting to get on my nerves. We are leaving. Alec can email the ritual details. You will leave us alone. Or you get my undivided attention. . .but only for as long as it takes for your smoldering pile of flesh to stop smoking."

With that, she got up off Alec's lap. Slightly dazed, he followed after her toward the door, but Stanishlough was too stupid to keep his mouth shut.

He got up from the table and pointed to them while making eye contact with Socar and as many members that would return his glance.

"You can't seriously think of letting them go! She's lying. The ritual will work. He has to show us how he did it! I can get it to work this time!"

"This time?" Alec turned sharply to face Stanishlough. "What do you mean?"

"Aren't others always in pursuit of the chance to walk under the sun?" Socar said evasively.

"Yeah, but why would you bother to do the homework when you can just steal it?" Diana asked, looking up to check Alec's reaction.

"You *stole* my research." Alec's tone went from incredulous to angry before he'd finished the sentence. "But you can't have. No one knows where I hid the research. No—" he stopped short. The look on his face was one of realization and. . .pain.

"What is it? Did someone else know where you kept it?" she asked quietly with a glance at his father.

"Yes, but not him," he replied. With a look of hatred, he focused on Stanishlough, "Where is Daniel?"

"Who?"

"My servant, Daniel. He is the only one that had access," Alec bit out.

His voice was arctic, colder than Diana had ever heard.

There was a pointed silence. It stretched so long the other members of the circle began to edge away from Stanishlough in a clear retreat of support.

Not noticing, Stanishlough drew himself up in his most arrogant and supercilious manner. "It was his own fault. He would have survived if he had been quicker to obey."

The silence stretched. The loyalty of a servant to his house was a point of pride. Kidnapping and torture of a loyal retainer was sufficient cause to declare war on another house.

Alec was frozen for an immeasurable moment until he suddenly blinked and lunged for Stanishlough. The older vampire broke his grip, and in the space between heartbeats, he twisted away from Alec.

In movements too quick for eyes to see, the two fought in vicious bursts, one getting the upper hand and then quickly losing it as the other wrested it from him.

Diana suppressed a flinch as one of the enemy's blows landed hard. She debated moving in and ending it, but the entire council was watching. As much as she hated it, Alec had to end this on his own.

The vicious fight continued in near silence. The other members of the council must have been too unnerved by her presence to take sides. She stood ramrod straight, fighting to keep her face impassive. Alec slammed Stanishlough against the table, the advantage clearly his when Diana saw Socar twitch his hand. A few nervous guards inched forward, responding to his sign in surreptitious movements.

They hadn't moved more than a few steps when a wall of fire rose in front of them. The guards reared back, and the wall became a circle around the two fighters.

"Don't even think about interfering," Diana hissed at the old man.

Socar sneered. "I bind you to the same rule, Elemental."

"You can't bind *shit*. I don't answer to you. But Alec doesn't need my help," Diana said firmly.

"Stanishlough is centuries older. Your mate—"

"Will still tear him apart," Diana cut him off sounding more sure than she felt.

She folded her arms and raising the fire circle higher and hotter so that Socar and the others had to retreat farther.

There was a sickening crack, a harsh sound that nearly stopped her heart. Diana turned to see Alec standing still with his back partly to her. Fear seized her until she saw that he was holding something. He dropped it and backed away, giving everyone a clear view of Stanishlough stretched on the floor. The older vampire's head was lying several feet away from his body.

She breathed a sigh of relief. *Well, that was fast.*

Diana walked through the fire circle and stood at Alec's side, taking in his frozen expression. Despite his strength and fighting ability, Alec was a scholar and gentlemen. He didn't take death lightly, and being its instrument would always be painful for him.

She cleared her throat slightly and whispered, "I didn't mean literally."

Alec's eyes met hers. It took a moment before they focused on her. A small coughing laugh escaped him.

"I'm sorry about Daniel," she said quietly. "Let's get out of here."

He took a deep breath but didn't say anything.

"Yes. Leave and don't come back," Socar said from across the room.

Alec's handsome face became hard and cold.

"I will leave, but I *will* come back. I'm keeping my seat on the council. If you oppose me, say so now."

"Now? While your witch is here to fight your battle?" Socar said. "Will you bring her to all of our meetings? Does she dictate to us now? Shall we bow before her?"

A rustle of whispers erupted behind him.

"If Alec wants to attend your boring ass meetings, I don't care. I won't be joining him. Frankly, I have better things to do. But rest assured, if he doesn't come home after one, I won't believe it when you say he got bored to death. If anything happens to him, there isn't a hole deep enough for you to hide in," Diana warned.

Socar stood up, his eyes shooting daggers at her. Then he straightened his suit jacket and stalked out of the room.

A few others followed him. The remaining company was silent until Daviel Saturne chuckled out loud. He got a few looks from his neighbors and subsided.

Alec walked to his father and said quietly, "I'll. . .be in touch. Will you be all right?"

"Yes," Alden said stiffly. "Stay safe, my son. I trust I'll see you soon," he added more graciously.

Alec nodded and followed Diana out of the council chamber.

42

lec watched Diana at the wheel as she drove straight to Boston.

She called me her mate.

She was his. And he was hers. He had lost Daniel. But he wouldn't grieve alone. Diana understood, and she would be there with him.

"Now what?" he asked her.

Hours had passed in relative silence.

"I can take you to your place. I guess you have stuff to take care of," Diana said.

"Yeah, some. I need to figure out what to do for Daniel."

"Did he have family?"

"No."

"Well, that's probably for the best. But I'm really sorry you lost him. I know he was important to you."

"Thanks."

It meant everything that she was there for him. And even though she would never say so, she needed him, too. He would take care of her and her secrets, if she let him.

"What happened to you in foster care?" he asked suddenly, surprising himself.

He'd meant to wait for a better time to ask.

Diana tightened her grip on the steering wheel as she glanced at him. He watched her quietly, but she didn't answer. She kept driving until she found a parking spot outside his apartment building.

He didn't ask again. He just kept staring at her.

"I killed my foster parents," she said finally, looking straight ahead into the darkened street.

"Did they deserve it?" he asked.

"Yes and no."

He waited patiently. Sighing, she sat back into the leather seat of her favorite car, a perfectly restored 1967 Shelby Mustang GT500. It had been waiting for them when they left the council chambers, courtesy of Logan.

"I lived in a lot of different homes after my mom died. Never lasted long in any one place. Stuff would happen that would spook the foster parents. Kitchen stoves going crazy until they broke. Electronics burning out. I was considered bad luck. And as I got older, things escalated, and fires broke out. I was labeled a problem case. I got stuck in some pretty rotten places after that. Till I ran away. But I didn't know where to go and eventually someone would find me. Then I would be sent somewhere else."

She stopped when he slid his hand over hers. As he gripped it tightly, she continued. "The last place was the worst. There was a husband and wife. They had three awful kids of their own but took in a lot of others for the checks they got from child service. Some of those kids were heading for the state pen, but I could handle them. Most of them found me. . .creepy. It was the parents who were a problem. The dad—I hated him. He beat some of the kids when they acted up, but it's what he did behind closed doors that made my skin crawl. Even to his own kids." She stopped and looked away. "I didn't have to wait long for it to be my turn."

He wanted to pull her into his arms, but he was worried she might stop. He settled for stroking her palm with his finger.

Eventually she continued. "The father waited for everyone to be out of the house. He kept me behind when everyone else had gone to school, telling them I was sick and that he would have to stay home and watch me. Only I wasn't sick. And I was done waiting for him to make his move. I sat quietly on my cot until he came to my room." She closed her eyes briefly. "He looked at me like he was having second thoughts. I think my calmness may have thrown him. But then he shrugged it off. He smiled and petted me, told me how pretty I was. And then I told him."

"What did you say?"

"That he was a monster. But it was okay. Because I was there to kill monsters—and no I didn't know what I was. Not back then. It just came out. And then I called the fire," she said, her eyes distant.

"It was the first time I did it on purpose. I wasn't sure it would come. It always seemed to happen when I didn't want it to. But it came. The cot burned, then the room. Eventually the whole house. I walked out of there without a scratch or singe. Not even my clothes were damaged. I went outside and sat in the front yard until the police came. The social workers took me away, and that's when I found out that my foster mother had gone back to the house after dropping the kids at school. She wasn't supposed to be there. And she died, too."

"She had to have known what was happening in her house," Alec said quietly.

"Yeah, she did. But I'm not sure that's enough of a reason for her to die. If she had chosen to fight him, she would have lost. He probably would have killed her."

"Maybe. Maybe not. All she had to do was inform the authorities. It's possible they would have been able to put a stop to it."

Diana cocked her head to the side. "I don't think it would have gone down that way, but there's not much point in speculating. I got locked up after that. They blamed the fire on me. I had a history with them. But I wasn't locked up for long. Gia came for me. And then everything changed. I had a calling, a purpose. And sisters."

She pulled his hand into her lap and held it with both hands. "Sometimes things still get to me. You're going to get frustrated, too. There are a lot of things we don't have the power to change. But you get to make a difference. Most of the time, it's enough. But not always."

"I get that," he said. She raised her eyebrows, and he insisted, "I *do*. But wouldn't it help to have someone to hold on to when it's not enough?"

She didn't answer right away, and he held a breath he didn't need.

"I need to move on soon," she said eventually.

Not what he was hoping to hear. But it was now or never.

"Yeah, I figured. Are you finally going to ask me to go with you?"

She smiled wryly. "I'm telling you to be ready to leave by noon tomorrow."

Alec laughed a little and then stopped and held out his hand. "And I'm telling you to come upstairs with me now," he said softly.

Diana stared at his outstretched hand for a long while before finally taking it. They got out of the car, and he stopped to admire it.

He put his arm around her. "Hey, do you think I can drive it tomorrow?"

"Not a chance," she said with a shake of her head.

"That's what I thought you were going to say. I'm going to have to teach you a little something about sharing. And we're going to start your first lesson right now," he said, tugging on her hand and pulling her in close before leading her upstairs to his bedroom.

THE END

Continue the Elemental's Series with Air, a Readers' Favorite Silver Medalist!

Grant Leishman for Readers' Favorite wrote:
"I can honestly say Air is one of the best books I've read this year. It was "un-put-downable" and I raced through it with little pause. An excellent read and definitely one of the best within its genre."
Read on Kindle Unlimited or listen to it on Audible today!

Thank you for reading Fire! Reviews are an author's bread and butter. If you liked the story please consider leaving a review.

Subscribe to the L.B. Gilbert Newsletter for a *free* novella!
http://www.elementalauthor.com/newsletter/

ABOUT THE AUTHOR

L.B. Gilbert is another name for USA Today Bestselling Author Lucy Leroux.

L.B. spent years getting degrees from the most prestigious universities in America, including a PhD that she is not using at all. She moved to France for work and found love. She's married now and has a polyglot 4 year old. The family moved back to California a few years ago.

She has always enjoyed reading books as far from her reality as possible but eventually the voices in her head told her to write her own. So far the voices are enjoying them. And judging by the awards, a few other people are as well. You can check out the geeky things she likes on Twitter or Facebook.

If you like a little more steam with your Fire, check out the author's award-winning Lucy Leroux titles, FREE to read on Kindle Unlimited

www.elementalauthor.com

or

www.authorlucyleroux.com

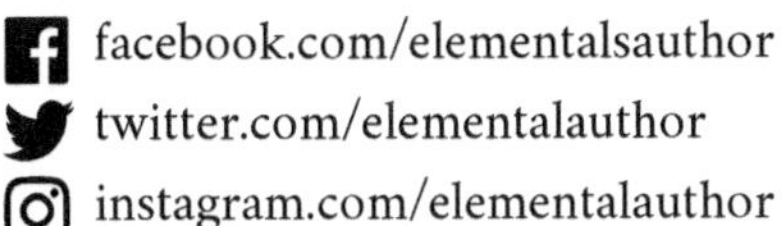